"Can one of these five rockstars fill the hole in my heart?

*Or will I
stay broken forever?"*

OTHER BOOKS BY

C.M. STUNICH

Hard Rock Roots
Real Ugly
Get Bent
Tough Luck
Bad Day
Born Wrong
Hard Rock Root Box Set (1-5)
Dead Serious
Doll Face
Heart Broke
Get Hitched

Tasting Never Series
Tasting Never
Finding Never
Keeping Never
Tasting, Finding, Keeping: The Story of Never (1-3)
Never Can Tell
Never Let Go
Never Did Say

The Rock-Hard Beautiful Trilogy
Groupie
Roadie
Moxie

The Bad Nanny Trilogy
Bad Nanny
Good Boyfriend
Great Husband

Triple M Series
Losing Me, Finding You
Loving Me, Trusting You
Needing Me, Wanting You
Craving Me, Desiring You

A Duet

Paint Me Beautiful
Color Me Pretty

Stand-Alone Novels

Fuck Valentine's Day (A Short Story)
Broken Pasts
Crushing Summer
Taboo Unchained
Taming Her Boss
Kicked

Fantasy Novels

The House of Gray and Graves
The Feed
Indigo & Iris
She Lies Twisted
Hell Inc.
A Werewolf Christmas (A Short Story)
A Werewolf New Year's (A Short Story)
A Werewolf Valentine's Day (A Short Story)
A Werewolf St. Patrick's Day (A Short Story)
DeadBorn
The Seven Wicked: First
The Seven Wicked: Second
The Seven Wicked: Third
The Seven Wicked: Fourth
Chryer's Crest

Books By Violet Blaze
(MY PEN NAME)

Bad Boys MC Trilogy

Raw and Dirty
Risky and Wild
Savage and Racy

Stand-Alone Novels

Football Dick
Stepbrother Thief
Stepbrother Inked
Glacier
Biker Rockstar Billionaire CEO Alpha

Groupie

Rock-Hard Beautiful

C. M. ♥ STUNICH

INTERNATIONAL BESTSELLING AUTHOR

This book is dedicated to the healing power of love

in all its many forms and incarnations.

CHAPTER ONE

Tears stripe my cheeks like melancholy stars, twinkling in the bright lights cast by oncoming cars. Their high beams streak over my face and away, rocketing off through the night, a night that for me has just come to a screeching halt.

I dash the tears away with the back of my hand, my mother's silver charm bracelet jingling with the motion, and lean my forehead against the steering wheel. My eyes might be crying, but I'm not making any other sounds. I sit there silent and still, the radio playing some gentle rock ballad to carry my pain into the night.

"Look into his eyes and say goodbye; never let another day go by; don't miss the quiet moments in between; never love and never leave again."

I sit up and grab my phone from the cup holder, pressing the home button and waiting for the screen to light up again. My stomach twists and catapults bile into my throat as I struggle not to throw up.

One text.

That's it.

All it takes to change the whole world.

In ten words, my stepmother has literally destroyed the last little piece of me.

Lilith, I'm sorry but your father passed away this morning.

No matter how hard or how long I stare, that sentence doesn't make any sense. Dad can't be dead; Dad's all I have left.

1

Just me and Dad.

My hands shake as I toss my phone into the passenger seat and run my fingers through the rich auburn strands of my hair. Same color as Dad's. Well, what Dad's used to be before the chemo.

"Fuck this."

My voice quivers as I turn the key in the ignition and start the engine, peeling away from the dirty, dry shoulder of the highway. I press the pedal to the floor, but no matter how fast I go, how many miles I put behind me, it doesn't change anything.

Dad is dead.

Next time I stop, it's at a gas station.

How?

That's the only word I can seem to type, but before I even press send, I know the answer to my own question. Dad was sick; Dad had cancer; Dad is dead.

I just left the city, is the text I send instead, because I really did *just* get off after a hard night's work and climb in my car with everything I own. The plan was for me to move in with my dad and stepmother, help take care of him until … he got better. Although I think I was the only idiot who ever believed he'd beat the cancer. Cancer can't be beat; it's a fucking monster. It killed my mom when I was in high school and now … "Dad is dead."

I say the words aloud, but I don't believe them, not really.

This is a very hard time for me, is what my stepmother, Susan, sends back in response. I stare at those words and feel anger ripple across my skin like a hot desert breeze. I'm in Arizona now; I just want to get back to New York. Even if my dad is gone, I want to see his body one last time. I *need* to see it.

I shove my phone in my pocket and climb out of my car, heading inside and digging around in my purse for some money. There's nothing left on my debit card; my bank account is currently negative. And my credit cards … maxed out. Dad had promised he'd have Susan wire me some money for gas … but now Dad is dead.

He's *dead.*

"Are you in line?" some guy asks gently, snapping me out of my stupor. I glance up and feel my throat get tight all of a sudden. He's looking at me with careful sympathy, like he can tell something's wrong. If I wasn't in total shock right now, I'd be into this guy with the beautiful mouth and the kind eyes. Something about his face, about the cool calmness of his expression makes my chest tight and brings a sudden surge of emotion crashing over my aching heart.

My lips part, like I could spill all my hurt into the air right now and he'd take care of it for me.

Fucking ridiculous.

Me and my pain, all we have is each other.

The gorgeous guy in the vintage band tee looks me up and down in my holey jeans and white tank. My body is all curves, falling out of my clothes in all the wrong places. Round hips, full breasts, skin the color of cream. My dad's side of the family is Irish and Scottish, so there's a sea of freckles across my nose that some guys think is cute. Clearly, the boy in front of me does, too.

"I, uh, seem to have misplaced my wallet," I say, shoving the offending item deep into the depths of my purse, so he can't see it and realize I'm lying.

He looks me over again with eyes the color of a tropical sea. I wonder for a moment as he stares at me if he's wearing contacts, but I don't think so. As I look at him, tears spring to my eyes unbidden. I try to choke them back, but he sees anyway.

"Here," he tells me, dressed in a rugged pair of jeans that look too expensive to be real. Something about the way they crease, something about the sharp smell of denim. His short auburn hair is shaped into a low mohawk, and he smiles at me when he passes over a wad of green bills. "For your tank."

"Thanks," I say as I curl my fingers around the money, my eyes drawn to his long fingers. Lines of fire scorch my skin where he touches me which only makes me cry harder.

There's a long, drawn-out sigh from this guy as he ruffles his hair with his musician's hands.

"Do you want a hug?" he asks which both surprises and

3

weirds me out.

"No," I say, taking a step back, curving my own fingers around the money. I look at him warily, like I think he expects to get something out of me for this cash. My eyes narrow and he sighs again, shrugging his muscular shoulders.

"Too bad." His smile is sharp and short. "I'm really good at them."

And then he steps up to the counter and tosses some money onto the glass, leaving with a pair of energy drinks and a bag of beef jerky. I notice he has a book tucked under one arm, too.

I breathe out suddenly as he disappears through the glass doors of the convenience store and into the hot desert night.

"Miss?"

I glance up at the clerk behind the counter and then down at the bills in my hand. Eight fives. Forty bucks. Wow. More generous than I expected.

I put it all in my tank and head back outside.

While I wait for my shitty AMC Matador to fill up, I check my phone again. I realize vaguely that my hands are shaking and my eyes are blurring with tears again, but I push all of that emotion down, tuck it deep inside and let it eat at what's left of my soul.

There's no need for you to come now, Susan says in her next text. I try to call her, but if the bitch can't be bothered to call me to tell me that my last living family member is now dead, then why should she pick up now?

I throw my purse to the ground and dump its contents on the oil soaked pavement, searching for any loose bills, any change. There's about fifty cents in dimes and nickels. When I bury my fingers in the pockets of my jeans, I find a five dollar bill.

Five dollars and fifty six cents.

That's what I have to my name.

I clamp a hand over my mouth and sit back on my ass, the vast expanse of a desert sky stretching above me like the domed roof of an amphitheater. Not caring that I'm lying on the ground at a gas station, I fall onto my back and let the tears drip down either side of my face.

When the pump ticks to let me know the gas is done, I sit

back up, sniffling, and gather my things back in my purse. As I do, I catch sight of a shiny strip of paper, shaped like a bookmark.

BROKEN HEARTS AND TWISTED SOULS TOUR featuring Beauty in Lies, Rivers of Concrete, and Tipped by Tyrants @ the Lyndon-Carter Stadium March 21ˢᵗ. Doors open @ 8 p.m.

It's a concert ticket, one that my last boyfriend bought me a few months back. When we broke up, he left the pair of them in our apartment, an apartment that I no longer have. I gave that up when he cheated on me, gave up my new apartment to move back to New York to be with my dad. I gave up my job. I even gave up my *cat*.

I search frantically through crumpled receipts and coffee stained napkins with little notes scribbled on them, until I find the second ticket.

The concert is *tonight* of all nights, but it's right here in Phoenix. I could take these tickets to the show and sell them outside the door to some kids looking for a good deal. Then, with the money, I could get to New York.

Dad might be dead, but surely even my wicked stepmother will give him a proper funeral?

I stand up and jerk the hose from the Matador's tank, shoving it back into place on the gas pump as I simultaneously look up directions to the concert venue. It's early yet, but I should still be able to hawk these tickets outside—looks like the show tonight is already sold out. Maybe I can even get some good money, enough to buy food and possibly a night or two at a motel? The drive from Phoenix to New York is *long*: thirty-six hours of straight driving.

I climb in my car, start the engine and head off in the direction of the venue.

As I drive, I think I see the guy with the expensive jeans and the tropical eyes on the side of the road, but I don't stop. I don't have any business with him, and boys that look like that can only mean trouble.

Whoever could've predicted he'd be one of the five ... one of *my* five.

Lily and her five rockstars.

C. M. Stunich

I'd give them my body, my heart, and my soul. I'd descend into their darkness as they embraced my own … and our connections would be pure poetry.

I'd become Lilith Tempest Goode, the ultimate groupie for Beauty in Lies.

In my own way, I would join their band, and sex … that would be *my* instrument.

The Lyndon-Carter Stadium is a massive beast, a large circular building with a revolving stage. Ever since I moved to Arizona with my boyfriend, I've wanted to see a show here. Tonight, I couldn't care less.

I stand on the sidewalk in the early evening dark, a cool, dry breeze chasing across the fine hairs on my arm as I stand there with the tickets tucked into my purse, watching the already massive line snake around the side of the building and into the parking lot.

I pray to god that nobody breaks into my car tonight; everything I own is in there. *Everything.*

Pulling in a deep breath, I approach the line, wishing I'd slipped on a jacket before getting out of the car. We might be in the desert, but it's in the mid-fifties and I feel a chill creeping across my skin. Maybe that's just the melancholia, slipping across my skin like a blanket?

Dad is dead.

I'm twenty-one years old and all alone. No family, no friends, no boyfriend.

I'm literally … nothing and nobody.

I march toward the gathered crowd and start to notice some men and women dressed in blue windbreakers, the word *Security* stamped across their backs in yellow capital letters. They look so fucking *stern* that I start to falter, watching people move around and chatter in excited voices. There's a hush to the air, like the calm before a tsunami breaks. The thought of being

7

in the audience when it finally does … is exhilarating.

Dad died today, bitch.

How can I even be *considering* something as shallow as a rock concert?

I cross my arms over my chest, my pink leather purse swinging in the crook of my arm as I try to decide how best to go about this. Do I just walk up there and start yelling about my extra tickets? I decide to just go up and ask; I *need* to get this money and get the hell out of here. If I have to drive day and night with no food and no sleep, just to get to my dad's funeral, that's what I'll do. I *have* to see his face one more time, so I can imagine his smile, so I can memorize the curve of his jaw or the shape of his lips. Pictures help, but … I need the real thing, one last time.

"Excuse me?" I ask one of the women in the jackets. She barely glances my way. "My father just passed and I can't attend the show tonight. Is it okay if I sell my tickets out here?"

I say the words, but I don't feel them, not really. How could I? Just last night Dad sent me a text telling me was looking forward to seeing me. How can he be dead? Shouldn't someone —Susan, his doctor, even Dad himself—have known how damn sick he was?

Maybe this whole thing isn't a surprise to anyone but me?

I chock back tears as the woman gives me a sympathetic look that I ignore, and nods briskly.

"Face value only unless you're more than two hundred feet away from the door." She turns, dirty blonde ponytail ruffling in the breeze, mimicking the whip of her navy blue windbreaker against her back. The woman smacks her gum as she points at a spot near the edge of the parking lot. "Just about there."

"Thanks," I say, moving away from the crowd and feeling stupid standing there in my white tank and jeans, a pair of heels on my feet. I was so eager to get home to see Dad that I didn't think clearly when I packed up the car. The heels I wore to work today were literally the only pair of shoes I could find. It feels sacrilegious, wearing these bright red heels when my father lies cold and breathless somewhere in Gloversville, New York.

Groupie

I only have to stand there for a few minutes when a young couple approaches me and offers up two hundred bucks for the pair of tickets. I'm pretty sure Kevin only paid about sixty-five for each, so I happily hand them over and pocket the money.

It's only as I'm walking back to my car that I see *him.*

There's this physical reaction in my gut, like I've been punched, and I almost topple over in my heels, putting out a hand to steady myself against the side of a random pickup truck.

He's sitting on the hood of some classic car wearing a *suit.* Like, who wears a suit in the middle of the desert? It's expensive, clearly tailored, dark as night. His cuff links glimmer as he lifts a cigarette to his lips and pauses, glancing over at me, eyes pale grey and apathetic as he stares at me. Tattoos peek out from under the sleeves of his white button-up, staining his hand with color.

"So you caught me," he says, which makes literally no sense. I can't stop staring at him, my heart pummeling my rib cage. I have to blink several times to steady myself, rising fully to my feet and damning my high heels to hell.

I stare down at the shoes and suddenly, I just start thinking of blood. I have no idea why; the thought just comes randomly and slams into my chest almost as hard as my reaction to Suit Guy.

He smokes his cigarette as I stand there and stare at my shoes, lifting my face finally to meet his bored, disinterested gaze. He looks like an asshole; I want nothing to do with him.

I keep walking.

"Where the bloody hell are you going?" he asks, sounding shocked and disgusted as I pass by him without a second glance. The sound of his accent draws my attention back, unbidden, and I catch more tattoos at his throat, just above the starched white collar of his shirt. He's even wearing a tie, this guy.

I watch as he drops his cigarette and puts it out with a pair of expensive loafers. I *know* expensive loafers. My ex-boyfriend of five years, his dad is a big shot attorney and he always wears shoes that cost more than my car.

"Here." Suit Guy holds out one of his tattooed hands and drops a laminate badge. It spins in the desert breeze as I wrinkle up my eyebrows. Rich auburn strands tackle my face and I scoop them away, trying to get a better look at this dude. He must think he's hot shit, for sure. "Well? Are you completely mental? Take it."

"I'm sorry," I say as I wrinkle my brow and turn to face him, crossing my ankles and lacing my fingers behind my neck. This is my strength pose; I do it all the time when I'm trying to stand up to somebody or something. In this case, it isn't the sexy British a-hole in the suit. This time, it's *grief.* Kevin always hated it when I stood this way; he said I looked like I was trying too hard. The thing is, I'm not trying at all. I never really have, and that's part of my problem. "Who are you?"

The man in the suit laughs and then he just drops the badge on the ground.

"Better hurry," he says, giving me this rapid flick of eyes that I guess is a once-over, "show starts soon."

And then he's turning and moving across the pavement with a crunch of desert dirt beneath his heels. I wait for him to snake through the parked cars and disappear before I head over and pick the badge up from the ground.

It's a backstage pass.

I turn it over several times, trying to decide if it's a fake or not, but it looks real enough.

That's when something occurs to me, something that Kevin said about the lead singer of Beauty in Lies being from some small town in rural England. Lots of things that Kevin said stick in my head; most of them are awful.

I search the band's name online and feel my entire body go cold when a ton of pictures pop up.

In almost all of them … the asshole in the suit is standing front and center.

Behind and to his right, the boy with the tropical ocean eyes is staring at me.

I slip the badge around my neck and head towards the front door of the venue.

CHAPTER THREE

Lilith

LILITH GOODE

This plastic badge around my neck, I guess it means I get treated like a goddamn *queen* in here.

I get in line with everyone else, but as soon as one of the security guards sees it, he gently takes my arm and leads me to the front of the line, briefly checking my purse and then ushering me through the metal detectors inside the doors. After that, he escorts me past the massive bottleneck near a second set of doors and through an elegant silver and black bar area.

Just past that, through *two* more sets of doors, we enter into a chaotic mess of shadows and people, cursing and the smell of sweat and excitement. Even standing here, I feel wrong, really wrong. Inside, I'm all twisted up and dead, like a winter killed tree in New York. The structure is all there, but the leaves—and most especially the flowers—are long gone. Somehow, unlike the tree, I feel as if there won't be a spring awakening for me.

My daddy is dead and I'm all alone.

I wrap my arms around myself.

"Hey, the contest winner is here," the security guard snaps at one of the roadies, pausing him in mid-step. He's this nondescript guy with short, wavy brown hair, a black tee, and jeans. He blinks at me several times and then rolls his eyes.

"Got it," he says, nodding and waving me forward impatiently. The smell of pot drifts behind him when he walks. "How did you find Paxton?" he asks me as we trail through the crowd toward a black curtain.

"Paxton?" I ask, but Roadie Guy doesn't really care about

the question he asked me, leading me through the curtain and ... stealing my breath away. As soon as we step out into the main part of the venue, the weight of the crowd settles around me and makes me feel like I'm suffocating. It takes every effort on my part to keep moving, following after him and avoiding the frantic sprint of other roadies as they try to desperately to get the instruments tuned under the watchful eye of the monstrous crowd.

The stage here is unique, round, set in the center of the room instead of the front. It even rotates during the show, making for an interesting viewing experience, but damn, it looks like a real bitch to set up for. People run back and forth on my right, to and from the center of the room.

Roadie Guy leads me all the way to the end of the hall—like a tunnel in a football stadium, the one that the players always burst out of—and into this circular dip that surrounds the stage. On all sides, the floor slopes up, carrying the crowd with it. I can hear them all around me, feel them vibrating the very molecules in the air.

Sweat starts to pool on my lower back and my breath hitches as I turn and look at them all, staring down at me, at the stage, cheering, screaming. My head spins and I feel dizzy and then suddenly *all* that I can think about is my dad.

I wish I'd taken that guy's hug in the gas station. Maybe then I'd feel a little better? I could really use a hug right now.

"Just hang out here and Paxton will grab you for the song."

"The song?" I ask, but Roadie Guy is gone, sprinting around like all the rest of them.

I clutch my laminate badge against my chest as I turn and stare up at the stage, the drums in front that say *Tipped by Tyrants* across the front, the shrouded daises behind it. The scene is simply set, with minimal props, to make the spinning effect of the platform that much more impressive.

I lean back against the wall behind me and feel a warm draft tickle red strands of hair around my face. If I were wearing lipstick or gloss, they'd probably stick to my mouth. As things stand, my lips are as dry as the desert that surrounds this town.

My phone ends up in my hands again, even though I know

that all I'm doing is setting myself up for more anguish, more heartache.

The background on my phone is a picture of Dad and me when he was young and healthy, when I was young and small enough to sit on his knee. This picture was taken before my mom died, before my sister was murdered, before I fell in love with a rich asshole that promised to give me everything, dragged me across the country, and left me with nothing.

I touch a hand to my stomach to try to help calm the nausea coiling inside me.

When I think of Kevin and Arizona and him cheating on me, dumping me with a smirk plastered across his face, I feel like I might throw up. And then because of all of that, I missed seeing my dad in his final moments.

Before I even realize I'm doing it, I'm crying again. Silent tears trickle down my cheeks as I stand alone in a crowd of thousands, just one lone redheaded girl with nothing and no one left to lose.

"Hey there, sweetheart," a soft velvety voice says from beside me. I glance over to find another roadie—this one wearing a black hoodie thrown over his head—leaning against the wall next to me. One of his boots—a pair of dark purple Docs—rests propped against the wall as he glances over at me. Even though we're standing close enough to kiss, I can't tell what color his eyes are. They just look black in the dim lights. "Don't cry. It's not all bad."

"How would you know?" I ask. I mean to snap at him, but I don't have the energy. My voice comes out breathy, low, and tasting of tears. I can feel the salt on my already dry mouth. This guy I don't even know reaches out and runs his thumb over my lower lip. "My dad died today," I tell him and he drops his hand suddenly. "I've been missing him for a long time, but the only thing that separated us was distance. How am I supposed to deal with missing him when it's life and death that are between us?"

"My mom died last year," he tells me, digging out a cigarette and lighting up, even though I'm pretty sure it's illegal to smoke in here. This guy with his quiet, careful voice doesn't seem to care. "Some guy broke into her house, raped her and shot her in the face."

That voice … it quivers and thrums with barely suppressed rage.

"How did yours die?"

"Cancer," I whisper, and I can't decide which story is worse —his or mine. But it's not a competition, and it doesn't matter. I breathe out and lean my head against the wall, closing my eyes tight against a new rush of tears. This guy's story doesn't make me feel better; it makes me feel *worse*.

"Stay and watch the show, okay? I know it doesn't seem like much, but it might help." His voice is back to being slow and sensual, unhurried. This is a gentle man tempered like steel in the hellfire of reality. He was born and raised sweet and gentle; the world has hardened him. I don't know how I know that or even if I'm completely full of shit, but it feels true when I think it.

"Does it help you? Music, I mean?" I ask as he reaches up and pushes dark hair off of his brow.

"It's the only thing that does," he admits, and then he stands up and glances at the badge hanging around my neck. "You found Paxton," he says, and again I have no idea what that means.

"Is Paxton hard to find?" I ask and he laughs, his voice as decadent and delicious like that as it was in a quiet whisper. I wonder if he's with one of the bands?

"Oh yeah. If he let you find him, you must be pretty special. There are hundreds of people combing around for him."

"Paxton is …" And then it dawns on me. Duh. "The guy in the suit?"

Hoodie Guy laughs again and shakes his head, reaching up to shove the material back. When he does, I feel a little dizzy, like he's just injected some sort of exotic drug into my bloodstream. His mouth, when he speaks, matches his voice perfectly. Full, curved up in the corner in an enigmatic smile. He's wearing a smidgen of eyeliner and I finally decide that his eyes are the color of dark chocolate, liquid and warm, like I could pour them over ice cream.

14

My chest constricts with guilt again and I wonder if maybe I'm just looking for a distraction tonight? Maybe this roadie guy could be it? I haven't had sex in over six months, not since I found out Kevin was cheating on me.

"That's right, sweetheart," he says, staring at me with bedroom eyes, half-lidded and sensual. "The guy in the suit." He watches me watching him for a long time and then pushes his hood back up, turning and disappearing into the shadows. I consider calling out, asking where he'll be after the show, but ... I just can't.

I reach a hand up and run my palm over my tear streaked face. Truthfully, I can't decide why I'm even here. I should be in my car, hurtling toward New York, toward Dad. But then, it's not like he needs me anymore. No, when he needed me, I couldn't bother to be there.

I suck in a sharp breath and check my phone again, this time pulling up my texts.

Did you get my message, Lilith? The house is already crowded. There's no room.

God, I hate the way Susan texts, talks, writes. Even the way she *breathes* is stiff and stilted and unnatural. I know Dad married her because he was lonely, but now, she's sitting in *my* childhood home, telling me that I'm not allowed to stay there, in my mother's art studio turned Susan's floral patterned guest room.

I hate her so fiercely in that moment that it makes my chest hurt.

My phone goes right back in my pocket.

A minute later, the lights dim even more and the music leaking into the room from the surround sound goes quiet. The crowd does, too, but after a collective breath, they let out a roar that could move mountains. Figures pour out the same door I exited no more than a half an hour ago and the room ... it explodes into violent chaos.

CHAPTER FOUR

Lilith

LILITH GOODE

The first two bands—Tipped by Tyrants and Rivers of Concrete —are good, good enough to make me smile and sway with the small group of roadies and venue staff that have gathered around me. From here, we have the best seat in the entire stadium, gazing up at the slowly spinning stage as musicians thrash and spill their guts onto the floor at their feet.

My ears are ringing from the bass, and I can feel every sound in my toes, tainting my blood, invading my bones. If I fell to pieces right here, broken apart by rhythms and beats, I wouldn't be surprised. Maybe that would be the best case scenario anyway? Because the more thought I give to my life, the less I feel like I want to live it.

Suicide ... doesn't sound like the *worst* thing in the world. And I mean, it's not like there'd be anyone to miss me, right?

As soon as that thought hits me, I know I'm in trouble, and I decide to let go. If I'm considering killing myself, then there's no reason for me to hold back, is there? If death is my best option, then I better start seeking out alternatives.

When someone starts passing around a cigarette, I almost take it. But then I remember that my father died of cancer and even if it *wasn't* lung cancer, I still don't want it. I feel a bit of relief because clearly, some small part of me does care whether I live or die.

I do accept a plastic cup full of frothy beer, lifting it up in toast and then tossing it back as the second band of the night wraps up their set.

I cheer with everyone else, feeling an unbidden smile steal across my lips. It's like a traitor in the night, this cloaked figure taking over my mouth. *Dad is dead.* But the beer's given me a pleasant buzz; my stomach is empty enough that it's cramping so even that small amount of alcohol makes me feel lightheaded.

Rivers of Concrete exits the stage dripping sweat, walking right past me and the small crowd around me, disappearing behind the black curtain over the doorway. Briefly, the stage stops spinning and the lights dim again, giving the roadies time to swarm the platform and drag away the instruments, pull the cloth off the beautiful drum set in the back, the one on the highest dais. Other instruments are brought forth and tuned.

It feels like it's taking forever so when another beer somehow makes its way to me, I take it in grateful hands; the last thing I need right now is extra time to think. As I take a sip, I glance around and notice that the roadies are just pouring cups of beer and passing them through the crowd. The security guards near us frown, their navy blue windbreakers crinkling, but they don't say anything.

My second beer goes down even quicker than the first, soothing some of the pain. That's when I decide to seek out a third, moving down the short, dark hall to the curtain and peeking through. There's a table covered in water bottles as well as an orange cooler with little cups next to it. On the floor next to all that is a silver keg.

"Can I have another?" I ask the original roadie guy, the one that smells like pot. He stares at me and shrugs, handing me a full frothy cup and watching as I swallow it greedily. "One more?"

"You're the VIP here," he says as I pass my cup back and he obliges my weakness. "Want to hook up after? I can get you on the bus," he brags, but I just smile tightly and walk away, realizing as I do that I'm stumbling a bit. I blame it on the heels, not the booze, but still, I almost topple over when I reach the dark curtain.

"Steady there," a voice says as a hand wraps around my arm and helps me to my feet. When I glance over, I find the Caribbean Sea gleaming in a pair of turquoise blue eyes. It's the boy from the gas station. Tears prick then and spill over onto my cheeks.

"Actually," I say, and I feel stupid when my voice stirs, "I do want a hug."

He doesn't laugh at me, just takes me in arms corded and banded with muscle and pulls me close. He smells good, like new denim and laundry detergent. I fight to hold back a sniffle, and keep my hand steady around the cup of beer; I don't want to spill it on him. He looks all dressed up. That's when I remember: he's in the band, in Beauty in Lies.

"Fuck," I say as I step back suddenly and almost trip over a loose cord. The guy grabs my wrist and yet again, gives me the privilege of staying on my feet. Beer sloshes over my hand and onto the cement floor. "I'm sorry. I just ... I've had a shit day."

I meet his bright eyes with my hunter green ones and he smiles softly. I notice then that he has a single piercing through the center of his bottom lip, a silver ring that winks in the light when he smiles at me.

"Did you ever find your wallet?" he asks, like he knows I was lying and doesn't care. Looking at him, there's this rush of feeling inside of me, all of these emotions bubbling up that I want to just spew into the hot air between us, get them out and see what he has to say. But then a woman in a tight black t-shirt and a headset steps up to him and puts her hand on his shoulder, saying something to him that's too low for me to hear. The boy nods and she steps away, but the moment's already been killed. "Enjoy the show, okay?" he says and then he's walking away, leaving me with the ghost of his touch hovering over my skin.

I breathe out and close my eyes, turning and heading back towards the curtain. I take up my spot against the wall, my feet burning in the too-high heels. After a moment, I kick them off and press my feet to the cement floor, breathing out a strong sigh of relief as my arches settle against the cool pavement.

I drink my next beer a little more slowly, cradling it against my chest and listening to the music from the surround sound, the noise of the crowd. If I think about my dad, I'll regret it; I know I will. Unbidden memories assault my consciousness until I give up and down the rest of my drink, padding back to the keg and finding it unmanned. I pour myself another cup and skip out of there before anyone sees me.

A few minutes later, a curtain drops down from the ceiling and the crowd gasps, going nuts as a projector hidden somewhere up above starts to play an animated video of sketched figures in black against the white fabric. Meanwhile, from my unique vantage point, I see five shadows slip from backstage and head down the hallway, disappearing into a small crack in the curtain.

It's Beauty in Lies.

My heart skitters a little, even though I only know a handful of songs. The ones I do know though, they're beautiful. That's why I agreed when Kevin asked if I wanted to come to the concert with him. Of course, that was *before* I found out he was fucking a good dozen other girls. My hand tightens around the plastic cup and it crinkles.

Glancing up, I watch as the five figures in the animated video climb into a convertible and then crash in a fiery explosion. Clouds roll over the wreck and pour bloodstained knives like rain. I have absolutely no idea what the images mean, if they're a reference to something I'm just not getting or if I've had too much to drink.

"*Now Introducing ... Beauty in Lies,*" a voiceover booms through the speakers as the curtain lifts back up, slow and teasing, flashing us four pairs of feet. That's enough to get the crowd into an animalistic frenzy. Hands claw the air above my head like zombie fingers, curling and begging and grabbing. The tension in the air gets so tight it feels like I'm choking all of a sudden.

"Good evening, Phoenix, Arizona," a familiar voice coos through the mic, his British accent making it sound like he's saying *Arizoner* instead of *Arizonuh.* I know just from the flash of expensive loafers that this is the guy from the parking lot, Paxton, the lead singer of Beauty in Lies. Somehow, through some strange twist of fate, I happened to win some weird contest for this backstage pass.

I clutch it tight as the curtain lifts even further, flashing me the man I thought was the roadie, the one I confessed to about

19

my dad's death. He's not wearing a hoodie anymore, just a tight black t-shirt and skinny jeans, fingers curled around a dark purple bass that matches his Docs. He's thrumming the strings, sending this warm vibration up through the bare soles of my feet.

The connection ... it's electric.

I swear, even though it shouldn't be possible, it's like he's looking right at me.

"We're Beauty in Lies"—the kick drum pummels the air and then the curtain's up and I get a flash of the boy with turquoise eyes sitting on his throne—"and we're here to welcome you to the first night of the Broken Hearts and Twisted Souls Tour." Paxton holds the mic in one tattooed hand and lifts the other up to loosen his black tie. His grey eyes twinkle as he takes in the crowd. "This song's called 'How I Say Hello'."

He gives one last jerk to his tie and then swings his free arm around, setting his bandmates on fire. Guitars rip from the speakers, played by a guy with razored blue-black hair and one with a tall silver and black mohawk. Confetti explodes from several machines set around the circular stage, and then it begins to move.

I hold up my left hand and wait for a piece to land on the sweaty surface of my palm, bringing it in close to examine it. It's one half of a broken heart. I slap the sticky confetti piece off on my jeans and glance back at the stage as it turns away from me.

The bassist and both guitarists are rocking out, tossing their hair as they rev up for a bouncy rock song and Paxton lets out this pained scream into the mic, riding a wave of drumming from the boy in the back. Suddenly, I just feel like I *have* to know his name.

I tear my phone from my pocket; I'm not the only one. All around me, people lift phones and tablets up, recording the show as it spins in an easy circle around the stadium. I don't even have to type in the band's whole name before information starts popping up.

Groupie

Lead Vocals, Keyboards, Pianos—Paxton Blackwell
Lead Guitar—Michael Luxe
Rhythm Guitar—Derek "Muse" Muser
Bass Guitar, Backing Vocals—Ransom Riggs
Drums, Percussion—Copeland Park

Copeland, the boy with eyes as bright as a tropical sea. And Ransom, the boy in the hoodie. Somehow, I've managed to literally run into three separate members of Beauty in Lies before the show even started. Must be some kind of record.

My breath catches as the stage comes back around and Paxton appears at the edge, reaching out, his arms directly above my head, fingertips just *barely* brushing the wild straining digits of the crowd.

"You aren't above it all, just say hello, descend into the darkness of this hellhole. So now I'm feeling like you came just to say I told you so, but down here, deep below, you're the kind of girl I'd rather told me no. You're the kind of girl that drowns hearts and leaves them in a deep blue sea, a siren, a songstress, always calling back to me."

"BACK TO ME!" That sensual velvet voice from earlier explodes through the speakers and wraps me up in dripping decadence, Ransom's scream the perfect complement to Paxton's smooth, careful notes. My eyes flick between them and then over to the boy with dark hair, the one that's just covered in tattoos, his eyes this sharp piercing violet, like Elizabeth Taylor or something.

Holy shit.

Why are they all so beautiful? I think frantically as my gaze swings to the second guitarist, his mouth quirked in an inviting little smirk, like he's used to smiling at people and getting his way. His tongue sticks out to the side in concentration as he taps his black boots against the floor and rides the wave of Paxton's voice all the way down into this growling scream that drops the lead singer to his knees at the front of the stage.

If I'd known then that their beauty hid so much darkness, would I have run? If I'd known that they were as broken—maybe more so—than me, would I have climbed the steps to

21

that bus?

I have no way of answering that.

Now, covered in the blood of their wounds, hindsight's twenty-twenty vision doesn't seem quite so clear.

CHAPTER FIVE

Paxton

PAXTON BLACKWELL

We're almost at the end of our set list when I glance surreptitiously down at the floor between songs, the lights flashing dark as roadies switch out my boys' guitars. *VIP ANNOUNCEMENT.* That's what's listed next on the piece of paper taped to the ground by my feet. Instead of starting our next song, I have to play along with this bullshit contest.

Parade for Paxton, please. What a stupid idea. I could've been killed trying to hand out that damn VIP badge. And now I have to serenade the damn winner?

Bleeding hell.

I curse under my breath and toss back a water bottle, finishing it off in few quick swallows and passing it off to a roadie to whisk away. By the time the lights come back up, I'm smiling, my suit sticking to my skin with sweat.

That VIP contest was *not* my idea, sending all the fangirls on a bloody race around the stadium to see who could spot me first. The record label came up with it, but they never specified I had to be *inside* the venue. So I sat outside and some girl with purple-red hair and eyes like emeralds had the audacity to stop in and act like she didn't have a damn clue about who I am.

I stare down at her now, as the stage comes to a brief stop, and then I flick my eyes back to the crowd. They're hungry for me tonight; I can feel it. The first night of our new tour, leaving all the bullshit of my past behind me in the dust, grinding it to soot beneath the soles of my Barker Blacks, the world feels like it belongs to fucking *me.*

"Alright, now," I say as I tuck the microphone back in the stand and play with my tie. They like it when I do that, run my inked fingers up the slick black silk like it's the inside of their thigh, when I curl my fingertips under my collar like I'm dipping inside their hot, wet core. "Would you like another song, then?"

The cacophony is fucking deafening, but it drowns the quiet, whispering voices inside my head, stills and silences them. I'm not bloody mad, but I do have a past as dark as pitch. Its gaping mouth yawns so wide that I can see all the way down its goddamn throat.

"Good. Because we have three more for you," I say and the people keep cheering. I almost wish they'd shut it for a moment, so I could fucking talk, get this little publicity stunt over with. "But first, we need to congratulate the winner of our *Parade for Paxton* contest, break down these barriers between us." I gesture at the gap between the stage and the general admission area with a flicker of my tattooed fingers. There's the silhouette of a dark forest there on my skin, the skyline and the trees, stretched across all ten of my fucking digits. "Come on up here, love," I say as I kneel down and reach out a hand to the girl with the purple-red hair. She's got a red plastic cup in one hand, her feet bare as she looks up at me from down below.

And goddamn. Goddamn, she's fucking *stunning.*

My jaw locks tight as I wait for her to take my hand. So much time passes before she does, that the crowd starts to murmur excitedly, hoping for a little drama. But I don't do drama; I left it far behind me. *Yeah, sure, right. Repeat that until it's true, Pax.* I'm a goddamn liar, even to myself.

I hop down off the edge of the stage and take the girl's beer away, passing it to a roadie as she blinks surprised eyes in my direction. Her mouth ... it's like this swollen bud, begging to be parted by my lips. I'd like to tear it apart with teeth and tongue, kiss her until those bright green eyes shutter closed and she melts into me.

"The hell are you doing?" I snap, and I don't even bother to whisper because nobody can hear me down here. "It's time to get onstage."

When the girl still doesn't move, this strange glimmering

shine to her eyes, I reach down and hoist her over my shoulder. She gasps, but that's it, the only sound I get out of her. She's curvy as hell, her body soft and enticing as it rubs against mine. I carry her straight up the steps and deposit her onstage quick as I can. Holy hell.

I snatch the mic back up and pass it over to her as one of the roadies puts a stool onstage and encourages her to sit on it.

"What's your name?" I ask as she stares at me and then lets her eyes trail across my bandmates; not once does she look at the crowd.

"Lilith," she says, her voice breathy but with this hint of steel, like she doesn't much care to be messed with. Shame, that. "Lilith Goode."

"Well, Lilith," I say as I kneel down next to her and get ready to sing, "tonight, this song is dedicated to you."

Her cheeks bloom with color and I grit my teeth. *What the fuck, Pax? You took two or three of these blushing virgins to bed every night during the last tour. Lost your nerve now, have you? Just because this girl has eyes the same color as Chloe's?*

But I really *don't* see that many girls with green eyes like this.

My band plays the opening notes to the song as I push back my dark thoughts. I won't let my fucking dead girlfriend ruin another concert, another day, another *second* of my life.

The audience shouts their approval as they wait for me to serenade this sad looking woman in her too-small tank top and tight jeans. There's a ribbon of pale skin between her shirt and waistband, and her breasts are practically spilling out the top. It's distracting, to be sure.

"*I knew from the first moment I met you, held your hand and saw you through, behind the locked door of your bedroom, felt your heartbeat flutter and bloom,*" I sing the words as gentle as I can, resting my tattooed fingers on the girl's holey knee, feeling her warm skin beneath me. I rest my chin on my hand and hold the mic close to my lips. "*Forever in my arms, I'll hold you close to my heart, protect your smile and keep it from harm, give our love an honest fresh new start.*"

What a load of bullshit.

The girl I wrote this song for, well, let's just say that didn't exactly work out.

I stand up suddenly and put the sole of my black loafer on the bottom rung of the stool, right between Miss Lilith Goode's legs. Surprisingly enough, she leans back and spreads her thighs, making the crowd ooh and aah behind me.

My mouth twitches into a smirk.

"Tell me how you feel when I smile against your lips, when I wrap my fingers around your hips."

I lean down into Lilith's space, but she just stares back at me like she's not sure how she got here. And that's when the lights shift and I notice the tracks of tears on her face. Hmm. *What the hell am I supposed to do about that?* I wonder as I stand up straight and back away for the next part of the song.

"Don't just speak the words; I want to hear you SCREAM!"

I let out the last word in a violent sound of my own, tearing my tie off and tossing it into the crowd as I open my shirt, letting my tattoos show as I back up and let my boys front and center for their guitar solos. I can't just sit still, and I can't look back at that girl, so I spin and twirl and swing my mic until sweat plasters my dirty blonde hair to my forehead.

When the song ends and I finally glance over at the stool, I see that the girl's already gone.

Good riddance.

She looked like trouble to me anyway.

CHAPTER SIX

Lilith

I squeeze backstage, pushing through the gathered staff as the crowd shouts from all around me.

"*One more song, one more song, one more song!*"

At this point, all I can think about is getting the hell out of there.

"Excuse me," the woman from earlier says, her headset still perched atop her mousy brown hair. "Lilith Goode? If you want to wait here, we'll gather up the boys in the lounge for the VIP experience."

"VIP experience?" I echo as my heart thunders and sweat pours down the back of my neck. I don't know why, but I just want to get out of there. Now. Get on the road and start heading towards my dad. "What VIP experience?"

She smiles tightly and puts a hand on my arm, gesturing at my badge with her tablet.

"Nobody's bothered to explain what you've won, have they?"

I just stare at her and I feel awful, but ...

I pull the badge from over my head and try to hand it to her.

"Here. I'm sorry. I have to go. I don't even know what I was thinking coming in here." The woman blinks plain brown eyes at me as I shake the badge in her direction. "Give it to somebody else."

"I'm sorry, *what?*" she asks snippily, like who could ever possibly turn down such a privilege. "You don't want to attend the meet and greet? That's the grand prize."

"Is there cash?" I ask, hating myself for even asking, but God, I'm desperate. I have two hundred bucks, but will that *really* get me and the Matador all the way to New York? Somehow, I don't think so.

"No cash—" she starts but then I'm turning and running ... right into the chest of the bassist. What was his name? Something weird and edgy. Ransom? His hands take hold of my shoulders and hold me in place as I blink up at him, rubbing my face with the heel of my hand. His chest is ... muscular as fuck and that *hurt*.

"Whoa there, baby doll," he says in that thick syrupy voice of his. He bends down and retrieves my badge, passing it back to me, dark eyes shimmering as he stares at me. He's quite a bit taller than me, six inches or more. I have to crane my neck back to meet his gaze. "Where are you off to in such a hurry?"

"So you're the lucky winner," another guy says, this the one with the silver mohawk, his dark roots shaved close to his head on either side, giving this ombre sort of effect that draws my eyes up and then snaps them back down to his face. His eyes are facets of color, rich and piercing as he stares at me and smiles. It's a smile that says *I always get what I want.* Only ... as he looks me up and down, I'm not quite sure what that is. "Come up and have a drink with us," he says, eyes sparkling as he meets my gaze and holds my stare unashamedly.

"I ... I'm sorry," I say as I weave around the two of them and make a run for the door. Since I'm coming from the opposite direction, none of the security staff tries to stop me as I sprint outside ... and into a torrential downpour. "FUCK!" I curse as I pound through puddles in bare feet. Like an idiot, I left my red heels behind. Now, I have no shoes.

No shoes, no dad, no mom, no sister.

Nothing at fucking all.

I sprint through the parking lot as fast as I can, but it's huge, bigger than I remember it being. By the halfway point, my shirt is plastered to my skin and completely see-through, advertising the red bra underneath. In the rain, in the dark, I find myself turned around for a moment and panic when I think I've lost my car. But then I pause and spin in a slow circle, catching sight of it and finding it parked only a few spaces away.

When I do, I almost wish that it had stayed lost forever.

Since such a large crowd showed up so early, I ended up having to park in the back corner of the lot, under a broken streetlamp. Well, I'm certainly paying for that now. All of my windows are broken, and across the wet pavement, most of what I own is broken and trashed and sopping wet. All the good stuff is probably gone—the flatscreen I hid in the trunk that Kev bought me for our anniversary, my iPod that was stuffed in the dash, my small box of vintage records that belonged to my mom.

I stumble over and touch the scratched and dented surface of the trunk with a shaking hand.

Looks like whoever did this popped it with a crowbar. The assholes also took the time to slit all four tires, smash my headlights, my taillights. And here I am, with a dead dad and two hundred dollars to my name, no car insurance, no apartment, no job.

I sit down numbly on the pavement, just sit cross-legged in the pouring rain and let it drag my red hair into my face. If there's a difference between my tears and the rain, I'm not sure anybody could tell.

A couple of people stop and ask if I want them to call the police, but what are the cops going to be able to do? Write up a report? Give me a ride to … nowhere. The crap apartment I signed up for when Kevin and I broke up is gone, the keys handed in, the security deposit lost to my a-hole landlord for 'carpet cleaning'.

As I sit there, I think about how it hasn't rained in weeks. Weeks of dry desert air and dust. And now … this.

I drop my face into my hands and wish I could just *let go* and sob. But I'm too stubborn and I've tried too hard for too long. If I give up now …

"I was coming out here to give you your shoes, but holy shit."

The silver-haired guy leans down next to me, his eyes on the chaos of my car, all my stuff tossed in tempest waves across the rapidly flooding parking lot. I think I'm sitting in about half an inch of water already, like a flash flood.

I glance over and find the red heels clutched in his fingers. He shouldn't have bothered, really. Why didn't he just have a roadie bring them out here?

"Thanks," I say, but it's hard to hear my voice through the raging downpour. The word gets lost in the rain as I blink gobs of water from my lashes, only to see them collect again almost immediately. I take the heels and drop them into my wet lap.

"This is your car?" he asks, but I can tell he already knows. He almost has to shout to be heard above the storm. "Come on, let's get you out of the rain."

He reaches out to help me stand, but I wave him away.

"I need to pick up my stuff," I say, but even as the words tumble out past my lips, I know it's useless. Even if I gather all my wet soggy clothes, my now dirty pillows and blankets, where will I put them? Back in the car with no windows?

That's when it finally hits me.

Dad is dead.

He's dead.

My daddy is dead.

The sobs tear through me, and I double over.

"Come on and we'll get you dry," the silver-haired boy … Derek? … says as he puts an arm around me. "Is there anything special you want to grab real quick?"

I nod and dash my arm across my face.

"My mother's ashes," I say and the guy's face flickers with some emotion I can't read.

"Where are they?" he asks, but all I can do is point toward the trunk. I'd stuffed them inside a pillow and wrapped that in yet another comforter. For all I know, Mom could be scattered in the running waters beneath my feet, carried away toward the storm sewer.

Derek digs through what's left in the trunk and pauses, picking up a small plastic bag and checking the seal.

My heart soars for a moment, but only until it realizes how pathetic that is, to be excited that my dead mother's ashes are still in the remains of my ransacked car.

"Here you go, Lilith," he says, like maybe he remembers my

name from onstage. "Let's go inside."

He drapes an arm around my shoulders and escorts me back to the venue.

CHAPTER SEVEN

Ransom

RANSOM RIGGS

When Muse appears in the VIP lounge with a soggy wet girl under his arm, I find myself rising to my feet.

"The hell did the cat drag in?" Paxton asks with a smirk. I turn my dark glare on him, and he returns the favor. There's no love lost there, between Paxton and me.

"Don't be a tool, Pax," I whisper because there's never much point in screaming—unless you're onstage. Things that are screamed, those tend to get lost in translation.

I move around the silver sofa, past a sea of rich teenage punks that paid for the 'VIP experience', some stupid fan get-together thing that usually brings pretty girls our way. Not tonight. Tonight, it's all middle-aged housewives and college age assholes.

"I'll get you a towel," Muse says, giving me a look over the girl's ducked head. She must've been out there a long time, since it's been at least an hour since she ran away. She's shaking and her eyes have that glossy, vacant look that I recognize so well.

"What happened?" I ask, but I'm not talking to her; I'm talking to Muse. He gets a stack of white towels from a roadie and drops them on the leather seat next to us, grabbing one and tossing it over the girl's red hair. In typical Muse fashion, he doesn't give a crap about personal space or boundaries and starts scrubbing at her head, drying her off with skillful caresses of his fingers, like he's giving her a scalp massage or something.

"Some assholes broke into her car, smashed all the windows,

32

slit the tires." Muse gives me a long, lingering look, like maybe there's a lot more to this story than he's saying aloud.

"What do you have there?" I ask softly, putting my hand on Muse's to stop his vigorous drying motion. I know he's only trying to help, but he never does anything in half-measures; it's all out, all of the time. I think he's scaring the poor girl.

I reach out and try to uncurl her fingers from whatever's clutched in them, but all I succeed in doing is making her drop her red heels to the floor.

"Sorry," she says with a sigh, tucking the object against her chest and finally lifting her head. In her eyes, I see that she wants to be strong but really, all she feels is weak. That, too, I recognize, that feeling. Fuck. "I …"

"You want a drink?" Pax asks and I turn my head to glare at him. What a fucking asshole. He's just leaning back on the sofa in his stupid suit, a woman on either side—the housewives that he definitely *won't* be fucking tonight because his standards are fucking ridiculous—and smirking.

"A drink," the girl says, and then she slides into the leather chair next to Muse like her legs can't hold her up anymore. After a moment, she unhooks the pink purse from her elbow and unzips the top, digging out a cell phone. Looks like the leather of the purse protected that at least. "I'd like a drink."

Pax lights up a cigarette and glares at me; I glare back.

"I need to call my stepmom," the girl says, starting to stand up. She doesn't even make it a full inch off the leather before she collapses and decides to stay. She tucks her bare feet up on the chair and curls into a ball. Seeing her vulnerable like that, it makes me want to … no. It doesn't make me want to do anything.

I turn away as Pax orders some bourbon for the redhead and ashes his cigarette in a silver tray on the table between us.

I'm wearing my hoodie again, and it takes a lot of effort not to throw the hood up and hide myself away from the world. I hate these VIP things, even when there *are* beautiful girls to choose from. Doesn't matter anyway, I guess. There'll be some waiting around outside, near the buses—even with the rain. I don't have to go to bed alone tonight; I never have to go to bed alone.

Just the thought of it makes me shiver with dread.

"Here," Muse says, reappearing beside me and handing me a full glass of Jägermeister. I don't realize my hands are shaking until I reach out to grab it. A few sips later and I'm feeling better, like there's a blanket over all the rage and hatred and fear I keep trapped inside.

I sit down on the arm of the girl's chair and try to listen to her phone conversation while Paxton drones on across from me and Michael sits next to him, pretending he gives a shit.

"Susan, please," the girl pleads. I glance down at her and decide that even if she's wet, if her lashes are dripping with rainwater, she's also crying. I reach out and sweep some hair behind her ear, drawing big green eyes over to my face.

"Don't cry, sweetheart. We'll figure this out."

"She just hung up on me," the girl says as Copeland appears and pauses at the edge of the lounge area, on the platform above the small staircase. He just rests his hand on the banister and stares at the wet creature trembling on the seat next to me. *"My dad died today."* Her words echo around my head as she stares at her phone like she's just been betrayed in the worst way.

I slide down the arm of the chair until I'm sitting next to her, and then I pull her wet body onto my lap. It's a stupid thing to do because it attracts Pax's attention, rivets his grey eyes on the girl's shivering body. Now he's interested. Whoever I look at, he fucks, just to prove that he can do it. Again, and again, and again.

"Do you need me to call somebody, honey?" I ask as I brush her hair back with the long black sleeve of my hoodie. I like to wear them oversized like this, makes me feel eighteen instead of twenty-five. Eighteen was a much better age for me; my mother was still alive then.

"There's nobody to call," she whispers, blinking rapidly, like she's just realized she's curled up on some strange guy's lap. I move my hand so she can sit up and lean over to grab the bourbon Pax ordered for her. When she does, her wet jeans drag low and her top rides up; I can see the enticing line of her ass crack. I want to run my finger down it, especially with her legs

34

slightly spread, her warm cunt balanced precariously on my knee.

I suck in a breath and look away, noticing that Pax is smirking at me.

Jesus.

The girl sits back, tosses her drink down like it's water and then stands up. Without saying anything, she moves to an empty chair as the punks from the love seat next to me start to check her out like crazy. Fuck, I hate teenage boys.

Copeland comes down the stairs and sits; Muse does the same.

And Pax, he orders the poor girl another drink. I watch her swallow this back, too, and wonder if she knows what she's really getting into here. She's wet and clearly upset about her dad. Where the hell is her boyfriend? Family? Friends?

"Listen, baby, do you want me to call you a cab?" I ask as the girl sweeps red hair from her face and looks over at me. She's ridiculously gorgeous in this old school pinup sort of a way. Curvy and feminine, with a large chest, white skin, big eyes and this crazy red-purple hair that I can't tell is real or not.

I want her then. Just like that. Instantly.

"My name isn't *baby* or *honey* or *doll*," she tells me firmly, "it's Lilith."

"Ignore him," Pax says, his accent slurred with alcohol, "he never uses people's names. It's always *sweetie* or *gorgeous* or something of the like."

I don't know why I do that, but he's right. I never use people's names.

"Shut the fuck up, asshole," I say quietly, hoping he can hear the hidden menace in my words. The last time Pax and I got in a fight, I gave him ten stitches in his beautiful face and he broke my wrist. That was years ago, but still.

"Can I get another drink?" Lilith pops up when the waiter approaches and clears away the empty glasses.

"Bring me one as well, yeah?" Pax asks as our manager appears on the stairs with a professional smile fixed firmly in place. She thanks the teenagers and the housewives for paying an exorbitant amount for tickets that got them sloppily scrawled

35

signatures on their t-shirts, pictures with the band, and two hours of sitting here listening to Paxton ramble on.

"I'm heading back to the bus," Michael says as soon as they leave, his signature leather jacket slung over his shoulders even though it's a hundred damn degrees in here. He stands up, doesn't acknowledge the sad girl with the red hair, and disappears up the platform Copeland came down.

"Are you sure there's nobody I can call for you, sweetheart?" I ask Lilith one more time, but she just shakes her head and looks up at me with this defeated expression in her eyes that gives me the chills. I look at her and wonder if I should step in and do *something* other than repeat the same question over and over.

"I'm fine," she says, but she doesn't sound fine at all, "really." Her gaze locks with mine and in the end, I just do what I always do and get out a cigarette, lighting up as I drift the way Michael left, towards the exit and the rain and the buses.

Usually, there are groupie girls waiting around for us here. New ones in every city, regulars that glom onto the tour and follow us like puppies. Tonight, there's no one. It's the first night of the tour, and we had bus troubles so we were late; we pulled into the venue about an hour before the doors opened. With the storm and the delay, it looks like we're shit out of luck when it comes to girls.

Fuck.

My throat gets tight and my hands start to shake.

I really, *really* don't like sleeping alone.

CHAPTER EIGHT

Lilith

Glass after glass, I slam the burning alcohol down my throat and try to wash all the pain away. Of course, pain isn't like dirt, something you can just scrub off. It's like a fishing lure, all those sharp barbs stuck inside your skin. The more you slap and pull and tug, the deeper it gets embedded until eventually … you just bleed to death.

I think I'm bleeding to death now.

"I should go," I announce suddenly, cutting off Paxton's, Derek's, and the roadies' combined laughter. The guy with turquoise eyes stares at me from across the silver table. I have nowhere *to* go, but how can I tell these people that? They won't care. They're rich; they're rockstars. And I'm just … a girl with no daddy.

The room swirls with pot and cigarette smoke as I pick up my red heels from the floor and stumble through the empty lounge toward the front doors. By now, the crowd's cleared out completely. It's just the band, their employees, and the venue staff.

I feel completely out of place here.

I walk all the way to the glass front doors before it *really* hits me. I stand there then, staring at the driving rain outside and wondering if I should call Kevin, the cheating piece of shit that dragged me all the way down here in the first place with promises of a perfect life. Instead, he fucked so many girls that he gave me an STD; it had to be him. I was only sleeping with him. I've only ever slept with two guys in my entire life. I lost my virginity at fifteen to a boy from school and we did it all of two times before his family moved away. Then I met Kevin. And it's been Kevin and only Kevin for five years straight.

I sit down on the shiny floor and put my heels and purse in my lap, watching the rain pound against the pavement, turn the surface of the parking lot into a small lake. I pull my phone out next, scroll to his number and then pause, my heart flickering with pain and betrayal.

The asshole gave me *syphilis*. Fucking *syphilis*. Luckily I caught it early enough, but it can literally kill people, cause brain or heart damage. That's how I knew he was cheating—because I got sick. I'm completely cured now—a single dose of penicillin will take care of it if you catch it early—but that kind of betrayal … it's bone deep. Bone fucking deep. I trusted him and loved him and all he gave me was disease.

I unzip my purse and dig through it until I find the results from my last STD panel. I keep it in there out of some fucked-up PTSD or something. If I don't have it, I start to panic, to worry that I might get sick again. But there it is, printed plain as day. Clean, clean, clean. I'm clean.

But looking at this, I know that no matter how desperate I get, I can't and won't call Kevin.

"Thought I might find you down here," Paxton Blackwell says as he swaggers down the steps, clearly drunk. Slightly drunker than I am, I think. He moves over to stand next to me, tall and imposing in his fancy suit. Even intoxicated, he has this apathetic look, like he just doesn't give a fuck about anything.

Right now, that sort of expression's appealing to me.

"I thought you might like to come back to the bus with me, party a little more?"

I stare up at him, his tattooed hands tucked in the front pockets of his black slacks. His hair is combed and perfect, like he's getting ready to head to Wall Street in the morning, broker billion dollar deals or something. It's just the tattoos that give him away, peeking out above his starched white collar, crawling out from under his sleeves and washing his fingers with ink. When he holds his hands still like that, it's easy to see the dark tree line, the night sky, tattooed across his fingers.

I glance back at the rain, down at my phone where the only names plugged into the contacts that I care about are dead. I look back up at Paxton, the leader singer for Beauty in Lies.

"Okay," I say as I get to my feet; he doesn't offer a hand to help me up.

"Right this way," he tells me, starting off down the dark hallway.

He doesn't wait to see if I'll follow after.

CHAPTER NINE

Lilith

My fingers trail across the wet metal surface of the tour bus as I stumble along behind Paxton, trudging through the rain to the door and waiting for him to open it. He's so drunk, it takes him a couple of tries to get the handle to work right. The security staff standing near the door don't even look at us.

I climb up behind him, the world spinning slightly around me, and find what looks to be a fairly normal RV sized living room—albeit a really, really nice one. When I was a kid, Mom and Dad used to take me on trips around the country in a rented RV. I was obsessed with that old movie, the one with Lucille Ball in it, called *The Long, Long Trailer.* I made my parents help me pick out a new rock from every city we visited and stored them in a drawer under my bunk.

This is … like that, only bigger, edgier, much more luxurious.

A black leather sofa sits directly across from me, two smaller leather swivel chairs facing it. To my right, there's a partition with a glass window. Through it, I can see a captain's chair where the driver must sit next to a matching passenger seat currently occupied by boxes. To my left, there's a slender galley kitchen and a sliding door that must lead to the bunk beds.

"Want a drink?" Pax asks as I sway and drop my heels and purse onto one of the leather chairs. In the other, the guy from the gas station sits watching us.

"Are you okay?" he asks me and Paxton curses under his breath, trying to pour two tumblers of bourbon and spilling it all over the counter instead. I don't look at him, focusing instead on the bright eyes of the boy looking over his shoulder at me. He seems genuinely concerned.

"I'm fine," I promise. I'm a little drunk, but I don't care. I want to be drunk right now. "Thanks for the gas money," I add, in case he doesn't realize how much that actually meant to me.

"It was nothing," he says, watching as Paxton appears behind me and offers a glass over my shoulder.

"Drink up, love," he tells me, smelling like cigarettes and soap. It's this filthy clean combo that starts up a tender ache between my thighs. The feeling is as surprising as it is shocking. For months I haven't been able to masturbate, haven't been interested in sleeping with anyone because of what Kevin did to me. And now, today, the day my father dies is the day my libido decides to come racing back?

I feel sick, but I drink the alcohol Paxton gave me anyway.

"Maybe you've both had enough to drink, Pax?" the guy from the gas station—Copeland—asks, setting aside a book and standing up to face us. I see that he's reading *Fifty Shades of Grey.* Even I've never read *Fifty Shades of Grey.* It makes me want to read it to see what all the fuss is about; it makes me want to like him.

"I'm twenty-six years old," Paxton says, the slur in his voice disappearing in a rush of contemptible admonishment, "I will drink what and when I damn well please." He nods his chin at me. "And she's an adult, aren't you Lilith Goode?"

I blink, surprised that he remembers my full name.

"I'm twenty-one," I say, in case there was any real question.

"Twenty-one," Paxton says, looking cold and bored and apathetic again. He swigs his drink and then watches as I finish mine. Collecting our glasses, he sets them aside and starts to pull me towards the back of the bus.

The door opens and Ransom Riggs appears, swallowed up by his black hoodie, his nostrils flaring as he glances from Paxton to me, this strange, feral look on his sleepy bedroom-eyed face.

"You're never going to stop, are you?" he asks in a voice so quiet, I'm not sure I'm even meant to hear it.

41

"*Never,*" Paxton drawls and then he's shoving Ransom aside with his shoulder and pulling me down the hallway. The other two guys are here, too. The silver haired one is sitting on the edge of a bunk with headphones around his neck, raising his eyebrows at me as I pass by. The other one, Michael according to the internet, is lying on his back, clearly having a private conversation on his cell.

Pax pulls me past them both and pushes open another sliding door. There's a room behind it, swallowed up almost completely by a king size bed. There's not even room to walk on either side of it, just a small narrow bit of space at the foot.

Pax doesn't bother to squeeze us both in there and close the door.

Instead, he steps close to me and puts his tattooed right hand up to the side of my face. It reminds me sharply of how he was onstage, resting his hands and his face on my knee, singing like he actually gave a crap about me. Just goes to show how talented he really is; clearly, we don't even know each other. In fact, when I first met him, I didn't think he liked me much. He probably doesn't like me much now either, but it doesn't really matter.

I don't need someone to like me tonight; I need someone to fuck me.

CHAPTER TEN

Lilith

Paxton curves his fingers around the back of my wet head and pulls me close, hovering his warm lips above mine. He pauses there for what feels like forever, making me realize how much I want this kiss, how much I want it to taste like oblivion, drag me under and drown my pain.

For the third time in my whole life, I kiss a boy for the first time.

Paxton's mouth slants over mine and his hot tongue slides between my lips, taking complete control of the situation. Clearly, he's done this before and quite clearly, he knows what he wants. He doesn't care that my father died today or that I'm soaking wet and shivering, doesn't care that I have nothing and nobody.

That sort of apathy ... speaks to me.

I feel like whatever darkness I might have inside of me, his is that much worse.

He kisses me not like that forgotten boy from so long ago, not like Kevin's sloppy acquiescence to foreplay, but like a man, an adult, someone who knows his way around a woman's body.

I moan against his lips, curl my fingers in the wet but still somehow perfect lines of his suit.

When he pushes me against the edge of the doorway, I don't fight him, letting him slide his inked hands over my curves and take me in. Now that my clothes are wet, plastered in some places, sagging in others, I'm even more exposed, my breasts tumbling out of my top, my ass falling out the back of my jeans.

Pax uses this to his advantage, running his warm hands over my entire body, sending hot thrills of fire through me. My sex feels swollen and eager and my thighs clench tight as I pull the edges of Pax's white button-up apart and lay my palms against his tattooed chest. He's so much more … *defined* than Kevin ever was, sculpted and muscular. I've never been with a man like this; I'm excited. It makes me realize how much I've been missing out on, having awful, sloppy sex with Kev all these years.

Pax is clearly dominant, his hands unforgiving, forging a path that can't be swayed. I wouldn't consider myself a weak person, but this feels so damn good. I don't want to be in charge of anything right now, not after all that's happened to me today, happened to me this year, happened to me *ever*.

"On the bed," Pax whispers against my mouth, his accent delicious and so different from the slow Arizona drawl I've been hearing from the locals. "And hurry, Lilith Goode; I don't like waiting."

He removes the silver cuff links at his wrists—a pair of finely crafted guitars in perfect miniature—and he does it with this slow, careful precision that scares me, especially when he looks me straight in the face with those eyes.

They take my breath away.

I climb up onto the bed, surprised to find that it's actually soft, the black silk duvet cover smelling of laundry soap. I bet with these boys and … whatever girls they bring back here, this has to be washed—and replaced—a lot.

I try not to think about that as I lean back on my elbows and catch sight of Ransom watching me from down the hall. He's leaning against a wall, one foot crossed over the other, completely casual in his stance. His eyes … they tell a different story.

He watches me like he's hungry.

I drag my gaze away from him and his dark eyes, dark hair, all closeted away in the shadows of his hood. When I look back at Paxton, he's got his jacket off, his shirt unbuttoned all the way down. I can see the flat expanse of his tummy, every square inch covered in colorful tattoos. He kicks his shoes off while I watch, takes his socks off slowly, watching me as he goes about removing each piece of clothing.

Meanwhile, I'm leaning back on my elbows in my wet holey jeans and tank top, my heart thundering, the alcohol keeping me from feeling too self-conscious about the whole thing. After a moment, Ransom moves away but he's quickly replaced by Copeland.

"Don't be cruel, Pax," he says, his soft voice a warning. His lead singer ignores him completely, taking off his belt and tossing it up onto the bed, like he plans on using it for something. My breath catches as he climbs up over me, the heat and weight of his body so new and exciting.

I reach a hand up experimentally, slide it along the side of his face and see how intimately he'll let me touch him. My fingers are just tangling in his dark hair before he grabs my wrist and pushes it aside. Wow. He's *really* closed off; all of that arrogant apathy must be just be one hell of a shield.

"Lucky you," he says, and I can't tell if he really believes that or not, "finding me out in the parking lot like that. And you pretended not to know who I am? Everybody bloody knows who I am."

"I didn't," I answer honestly as he lifts one hand and lays his fingers across the front of my neck. When he pushes me back down into the blankets, I don't resist. Sweet, sweet oblivion. I need that right now.

"Sure thing, love," he says and then he's kissing me again, tasting like cruelty and bourbon. This guy … he's hot as hell, but he's also a little bit scary. If this were for more than just one night, I'd be worried.

'Don't be cruel, Pax.'

I wonder what that was all about.

I don't have to wonder for long.

Paxton grabs hold of my hair—*hard*—makes my scalp sting a little as he fists mahogany strands around his knuckles and pulls. His tongue is merciless as it drives between my lips, claiming every single last part of me, leaving no stone unturned. I hardly notice when his hand drops down and unbuttons my jeans.

45

His fingers slip easily inside, one hot tip trailing down the front of my panties and then under the fabric, testing to see how wet I am. I'm soaked, and not from the rain. Paxton pulls his hand out and slides his middle finger against his thumb, rubbing my juices against his skin.

"Well, that was easy, wasn't it?" he asks and his voice is as cruel as his kiss. When he reaches over and grabs the belt, my heart starts to hammer and I feel sweet trailing down between my breasts. He wraps the leather around my wrists and around a spindle at the bottom of the headboard, pulling it taut and then poking the metal clasp through a hole near the center of the belt, one that he clearly doesn't use to keep his pants up.

He's done this before.

I'm not sure whether that should bother or excite me as I lay there with my arms tied up above my head, watching him. He sits up, his white button-up hanging casually off one shoulder and then he drops any residual hope of a smirk or a smile, staring down at me with grey eyes full of tempest-tossed storms and angry seas.

"If you want me to stop, just say it. I don't play games."

And that's it, the only warning I'll get.

Pax stays sitting propped up long enough for me to examine some of his tattoos, and although I'm pretty drunk, I recognize that there are words scrawled in black cursive all the way down his chest, dipping underneath his waistband. I wish I could read some of them.

Light filters in from down the hall but for the most part, it's dark in here. The two small windows have their curtains closed, and even from in here, the rain sounds loud and angry and raucous.

Pax pushes my sticky wet tank top up and over my breasts, sliding one steady hand around my rib cage to undo the clasp of my bra. Now that my arms are tied up, he can't remove it completely, so he just pushes that up, too, exposing two aching mounds of tender flesh, cool and wet from the rain, desperate to be touched.

When his hot hand closes over one, I don't even care that his touch is just this side of too much. He squeezes and kneads my

46

flesh before dropping his mouth to my nipple, grazing his teeth over the hard points and making me gasp. Automatically, I try to bring my arms down, curl my fingers in his hair and take some control over the situation. But the leather belt is tight and tugging on it only seems to make it feel tighter.

You just met this guy and you're letting him tie you up? What the hell, Lilith? I think that, but I don't ask Pax to stop and untie me; I don't want him to stop. If I make him back up, undo his belt, send me back out into the rain, I'll have to remember that I am nothing and I have nothing and ... there's no one left.

I gasp as his mouth closes fully over my left nipple. Pax bites down hard enough to draw my rib cage up off the bed, but not so hard that I tell him no. Without ever having met me before, without knowing anything about me, he somehow has this innate knowledge of how to ride the fine line between pleasure and pain.

"Lilith Goode," he whispers against my breast, flicking his grey eyes up to stare at me over the pale mound of my breast. Paxton raises his head and leans forward, putting our mouths close together again. "I'm like a connoisseur," he says, brushing some wet, red strands of hair from my forehead. Unlike when Ransom did it earlier, there's nothing kind about the gesture. "A collector, if you will."

"A collector of what?" I just have to ask, even though I know he's baiting me.

"Of names," he says, surprising me. "What's your middle name?"

"Tempest," I say and his curved dark brows go up.

"Tempest," he repeats, and I like the way the name sounds with his accent.

"What's yours?" I whisper back, liking that for just a split second there, Paxton Blackwell looks almost vulnerable, almost human.

"Nah, I don't give my name out to strangers," he says and just like that, the moment's passed and he's sliding down my body, hooking his colorful fingers under the waistband of my jeans. He slides his right hand to the button, flicking it open

47

with his thumb.

I watch him, my head slightly raised, as he drags the denim down my legs and tosses it aside in a soggy heap. By the time I hear it hitting the floor, he's spreading my thighs and pressing a hot kiss to the inside of me.

His touch feels … charged. It's like that kiss sinks into my bloodstream and travels straight to my core, making me gasp and struggle against the restraint on my wrists. Only, there's nowhere I want to go, nowhere but here. Hell, there *is* nowhere but here for me.

Paxton takes his sweet time working down my thigh from my knee. I swear, it takes *hours.* The pleasure is both exquisite and sadistic, too much and not enough at the same time.

I make a plaintive whimper, but my brain is firing on so many primal levels, there's no room to think treacherous thoughts—not about Dad, not about my car, not about anything.

Pax *finally* presses his mouth to the crotch of my red lace panties and white-hot color explodes behind my eyelids. Kevin went down on me maybe a half-dozen times during our entire five year relationship, and I got the impression that he just wasn't into it.

Paxton, he's *definitely* into it.

He makes these … these male sounds when he's between my thighs, like that's where he wants to be. And his mouth, it's just as ruthless between my legs as it was on my lips.

His fingers curl under the fabric and pull it aside, finally exposing my pussy to the scorching heat of his bare tongue. It's about all I can take, dropping my head into the pillows and letting out a loud, pained sort of a sound.

"Your past lovers not take care of you right, Miss Lilith Goode?" he asks, and I can feel his cruel laugh against the bare heat of my throbbing wetness. "Because you're wound up real tight."

Paxton thrusts a finger inside of me, punctuating the word *tight* with the motion.

I scream then, a real, full shout that makes my throat feel dry and sore.

"What the hell, Pax?" a voice asks quietly from the hallway

48

—I think it's Ransom again.

The bed creaks, and I take the guess that Pax is glancing over his shoulder. I'm trembling too much to lift up my head and see for myself.

"Fuck off, Ran. Can't you see I'm busy here."

Pax inserts a second finger and I cry out again. It's a little overdramatic, but it feels so good, and the sensations shoot straight up into my brain, like lasers destroying all the horrid little thoughts and memories biting at my subconscious.

I'm sweating all over the pretty black duvet cover, leaning my head back and focusing my blurry eyes on my bound wrists. I'm crying again, but I can't decide why that is, so I ignore it, leaving my head where it is so Paxton won't see and stop.

I don't hear anything else from Ransom, so I just assume he's left because Pax starts fucking me with his fingers, deep and hard and fast. My body loves the unfamiliar shape of his hand, tightening dramatically as I take fluttering breathless gasps. He even drops his tongue back down and tastes my clit, the hot flesh of his mouth pressing too hard, flicking too sharply.

I love it all.

"I want you inside of me," I whisper and he laughs again.

"I'll bet you do," he says, but he withdraws his hand and I glance up again, finding his grey eyes on mine, watching as he wipes his wet fingers on the open edge of his white button-up. He might've just laughed, but he's definitely not smiling. Our gazes locked, he reaches into the pocket of his expensive slacks and draws out a condom. "Safety first." Even that, in his cold, sharp accent, sounds mean.

Pax unzips his pants, but I can't lift my head up enough to examine his cock. It's too dark anyway to see much, so I lay my head back again and listen to the rustling sound of his clothing, the rain outside the window, the gentle creak of the bed.

His hand takes hold of my face and tilts my chin down as he hovers above me, his hard warm body settling between my thighs.

"Look at me while I fuck you," he says, and I don't even have a chance to breathe before he's thrusting his cock inside of me. It's been so long, and he's only the third man I've ever been

49

with, so the sensation is ... it's so intense that I feel tears prick the edges of my eyes. "There it is again," Pax whispers, like he's fascinated with me, with my emotions. "What the hell is wrong with you?"

He asks that question even as he stares into my eyes, one hand holding my face, his opposite forearm keeping him propped up. My hard nipples scrape against his bare chest as his white button-up gapes open and his hips piston into mine. He's big, much bigger than Kevin, and I feel for a second there like he's going to break me.

Well, if I weren't already broken.

I squeeze my thighs around him, trying to get him to slow down a little, feeling a hot flush coloring my cheeks. When I try to close my eyes, he squeezes my face with his pretty fingers.

"No. Look at me."

"Why?" I ask, but the word is strained and thready, and he doesn't much look like he gives a fuck about what I have to say. Good. I don't want him to care; I just want him to fuck me. His cruelty, I almost feel like I deserve this. Dad was dying; I knew that. But I didn't go home right away because ... oh God, for so many reasons that don't even matter anymore.

Before I know it, tears are streaming down my cheeks again and Pax is slowing, stopping.

He just stares at me.

"Please don't," I whisper against his lips as he puts his mouth so close to mine that we're sharing breaths. "Don't stop. Not yet."

"Fuck," he says, but he keeps moving, filling me up, stretching my body with his cock. He's so long that when he thrusts in, I get this weird tingling sensation deep inside. I squeeze my thighs tighter, pull my legs back, give into the sickening rush of pleasure that I *don't* deserve. I want Pax to be crueler, rougher, meaner.

"Harder," I whisper as he kisses me again, steals my breath with his tongue. He takes my instruction as carte blanche to go as fast and deep as he can, letting go of my face, dropping his hand and cupping my ass. Paxton drives into me and pushes everything else out—my doubts, my worries, my fears. He fucks me until I'm a sweating, aching mess, looking into his face as he kisses me with his eyes open.

We stare at each other, and when he comes, he drops his forehead to mine, shuddering and gasping, digging his fingers into my ass ... and then looking at me like I'm fucking crazy.

"The bloody hell ..." he starts and then he's pushing away from me, pulling out. I feel the bed jostle as he stands up off of it, and lift my head to watch him. "The fuck ..." He's still cursing as he tosses the full condom into a trash can and zips himself up.

Without even bothering to untie me, he walks away.

CHAPTER ELEVEN

"Paxton?" I call, lying there naked and sweaty and desperate as hell. "Paxton!"

I pull against the belt and curse him under my breath, wanting to cry some more—this time from frustration.

What. An. Asshole.

What a fucking asshole.

I even hear the front door of the bus open, the storm thundering and raging, and then I hear it slam behind him.

"Paxton!" I scream, thrashing at the stupid fucking belt on my wrists. I liked it before; now I just want it off. Preferably so I can wrap it around the lead singer's neck and pull *tight.*

"Holy shit," a voice says and then somebody's climbing on the bed next to me.

It's the boy from the gas station, the band's drummer, Copeland Park.

"God, are you okay, Lilith?" he asks, and I like how he, too, seems to remember my name. "Fucking Paxton. Jesus, I mean. This is the first time he's ever left a girl tied up like this ..." He trails off as he undoes the belt and I drag my wrists to my chest, cradling them and trying to get back some sensation. "Damn it," Copeland's cursing, but I see him glance over at me and then away sharply.

I'm aware of what I look like, lying naked and pale on the black bed, drenched in sweat, red hair wet and stuck to my forehead. I wonder if he can see the green of my eyes; I can certainly see the bright blue-green of his, even in the dark.

Some distant part of me, buried beneath sex and alcohol and pain realizes that I should probably be scared, sitting naked and alone on a bus with a bunch of men that I don't know for shit, that could do all sorts of horrible things to me and probably get away with it.

But I'm not.

"Are you alright?" Copeland—I heard his bandmates call him *Cope* earlier—asks softly, still not looking at me. I think of that hug he offered that I turned down, that he gave when I asked a second time. No, I'm not scared of him at all.

But I am ... I need ... something. More. The pain and fear is starting to creep back up on me and I feel like I'll collapse under its weight if it gets me now. Just a few more moments of oblivion. Is that too much to ask?

"I'm cold," I say and Cope turns to look at me.

That's when I reach up and take the side of his face in my hand, kissing him hard and quick on the mouth, hoping that he can taste my feelings on my lips. Maybe he won't want me after he just saw another man fuck me, but I don't care. I'm asking with my kiss ... and he's answering.

Copeland turns to face me, pulling me into his lap. We've just started kissing and already, I can feel him hard and ready beneath his expensive jeans. Maybe he's been hard this whole time, listening to Pax and me fuck? I hope so. The thought turns me on even as a wave of giddy, nervous energy shoots through me. Two men in one night? Two men was the whole total of my entire sexual experience until about forty minutes ago.

It feels ... dirty and wrong and ... I want it so badly it hurts.

"How drunk are you?" Cope asks after a minute, putting his fingers in my hair, his touch soft but firm. I realize he's dead serious about his question, this guy who reads *Fifty Shades of Grey.*

"I'm buzzed, but not as drunk as Paxton," I say, looking into his vibrant eyes, wishing I could swim in them. I bet the water's warm. "Not drunk enough to regret this in the morning."

"Okay," he says simply, and then he pulls my face gently towards his. His kiss is *nothing* like Pax's. It's sweet and comforting, but somehow more invasive, like he could crawl inside of me and pull all my secrets out. I think about the way I felt when I first spotted him at the gas station, how all of my emotions rushed up through my skin, flooding me with feeling.

I wrap my arms around his neck, like he's my boyfriend and not some random one-night stand.

It feels good, to hold him like that. He holds me right back, putting those musician's hands of his on my bare waist. His long fingers curve around my body and make me feel grounded, steady. It's such a different rush, such a change from Paxton's cruelty that I feel little butterflies tickle the inside of my belly.

I kiss Cope and feel the warmth of his single lip ring brush against my mouth. He's a good kisser—a *really* good kisser—and he kisses with his whole mouth, every bit of it. Lips, tongue, a very soft brush of teeth, breath, even rubs his nose softly against mine.

Holy crap.

This is the kind of boy you fall for without even realizing it's happening. This kind, he's *ten times* as dangerous as Paxton Blackwell. With a guy like Pax, it's clear what he wants and why. With a guy like this … it could be anything.

I feel thankful I've never fallen in love with a man like this. Kevin was hard enough, broke my heart right in two, and he was a complete douchebag. A boy like Copeland with long fingers and soft hands, that smells like denim and laundry detergent, that tastes bright and fruity like the red drink he was sipping at the bar … he's heartache waiting to happen.

The more he kisses me, the warmer I get, the more tender my skin starts to feel, until I'm afraid that I might just crack in half completely.

"I want to come," I whisper and Cope actually laughs, this soft, easy sound that probably melts women's panties. If I had any on, it would melt mine.

"Pax couldn't get you there?" he asks, and there's this sharpness to his voice that makes my heart hurt. "What a tool."

Cope turns and deposits me onto my back again, pausing for just a split second to glance at the open door. Unlike his lead singer, it looks like he might actually mind being watched. But

54

for whatever reason, he leaves the door open and sits up, tearing his white band tee over his head and tossing it aside.

His body is … oh my god.

Big strong arms, broad shoulders, a wide chest. I could tell he was the drummer just by the strength of his upper body. Unlike Pax, he's almost completely free of tattoos, with the exception of a pair of hearts right over the left side of his chest. He's still wearing sweatbands at his wrists, but I think I see some ink peeking out from there, too.

"Is there something in particular that you like?" he says and I blink in surprise. I did not expect to be asked that by a rockstar. His eyes … they pierce right through me.

"Um …" I have literally no idea how to answer that. What do I like? It's been so long since I even thought about it. *I hate you, Kevin. I hate you so much.* A stranger is asking me what I want, and my boyfriend of five years never bothered. "Just an orgasm," I say because I haven't had many of those in my life. Actually, I'm not sure if I've ever had one. Don't people generally say if you're not sure, then you haven't had one? I've gotten close though—mostly by myself.

Cope chuckles again, sounding like the boy next door, that heartthrob that all the girls fall in love with because he's so damn nice. He fucks them all, never commits to any of them. That's what I see when I look at Copeland Park.

"One orgasm, coming right up," he says as he ruffles his auburn-red hair with his hand. Looking at him, I think he's Irish or Scottish, like I am. And I like the easy, casual style of his hair. It's not all crazy and huge and gelled into spikes like some punk rocker from the eighties, just put together enough to show the world that he gives a fuck. "Lucky for you," he says as he leans over me and I get that butterfly feeling again, "that's my specialty."

Cope's warm breath against my ear makes me squirm, and I'm suddenly so damn glad that my wrists aren't tied anymore. I wrap them around his neck, play with the short hair on the back of his head with my fingertips. Cope kisses me like I'm his real girlfriend, not some random girl he gave money to at a gas station.

The way he holds me, it's like he's hugging me again and it feels so fucking good. If I let myself, I could fall right into his arms and never want for anything again.

With bad boys—like Paxton Blackwell—it's so easy to tell what they're thinking, what they're going to do. But the good boys ... they make you feel safe before they drop you on your ass. See, told you Cope was dangerous.

The nice ones always are.

CHAPTER TWELVE

Copeland

I press my lips to the thundering pulse in the sad girl's throat, feeling her heart beat against her bare chest, pressing mine close so we're skin to skin. I like that, feeling people's emotions through their body.

And this girl ... she's absolutely thrumming.

I wonder what happened to her, even as I kiss my way down her neck, trail my fingers down her side. She's absolutely beautiful, like Marilyn Monroe but with red hair and green eyes. As soon as I saw her in the gas station, I wanted to be all the hell over her, worshipping her body with my hands.

And asking me for an orgasm like that? That just kills me. What else can I do but give one to her?

Fucking Paxton, that piece of shit. I would totally kick his ass if I thought it would help, but Pax is just Pax. He's been a dick since I first met him, when he was nineteen. He's an even bigger dick now, has been ever since Chloe and Harper died in that accident.

Well, since Chloe *killed* Harper in that accident.

Still, how could he leave this naked, trembling girl in here like that?

"You're beautiful," I tell her because I get this sense that she doesn't hear it enough. I see a lot of girls like this, lonely and sad. They need somebody to want them, and I want to want them. I want to take care of them all. Inevitably, I let them go after the night, but I always pray that when I do, they'll find their feet.

This girl in particular, there's just something about her. When she asked for that hug backstage? Well, fuck, I was thrilled to see her there.

I help her out of her wet tank and loose bra then kiss her breasts gently, noticing the marks that Pax left in his wake of destruction, hickeys and the slight indentation of teeth. I pay extra close attention to those spots, leaving a trail of warm, gentle kisses against Lilith's pale, white skin.

Her moans are throaty and uninhibited, possibly from the alcohol, possibly from whatever emotional trauma she's been through today. I could see it reflected back in her eyes when she was onstage with Pax, this deep-seated pain gnawing at the edges of her soul.

Poor Lilith.

She tangles her fingers in my hair and hugs me close, squeezing my face to her chest, using my body for comfort. I like that. A lot. Pretty lips and nice hair, curves and breasts, those are great but it's moments like this that really turn me on.

I kiss all the way down her belly, pausing at the small strip of red hair on her pussy. It's waxed into a shape that I like to call the *champagne* because it looks like a champagne flute. I brush my thumb across the hair and Lilith shivers. It's crazy, how vibrant and wild her hair is against her skin. I was sure it was dyed when I first saw her, but unless she dyes her pubic hair, it's as real as those vibrant emerald eyes of hers.

"Fucking gorgeous," I murmur against her hip, curling the fingers of my left hand around her curves and squeezing gently. Her soft flesh fills my hand, just enough to grab onto, enough to cushion the hard planes of my body against hers.

I glance up and find her panting, staring up at the ceiling, her fingers still clutching my hair.

"Are you okay?" I ask and she nods, her gaze drifting down to my face.

"I'm … yeah, I'm good." I lift myself back up, prop my face up on an elbow and stare down at her, letting the heat and weight of my body make her wiggle underneath me.

"Just tell me what you want. Whatever is, I'll do it." I smile and her cheeks flush. "Well, with few exceptions. There are

58

some things even a rockstar won't do to get laid."

"Like?" she asks, breathing hard, her heart still pounding against my own.

"Oh, stuff you don't even want to *know* about," I joke and then I kiss her mouth again. She responds like a flower tilting toward the sun, raising her chin, pressing against me with her whole body. Her legs fall apart, and I know what she wants. Pax teased the hell out of her; more foreplay at this point is just torture.

I break our kiss and roll onto my back, reaching up behind me to one of the small drawers on the headboard. This room back here, we all take turns using it, bringing girls back here. It's a lot easier to play around on a custom king size bed than it is on a little bunk shoved into the wall. Anyway, there are plenty of condoms in that drawer. I pull one out and glance over at Lilith. She's turned toward me now, her hands cradled beneath her head.

"You're really nice," she says and I smile again. "Is it all bullshit?"

"Bullshit?" I ask with a raised brow, turning onto my side to face her fully, propping myself up on an elbow. "No, not at all."

"Why did you give me money at the gas station? You knew I hadn't lost my wallet."

I shrug.

"You needed money; I had some on me."

"And the hug?"

I sigh and lean in, kissing this stranger's lips like they belong to me. I like to pretend that they do, sometimes. All these girls. Like maybe one of them is actually mine.

"What about it? You needed a hug; I had one on me."

Lilith sighs, but it's a good sounding sort of a sigh.

"Want me to fuck you now?" I ask against her mouth and she nods, breathing out, the warmth of it fluttering against my lips. This girl, she smells and tastes like rain. Maybe she sat too long in the storm?

"Please do."

I roll onto my back, unbutton my jeans, and slide the pre-lubed condom down my shaft. Lilith's more than ready when I turn toward her again, pulling me between her thighs and rolling so that she's on her back with me on top.

She closes her eyes tight, cutting me off from that gorgeous gaze.   I struggle to describe the color in my own head. Something like … like rolling hills or fresh spring leaves, vibrant and alive.

But if she wants them closed, that's okay with me.

I find her opening with my cock and she gasps, panting and curling her fingers around my shoulders before I'm even in. Her nails dig into my skin, but I don't mind. I smile and kiss her mouth until she relaxes and her thighs loosen up a little against my sides.

"It's okay, Lilith," I tell her, "we'll get you there."

"Okay, Cope," she whispers back, and I really like that she uses my nickname. She must've picked it up from one of the guys, or maybe she's a really big fan of Beauty in Lies. I don't think she's a groupie, doesn't act like one at all. Besides, she definitely didn't recognize me at the gas station.

Makes me like her more.

I push inside slowly, pausing when she tenses up again, and only moving forward when she calms down. It takes a few minutes, but I end up fully sheathed in her warmth, ripples of pleasure tracing across my skin as I breathe out, long and low.

"That feels good," I say and Lilith makes a murmuring agreement in her throat, her voice soft but strong underneath, like she wants to be a nice person but she's seen too much shit. I like that, too.

I reach down and adjust her hips, adjust my position a little, making sure that when I thrust, I grind against her clit, too. It's already swollen and firm, as desperate for an orgasm as she is.

"So tight, Lilith," I whisper against her ear and she shivers all over, tightening around me.   The sensation is hard to describe, an intimate sort of hug, a caress. I keep moving with deep, easy strokes. I know the shape of my own body, the way it feels inside of a woman. I've asked, many times before. My shaft is slightly curved, so if I get the motions right, my cock stimulates the top wall of a woman's vagina just right, hits that G-spot, makes her shiver.

It definitely makes Lilith tremble beneath me.

Her pink lips part with a pop, and she makes this sound.

"Oh."

Just that. I smile again and lean down, kissing the top of her head, pretending like the two of us have some reason to be in this room other than just sex. It's a nice fantasy anyway.

Her hips start to move with mine, and I encourage that, putting a hand on her hip, helping her rock into me so that it feels good for us both. Lilith's so wound up that it doesn't take her all that long to start gasping, thrusting hard against me, that steel band of muscle inside her taking me prisoner.

I move a little faster, listening to her heartbeat thunder through her body and into mine.

When she comes, there's this rush of relief that floods her and washes over me, too. Her back arches and she locks her legs behind me, holding me inside of her as her body flutters around mine, pulses and begs me for something that I can't give her. But I wish. I would *love* to come inside of this girl.

I take the next best option, kissing her deep and hard, moving my hips through the aftershocks of her orgasm and finding my own. I groan deep and rough against her mouth, coming hard inside the condom.

For a moment, I let her hold me like I'm hers.

Lilith clutches at me, and when I glance down, I see that she's crying again.

Poor, poor Lilith.

"It'll be okay," I say as I grab the base of the condom and pull out, chucking it in the trash and fixing my jeans. And then I take her in one arm and let her cry against my chest for an hour. But after this, I have to go.

Because I'm not hers, and she's not mine.

Although for some reason, with this stranger, this time ... I kind of wish she was.

CHAPTER THIRTEEN

I think I drift off to sleep, but not for long.

I wake with a start, and my first thought is *Dad is dead.*

He died.

Without me.

My heart clenches with pain and I sit up, the black silk blanket falling down to my hips. Copeland is gone; so is Pax. I rub at my eyes and then start to panic. *What time is it?! How long have I been here?* But when I get up on my knees and pull the curtain aside, I can see it's still dark, still raining, still Phoenix.

I breathe out a sigh of relief and pause when a knock sounds at the door.

It's the other guy, Derek, the one who found me in the parking lot. He's wearing a pair of thick rimmed glasses in black and trying not to smile. He's also pretending to cover his eyes with his hand.

"Hey there," he says as I feel my body start to tremble. But it's not because of him. It's just ... after a tragedy, sleep feels so good, like a reprieve. Waking up becomes this horror because every time you do it, you have to relive the shock and loss again, until it becomes as familiar to you as the whorls of your own fingertips.

My daddy is dead.

And he was my best friend, my rock when Mom died. When Yasmine was murdered. We were it for each other until Susan came along, until Kevin. I never should've moved away and left him when I knew he was sick.

I'm a terrible human being.

"Sorry to bug you, Cutie, but we're shipping out soon."

"Oh," I say, liking the feel of this bed beneath me. It's warm and cozy, and even if a hundred girls—or more—were fucked in here, I don't care. The little room at the end of the tour bus has silver striped wallpaper and a black headboard shaped like a bat with spindles its in gaping mouth. There are records hung on the wall in different colors; I have no idea that they mean.

When I leave this bus, I'll be standing in wet clothes with a purse full of my mother's ashes. Two hundred bucks and nowhere to go. And I'm tired. And sad. And so hungry.

As if it can read my thoughts, my tummy rumbles and I clamp a hand over it, pulling the silk blanket up around my breasts. Derek drops his hand when I do, proving that he wasn't *really* covering his eyes up.

"You're kicking me out," I say blandly, but he just tucks his hands into his pockets and stares at me. His hair is so … well, *cool*. It's silver-white on the top, darkening into black at the roots. Looking at it, I guess that maybe Copeland's hair is a *faux hawk* because this look is more 'mohawk'. I mean, I guess. I'm not really an expert on this kind of thing.

"Not really, not yet. You can stay for a little while longer. Or all night, if you want."

"All night?" I ask, my heart thundering.

"If you fancy a trip to Denver?" he says with a small laugh, sliding one hand over his crazy hair. His eyes are taking me in like I'm a statue, a piece of art to be examined and appreciated. I'm not sure how to feel about that. His gaze is openly curious and tinted with a mild sort of humor. It's hard to tell in the shadows, especially with his body limned in light from the hallway, but I think his eyes are a rich hazel, warm and gold-grey and inviting.

I breathe out, tempted by his offer. If I at all thought he was serious, I would jump on it. A free ride to Denver? That would take me at least part of the way to my destination. And then maybe I could rent a car or something? No. No, you need a credit card for that. Fuck.

"I just wanted to say, if you need the shower, it's free. Also," he kicks his foot back and taps his toe against a box sitting in the hallway behind him, "I went outside and picked up some of your stuff, anything that looked important or was in good shape. I put the rest in your car and taped the windows up with plastic bags. Won't keep the thieves out, but at least it won't rain inside anymore than it already has."

"Why?"

The word pops out of my mouth before I can stop it. I feel like such an *asshole*. Why? I should be telling him … "Thank you," I say quickly. He's still smiling at me, this sexy, sly little smile that says nothing at all about his personality. "Seriously, it means a lot."

Deep breath, Lilith. Don't cry again. You're stronger than that.

But … there's nothing wrong with grieving, with tears. I need to remember that.

Dad died today.

Sharp breath.

"All your stuff is wet," he says, glancing at something on the floor. My jeans, I think. "You want some clothes? I have a ton of extra shirts; you could have one. Maybe some sweatpants?" His smile twitches a little. "No bras or panties—I usually send those along with the girls who bring them."

"How very kind of you," I say, gathering the sheets close and watching him watch me. If I invited him, I think he'd fuck me right now. At least, he's looking at me like he would. "Yeah, if it's not too much trouble, I'd like a dry shirt."

"Abso-fucking-lutely." He tosses some stuff at me and I see that he already anticipated that I'd say yes. There's a huge black band tee with the words *Beauty in Lies* in pale pink; broken white hearts oozing red blood decorate the fabric in a random pattern. This thing, it'll be like a dress on me. The sweats are black, generic, definitely well-loved but clean and smelling of laundry soap.

My stomach grumbles again and Derek smiles.

"Want something to eat?" he asks me. I hate feeling so vulnerable, but … I'm *starving* right now. And it's not like I have a lot of money for food.

"If it's not—"

"No trouble at all," he says, intercepting my words and disappearing down the hall. I have no idea what to do now, where the shower is, if I should try to get dressed under the covers. I'm sitting there thinking when I see Ransom again. He just pauses in the hall and stares at me with his dark chocolate eyes.

My heart almost leaps from my throat when he walks down it and puts a hand on either side of the doorframe, blocking out all the light, completely cloaked in his black hoodie and shadows.

"Just so you know, Paxton is back. If you want to beat the shit out of him, honey, I'll hold his arms for you." Ransom speaks so quietly, I have to concentrate to hear him properly. My skin shivers and the aching warmth between my legs pulses, like I didn't just fuck *two* different guys.

"It's okay," I say as I pull the covers closer and meet his hooded stare. Somehow, even with his lids covering half his eyes, it looks like he's putting effort into keeping them open. It's so beyond sexy I can barely breathe. He's the only person I've spoken to today that I told my secret to. It makes me feel stupidly connected to him, even though we just met. "I don't care about Paxton. Fuck him."

Ransom laughs, and the sound … it's like a ribbon of shadow curling around my shoulders, making me lean forward. The sheets fall to my waist, exposing my breasts. It's an accident—or maybe a Freudian slip—but I see the darkness flash across Ransom's face.

He runs a hand across that tortured expression and glances away, moving to the side when Derek reappears with a plate.

"Okay, Cutie," he says, crawling across the bed on his knees as I scramble to cover my breasts up. When he hands the plate over, I see a big fat sandwich brimming with something that looks like roast beef, a pile of potato chips, and a handful of cookies. He's even brought me a soda. "Here ya go. Eat up. Wouldn't want to lose all those juicy curves."

"Leave her alone, Muse," Ransom growls from the doorway

and Derek Muser—Muse, I guess—glances over his shoulder.

"Cool it, Ran. What's your problem? Don't take your Pax hate out on me, man."

Ransom shakes his head suddenly, shoving his hood off his dark hair and spinning on his boot, storming down the hallway and slamming the sliding door at the end of it, cutting all the light.

I feel my hand start to tremble and the sheets fall around my waist again.

Fuck.

I don't want to be in complete darkness right now.

"Shit," I curse, suddenly very aware that there's some strange guy in the bed next to my naked body ... that I fucked *two* other strange guys not all that long ago. "How long have I been asleep?" I whisper.

"Um, about a half hour after Cope came into the living room. Are you sure you're okay?"

"My dad died," I blurt, setting the plate down on my lap, cracking the top on the soda just so I can hear the sound of it fizzing. "Today. He died. From cancer."

I swallow huge mouthfuls of the soda and it feels too sweet running down my throat. I just want it to stop. I reach back, looking for the shelf on the headboard I saw earlier. I set the can down with the click of aluminum.

"I'm sorry," Muse says quietly, his voice a sort of strange brightness against all the dark around me. "So that's why you look so sad then. And here I was feeling bad for you about the car. I mean, not that that doesn't suck, too."

He pauses, like he's rethinking his words.

"Sorry, sucks isn't the right word."

"No, sucks is exactly the right word," I say with a small sniffle.

"Where's your dad now?" he asks, like he can tell I wouldn't have come to the concert if I could get to my dad.

"In New York. I found some extra tickets in my purse, so I came here to sell them, to get gas money for the trip." I pause and think of Paxton, sitting on the hood of a car, smoking a cigarette. My cheeks flush and my body feels warm all of a sudden. But seriously, what a fucking prick. "Then I somehow managed to win the backstage pass thing and ... I never should've gone inside."

There's a long stretch of quiet, and I tentatively place a chip in my mouth, closing my lips and letting it melt there for a second.

"So now you have no car, still have no money, and I'm guessing ... all that stuff ..."

"I was moving there, to be with him, to take care of him." Tears spill down my face in fat, hot drops, but I don't make any sound, eating the chips slowly, one by one. "The stuff in that car was everything I had."

"Fuck."

I seem to make these guys say *fuck* a lot. Not sure what it is. My life is just screwed-up and weird, I guess. Maybe I attract unhappiness? Maybe there's something wrong with me? Either that or I was just a complete and total bitch in my past life.

I reach up and run my fingers through my hair. It's still wet in some places, tangled as fuck. It'll take me hours to comb it all out. I shift and the blankets rustle loudly in the sudden quiet.

"What are you gonna do?" he asks me. "You have family around here or something?"

I don't answer that, choosing instead to take a bite of my sandwich. It is roast beef, and thinly sliced cheddar, tomatoes, lettuce. He even took the time to put mayonnaise and mustard on it. And I'm so damn hungry that it's *good*. Like, really, really good.

"Guess not or you wouldn't be here, huh?" he asks, and then I feel his hot hard body leaning across mine. I go still for a second, but then light blooms from a lamp on the side of the headboard. It's got a red shade, so the color is muted, bathing the small bedroom in this hazy, sexy sort of glow. "You have a plan?"

"Not really," I say, blinking and trying to let my eyes adjust to the light. That's when I remember that I dropped the blankets and that my tits are hanging out, but at this point, I honestly just don't care anymore. I hope Muse looks; I want him to look.

I keep eating my sandwich as he leans back into the pillows

and puts an arm behind his head. Cope was nice; Ransom was interesting to talk to; Paxton was hot. But Muse is the only man I've met today that had the decency to think about basic human needs. Well, besides sex.

"You want a plane ticket?" he asks suddenly, and I look over at him. I thought he'd be staring at my breasts, but his eyes are closed. I notice then that he's wearing a set of sweatpants that are exactly the same as the ones he gave me. I can't remember what he was wearing onstage. Jeans, probably.

"A plane ticket?"

"Sure. I could buy you a plane ticket, so you can go and see your ... family." I'm glad he doesn't say the word *dad*. I just don't want to hear that word spoken aloud again right now.

I finish off my food and then set the plate on the same shelf as the soda. In the red light from the lamp, the little room is even cooler, even more hip. I could live here.

"I'm sure they're expensive ..."

"I'm loaded," he says, like it's no big deal. I glance at his face and he cracks one eye, the color mysterious and shifting with every micro movement that he makes. I decide that they're definitely hazel in color, blue and green and brown and copper all at the same time. Beautiful. "Here." He takes his phone out and hands it to me. "Go online and find your ticket and I'll buy it for you."

"Why?" I ask, and yet again, I feel like a complete bitch. I should just be saying thanks.

"You remind me of me," he says which is weird because I don't feel like we have anything in common at all. His other eye cracks open as I take the phone in my hand and lay back. Sitting together like this, though, I feel like we could be friends. Muse is easy to talk to.

Silence falls again and I hear raucous arguing from the front of the bus; I ignore it.

I search for Phoenix Sky Harbor airport on a travel site and then try to set up a trip to New York. The more I search, the more depressed I get. Either everything is sold out, or grounded from the storm. I make a frustrated sound under my breath and drop the phone in my lap. My first streak of luck today and the

weather—and some stupid awards show happening in NYC—
are destroying my chances of getting home.

"No luck?" he asks and I toss the phone his way. "Fuck."

See, there it is again.

"There's nothing—*nothing*—until next week," I whisper, and
even though I *can* wait, I feel like I'll die if I do. I *have* to find
some other way to get home.

"Book it for next week; I'll pay for a hotel."

I sit up suddenly on my knees. It's a move that quite literally
flashes the whole of my naked body to Muse, but it's over and
done with, so I just sit there and stare at him.

"Stop that," I say as he sits up and gives me a weird look,
raising an eyebrow that's pierced with four black metal balls,
spaced horizontally above his left brow.

"Stop what?" he asks, but his hazel eyes rake my body with
a sudden fervor and he sucks in a sharp breath.

"Fuck."

Third time's a charm, I guess.

"I should go," Derek … Muse … whatever, says and acts
like he's about to get up from the bed.

"Please don't," I say, reaching out a hand, curling my fingers
around his muscular arm. He glances over at me, staring at me
over the rims of his glasses. When he pushes them up his nose
with his middle finger, I lean in and kiss his mouth. I'm not
even sure *why* I'm doing it, but it just happens and then there's
this spark that ignites between us. He reaches up with both
hands and takes hold of my face, kissing me long and deep,
drawing me forward on my knees.

When I swing my leg over his, he reaches out and helps me
straddle his lap, still kissing me, hands still on my face even
though I can feel his cock beneath the fabric of his sweatpants.

Oh my god, Lilith, what the fuck are you doing?

Didn't I just screw two other guys? A third one … that
would be crazy, wouldn't it?

I'm such a slut, I think as I put my palms on his pale purple
wifebeater, digging my fingers into the fabric. I realize in the
back of my mind that this probably isn't the healthiest decision
in the world. Dad just died and I'm not thinking clearly, not

even close.

I keep thinking Muse is going to push me away, ask me what I'm doing, but he doesn't. Instead he reaches down and pushes his sweats out of the way, freeing his cock. I don't even look at it, just keep kissing him as he takes my wrist and guides my hand down between us. My fingers wrap his shaft, gripping hard, working him as I lean in close and push my breasts to his chest.

I think about maybe giving him a blow job, but my mind's just not there; I need oblivion.

I copy what Cope did and reach up to a drawer on the nightstand. When I dip my fingers in there, I find a lot more than just condoms. My cheeks flush, but I don't care to analyze what else these boys have stashed on their bus. I just take one of the little packages out and break our kiss long enough to open it and slide it down Muse's body.

He groans as my fingers trace his shaft, letting his head fall back against the headboard. He lifts his muscular arms up and crosses them behind his head, eyes closed, thoroughly enjoying himself. He's not cruel and desperate like Pax, not sweet and attentive like Copeland, but relaxed, easy, willing to go wherever the flow takes us.

I stare at his face in the hazy red glow, at his glasses, his silver-black hair. He has one sleeve of tattoos, all in black, just a whole flock of bat silhouettes that explode from the fingertips of his left hand, fly in a burst up his arm and onto the back of his neck where they disappear into his hair. I wonder if he has them on his scalp, too?

He opens his eyes and looks back at me.

"You don't have to fuck me for the plane ticket or anything," he says with a slight shrug. "That stuff's just free."

"I know," I say and then I almost smile. Not quite. Almost. "I wouldn't fuck you to get any of that. I'm not a whore."

"Didn't think you were," he says as I put one hand on his shoulder and lift up onto my knees, straddling his cock and using my other hand to guide him where he needs to go. Derek settles his hands on either side of my hips and helps ease me down the length of his shaft.

Groupie

I breathe out sharply as I settle myself onto his lap, my skin prickling with new sensations, the brush of foreign hands, the feel of a foreign body buried deep inside of mine. Somehow, knowing this is the third guy I've slept with today … excites me. It stirs some deep, primal part of me that wants to mark all of these boys as my own. The thought's as foreign as it is different; I've always strictly been a one man sort of a girl. Other than that guy I slept with twice as a kid, it's just been Kevin, Kevin, Kevin. I devoted myself to him and look where that got me?

I'd much rather have a menagerie of men.

I giggle—stupidly and inappropriately and randomly.

Muse smiles at that.

"Nice to see you've still got a sense of humor," he says as I drop my right hand onto his other shoulder, right over a sea of bats, and start to move. His smile doesn't last long as I rock my hips, slow at first, and then faster, faster, faster.

Sweat drips down the sides of my face as I push the emotions aside with sex. It really is the best drug. I'm surprised because the alcohol I downed earlier in the lounge didn't seem to do nearly as much to take my mind off my problems. This … with Muse's cock inside of me, there's no room for anything else.

I bite my lower lip to keep back a barrage of sounds, but my teeth slip and I end up letting them all fall out anyway. I groan and sweat and grind against a man that I don't know, looking up to find him with his head tilted back, his hands guiding my hips. As if he can feel me staring at him, Muse drops his gaze and leans in close, taking my lower lip between his teeth, sucking it into his mouth.

I groan as he slides his hands up my back, soothing my heated skin with his fingertips. He smells vaguely of cigarettes and something pleasant and smoky, like a fragrant incense. As I ride him, I listen to the soft creaking of the bed, the rough gasps of his breath. I'm surprised he lets me go as fast and frenzied as I am, that he doesn't come right away. I work him hard, too, pressing my pelvis into his, rubbing my clit with each thrust.

My head drops to his shoulder, but I don't stop, biting one of his bat tattoos. Muse tastes like he smells, smoky and spicy.

Maybe like cloves? I'm not sure.

We don't talk as I grind myself into him, feel my orgasm catch, and gasp again, biting his neck this time. Muse clutches me close, wrapping an arm around my waist as I arch my back and let my head fall back, wet hair clinging to the sweaty, sticky surface of my skin.

His mouth meets my nipple, sending me crashing completely over the edge and before I know it, I'm on my back again and he's fucking me hard, finding his own release with a sigh and a deep, masculine groan.

When we've both had a chance to catch our breath, he sits up and looks down at me, adjusting his glasses with a single finger. That, too, has bats on it. I try to remember if I saw him wearing glasses earlier and decide that I didn't; he must wear contacts onstage then.

Muse opens his mouth to say something—hopefully to offer to stay in here with me because I think I might need more, more, more. His mouth, his hands, I don't care.

"What the fuck is going on in here?"

I glance up past Muse's shoulder and find the guy with the leather jacket, the one with the violet eyes. He's not wearing his jacket now, standing there shirtless and glaring. Muse makes an annoyed sound in his throat and rolls off of me, fixing his sweatpants.

"We're just playing around," Muse says, still breathing pretty hard as he gets rid of the condom and the guy ... Michael, I think it was ... scowls down at him. He's covered in tattoos, too. Not a whole layer of them like Pax, but he has two full sleeves and a big chest piece. Also like Pax, he looks like a complete dick.

But I'm attracted to him, too. Maybe there's something wrong with me tonight? Maybe I'll wake up tomorrow and realize this was all a dream, that there was no way I was surrounded by five hot guys on a bus ... or that I had sex with three of them.

"You could play around, too," I say and I hardly recognize the sound of my own voice. Who is this person, this woman that's confident enough to invite yet *another* man into her bed?

But then, it's not really my bed is it, and maybe I'm not this woman? Maybe I, too, am playing around?

Who the fuck cares?

I hold up a hand to Michael as Muse whistles under his breath and scoots off the bed, leaving to give us some privacy, I think. Michael looks my body up and down, his feathered black hair falling into his face, his beautiful eyes passionate and wild. I bet he's an amazing lover.

He looks at me with fire rearing in his eyes, parting his lips, darkening that violet gaze to black. I can almost see his pulse in his throat, can swear I hear his heart beating. As I stare up at him, I even catch sight of a single drop of sweat sliding down the side of his muscular neck, over the jewel toned firebird tattoo on his chest.

Michael runs his tongue across his lower lip and rakes his fingers through his hair; I can see the bulge in his sweatpants from here.

"No," he says after several long moments. I feel my hand drop to my side, feel my heart thundering, my cheeks turning red with embarrassment. "I don't fuck groupies."

Groupies? I think as he turns away, climbs into a bunk and slides a curtain closed. The sound of the metal rings grating against the metal bar makes my teeth hurt. *Groupie? I'm not a* groupie.

That was the first time I'd heard that word used on me; it wouldn't be the last.

CHAPTER FOURTEEN

Lilith

I dress myself in Muse's giant t-shirt and sweats, listening to the chatter from the front of the bus. The door to the bedroom itself is still open, but the one leading into the kitchen area is closed. As far as I know, there's nobody back here but me and that asshole Michael guy. My cheeks flush as I dig my bra and panties out of the wet clothes on the floor and tuck them into the giant pocket on the sweats. My jeans and tank are sopping. No way I'm putting those back on.

I'm finishing off my soda and trying *not* to glance at the three full condoms in the trash can by my feet when the door at the end of the hall opens and spills weak light across the shadowed floor.

It's Ransom again.

"Hey, honey," he says when he sees me sitting there and looking at him. I want to hate that he says *baby* and *sweetie* and *honey,* but I don't. There's just something about his soft, sleepy voice and his bedroom eyes that makes it sexy. "Muse says you have free reign to use his credit card to book whatever you need."

He comes all the way down the hall in his black hoodie and grey sweats, holding out a hand with a smartphone and a credit card tucked inside it. I notice he's barefoot and casual, leaning against the doorframe and staring down at me on the edge of the bed.

"Thanks," I say as I take the phone and the card, my body humming and singing while my heart whimpers and cries. It's a strange feeling. This night ... this wasn't the way it was supposed to go. I was supposed to drive my shitty Matador to Dad's place, move back into my old bedroom, take care of him during the day and start night classes at the community college.

A drop falls on the bright surface of Muse's phone before I realize I'm crying yet again.

But then, it's been—I glance at the time on the phone—about twelve hours since I found out that I was alone in the world. Twelve hours. Half a day. I think I can cry still and not feel like I owe the world a strong face to look at.

"Where *is* Muse?" I ask as I look up, wondering suddenly why Ransom, one of the only guys I *didn't* sleep with tonight, is the one bringing me the phone.

"He called a tow truck for your car; he's outside with our manager and some roadie that says he knows a good auto body shop."

"He's towing my car?" I ask, and I can't decide whether or not I should be excited about that. "Can they fix it?" I hear the wistful hope in my voice at the same time Ransom does.

His full lips twist to the side in a sad sort of smile, dark eyes focused wholly on me and my tear streaked face.

"I don't know, sweetie," he says, and his voice wraps around me and holds me tight, like a caress, like one of Copeland's hugs.

"I can't believe it's six in the morning," I whisper next and then I just break down, dropping the phone and credit card into my lap and covering my face with my hands. I can't even *believe* that my daddy died today. How? Why? He was smart and strong and the kindest man I'd ever met. He was young, too. He was only forty-eight years old and now he's *dead*? How can he be dead?

"It's okay to cry, baby doll," Ransom says, sitting down on the bed next to me. He takes the credit card and phone away. I'm not sure what he does with them, but he puts his arms around me and even though it's not the same kind of hug that Copeland gave me, I feel some sort of connection to him. "Come 'ere," he says, turning and crawling up the bed, flicking off the light.

I can barely see his hand when he offers it to me.

I sniffle and even though I'm a little suspicious of his motivation, I take what's being offered and follow him to the pillows. He gets us both under the covers and then gently turns me so I'm facing away from him. My throat gets so dry and my body throbs in response to his touch as he curls his own around me, spooning me nice and tight.

It's literally the most intimate thing I've ever been a part of—and that includes all of the sex I just had.

"Let the tears out, baby doll," he says as he buries his face against my neck and breathes out slow and deep. I swear, he smells like my mother's violets. Or maybe he just smells like cigarettes? Doesn't matter. I like the way his arms feel as they curve around me and hold me tight. "When my mother died, I locked myself in a bathroom and cried for two days straight."

"I'm sorry," I whisper as he presses a strangely intimate kiss to the side of my forehead.

"Thanks," is his response.

"For what?" I ask, trembling and shedding messy tears all over the black silk pillow beneath my head. "You seem to be the one comforting me."

"For this. I hate sleeping alone, baby girl. I *hate* it."

I start to tell him that I'm not sleeping here, that I have to go, that I'm sure their bus is probably leaving for Denver soon.

Instead, I drift off in a stranger's dark arms, swaddled in heat and hoodie and most definitely, the flirty scent of violets.

CHAPTER FIFTEEN

Lilith

A pleasant jostling wakes me out of sleep, this gentle rocking motion that brings primal memories to the surface, like a baby in a cradle. It's soothing, especially when combined with the soft, warm breath feathering against my ear, the rhythmic breathing of the body curled protectively around mine.

This is nice, I think as I snuggle into the pillow and then ... that awful feeling sweeps over me.

My father died yesterday; cancer *stole* him away from me.

A hiccuping sob rises in my throat and chokes me as I sit up straight, tearing myself away from the warm arms that held me.

Ransom Riggs.

The bassist for Beauty in Lies.

I rub both hands down my face and feel the gentle jostling motion again.

It's the movement of the *bus.*

"Oh my god."

I scramble to the window on the left side of the room and push the heavy blackout curtains aside, letting golden light spill across the black surface of the bed. We're rocketing down a highway, flat, dry ground stretching out for miles and miles, covered in nothing but shriveled sad looking shrubs. Makes me feel awfully lucky to be inside this dark, air conditioned bedroom.

A groan sounds from behind me and I glance back to see Ransom pulling his hood over his eyes.

"Close the curtains," he mumbles, and I do, shoving them

back into place and spotting my purse on the floor near the foot of the bed. Someone must have brought it in here for me, but I have no idea who. I dive for it and snatch my phone from inside, checking the time.

It's almost two o'clock in the fucking afternoon.

"Holy shit," I whisper, checking my texts and finding ... nothing. Literally, nothing. Nothing from Kevin or Susan or my estranged aunt, Bess. It really hits me then, how truly sad and alone I am. I disappear all night, half of the next day, and nobody knows where I am. Nobody cares.

I drop the phone in my purse and sit back on my heels with a deep sigh.

"What's the matter, honey?" Ransom murmurs from behind me. The sound of his voice is dark and sensual and soothing. I get the impression that he's broken and sad inside, but he does a good job of hiding it.

"Where are we?"

He sits up, yawning and stretching his arms above his head. The motion causes his hood to fall back, revealing a headful of messy dark brown hair, the same color as his eyes, like chocolate or a hot cup of coffee tucked in tired hands.

"I have no idea," he murmurs, leaning over and peeking through a curtain. His face wrinkles up and he blinks stupidly at the bright sunshine. "Ugh. Gross." I'm not sure if he's referring to the sun or the scenery, but he drops the curtain back in place and looks over at me. "We're on the road," he says, like he's afraid I'm going to freak out.

I almost do.

But then I wonder why. Why the hell should I care? We're driving, aren't we? And it's not on my dime with my gas or my food. If these boys can get me to Denver, then why not? Maybe I can get a flight from there to New York? Muse said I could use his card ...

"Who decided to just take me along for the ride?" I ask as Ransom yawns again and scratches at the front of his hoodie with lazy fingers.

"Probably Muse," he says in that soft, velvety voice of his. "He overreaches a lot, makes assumptions, acts like he knows people when he has no fucking clue. Need me to hold *his* arms back for you, baby?"

"No," I say, my voice just as soft as his. I scoot back up to the pillows and watch as Ransom shrugs his hoodie over his head … revealing a bare chest etched in scars and ink. He has three deep gashes across his sculpted pecs, long healed and slightly discolored from the rest of his skin but visible nonetheless. When the bus hits a particularly big pothole, the curtains flap and sunlight flashes across Ransom's face. I realize with surprise that he has a scar there, too, down the side of his left cheek. It's not visible without the bright light to highlight it, but it's there. I decide not to comment on any of it. "I … need to get to New York anyway and my car clearly isn't going to make it. Maybe I can get a flight out of Denver?"

I watch as Ransom struggles with his hoodie, yanking out a black t-shirt from inside it. I guess he took both off accidentally. He slips the shirt over his head and then turns to look at me with his heavy lidded gaze.

"That sounds like a good plan, doll. But why New York?"

"It's where my dad is," I say. I can't make myself say *dad's body*. His corpse. This shell of flesh and bone that used to be the greatest love of my life, the only man I ever truly loved. My daddy. I suck in a sharp breath and wrap my arms around myself.

"You have family there?" Ransom asks, but when I don't answer, he makes this soft, sad sound in his throat that manages to light me up completely. I glance back at him and see that he has his hand out again. "Sleep with me a little longer?" he asks, and I turn and go to him. What else is there to do? I don't know anyone on this bus and it's a *long* drive. If I had to hazard a guess, it looks like we're near the Arizona/Utah border. It'll probably be another six or seven hours until we get to Denver.

I curl my body up against Ransom's side and realize with the sharp sting of butterflies that I'm doing something weird with a stranger—*again.* Four strangers, four weird encounters in one night. *Five if you count that asshole Michael guy staring at me like he wanted to jump my bones and then storming off.*

I refuse to think about him; I have enough to worry about.

"My dad was my hero," I say absently.

"My mom was mine," Ransom says and I shiver when I think about his story. "*Some guy broke into her house, raped her and shot her in the face.*" Harsh words to say to a stranger. "You're probably curious about my scars," he says mildly.

"No," I say, but that's a lie.

Silence falls between us and I close my eyes, drifting in and out of sleep for a little while.

I wake up when I hear Ransom make a sharp, terrible gasping sound.

Snapping to, I sit up and look down at him, finding his legs tangled in the sheets, his breathing hard and uneven, sweat soaking his forehead. Immediately, I drop my hand to his face and brush sticky wet strands of his hair back.

"It's okay, baby," I say, and realize stupidly that I'm imitating his weird pet name habit. "It's okay, wake up." I stroke his face until his eyes flutter and he flicks them up in my direction, meeting my gaze. Before I can stop myself, I'm leaning down and kissing his mouth. It's full and warm and his response is priceless. He makes this sound that turns my body to liquid, makes my sex clench in anticipation of feeling him inside of me.

Ransom pulls me on top of him, wrapping me up like he did last night, kissing me with a mouth that tastes like shadow and heartbreak; I can't explain it. That's just what he tastes like.

His hands glide down the back of the t-shirt, and he grips my ass in strong fingers.

We make out like teenagers, kissing for what feels like years, tasting and exploring each other with our hands. He manages to get one up my shirt, fondling my breast with this fervent desire he holds firmly in check, like he's afraid to let it out and see what might happen.

Feeling him hold back like that makes me want to shake him loose, so I pull away and slide down, my entire body on fire, my skin so sensitive that the touch of my clothing feels painful. I catch the grey waistband of Ransom's sweats and start to tug them down.

He stops me with a hand on his waistband.

"Wait," he whispers, voice still delicious and decadent, but laced with need. "There are scars all over me, down there, too."

But I don't care, so when he lets go, I pull his sweats down and see what he's talking about.

There are several sharp lines down here, too. None on his actual genitals, but his hips and thighs. Now I'm *dying* with curiosity; I want to know.

Then a horrible image pops into my mind, of those leaked pictures of my sister, all those gunshot wounds, and I clamp down on that curiosity. I don't need to know everything; I've learned that lesson before.

I focus instead on Ransom's cock. He's thick, bigger than stupid fucking Kevin for sure. And I've always sort of hated giving blow jobs before ... but I need to see Ransom let go a little.

I kiss my way down his shaft, fondle his balls with my hand, feel his tension leaking out little by little. And the sounds that escape his throat, those are like foreplay in and of themselves. I've never heard noises like that, these velvety little kisses of sound that get stuck in my head, travel through my blood, and wet my borrowed sweatpants with desire.

"Too much, sweetheart," he gasps when I slide as much of him between my lips as I can. "Too much."

I don't stop, sucking and caressing him with my mouth, my tongue, enjoying the way he writhes beneath me. I don't take him to the edge though. When his breath starts to flutter and he curls his fingers in my hair, I move back up to lay next to him.

Ransom doesn't waste any time getting a condom and slipping it on. He doesn't climb on top of me though, instead encouraging me to turn around. I get on all fours and gasp as he slips the sweatpants down to my thighs. I can't spread my legs with them on, but that doesn't seem to matter. I'm so wet that when he grabs hold of my hips with one hand and guides his cock to my opening with the other, he slips right in.

I'm shocked at the full, heavy feeling of him between my legs like that. Like he said, *too much.* It's too much. It gives me something else to think about though, keeps my mind occupied with the delicious slide of his body inside of mine.

Ransom is different from the other boys, restrained and

desperate, and sad, so sad. He's got this dark, twisted soul that I can feel through the connection of our bodies. It makes me want him at the same time it scares me enough that I wonder if I should stay away from him.

Doesn't matter, I tell myself as I put a palm up against the shiny black lacquered surface of the wooden bat headboard. *This won't happen again. Just this one time. One time.*

I repeat that mantra as his hips slam into me, the slightly uncomfortable feeling of tightness morphing into pure pleasure, tearing through my body in violent waves. I gasp and shudder, even as his skillful hands slide down and underneath the baggy t-shirt, cupping my breasts. Ransom leans over me, puts his mouth to my ear and whispers something.

"I wish I could see your face."

I think that's what he says, but he doesn't stop fucking me long enough for me to decipher it. Instead he moves inside of me until he comes, slamming into my aching body with deep, wild thrusts. The rough, broken sound that tears from his throat almost shatters me into pieces.

I'm still recovering from that when he pulls out and turns me over.

He gets rid of the condom, fixes his pants and reaches into a drawer above my head.

"What are you …" I start, but he's got this silicone cock in his hand, smiling wryly at me when I make a face.

"It's just a dildo, sweetheart," he says as he runs his long fingers down the length of it. "And it's brand-new. No worries." Before I can protest, he's slipping it into his mouth, lubing it up like he doesn't give a shit what that looks like, how hot it is.

He lays down next to me, curls an arm under my back and pulls me close.

Our eyes are locked when he puts the toy inside of me. It's not as warm as he was, but it feels so good, especially when I see the way his pupils dilate, the way his gaze lights on fire when he watches it move in and out.

I relax into the pillows, turn my head and bury it against his t-shirt, breathing in that sweet fragrant scent of his as I drop my left hand to my clit, tease some juices over it and masturbate myself all the way up to the edge and over the other side. It's so weird to do this with a stranger watching, but something about Ransom ... his pain calls to mine. We could be twins.

I come around the toy, soaking his hand in shining heat, gasping as I push my head into the hollow of his throat, feel the slight brush of stubble rub against my skin.

"There you go, sweet thing," he whispers, kissing my forehead, putting the toy into a different drawer and pushing it closed. I wonder what they do with those? Throw them away and buy new ones? I'm not exactly an expert on sex toys, but aren't those things expensive? I suppose it doesn't matter; I won't be here long enough to find out.

"When your—" I start, intending to ask about his mom again, but the door to the bedroom opens and I turn to find Paxton Blackwell standing in it, smoking a cigarette and staring at me with his steel grey eyes.

"Get the fuck out, Pax," Ransom growls, and even though his voice is quiet and dark, it's terrifying. Clearly these two have a history,

I pull away from him and sit up, tucking tangled red hair behind my ear as I watch the two men stare at each other. The two men that I *just* fucked.

Holy fucking shit.

I just slept with four dudes in a row.

My cheeks flame and I snap my gaze down to my knees; I can't seem to look at either of them right this second.

"The fuck is going on in here? Are you poaching my groupies now, Ran? That's low—even for you."

"You left a girl tied up with your belt," Ransom says, and I close my eyes. I do not need him to defend me, but I have the sense that this is about a lot more than just last night. These two are letting some old hurts boil up. "What the fuck is wrong with you?"

I finally get the courage to look up, finding Pax staring at me with a bored, neutral sort of expression on his face. It's weird, looking at him like this, thinking about his cruel mouth on my pussy, his cock driving inside of me. One-night stands ... this is my first experience with them and I'm not sure how to act.

"I'm not a groupie," I say finally and they both turn to look at me. I know what it looks like: I got on their bus, proceeded to invite all *five* of them to fuck me, and ended up actually doing it with four different members of the band. So yeah, I *guess* groupie would be the word, but that's not why I came here or why I slept with them. "I'm not starstruck and I'm not here for Beauty in Lies. I … just needed to forget for a little while."

"Yeah, well, hate to fuckin' tell you, love, but that's what we're *all* here for."

"What do you want, Pax?" Ransom asks, voice low and simmering, drawing the other man's grey gaze back to his face. Seeing Paxton again this morning, after what he did to me last night, I should probably be pissed off, too. My tired soul just doesn't seem to have room for that kind of emotion though and instead, I end up studying Pax almost as apathetically as he seemed to be looking at me. He's still wearing his slacks and button-up from last night. The shirt hangs off one shoulder, exposing most of his bare upper body to me.

That's when I realize that the cursive words on his chest are accompanied by musical notes and when I squint, I start to read the lyrics.

"Look into her eyes and say goodbye; never let another day go by; don't miss the quiet moments in between; never love and never leave again."

Holy shit.

Those are the lyrics to that song, the one I heard in the car when I first … got that fucking text. The only difference is that in the actual song, the words say *his* eyes; Paxton's chest clearly says *her.* He notices me looking, adjusting his position in the doorway so that he's facing me fully, smoking his cigarette with inked fingers covered in trees and night sky. He's gorgeous, just as gorgeous as he was onstage—maybe more so. But he also looks like he's had a hard fucking night. His dirty blonde hair is mussed and tangle, his eyes shadowed, black liner smeared next to one eye. Pax looks seriously hungover.

"Want?" he asks, finally, studying me with that practiced cruelty that he does so well. Obviously, it's a mask for a seriously fucked-up individual underneath. I don't let it bother me. "I want to know what the hell you're doing back here, all shacked up through the afternoon with this girl." He gestures at me with his cigarette like he doesn't give a fuck, maybe even like he's somehow disgusted with Ransom for staying in here with me. But there's a sharp undertone there that I don't miss. "With this *Miss Lilith Tempest Goode,*" he adds, tilting his head slightly to the side and smirking at me with his mean mouth.

"I'm like a connoisseur. A collector, if you will."

Pax's words ring in my head and I take a deep breath, meeting his gaze without flinching.

"None of your goddamn business," Ransom says quietly, grabbing his hoodie and putting it back on, like it's a security blanket or something. No, maybe more like it's a costume, as much a shield for his emotions as Pax's wicked mouth and steely glare. "How does that sound?"

"It sounds," Pax starts, glancing down at the trash can on the floor by his feet. My cheeks light up with red and I make a groaning sound, putting my head in my palms to hide my face. There are four condoms in there … from four different guys. From last night and this morning. Oh. My. God. "Like you're getting awfully defensive of something that doesn't belong to you."

"That would be your specialty, not mine," Ransom breathes, his voice so low and dangerous that I have to lift my head up.

"Please stop," I say as I grab Muse's phone and credit card off the shelf, scooting forward on the bed and swinging my legs over the end. I put my feet on the narrow strip of floor, surprised to find that the wood is pleasantly warm. Wow. On a bus, no less. The only place I ever lived in that had heated floors was in the apartment Kevin moved us to when we first came down here, the apartment I left when he gave me … his awful parting gift. "You two don't need to fight on my account. As soon as we get to Denver, I'll be out of your hair."

I look up and find myself so close to Pax, close enough that I can remember why I let him take me to bed last night.

"Is there a bathroom I can use?"

"Right this way," Pax says, flicking his gaze back to Ransom with a flash of triumph. I have no idea what that's about, but whatever's going on between these guys, it'll take a lot longer than one day to fix it. Not that I have any interest in doing that anyway.

Pax backs up down the hall, dragging his fingertips along the wall, his cigarette shedding ash as he walks. I follow him, a little nervous at the exchange between us, like we're playing a game of cat and mouse. Clearly, *I* am the mouse.

Jesus.

"Toilet's here," Pax says with a smirk, pointing to his left. His white button-up finally gives up the ghost and slides down his other shoulder, leaving his glorious body open to my gaze. I swallow hard. "But clearly, there's no *bath* in there. The bath," he starts, using his bare foot to slide open a door on his right, "is in here."

I glance around the corner, surprised to find that the entirety of the little room on my left *is* a bath with a showerhead in the ceiling, black and silver tiles covering every square inch of floor, ceiling, and wall. To even get in there, I'd have to step over the edge of the tiled half-wall that makes up one side of the bath.

"Take your *pick*," Pax says, still bracing himself in the narrow hallway with his forearm. He smokes his cigarette and then drops it in the toilet on his left. It sizzles out with a small sound. Behind him, the door to the kitchen is closed, but my heart starts to pound when I think of Copeland and Muse, sitting out there, possibly wondering what I'm doing, possibly judging me.

I can't quite bring myself to care.

"Excuse me," I say and I try to duck under his arm into the toilet. He doesn't let me slip past him, caching me around the neck with his forearm and pulling my body against his.

"What's your story, Lilith Tempest Goode? You follow me onto my bus and then fuck all my bandmates? I didn't peg you for such a naughty girl."

"My dad died yesterday," I say and it has exactly the sort of effect I thought it might. Pax releases me like I've tossed cold water in his face, giving me just enough time to slip into the little room and close the door behind me. I lock it and flick the switch for the overhead fan, putting my back to the wall and sliding to the floor.

Silent tears stain my face as I weep quietly for everything that I've lost.

I guess I don't realize yet just how much I'm about to gain.

CHAPTER SIXTEEN

Michael

"Why the fuck is that girl still on our bus?" I demand as I watch Pax let himself out of the hallway with a disturbed sort of a look on his face. I know that look; I'm just not sure *why* I'm seeing it right now. "Are you okay, man?" I ask, changing my tone suddenly. My friend looks like he's just seen a ghost or something.

"Why does it matter if she's on the bus?" Muse asks from behind me, drawing my attention around and finding him standing in front of the counter, making himself a cup of tea. Tea. Like he's not already weird enough. "It's not really your business, is it?"

"Who is this chick that all four of you would fight over each other's backs to stick your dick in her? She have some kind of special vagina magic or something?"

"Hey, watch your mouth, Michael," Cope says, slamming his book on the table next to the sofa. The look he throws me is dripping with disdain. He thinks he's better than me, charming the panties off girl after girl after girl. Because he's *nice* to them, that makes him a sweetheart or something, some heartthrob boy next door or whatever. Fucking hypocrite. "Muse is right; what do you care?"

"Because we don't generally drag groupies from one city to the next. I like my peace and quiet when I'm on the road. After that nightmare roadshow you all put on during the last tour, we had an agreement."

"Seriously, Michael, you need to get laid," Pax says,

pretending he's perfectly fine when he didn't sleep a damn wink last night, drank himself into a stupor and passed out on the kitchen floor. "That girlfriend of yours make conjugal visits?"

He doesn't look at me as he pours himself a cup of coffee and lights up another cigarette.

"How long is this chick going to be here?" I ask, knowing I'm being a hard-ass and not caring. I don't want her on my bus, stirring up shit from day one. Last night's gig was the first of this tour—a *world* tour—that starts in the states and takes us everywhere: Montréal, Dublin, London, Sydney. One little hiccup on this tour and everything could go to shit.

And I for one have plans: tour, new album, marriage proposal, kids.

My longtime girlfriend, Vanessa, is waiting for me back in Seattle. I won't let anything fuck that up—not even a curvy redheaded groupie with dark green eyes.

My lip curls as I lean against the counter between Muse and Pax, trying not to think about how hard I got when I saw that girl stretched out on the bed in front of me, holding up her hand, inviting me in. Jesus. What kind of man am I? I won't do that to Vanessa, not ever again.

She was *thrilled* when I called her for a little round of phone sex though; I put my stiff cock to good use.

"I don't know," Muse says, lifting the black mug to his lips and glancing at me from the corner of his eyes. "As long as she wants, I guess."

"Oh, hell fucking no—" I start and then pause when Ransom lets himself out of the hallway, closing the door carefully behind him. He's got his hood up, hands tucked into the front pocket. He ignores me as I focus my glare on him, watching as he moves to the fridge and gets out a beer. "You, too, huh?" I ask as he continues to ignore me. "Guess everyone's drank the Kool-Aid, but me."

"Guess so," Ransom says in a low voice, flopping into one of the two leather chairs facing the sofa. He swivels it around to face the hallway and tucks his bare feet up underneath himself. When he looks at me, his dark eyes hold a challenge. We never really had any problems before, but since I refuse to alienate

Pax the way he's done, I guess I'm the enemy by proxy. "Why are you in here so early in the morning bitching about some poor, lost girl? Does that make you feel good about yourself?"

"I just don't want some random fucking groupie digging her nails into *all frigging four* of you and causing drama. The last time you fought over a girl, bones got broken and people got sent to the hospital."

Ransom tosses his hood back and stands up, getting in my face. Sometimes I forget how fucking big he is, since he's always swimming in sweatshirts and talking in low voices, calling everybody sweetie and honey and darling.

I slide away from the counter and take a step back from him.

"What happened with Kortney is hardly the same as what's happening now," he says. I expect him to yell, but he doesn't. He never does—unless he's onstage. "Why would you even bring that up?"

Paxton keeps his back to the situation, but Ransom doesn't miss the smirk that crawls across his lips.

"I swear to fucking god, I will kill you if you don't wipe that look off your face."

"What bloody look?" Pax asks, turning around and challenging Ransom with a stare. "I haven't the faintest idea what you're fucking talking about."

I step forward, prepared to get in between them again when the door slides open behind me. I turn and find myself staring at the girl from last night, the one with the VIP badge. As soon as our eyes meet, her cheeks flush and she sucks in a deep breath.

"Good morning," she says, meeting my stare head-on and refusing to look at all ashamed about bagging the entire band last night. She doesn't look coy either, just neutral, distant, but like there's this inner core of steel inside of her soul that she's fighting to hang onto.

I hate her instantly.

My mouth gets tight and I step aside. Let her talk to one of her lovers instead.

"If it's still okay, I was hoping I could book a flight out of Denver?" She holds up a phone and I notice she's looking at Muse. Of *course* this is all his fault. I bet he's the one that invited her to stay the night. He has no fucking boundaries, that guy.

I follow her gaze and step back, leaning against the counter opposite Pax.

"Oh, definitely," Muse says, stirring a second cup of tea in a pink mug. He hands this out and the girl steps forward to take it. "There's coffee, too, if you want some of that instead."

"This is great, thanks," she says, dressed in a massively oversized Beauty in Lies t-shirt and some black sweatpants. Her red hair is wet from the shower, curling halfway down her back in mahogany waves. The way she moves, the way her face is pinched tight, I can tell there's something weighing heavily on her mind. Not that I give a shit. It's just, like calls to like or something.

I slide a smoke from my own pocket and light up as I watch her sit in the chair next to Ransom's. He swivels his own to watch her playing with Muse's phone, shoving his hood back up to cover his hair.

"Having any luck, darling?" he asks after a few moments, and I notice the way Pax's eyes watch their interaction, the fingers of his left hand curling into a tight fist. It's been like this between the two of them for years now, ever since Pax fucked Ransom's ex-girlfriend, Kortney. No, before that maybe, when Ransom was crushing on Chloe.

"There's a flight that leaves around ten tomorrow morning, from Denver to Syracuse," she says, her voice detached and empty, but then she cringes. "But it's almost six hundred bucks for an economy ticket."

"Book it," Muse says, sipping his tea, looking at her over the tops of his glasses.

"I don't want to impose on you for another night—" she starts to say.

"I'll pay for a hotel room," I say and five sets of eyes swing my direction.

"For fuck's sake," Copeland scoffs as I meet the girl's eyes dead-on. "Would you lay off, Michael? She can stay with us if she wants."

"Maybe she doesn't *want* to stay here?" I say, standing up

91

and taking a drag on my cigarette. "Have you ever thought of that? Maybe she'd like a hotel room?"

"*She* is named Lilith," the girl says, standing up and turning to face me. "And I appreciate your offer. After last night, I can understand why you might not want me on this bus. I shouldn't have said what I said to you; I'm sorry."

I blink at her, wrinkling up my nose. This is the first time a groupie's ever apologized for hitting on me. I'm seriously fucking confused.

"Whatever; I just have a girlfriend. It's not like I really give a fuck. I just don't like groupies spending the night on my bus."

"A girlfriend that you whored around on and got caught by," Pax says from beside me, turning and lifting his coffee cup to his smirking mouth. Without thinking, I toss my cigarette into his mug and he curses, sloshing hot coffee all down his bare chest. "You fucking wanker!" he snarls, and then he throws the full cup in my direction. It hits the cabinets near my legs and shatters into pieces, burning my feet with hot liquid.

"Hey!" that Lilith girl says, stepping up between us. "Look, I can see I'm causing problems here. As soon as we get to Denver, I'll take a cab to the airport, spend the night in the terminal. It's not a big deal; I've done it before."

"You don't have to do that on their accounts," Cope says, running a hand over his red hair. "It's not a big deal if you want to stay the night again." Is it just me or does he sound a little eager? I kick a shard of porcelain at Pax and he narrows his grey eyes on me.

"No, really, I appreciate everything you guys have done for me, but I think I've overstayed my welcome." Lilith smiles tightly and heads down the hall, barricading herself in the room we jokingly refer to as 'the Bat Cave'. Only, no crime fighting superpower prowess happens in there, just lots and lots of sex. I've had my fair share of groupies back there, before Vanessa and I got serious again.

I cheated on my girl before; I won't make that same mistake again.

CHAPTER SEVENTEEN

I close the door in the back, lock it, and spend a good hour trolling my father's Facebook page to read all of the condolences from his friends. And he had a lot of them. Man, my dad ... he was a volunteer firefighter and he knew *everybody* in our small town. I mean, *everybody.* Looking at the messages people have left, I start to miss him all over again.

I trace a picture of his face with my thumb and feel my heart leap into my throat when I get an incoming call from Susan.

"Hey," I answer breathlessly, trying *not* to think of our conversation last night. When I called to tell her about my car and ask if she could wire that money Dad promised, she basically called me a gold digging brat and hung up on me.

"Lilith," she says with a sigh. Clearly, she's hurting and upset, but so am I. She was with my dad for six years; I was with him for twenty-one. I have a right to be sad and angry, too. "I just wanted to call to see if you'd gotten things straightened out back home."

Back home.

What a bitchy thing to say. I can't even remember the number of times I told her and Dad together that Phoenix was not my home, that I missed Gloversville, that I wanted to *come* home. Dad just used to say, *"Well, why don't you then?"* Back then it seemed impossible. Kevin and I had a gorgeous apartment; he was just starting at his dad's firm. I spent most of my time painting and waiting around the house for him to get off work.

Now all my paintings are gone; Kevin burned most of them and he took the laptop with my digital work on it. He even changed the password on my cloud account, so I can't get online and access any of it.

God, I hate him.

"Things did not get straightened out, Susan," I say, feeling my anger burn hot and fierce inside of me. "Didn't you hear what I said last night? I had two hundred dollars in cash and no credit cards. All my stuff was tossed across a parking lot in the rain, and I had nowhere to go."

"You could've taken a cab to a motel," she says with another sigh, like I'm being dramatic.

"The kind of *motel* that rents a room to someone *without* a credit card is generally the kind of place where a single, young girl with no weapons, no money, and no family goes to disappear."

"I don't know what you want me to say, Lilith. I'm sorry? My husband died yesterday."

"My *dad* died yesterday and you didn't even have the decency to call me! You *texted* me. You *texted* to tell me that my best friend and only family in the world was gone and I didn't even get to say goodbye." More tears are rolling down my face, but I don't care to stop them.

"Lilith, you haven't been here. You didn't have to watch your father fade and wither away, and you didn't have to hold his hand when he took his last breath. Be glad that you didn't have to see any of that."

"Any extra seconds with him would've been a privilege," I whisper and somehow, that just makes Susan angry.

"Nothing stopped you from coming here, Lilith! Nothing! You could've been here months ago if you wanted to be."

"I had no money, no way to get there, Susan. You and Dad were struggling, couldn't afford to give me any money. I had a job and an apartment. I took care of things as fast as I could; I was trying to be practical."

"And look where that got you," she snaps.

"Look where that got me," I whisper back. I don't have the strength to yell. "I'm working on a way to come home. When's the funeral?"

There's a long pause that scares the crap out of me.

"Don't come here, Lilith," she says, her voice wet with sadness and tears. "There's nothing here for you. Not for me, either. I'm selling the house and leaving to be with my mom in Florida. I already have my brothers up here helping me clean out the place."

"Dad died *yesterday,*" I say, my voice shaking with rage. "And you're already getting rid of his stuff?"

"If you can afford this mortgage payment, I welcome you to take it over. But I *can't.* Is there something of his that you want? I'll save it for you; I can ship it down there."

"I want to see him," I state firmly. I am *not* backing down on this one. Not being able to see my dad before he's buried … that scares the shit out of me. I can't even imagine not looking at his face again, memorizing the fine wrinkles by his eyes, the shape of his nose, so like my own, or the cleft in his chin. "When is the funeral?"

"Lilith," Susan says again, "please don't come here. There's nowhere for you to stay. The house is already half-empty and my brothers are staying in the guest rooms."

"You mean the guest room and *my* old bedroom."

"I'll have them pack your stuff up and put it in storage. You can come pick it up when you're ready. Just come up with a list of what else you want and text it to me."

"Susan, when is the funeral? I need to see him before he's buried. *Please.*"

"Listen," Susan says, calming her voice a little, breathing deep, "there's not going to be a funeral."

"What do you mean?" I ask, feeling icy prickles tease my spine.

"Funerals cost money and we just … your father and I don't have it. He's going to be cremated. I'll give you half of the ashes."

"Half of the … ashes," I say, my hands shaking, my body going cold all over.

Ashes? That'll be all that's left of dad? Just grey-white powder?

Just like Mom, I guess ... I think of her ashes sitting inside a plastic bag, tucked into my purse. How sad and pathetic and meaningless they seem. But Mom made pre-need arrangements and asked to be cremated; Dad wanted to be buried.

"I don't want him to be cremated," I say, and Susan sighs again, sounding so tired I almost feel sorry for her.

"Lilith, I'm his wife. I get to make that decision, not you. I'm sorry, but arrangements have already been made."

"How long do I have?" I whisper, feeling this violently desperate urge to get home to my dad.

"It's ... I'm sorry. It's too late. I'll mail the ashes to you; text me your new address. Please don't call me again. It's too painful."

And then my stepmom hangs up on me.

CHAPTER EIGHTEEN

Muse

DEREK "MUSE" MUSER

"Maybe I should go and check on her?" I ask after a few hours have passed and there's no sign of Lilith. Ransom and Pax have disappeared to their bunks, and Michael's on the phone having a hushed argument with his girlfriend, Vanessa, but Copeland puts his book aside to look at me.

"Her dad just died," he says, and there's some strange catch in his voice, like maybe he's a little pissed off that Lilith didn't tell him that personally; he had to hear it from me and Ransom. "Give her some space, Muse."

"We've given her space," I say, gesturing at him with my phone. He stares back at me with his weirdly bright turquoise eyes and then sighs, teasing his fucking faux hawk with his fingers. "Now it's time to check on her, for her own well-being. She hasn't even booked the flight yet. What if it sells out or something?"

"You're going to do whatever it is you want to do anyway, so why even pretend to ask me?" Cope asks, clearly annoyed with me. I stand there and cross my arms over my chest as he plays with the pages in some weird book with cuff links on the cover. I have no idea how he reads that crap.

"Wait a second. Are you mad because I slept with her, too?" I ask and Cope just sighs, shaking his head and standing up from the couch. He moves around me to get a soda from the fridge. "Seriously. That's what this is about, isn't it?"

"Look, Lilith's an adult. That was her decision to make, not mine."

"But really, what you're trying to say is, *I'm pissed off.*"

"Muse, fuck off," Copeland says, but he says it nicely, you know, like he always does. He sits back down on the couch, dressed in powder blue Chucks, a matching tee and torn jeans. The watercolor tattoos on his wrists look extra bright against all that pale blue, these swirling spots of ink on either side. He's got one per arm, these twisted, brilliant streams of color with bass clef hearts on one side and eighth notes arranged into stars on the other.

I watch him as he drops his head on his fist and pulls his book into his lap. Unlike the rest of us, Cope refuses to convert to modern technology and read shit on his phone or an eReader. He can barely even get into his bunk anymore because he has paperback and hardcover books stacked on three sides. Sometimes at night, I hear them topple off the bed and onto the floor—usually followed by a bout of heavy cursing.

"But you are," I say as I cross my arms over my chest. "Pissed off, I mean."

He ignores me, but I decide he's jealous anyway. Why shouldn't he be? That girl, there's just something about her that I like. I liked her as soon as I saw Pax pull her onstage for that song. She's a real cutie, that's for sure, but there's something else … Obviously I can't be the only one that sees it or she wouldn't have the four of us scrambling after her like she's the second coming of Jesus.

"Suit yourself then," I say and turn, heading down the hall and rapping lightly on the black door at the end of it with my knuckles. "Hey, cutie, you in there?" I ask.

There's no response, no sound at all actually which kind of freaks me out.

With all the things she told me, about her dad, about having no family, how she looked sitting outside all alone in the rain … My heart clenches and I take a deep breath. Man, I hate being so … empathetic. I swear, I have to feel everything everybody else is feeling all the time. Sometimes I even forget how it is that *I'm* supposed to be feeling. Maybe like anything else, I use it to protect myself from my own emotions? That wouldn't surprise me much.

"Lilith?" I ask again, tapping my tattooed knuckles against the wood. "Just let me know you're okay in there and I'll leave you alone."

Another few moments of strained silence. I'm about to head into the kitchen and grab the key when I hear the lock flick. The door slides back to reveal a girl with sad, sad eyes and a drawn face. Immediately, she turns around, crawls back into the bed and curls her knees up to her chest.

I let myself in and close the door behind me. There's basically zero room to stand in here, so I end up sitting on the bed, too.

"What if I'm not okay?" she asks me, like she's genuinely curious to see what I might have to say. Her eyes pool with tears, but she blinks them back like they're traitorous and lifts her chin to stare at me. "What if everything's just … fucked-up beyond belief?"

I kick my boots off and scoot up the bed until I'm sitting next to her, close enough to touch but with a careful cushion of distance between us. If she chooses to close it, that's her business. I won't touch her unless she wants me to. But if she does … God help her, I will be all the fuck over her.

"Talk to me," I say, leaning my head back against the headboard.

Lilith makes this frustrated sound in her throat and runs both hands over her face. I get this compulsion to reach out and touch a strand of her red-red hair, but who knows where the fuck that comes from so I ignore it.

"It's not fair," she says, dropping her hands into her lap. Seeing her curled up, knees tucked to the side, dressed in my clothes … it's beyond sexy. I mimic her motion and swipe a hand over my own face, glancing away to get a reign on my crazy hormones. I've always had a seriously healthy libido, but damn, this chick, she's something else entirely. "And I know, I know, *life's* not fair, but isn't it okay for me to notice it? Call the universe out on its bullshit?"

I glance back, pushing my glasses up my nose with two fingers. Whenever we're onstage … hell, whenever we're anywhere but the sanctity of our own bus, I wear contacts. But here or wherever else I feel comfortable, I prefer to wear my glasses.

"Yeah, of course. You won't hear me telling you that God works in mysterious ways or any of that shit. Life can be a thorny path to follow; sometimes you just bleed."

"I didn't even know he was sick at first," she says, looking over at me. I notice her eyes are the same green as the feathers on the hummingbirds that used to collect outside my bedroom window. Shimmery, glittery, alive.

"They hid it from you," I say; it's not really a question.

"They told me he'd been diagnosed, but they never really went into specifics." Lilith smiles tightly over at me. "I wanted to, you know, Google everything. Look at treatment options and stuff ... but even now, even with my dad lying alone and cold somewhere ..."

"Wherever he is, he's not alone," I promise, wishing I actually knew this girl so I could reach over and take her hand. I remember what Ransom was like when his mother died. It's been a year and I'm not sure he's really ever recovered from that.

"How can you be so sure of that?" she asks, turning to face me, leaning sideways into the mound of pillows behind us. "Like, how do you know his spirit isn't trapped there, waiting for me?"

"You're putting too much pressure on yourself," I assure her, crossing my arms together behind my head and looking up at the pale grey color of the ceiling. It's the same color as the stripes on the wall, this soft dove grey to make up for the stripes of metallic silver. "That's your guilt speaking. No matter what you believe in, you know your dad isn't waiting for you up there. Whatever your reasons for going to New York now, they're *your* reasons. Whatever we do when loved ones die— grieve, sob, hold funerals, erect gravestones—it's all for us, not for them."

"How would you know that?" she whispers and I expect to see her crying when I glance back over. Only, she's not. She's staring at me like she's in desperate need of a friend. Luckily for her, that's something I'm pretty damn good at. "Have you ever had anyone die before? Because I have. It's important to honor their memories."

"Because it's important for you to remember them," I say as the air conditioner murmurs, spitting an icy cold breeze into the darkened room. All of the curtains are still closed which is fine by me. This part of the country, there's not much in the way of scenery to look at outside. "But if you have had people die, then you really do understand." I look back at Lilith. "Punishing yourself, that won't help your dad, not at all."

"If I'd have known how sick he really was …" she whispers and then she crawls over to me, putting her head on my chest, her arm around my waist. I freeze up for a moment, but then I drop my right hand to her head. Unlike last night, her hair is soft and shiny today, so easy to run my fingers through. "I'm sorry," she says after a few moments, but she doesn't try to pull away. "I just don't … have anybody to talk to right now."

"Did you want me to book your ticket?" I ask softly, but when she doesn't answer, I figure it out. Whatever happened after she came in here, she no longer needs to go to New York. I decide not to say anything, not yet. If this girl is sad enough to cuddle up to a stranger, then she must really be alone.

Truly and completely and utterly alone.

But that's okay, because so am I.

In the end … aren't we all?

CHAPTER NINETEEN

Lilith

LILITH GOODE

I can't seem to stop myself from falling into oblivion every chance I get—alcohol, sex sleep. And Dad's only been gone for a night and half a day. Will the pain get better as time passes? It did with Mom, with my sister, Yasmine, but that's because I had Dad to hold me, hug me, tell me everything was going to be okay.

Now, he's gone, too, and all I have is a bus full of rockstars that I slept with last night.

I groan and sit up, realizing suddenly that the gentle jostling of the bus is gone.

We've stopped.

I scramble out of the bed, push the bedroom door open and peer down the dark, narrow hallway. The kitchen door is closed, but I can hear the murmur of several voices. Suddenly I feel completely self-conscious in my borrowed sweats and t-shirt. I clutch the front of the black cotton, fisting my fingers in the fabric. I have a large chest, so not wearing a bra all day … and I even went out and talked to all five of the band members at the same time?

I must've really been blinded by grief.

Even now, with my throat tight and my dad's laughter ringing in a cruel string of memories in my head, I can't even *imagine* walking out there now.

I bend down and open one of the stacked boxes Muse left for me. My heart constricts a little. It's fucking cruel for him to be so nice to me like this; it'll only make things hurt worse when reality hits again, when I realize I have *nowhere* to go. No home. No job. No family.

Practical concerns sweep over me, freezing me with panic as I stare at the familiar collection of objects inside the box. The whole thing even smells like me, this rose water perfume that I like so much. I lean down and put my face to the items inside, breathing deep. These things, they smell like my past. I want to get high on them, forget that my future smells like bullshit.

Male laughter echoes back to me from up front, snapping me out of the moment. Frantically, I dig through the items inside. These, at least, aren't really that wet. They must've come from inside the car or something.

I manage to score a decently acceptable dress. It's far too short to be a proper funeral gown, but at least it's black, and I won't feel like a complete slob in front of those guys. My stomach twists with butterflies as I pause to grab my red heels from the floor and tiptoe back to the bathrooms. I pop in the shower real quick and then wrap myself in a towel to scramble to the toilet/vanity side of the equation.

What a weird setup, I think as I force my numb fingers to pull a tube of red lipstick from my purse. It's too much, not right for a day of mourning, but I feel like I need a bit of a mask to face the world right now.

Once I'm dressed, my face made up with careful, even strokes, like my skin isn't really mine at all, like it's one of my paintings instead, I head back into the hallway and pause next to the door. I don't hear anyone talking anymore, just empty silence.

My heart starts to pound and a wave of loneliness creeps over me, prompting me to push open the door and step into the kitchen, my heels loud on the wood floors beneath them.

Ransom is standing in the middle of the room in a loose black tank, the armholes cut so low that when he turns, I can see his chiseled chest and back underneath the fabric.

"Hey, sweetheart," he says, voice dripping velvet, a cigarette dripping ash from his fingers. The way his gaze sweeps me, from my red heels to the short hemline of my dress, I can tell he likes what he sees. A bit of the loneliness recedes and even though I know it's not exactly healthy to drown my feelings with lust, I let it happen. It seems to work okay.

"Hi," I say as I close the hall door and lean against it. "We're in Denver?"

"We are," Ransom says, chocolate dark hair falling across his brow as he smokes his cigarette, the lower half of his face decorated with a thin layer of stubble. And his arms ... they're big and muscular, wrapped in swirls of black and grey ink. Immediately, my eyes catch on a woman's portrait on his left bicep. Without even having to ask, I know that's his mother; it has to be.

I draw my eyes back to his face.

"We just got here," he adds as he takes a few more drags on his cigarette and puts it out in a nearby ashtray. "I was about to come in and wake you up. You sleep okay, honey?"

"I slept too much," I say, feeling a little groggy and disconnected from the world.

Ransom nods and turns to me, reaching up and putting a thin hood over his head. Wow, even his tank tops have hoods on them.

"Last year, when my mom died, I slept for a week straight. So, in my scorebook, you're doing a fuck of a lot better than I did." I close my eyes as he speaks, just telling his words brush across my cheeks like sensual caresses. I *love* the way he talks.

When I open them, I find him studying me with his rich brown eyes. In this light, I can actually make out the faint scar on his left cheek.

"We don't have a show tonight," Ransom says, breaking the moment as he turns away from me and picks up a dark brown bottle from the small table between the swiveling leather chairs. "Most of the guys are off stretching their legs; Cope always runs a mile or two when we get to a new city."

I force myself to stand up straight, moving away from the door and pausing awkwardly in the center of the room. The truth is, I don't have anywhere to go. And now, I'm not even in Phoenix, a city that I actually know. I'm in fucking *Denver*, Colorado. I don't know anything about Denver.

"Can I get you a beer, honey?" he asks as I cross my arms

over my chest, aware that the square neckline of my dress reveals a whole lot more of my breasts than I'd like it to. It's not that I'm generally a modest person, just that it feels disrespectful to Dad. But then I think of what Muse said to me and I feel a little better. *"Punishing yourself, that won't help your dad, not at all."*

"Sure," I say, tucking some wet strands of reddish purple hair behind my ear and gratefully taking the cold beverage from Ransom's outstretched hand. When our fingers brush, I get this wild tingle that shoots up my wrist, my arm, straight into my chest. I can't even believe that I sucked this guy off this morning, that he fucked me from behind, that he used a toy on me. Kevin hated toys of any kind—probably because he knew that no matter how cheap the vibe or how small the dildo, they'd be better at sex than he was.

"I'll just, you know, get my shit together and be out of your hair," I say as I think about maybe booking a plane ticket from here back to Phoenix. As much as I want to go back to New York, what's the point? What'll I do once I'm there? At least if I go back to Arizona, I can maybe get my car back. I need to ask Muse where exactly he had it towed, figure this all out.

"There's no rush, baby doll," he says, and he sounds pretty genuine about it. "Have some beers, hang out for a while."

I smile at him and move over to the couch to sit down, twirling my beer on the arm and picking at the label with my other hand as Ransom sits, not across from me, but right next to me. He's wearing these long black cargo shorts, so the skin of his calf is pressed up tight to mine. Looks like he has a tattoo there, also, this big black and grey owl that I'm envious of.

"So, what do you guys usually do on your nights off?" I ask, glancing over at him, wondering if I'm going to regret that question. I know I just met Ransom yesterday, but I guess I just don't want to hear if what he and his friends do for fun is pick up ... well, *groupies.*

He shrugs his shoulders loosely, his warm skin brushing up against mine, and takes a swig of his beer.

"Sometimes we work on music together, practice, party, but usually by about halfway through the tour we're so fucking tired that we just sleep."

I smile at that.

"How popular are you guys exactly?" I ask, wishing I had my phone so I could look them up again. I keep thinking of all those professional pictures I found when I looked them up before, to find their names. They seem so stern and posed in all those shots, when really they're just regular guys. "Like, Metallica in their heyday popular or ... ?"

Ransom laughs and even that sound is low and languid and dripping sensuality.

"No, not that popular, but our newest album went multi-platinum." He doesn't even sound like he really cares when he says that, staring ahead, towards the door of the bus and drinking his beer. Even the way Ransom moves is slow and sexy, inviting me in.

I look away and take a drink of my own beer. I'm so numb right now, I barely even taste it.

I can only keep my gaze away for so long and after a moment, I glance back. *I can't believe I fucked this guy,* I think as I stare at him. He's about a million levels above Kevin in the looks department and about a billion above him in the *niceness* category. Sitting here now, I feel like a complete tool for dating the guy for so long.

I sigh.

I guess I thought I was in love; love makes people crazy stupid.

And I was about to do just that ... five times over. If I'd known that in that moment, sitting on the couch with Ransom, I might've run out that door and into the cool dark Denver night and never looked back. Okay, so maybe not, but things were definitely about to change for me—forever. I'd never be the same after that tour.

"After your mom died," I start, looking up at Ransom through my lashes, wondering if I'm making a bad decision by bringing this up again, "did you have family around to comfort you?"

His caustic laugh answers that question for him.

"No family, honey," he says, finishing his beer and setting it on the floor by his feet. He turns to look at me and I get swept into the darkness of his gaze. "Single mom, tough luck, hard times. You know the story. My dad died in a motorcycle accident when I was six, and I never really got to know his side of the family. Mom didn't have any family."

"I'm sorry," I say, and I mean that, even if it sounds like a canned response.

"This band, the music, that's what got me through," he says resolutely, meeting my eyes, making my heart pound wildly. In his darkness, I see my face reflected a thousand times over. We could be ... either perfect soul mates or terrible toxins for one another.

I breathe out sharply and shove the end of the beer bottle between my lips, flicking my eyes to the door of the bus as it swings open and Paxton walks in. No, he swaggers in. Definitely swaggers.

As soon as our eyes meet, a rush of heat shoots through me, cutting into that numb feeling like a knife. It's nothing but sexual attraction, obviously, because Pax is a serious dick, but it's a nice distraction.

"Still here, Miss Lilith Tempest Goode?" he asks, dressed in another of his stupid suits, all pressed and polished and looking like a damn CEO or something ... I mean, except for the tattoos. Before I can come up with a response, he's sauntering around the couch, putting a hand on the back of it and leaning it to press a scalding kiss to my mouth.

I can't help myself; I lean into his touch, arching toward Paxton, curling the fingers of my left hand around his starched collar. *God, he smells good,* I think as his wicked tongue parts my lips, takes over my mouth, my thoughts, my pulse. He sends it racing a million miles an hour.

From beside me, I hear Ransom make a noise of frustration and manage to pull myself away.

"You going to stay the night, then?" Pax asks against my right cheek, the feel of his mouth on my skin sending goose bumps up across my arms. Wow. He's a serious prick, but he oozes sexuality. Maybe it's his only redeeming quality?

"I ... I don't know," I say, because the thought of walking

down the metal steps and leaving this bus behind makes me feel queasy. I know I don't *know* any of these guys, but I feel like I have a connection with a few of them: Muse, Cope, and Ransom. And then there's this sex thing with Pax …

"Well, if you are, I'm up for another shag," he says, standing up straight, tucking his fingers into the pockets of his black slacks. His button-up, tie, and jacket are also all black today, making him look sinister but irresistible at the same time.

"After you left her tied up last night?" Ransom asks softly and Pax's grey eyes drift over to him. His look switches from cocky but bored to disgusted but triumph. Um. I watch their interaction play out with undisguised curiosity. Clearly, these guys have issues of their own to deal with. "Why the *fuck* would she want to screw you again?"

"Because I'm bloody brilliant," Paxton says, looking back at me, like he's waiting for some sort of confirmation from me.

"Why did you run away like that?" I ask him and he raises both of his blonde brows.

"Run away? Oh, love, I didn't run away. I was just done with you."

Ransom tenses up beside me, like he plans on kicking Pax's ass, but I stand up off the couch instead, looking the man in his grey eyes.

"No, you *ran* away. Because of something I did. Why?"

Pax runs his tongue across his lower lip and drops his hand to my beer. When he tries to take it, I let him have it. He tosses back the remaining half, smiles at me, and walks away, dropping the empty bottle in the sink. Then he disappears into the hallway and closes the door behind him.

"Don't let him get to you," a voice says from behind me and I turn to see Cope and Muse coming up the steps. Copeland smiles at me, his turquoise eyes focused wholly on my face, completely ignoring my little black dress. Muse takes me all in, starting at my toes and working his way up. He grins when our eyes meet.

"I managed to get everything you asked for, Ran," Muse says, a giant cardboard box in his hands that he carries over to the coffee table. A heavenly smell drifts in along with him, and suddenly, my stomach grumbles. I'm *starving*. In the last forty-eight hours, I've had a stale donut and a strawberry milk, plus the food Muse made for me. That's it. "There's plenty for you, too, Cutie," he says as Copeland takes his white t-shirt off and rubs the sweat dripping down the sides of his face. Based on his flushed cheeks and heavy breathing, it's obvious that he was out running like Ransom said he was.

"I ..." I don't even have the energy to be polite. Now that I've realized how hungry I actually am, I feel dizzy, and buzzed from that half of a beer. Happens to me on an empty stomach. "Thank God," I breathe and Muse chuckles; Ransom grins.

Cope moves to the cabinets, gets a glass and fills it up, chugging water and letting some of it sluice over his lips, down his throat, across the pair of heart tattoos on his chest. I stand transfixed for a moment before I manage to pull away, feeling my nipples harden and crossing my arms over my breasts to hide it.

I have no idea what the fuck happened to me last night. It's like ... like my grief broke something open inside of me, killed my inhibitions, and thrust me into the midst of a wild sexual awakening. I just ... I want one of these boys to fuck me again. And then I also feel awful about it because I'm supposed to be grieving ...

"Burgers and fries?" I ask with a smile as Muse hands me a brown paper bag and I peek inside. "I'm ridiculously excited about this."

"Um, now that I've seen you wearing that dress, so am I." He smiles at me again and passes over a frosty cup. When I take a quick sip, I get strawberry milkshake. What a weird coincidence; I'm literally obsessed with anything strawberry flavored. "Eating that, you'll look like the star of a naughty Carl's Jr. commercial."

A laugh escapes from my throat, and I clamp a hand over my lips, smearing my red lipstick. When I pull my palm away, I see it bright and vibrant against my skin, like blood. Yeah, maybe it was a mistake to wear it. It's definitely too red for the day after my dad died.

"I'll take that as a compliment," I say as I sit back on the couch and start in on my food.

"Oh, it was meant to be," Muse adds as Cope collapses in the chair across from me, still shirtless, totally beautiful. Muse takes the other chair, and all three of the guys dig into the food with gusto. Looking at them all, I guess I should feel self-conscious about having slept with them, one after the other. Only ... I don't. Right now, I'm just sort of drinking in their companionship. They're making it really easy to want to be here, and I just don't want to leave and be alone yet.

We eat in silence for a few moments before Michael appears in the doorway, looking pissed.

"Have another fight with Vanessa?" Ransom asks quietly, but Michael ignores him, shrugging out of his leather jacket and tossing it over the back of Muse's chair. Muse makes a face when the zipper smacks him in the back, but he doesn't say anything about it.

"She's acting like I'm on some leisurely vacation or something, like I *want* to be trapped on a fucking bus day in and day out. She basically implied that *I*, personally, made the decision to tour again so soon. I fucking *told* her that it wasn't my choice, that the record label made the decision, but all she does is act like I'm in love with the goddamn idea of being away from her."

Michael runs his hand down his face and pauses his rant suddenly, turning to look at me with his beautiful violet eyes widening in surprise.

"You're still here?" he asks, and I feel my stomach drop. Suddenly the burger clutched in my fingers doesn't look all that appetizing.

"I'll get out of your hair as soon as I can," I say, keeping his gaze, refusing to look away first. He challenges me for a long moment and then shakes his head.

"Whatever. I don't care."

"Bugger off, Mikey," Paxton says, swaggering back into the room and snatching another bag from the cardboard box. He peers inside and makes a happy sounding sigh. "If the girl wants to stay, let her stay." He gives me a measuring look and lets his mouth quirk in a seductive smile. But if he thinks I'll stay just to fuck him again, he's wrong. This guy has a serious attitude problem.

"Don't call me Mikey," Michael growls at Pax. "I fucking *hate* it; you know that."

"I just want to know why you're shitting in your fucking knickers over a beautiful girl? Are you tempted, Mikey? Is that what it is?"

"Fucking Christ, Pax," Michael says, grabbing his own bag and pulling down a panel from the wall with his right hand. I watch, fascinated, as he grabs a folded chair off a hook from inside and opens it up with a flick of his wrist.

"Vanessa won't last," Ransom says softly, and Michael's face gets tight and angry. He's staring at me again, but I don't care. I take a bite of my burger and try not to let him get to me.

"Why the *fuck* would you say that?" Michael growls—he seems to like growling a lot—and then tears into his burger with rage. I've never seen someone eat so angrily before; it's actually fascinating to watch. "After all the shit Vanessa and I have been through, why wouldn't we last? We've invested years into this fucking relationship."

"If that's your reason for staying in it, then you won't last much longer," I tell him seriously. I know this is none of my business, but I can't help myself. The words seem to just pop out of my mouth. "I just broke up with my boyfriend of five years and honestly, even though it broke my heart, it was also kind of a relief."

Michael stares at me like he wants to stab me in the eye with his French fry.

"See," Ransom says softly, smiling at me from inside his hood, "Lilith agrees with me. Now you have a female perspective on the situation."

"And, uh, who the fuck *is* Lilith anyway?" Michael asks, and I figure he's gearing up for something mean, so I put a stop to his words by standing up.

"I'll save you the trouble," I say and for whatever reason, Michael stands up, too. "Please don't." I hold my burger up to my chest like a shield, wrinkling my brow and trying to take deep breaths. Fuck. I knew this would happen. It happened with Mom, with Yasmine. Whenever I lose somebody, I go in and out of grief. Like, I can push it down for a while, but it comes raging back at the most inappropriate fucking moments. "Whatever you want to say about me, can you wait until I leave?"

"And when, exactly, is that going to be?" Michael asks as Paxton walks around to his side of the room and grabs a second folding chair from the hook on the wall, snapping it into place. "Look, I'm not trying to be rude, but we've had groupies try to hang around here before. I'm sorry, but you really need to go."

"Duly noted," I say, feeling pain well up from deep inside as I shove my food into the bag and toss it onto the couch.

"What the fuck, Michael?" Ransom asks, his voice never raising above a low half-whisper. "This isn't just your bus." He rises to his feet and manages to catch my arm before I pull away. I'm not just going to run off into the night. I want to ask Muse maybe if I can buy that ticket to Phoenix, but the tightness of Ransom's grip on my arm makes me want to look at him. "I'm inviting you to stay," he says, looking me in the eyes. "Me. I know what it's like to lose your parent, and I know what it's like to be alone. If you want to stay the night again, you can have the Bat Cave all to yourself."

"Jesus Christ," Michael curses from behind him as I stand there and stare at Ransom Riggs for a long, aching moment. "We have a rule: groupies on the bus for one night *only*."

"Yeah, well, special circumstances and all that," Muse adds, drawing that violet eyed glared over to his face. "What's it matter to you? It's not like you use the Bat Cave anyway."

"It matters to me because I have to live here, too, you fucking asshole." Michael shoves his wrapper back in his bag and tosses the whole thing back into the box. "Because all four of you fucked *one* chick last night and you're all staring at her like you want to be in her polygamist collection of husbands."

"Polyandrous," Muse says, lifting a finger up. "When it's one wife with several husbands, it's called polyandry."

"Fuck *you,*" Michael says, storming around the swivel chairs and through the kitchen. He pauses at the hallway door and glances back at the rest of us, his violet eyes staring straight at me. "If you're going to insist on her staying, then here's the deal: no other groupies on this fucking bus. I'm goddamn serious about it. Not even *one* other girl or I will walk the hell off of this tour, contracts and obligations be damned."

He narrows his eyes at me and then smirks, pulling a smoke from his pocket and lighting up.

"Let's see how long you last *now,*" he whispers cruelly, and then he's slipping into the hallway and doing his best to slam the wooden door on its slider.

Ransom releases my arm and I sit back down, reaching back into my crumpled bag to finish off my now lukewarm fries. Might as well not let the food go to waste.

"After this, Muse, if it's still alright with you, I'd like to book that ticket," I say casually.

"Sure thing, Cutie," he says, but the way he looks at me, I get the feeling he can see right through my false bravado and straight into the depths of my tired, empty soul.

CHAPTER TWENTY

Lilith

LILITH GOODE

I take Muse's phone into the back room—what I guess they call the *Bat Cave,* probably because of the giant bat shaped headboard—and sit on the edge of the bed. Quickly, I look up flights from Denver to Phoenix and find one that leaves at eight tomorrow morning. It's cheap, too, a fifth of the price of the one to New York.

I feel a little better taking Muse's money that way, purchasing the ticket and then pausing when he appears in the hallway, padding down to stand in front of me with his arms crossed over the front of his white wifebeater.

"I had your car towed to an auto body shop. It should be ready by next week. It's my number they've got on file, so if you want to plug yours into my phone, I'll give you a call when they call me about it."

My heart jumps and skitters a little with anxiety.

"That's really nice of you, but I can't afford—"

Muse leans his forearm against the doorframe and gives me a sad half-smile.

"I told you I was loaded; don't worry about it." I find my eyes drawn to his silver hair. It's such a strange color; I wonder what it takes to dye it like that. Probably buckets and buckets of bleach. It's so ethereal and sexy, fading into the perfect darkness of his roots.

"Thank you," I tell him, feeling this huge surge of relief. I don't feel like I have a right to accept such generosity, but who am I to look a gift horse in the mouth? I plug my number into his contacts and hand the phone back, feeling a cool wash of sensation when our fingers brush.

He smiles at me, but I have a hard time smiling back. There's something about Muse that says he gets it all, all the tiny, practical little life things that the others don't seem to be aware of.

"Are you sure you're going to be okay?" he asks finally, and this time, I make myself smile.

"Yeah, I'll ..." *Daddy is dead; Daddy is dead.* "I'll be fine."

"How are you going to get your car if you're in New York?" he asks casually, scrolling on his phone with his thumb. I see the screen reflected in the lenses of his glasses; he's looking at the travel site. I feel my throat get tight. "Ah," he says, like he expected this all along, "you're not going to New York anymore."

"She's already scheduled him to be cremated," I blurt, shoving red hair over my shoulder. It's so long, halfway down my back. I just want to hack it all off with a pair of blunt scissors, take my frustration out on my hair. "My stepmom. She's having Dad cremated and she's not having a funeral and she's selling the house ..." I trail off and force myself to take a deep breath, looking away, toward the framed records on the wall. All those awards for Beauty in Lies. Looking at their accomplishments, I feel sick. What the hell have I done with my life?

The answer is heartbreaking.

Nothing.

I've done nothing.

"May I come in?" Muse asks, looking down at me with his hazel eyes.

"It's your bus," I say, but that's not a good enough answer for him. He crosses his arms over his chest and takes a deep breath. "Yes."

"Thank you."

He steps inside and closes the door behind him, crawling onto the bed and tossing his phone onto one of the shelves on the headboard. I kick off my heels and join him, my tight black dress riding up as I scoot across the bed and nestle into the pillows.

When I notice Muse watching me with dilated pupils, I get this hot, achy feeling all over my body. He must see something of that feeling in my face because his hazel eyes get wide.

"You don't owe me anything," he says suddenly, holding up his palm. "I came in here to talk."

"What if I don't want to talk?" I ask and he smiles again, reaching out the hand with the bat tattoos all over it, running his heated palm up my exposed thigh. I close my eyes and feel my breath rush out of me. Holy shit. My heart and soul feel dead … my body feels almost desperately alive. Like, if she can get all these touches and sensations inside of me, maybe they'll jump-start my heart?

"I'm more than happy to fuck you," Muse says, "but I want it to be mutual."

"It's mutual," I say, and then I'm leaning over his chest and kissing his mouth again. He tastes smoky again, but not like cigarettes, not at all. Like Earl Grey tea maybe? Definitely tea. That's what that taste is.

Kevin would've laughed cruelly if I'd offered him a cup of tea.

"I drink fucking coffee," he'd bitch and I get frustrated and annoyed at him all over again, curling my fingers in Muse's shirt and letting him push my dress up in the back so he can cup my ass. He does it with a fervency that makes me feel like this is urgent, like I need to be touched and held or I might die. It's overdramatic, sure, but it feels so much better than the blank emptiness of shock.

I embrace it as Muse embraces me, the hot warmth of his body soothing as he rolls us over and puts a knee between my thighs. When he reaches up to take his glasses off, I put a hand on his wrist.

"Leave them on?" I ask and he laughs, but he obliges me, dropping his mouth back to mine, taking hold of the side of my face and savoring the taste of my mouth. Muse is a confident lover, and it's obvious he enjoys the physicality of sex, but there's … something else. It's hard to explain, but I get the sense that there's something more here, too.

He tastes almost as lonely as I feel.

Muse's knee presses up against the vibrant heat between my thighs and I find my body arcing forward of its own accord, rubbing against the black denim of his jeans. As we kiss, I feel him grinding his erection into my hip.

"Oh, Derek," I moan and he stops kissing me for a moment, letting out this long, sharp breath against my ear.

"I like hearing you say that," he whispers, kissing the side of my neck, making my body go pliant in his hands. "Nobody calls me Derek anymore."

He drops his tattooed left hand down and slips it under the red lace lingerie covering my sex, slipping a pair of fingers inside of me before the door slides open behind him and I gasp. My fingers curl into Muse's shoulders as I find the plain-faced ponytail girl standing there, the one from backstage with the clipboard and the headset.

And she could not have interrupted at a worse possible moment.

"Oh, sorry," she says, blushing profusely. "I didn't realize … I'll come back."

The way her eyes sweep me, there's a sort of predetermined judgment there that feels heavy and ragged as it falls across my exposed skin. I don't like that, not at all. She's looking at me like I'm a slut. And … I don't think there's really anything *wrong* with that, but … that's not who I am either. Until yesterday, I'd basically only had sex with Kevin.

Ponytail Girl turns her face away, but she doesn't bother to actually leave like she says she's going to. Oh my god, but it's so damn awkward when Muse slides his fingers out of me, out of my panties, and sits up.

We exchange a long look as I adjust my dress and sit up, too.

"Lilith," he says as Ponytail Girl turns back towards us with a disingenuous smile, "this is Octavia Warris, the band's manager."

"We met last night," Octavia says, still pretending to smile sweetly, but giving me that same awful look. "Lilith Goode, the *Parade for Paxton* contest winner, right?"

"Right," I say as I tuck my legs up and try not to hate this woman. She's just doing her job, I'm sure. "It's nice to meet you. Sorry it's under such … unusual circumstances." I gesture at myself, the bed, Muse.

"Oh, don't worry about it," she says gently, and for a second there, I feel bad because I think I must've misjudged her a little. "These aren't unusual circumstances."

I think my mouth pops open in surprise as Octavia turns her attention to Muse.

"I need to see you in the living room for a moment, please," she says, but he holds up a hand—thankfully not the one that was inside my underwear.

"That was rude, Octavia," he tells her, but she's already turning away and disappearing down the hallway. Wow. So it's not just Michael that wants me off this bus. I think about leaving now, getting a hotel room, but then I can't ask Muse for anymore money and I don't have a credit card … No, it just makes sense to stay here for the night. Ransom and Muse invited me; Copeland and even Paxton didn't seem completely opposed to it. "I'm really sorry about that," he tells me and I shrug loosely. What one random stranger thinks of me doesn't matter in the long run.

Dad is dead; who gives a *fuck* what *Octavia* thinks.

"She's usually pretty nice, just not to gr—" Muse stops suddenly and gives me an apologetic look. "I'm sorry. I know you're not a groupie, not even close."

"It's fine," I say with a tired sigh and even though I've been sleeping all damn day, it's suddenly all I want to be doing. "Don't let me hold you back from work."

Muse scoots back towards me and puts his hand on my hip.

"I'd much rather stay in here with you," he says and even though I know there's nothing between us but sex, it feels good to hear someone tell me something so nice. It might be the last time I hear something like that for a long time.

Muse kisses me, and my heart thunders at his touch, but the moment's passed and we both know it. He pulls away and looks at me for a long moment. I can tell that this is the part where I invite him back after he's done with his meeting, but it takes me a second to get up the courage and then he's pulling away with an understanding smile.

"If you need anything from the kitchen, feel free to help yourself."

He scoots off the end of the bed, grabs his boots off the floor and disappears, closing the door behind him.

After a few minutes, I decide to take my dress off, shoving it back in the box and replacing it with Muse's t-shirt and sweatpants. I drag my phone from my purse and curl up in the dark, underneath the black silk blanket. I think it's stuffed with feathers or something because it's light as air, fluffy and soft, but warm, too.

I open up my gallery and start scrolling through pictures. Pictures of Dad and me, of Mom, of Yasmine. I should probably cry again, but my eyes hurt and I'm just done with tears for right now. There's a small possibility I could be in shock of some kind. I mean, tucked in here on this giant bed, in this room with its silver wallpaper, I feel like I'm in a different world.

Tomorrow, when I get off that plane back in Phoenix, *that's* when it'll all come crashing down; I'm sure of it. After a while, I decide I can't stand the silent, smiling faces of my dead family, and start some mindless sitcom on Netflix, staring into the tiny screen of my phone and wishing I could get sucked away into a happy, little world with a laugh track and a conclusion at the end of every episode.

Hours later, when the door opens, I see Ransom standing in the darkness in his hoodie and set my phone aside.

"Hey, doll," he says, his voice warming up all the cold places inside of me. "I'm not looking for sex or anything, but could I sleep with you? I just … fucking hate sleeping by myself."

I want to tell him no, to sit here and wallow in my own misery, but then I smell that faint violet scent that clings to his baggy black sweatshirt and I can't help myself.

"Sure," I say, and like he did last night, this complete stranger crawls into bed with me and tucks me against him, like I'm something precious to be held and cherished. I don't want to admit that the sound of his breath, the feel of his heartbeat against my back, or his sweet scent are almost as comforting as one of my dad's bear hugs.

I squeeze my eyes shut tight and when I open them again, it's to the sound of my alarm going off.

Time to go.

Only … there's literally zero part of me that wants to leave this place.

CHAPTER TWENTY-ONE

Lilith

LILITH GOODE

It feels almost impossible to crawl away from the comfort and warmth of Ransom's arms—especially when I had to wake him up and soothe him back to sleep no less than six times last night. How does he manage without someone by his side?

I get a stab of jealousy as I realize how easily he cuddled up to me. He probably just picks girls at random and brings them back to the bus. If he could do it with me, there's a good chance he does it with lots of others, too. I wonder if it ever scares them away? He gets pretty violent in his sleep, although he didn't hurt me at all.

With a sigh, I push his arm off and crawl down to the end of the bed for the last time, taking my phone with me. After a quick perusal of the items in the top box, I realize there's nothing else in there that's black. Moving onto the next box, my breath catches sharply as a framed photo of my dad stares up at me. I have this exact same picture on my phone, but knowing that I almost left it behind in that rainy parking lot makes me sick.

I shut the top quickly, toss it aside and start on the third box. All in all, there are four total. Muse probably spent a lot of time in that parking lot picking my shit up. With a small sniffle, I drag a pair of black leggings from the tangled pile of clothes and wrinkle my nose. They smell musty, like clothing that's been left in a washing machine for too long.

"Fuck," I whisper, deciding it doesn't really matter. I'm taking a two hour flight home and then … I'll probably be staying in one of those shitty motels that I'm so scared of. But it'll be fine. Just fine.

I struggle through the boxes one more time, trying to find a pair of shoes that *aren't* shiny, loud red heels, and come across a pair of pale pink leather Docs. The inside of both boots are wet, but I decide that's better than wearing heels to the airport and slip them on.

I toss my purse over one shoulder and grab the top box from the stack.

Muse is waiting for me when I step through the hall door and into the kitchen.

There are two cups of tea on the small table between the two swivel chairs, steam rising from them still.

"Sit and talk with me a sec before you go?" he asks, leaning against the counter. His silver-black hair is styled into a perfect mohawk, eyes dark with liner and strangely bright without his glasses to block them. He's even dressed up like he was onstage, wearing a pair of skinny jeans with pins all over the right thigh, a plain green t-shirt and a dark denim jacket over an unzipped hoodie. That, too, is covered with pins. He looks very punk rock, and I find myself smiling a little.

"I don't have a lot of time before my flight," I say as Muse stands up and takes the box from my hands.

"If you still want to go after our talk, I'll drive you. One of the roadies drives a truck with a trailer on the back, but it's unhitched right now. I could take you straight to the terminal."

"Our talk?" I ask as Muse puts the box down by the front door and gestures to one of the chairs. I decide to sit down anyway and take the warm cup of tea between my palms. I hadn't realized how cold I'd gotten since I pulled away from Ransom until I was holding this mug. "What do you want to talk to me about?"

I watch him as he takes a seat but for the life of me, I can't imagine what this could possibly be about.

"You're going back to Phoenix?" he reconfirms and I nod slowly. "To what?"

"What do you mean *to what*?" I ask as my heart starts to beat uncontrollably and I stare into the kaleidoscopes of color that make up Muse's eyes. He sips his tea carefully and watches me like he already knows the answer to my question. "To nothing, okay," I say and it feels so goddamn good to get it out that I keep going. "No apartment, no job, no family, no friends, no boyfriend. I'll be getting off that plane with two hundred bucks and everything I own."

It occurs to me in that moment that I probably don't even have enough money to cover the baggage check fees for my boxes, and my entire body goes cold.

"I've been where you are right now," Muse tells me as I sip my drink, and the sweet clove-orange spice of the liquid reminds me of his hot mouth on mine. He leans back in his chair, looking impossibly young and hopeful, the four black piercings above his brow catching my attention. "I don't have any family left either. When I auditioned for Pax's band, all I had was my guitar and a gun with three bullets in it."

I raise my own eyebrows, but all Muse does is stare into his cup.

"I'd tried out for a lot of spots in a lot of bands, even tried starting my own. It was," he pauses to laugh and drink some of his tea, still not looking at me, "it was a clusterfuck, let's just leave it at that. I had no place to live, no job, and no family. I figured if I didn't make Paxton's band, I had two more bullets than I needed to make it all stop."

"Derek," I start and he shivers a little, glancing back at me, the green in his shirt bringing out the flecks of emerald in his eyes.

"My point is, why are you going back there? What are you going to do when you get there? I see too much of myself in you to just let you go without asking."

"I'm not going to kill myself," I say because I don't feel suicidal. If anything, beneath the icy cold numbness inside of me, all I want is to fucking live. I look away sharply, but I can feel Muse's eyes on me still. "What else am I supposed to do? There's nowhere for me to go."

"Stay here," he says and I snap my attention over to him, spilling tea into my lap with a curse and then pausing to push some red hair away from my face.

"Stay here?" I ask, heart pounding, this strange feeling taking over me, burning me up from head to toe. "Like, as a …" I start to say, but I'm not sure how to finish that sentence except with the word … "Groupie?"

Muse shrugs, and even the heavy jacket and sweater he's wearing can't hide the muscular breadth of his shoulders or the strong biceps hiding underneath. He continues to stare at me, making me feel like I need to fidget. I tuck my legs underneath me and then untuck them again.

"No, not like that. You wouldn't be expected to do anything you didn't want to. If what you want is to just camp out in the Bat Cave and sleep, you could do that. You could also come to our shows; I'll get you a backstage pass and you can hang out."

"I don't understand," I say, looking at him and trying not to notice that my hands are shaking a little. His offer sounds too good to be true, and I don't trust stuff like that. Life is never kind or friendly or easygoing; she's a raging bitch. "Why?"

Muse smiles and I realize I'm doing exactly the same thing I did before, when he told me he cleaned up my stuff, when he offered to let me use his credit card to buy a plane ticket. He sighs and sets his cup aside, leaning over and putting his elbow on his knees, his fingers in his hair.

"When …" he takes a deep breath and closes his eyes. "When you see another lonely traveler walking the same sad, strange path you almost fell off before … it's only right to see if you can guide them down a different road." Muse opens his copper-emerald-sapphire flecked eyes and looks back at me with a half-smile that matches his words: sad and strange. "If Pax hadn't brought me into Beauty in Lies, I'd be dead right now." He chuckles and sits up, the pins on his coat rustling with the movement. "And let's be honest, when I joined, I was shit at the guitar. I had no clue what I was doing. But he didn't hire me because I could or couldn't play music, he hired me because he recognized the same thing in me that he had in himself."

Muse stands up and looks down at me.

"It's not technical skills or schooling or even passion that makes good music: it's pain. Pax has it; Ransom has it; Cope has it; Michael has it. He picked me because he knew I had it,

124

too. He could teach me to play guitar; he couldn't teach me what it's like to suffer and survive."

"But what happens if I stay here?" I ask him and he smiles a much happier sort of smile.

"That's up to you. *You* decide what you do with your time here. And when we play our last stateside gig in New York, make a choice. Stay there, go back to Phoenix, move to Hong Kong if you want."

I can't help but smile at that, but my hands ... the shaking has doubled, tripled.

"You can have the Bat Cave. Consider it yours for the remainder of the trip. Two straight weeks to grieve your dad, to figure shit out."

"Did you talk to your bandmates about this?" I ask, even as I'm dying inside to say *yes.* It crosses my mind that if I agree to this, I'll be spending two weeks with *four* guys that I fucked. Things are bound to get ... messy and awkward.

"Cope and Ransom," he says, slipping the fingers of his tattooed hand into his coat pocket and watching my face carefully as his full lips twist into a mischievous smile. I think about what Ransom said, about Muse being overreaching, acting like he knows people when he doesn't. I can see that. I also wonder how many lives he's saved by doing that. Because right now, it feels like he's saving mine. "Pax and Michael, we'll deal with when they get up. But it's three versus two, and we have a majority rules plan in place for disagreements so it doesn't matter."

A drop of liquid plops into my tea and I look down in surprise, only to realize that I'm crying yet *again.* But it's only because I'm thinking of Dad. He would never approve of me hanging out on a bus with five dudes, but if it's what I wanted to do, he'd support me. He was old-fashioned in some ways, but he loved me more than he loved his traditions or his values.

I open my mouth to talk, but Muse steps forward and gently covers my lips with his hand.

"Don't ask *why,*" he tells me and I smile beneath the heat of his palm, "just say yes or no."

"It sounds like you're asking me to marry you," I joke when

he drops his hand and grins a little.

"Who knows? I'm definitely into you. Maybe by the end of all this, I will be?"

I laugh, but the thought of hanging out here, drinking spicy cups of tea with Muse, hearing Ransom call be *baby doll,* eating burgers in this living room, that all sounds like heaven. Then again, maybe they've only been so nice to me thus far because they expected me to leave? I could be in for a completely different sort of two weeks.

But it's better than lonely Phoenix and motel rooms that take cash and wondering if I can get a food stamp card from the human services office.

"I'd be an idiot to say no," I tell him, setting my cup aside and standing up. I throw my arms around Muse's neck and he wraps his around my waist. I'm not sure it's ever felt so good to hug a stranger ... except for maybe Copeland. Those two definitely rank up there in the hugging department. "Who knew a stupid one-night stand would get me on your fancy bus for two weeks?"

"It wasn't the sex; it was your eyes," he tells me and I squeeze him tighter because he sounds so serious. Underneath my brief flicker of happiness, I feel melancholia leaking through, but I ignore it, push it back. I won't waste these two weeks wallowing in misery; I need to come up with a plan, something that would've made Dad proud if the cancer hadn't stolen him away from me.

I hear the sound of the hall door and glance over to find Ransom staring at me from his dark eyes. He lights a cigarette as he watches me let go of Muse's warm body with a strange sort of reluctance that I don't quite understand.

"Guess this means you're staying, honey?" he asks in his leather and lace voice.

"Staying?" Paxton asks, pushing past him and moving into the kitchen wearing yet another fucking suit, all perfect and pressed and polished. "Who's staying?"

He pours himself a cup of coffee before he turns and spots me standing there.

I have no idea what to make of the impression in his cold grey eyes.

126

CHAPTER TWENTY-TWO

Paxton

I can't spend my bloody time worrying about some girl who blushes and cries when I fuck her; I have a show to think about. I run a hand down the rich royal purple color of my tie and stick a cigarette between my lips.

"You're okay with this?" Michael asks, looking like he wants to punch somebody. Nothing new there; Michael always looks like he wants to punch somebody. "With this girl staying on our bus?"

I pause and check out a gaggle of girls in the corner, all dressed in expensive VIP badges, biting their lips and staring at the two of us like they'd enjoy eating us for dinner. I ignore them; they'll be here whether I give them any attention or not.

"What's the problem? A hot groupie in permanent residence? Why should I complain?" I might not have time to worry about that girl, but I'd take another shag or two or ten. I feel like her curves are tattooed across my body along with all the song lyrics. *"My dad died yesterday."* Well, shit if that doesn't make me feel like a right arsehole. Maybe that's why I ran away from her, out into the fucking pouring Arizona rain?

And she knew it, too, that I was running away.

Wish she could explain to both of us why I panicked like that.

"Because what I said before still stands: if she's on the bus, no more groupies. You guys are not going to start collecting them like souvenir fucking postcards."

"Are you fucking serious?" I ask him in the hazy backstage darkness. Up ahead and to my right, there's a set of steps that lead to the stage. I can hear Rivers of Concrete playing their set now, hear the crowd getting warmed up and ready for us. This is probably my favorite part of the whole night, all the anticipation, the expectation, the excitement. "That's ridiculous. You're not punishing me for a decision that Muse, Cope, and Ransom made. If I want to fuck a girl on the bus, I damn well will."

"Where? With some redhead in Muse's baggy t-shirt walking around and sleeping in the Bat Cave? I will *not* have this shit turn into some sort of catfight-fuckfest."

"Because you can't have a bloody lick of fun doesn't mean you have the right to cut the bollocks off the rest of us," I say as I turn and look my friend in the eyes. He's wearing too much eyeliner and a leather jacket with a sweater underneath it, his dark hair falling across his sweaty forehead. We haven't even taken the damn stage yet and already it's hot as the surface of the damn sun in here.

I straighten my collar and adjust my cuff links as I return Michael's sharp look.

"If I didn't know any better, I'd think you were just jealous. Maybe that curvy little redhead is tempting you more than you care to admit?" I smirk when I say that and watch as his hands curl into angry fists.

"Like I'd want to touch some girl all four of you fucked. That's disgusting."

"Tell yourself whatever you want," I say as my smirk gets deeper, darker, "I had her first."

I saunter past him over to the steps and smoke my cigarette, eyes scanning for Lilith Goode. I find her near the refreshments table, drinking a red cup filled with beer, wearing that little scrap of a black dress I saw her in yesterday. Admittedly, I like the look of it. Sharp red heels, scorching red lips, vibrant red hair.

When I see the others clustered around her, my eyes narrow a bit. I did bloody have her first, didn't I? And what's she done to get those three panting at her heels like that?

I lean against the wall and watch her until our set comes up and she moves away, disappearing down a different set of steps, heading towards the audience instead of the stage.

"Looking for a replacement for Kortney?" I ask Ransom when he moves up next to me. Anger ripples through him, but he doesn't react. That's one of the things that drives me up the bleeding wall, watching him coil up inside of himself like that. He never fucking shouts, hardly gets visibly angry. And I want that, crave it really.

It's his fault that my girlfriend, Chloe, and my sister, Harper are dead. His fault. We used to be friends; he's the reason I'm a musician after all. But I can barely look at him anymore.

"Leave Lilith alone or I'll give you another concussion," he says softly, voice hardly audible above the cheering of the crowd. But I don't intend to listen to that. If I can get that girl into bed again, I will—especially if that fucker Michael intends to keep other girls off our bus. I almost believe he'd do it, too, walk away from all of this just to prove to himself that he's not an asshole like the rest of us, run home to Vanessa and marry some girl he hates.

"Lilith," I say as I smile wickedly at Ransom and he narrows his dark eyes, "doesn't belong to you, now does she? She's a free woman, and if she's going to be our houseguest for the next few weeks, I may as well have another go at her."

"She's not your whore, Pax," Ransom says, his voice edgier but still no louder than a whisper.

"Did I say she was? She's clearly into me is all. I wouldn't be surprised if she fell on my dick before the end of the night."

"I could slit your throat and not lose a single night of sleep," he whispers back and I smile even bigger.

"Didn't you already do that and get away with it once? I'd hate to see you try it a second time." I pause as our manager, Octavia, listens in on her headset and then gives me a firm nod of her head. I've got a pretty good idea that she's in love with me, but I don't shag my bosses. Doesn't usually turn out well, that. "Oh, but wait, you didn't just slit his throat, did you? You stabbed him, what was it, a hundred and fourteen times?"

"You're a monster," Ransom says, but I can barely hear him because I'm heading up the steps to the stage and listening to the crowd explode in wild excitement. I wave at them and then pause at the front of the stage to take a deep bow, grabbing the mic when I stand up and waiting for them to quiet down a little. Takes 'em awhile, but I just wait there and glance into the shadows at the base of the stage, at the small cluster of VIPs behind the bodyguards. Lilith's hair is such a strange color that I pinpoint her position right away.

"My name is Paxton Blackwell," I say as I put my hand on the mic stand and walk in a tight circle around it, my black loafers loud against the surface of the stage as I look up and across the glittering crowd. "We're Beauty in Lies." More cheering, always with the bloody cheering. It's not that I mind —who the fuck doesn't want to be worshipped—but sometimes it just gets annoying. "And we're from Seattle, Washington." Well, that's where our band started. Really, I'm from a small rural town outside of York, but who the fuck here cares about that? "We're starting off with a song I wrote for an ex-girlfriend."

I look up at them and smile like I've just decided this. In all reality, our manager's had our set lists for each city predetermined and ready to go since we announced the tour six months ago.

"This one's called *Chloe,*" I say and I try not to sound disdainful when I say her name. She *is* dead after all, and even if I started hating her before that happened, I try not to let my voice drip with irony when I sing this song.

I clear my throat and the band starts up behind me. Michael first, then Copeland, Muse and Ransom. The mic lifts to my lips.

"Since I met you a year and yesterday, you've done nothing but take away my heartache and my pain. Without you, it's only darkness that I breathe. The sunshine never smiles down on me, and I'm left pining here; I bleed. Empty and broken. A mirror of shattered glass, in love with a razor's reflection, feeling my end coming on so fast. Oh, Chloe, sweet thing, you make me want to breathe again."

I take a deep breath and a step back as Ransom screams into his microphone.

"LIVE AND LOVE AND LEARN TO BREATHE AGAIN!"

I don't bother to move around, not for this song. I clutch the mic stand and let my head and foot move in time with the beat.

"Hair like roses, smirking lips and beauty queen poses. Of all the stars in the night sky, you're the only one that makes it bright. Chloe, sweet thing, in your arms I breathe again. That shattered glass and silent moments, with you I feel the truth it poses."

Taking the mic in both hands, I slip it back into the stand take off my cuff links as I sing, the right and then the left. I stick them in my pockets and glance down at Lilith Tempest Goode, standing there watching me with a red Solo cup and an enigmatic expression that frustrates me to no end.

I ignore her, wondering why I even give a fuck what some random groupie thinks. And she might say she's not a groupie, but why the hell did she follow me back to the bus then? Because her dad died? Just a little grief filled fucking then? I suppose I could understand that. Did the same when my sister died in Chloe's drunken car accident.

But the thing is, I learned my lesson with that shit before. I may never trust another woman—another *person*—ever again. Maybe I should've put my foot down about this girl being on our bus? This majority rules bullshit shouldn't count when it's something as big as this, as big as carting around some crying-blushing redhead.

I finish that horrid song and smile as Muse and Michael toss their guitars up in the air, across the stage and towards a pair of waiting roadies on either side. The crowd cheers dramatically as the confetti machines explode and drench them in vibrant bits of colored paper.

"This one," I say as I shrug out of my suit jacket and hand it to another roadie, pushing up the charcoal grey sleeves of my button-up, "we've never performed it live before."

I raise my brows and catch Lilith's eyes yet again. Seems strangely impossible in a room full of two thousand people that I would keep looking at her, but it happens and I feel a slight frown crease my mouth.

"A few years back, my sister, Harper, was visiting the States from England." I take a few steps back as some roadies roll a gleaming black piano onstage, front and center. "When she died in a car accident. This song is for her."

I sit down on the bench in front of the piano, letting the roadies adjust my mic as the crowd bubbles excitedly. Truth be bloody told, this is the *last* song I'd ever want to perform live, but our record label has spoken and so shall it be done.

Taking a deep breath, I place my fingers over the keys.

"Of course, this is called *Harper B.*," I say and then I start playing, closing my eyes for a moment, letting myself fall into the music. If I don't, if I have to sit here and listen to Ransom play his bass guitar and sing alongside of me, I might just kill someone. The other boys sit this one out; it's just me and fucking Ransom Riggs.

I hit the keys hard and listen to him strumming softly behind me; he plays his instrument like he talks, quiet and sensual, like he's trying to seduce some poor chick into his fucking bed, to lay there all damn night and listen to his nightmares.

Ironic, too, that it's at least partially his fault that she's dead.

"*Harper B., the night you said goodbye I cried, so loud the angels came to say goodnight. How can I live another day knowing you won't be there to hear me play? Why is the world so fucking cruel? Why did God take someone as beautiful as you? Remember that summer day we flew to Seattle just to stay? I wish I'd hugged her, kissed her, Dear God, how I miss my baby sister.*"

My fingers strum across the ivory keys as I suck in a deep breath and push my anger, my pain, my rage away. That night she came to visit, Harper and I were supposed to go out and party, but I was so goddamn upset with Ransom and Chloe that I just couldn't be bothered. Chloe showed up at my place after I left to cool my head, and took Harper with her; they never came back.

If Ransom hadn't tried to steal my girlfriend, if he hadn't picked a fight with me that night, Harper would probably still be alive. Of course, I blame Chloe, too, since she was the drunk idiot that was driving that car, but she's gone, too, payment extracted and served. Good riddance.

I hit the keys harder, pushing my fingertips into the piano

like I blame the instrument for my pain and my frustration. I feel myself gritting my teeth and almost miss the next verse. But I'll be *damned* if I let Ransom sing about Harper without me.

"Harper B., please wait for me, I'll be coming to see you soon. Because in the end, it'll just be me and you the way we've always known. Baby sister, oh God how I miss her, please tell me why it had to be this way? Tell me why I should I even stay? Harper B., baby, just know that I love you more than I can ever say."

Once more, I glance down into the shadowy space in front of the stage and catch Lilith's eyes. This time, she's crying again and when our gazes lock, she smiles softly.

What the fuck is that supposed to mean?

I tear my eyes away from her and force myself to finish the song, the set, and I don't look at her again until I'm tearing down the steps and into the hazy glittering darkness backstage. It's like a gathering of dark fae back here, all of this raunchy beauty, like the Unseelie court's finally crossed the veil and managed to spread their wicked revelry.

I make it all the way to the bathroom before I slam the door, close it hard and slide to the floor, putting my fingers in my hair. And then I finally let out a scream I wasn't sure I was holding in until just now, until tonight.

Fuck that girl who thinks it's okay to cry like that? Out in the open where everyone can see?

There is no way in *hell* I'm letting her stay on my bloody bus.

CHAPTER TWENTY-THREE

Lilith

LILITH GOODE

I let myself get pretty drunk backstage, enjoying the easy camaraderie of the roadies and the staff, the way they accept me into their group, laughing and sharing cigarettes—which I don't take—telling stories about the road, about the bands, anecdotes about their own lives.

Truly, I'm curious to see what the members of Beauty in Lies are doing, but they have their VIP get-together, and I can just vaguely see them snapping photos with fans and signing things from my position in the sky bar, up high on the balcony overlooking the venue. Most of the fans have cleared out already, but there are enough people here that for a while, I don't feel so lonely.

When Pax and Ransom started singing *Harper B.,* I almost lost it, but I feel okay now. I Googled Paxton's sister and found some vague news articles about a drunken car accident, but the details are few and far between. Somebody really didn't want the press digging too deeply into this. I wonder about it, wonder if that explains the pain and darkness and cruelty in Paxton's gaze, in his touch. It would make a certain awful sort of sense.

After the roadies disappear, I follow the curving gold carpet downstairs, my fingers brushing the wall as I try not to fall over in my tall red heels. I didn't really want to wear them again, but the rest of my clothes are musty and damp and dirty from being strewn across oil soaked pavement. This dress is all I have, and I couldn't really wear any of my other shoes without looking ridiculous.

When I get back downstairs, I find Octavia in the lobby, directing roadies to clear out the merch tables—covered in t-shirts, shrink-wrapped vinyl records, CDs, hoodies, pins, stickers. She sees me coming into the lobby and pretends to smile at me.

"Did you enjoy the show, Lilith?" she asks, tucking her iPad up against her black t-shirt.

"It was incredible," I say, and I mean that. I've only been to a handful of concerts in my life, but the depth of emotion in Pax's voice when he was singing about his sister … I don't think I'll ever hear another sound as hauntingly beautiful as that in my entire life. "I've never—" I start, and Octavia holds up a hand, glancing away and listening to someone talk to her in the headset. She reaches up and presses a button on the side of her earpiece.

"Absolutely, thank you so much." She glances back at me and smiles again. "Lilith, I was wondering if you wouldn't mind stopping by my trailer tonight. Mr. Muser discussed having you stay on the tour and although I'm firmly against it, it's not my choice to make. What I would like, however, is for you to sign an NDA—you know what that is, don't you?—so if you could make the time, I'd appreciate it."

She smiles again, her sweet midwestern farming face turning into a straight mean girl's expression for a minute. When she turns, her ponytail whips me across the face and I stare in shock at her back as she bounces away.

What a fucking bitch.

I take a deep breath and close my eyes. She's not worth it. I learned a big lesson when Kevin paraded one of his girlfriends in front of me after we'd broken up and I was moving my stuff out of our apartment. All of that seething rage and anger inside, if you unleash it, it creates an unpredictable, uncontrollable storm, one that doesn't judge what or who it destroys. Sometimes, even if you're the one that let it all out, it can destroy you, too.

I head back towards the buses, showing my badge to every member of security staff along the way and pause hesitantly at the bottom of the steps. Derek invited me to stay here, but it still feels strange, absurdly surreal. Two weeks ago, I was wiping tables down at a shitty diner and dreading calling my dad back, terrified that when he said we should *talk,* that he had bad news to share. Then he suggested I come and stay with him and the whirlwind of packing and sorting things out started. I sold what little furniture I had, gave my poor cat away to a girl from the diner, gave notice at my job, at my apartment.

And then, on the day I was supposed to drive to New York, he died on me. My dad left me alone to figure out how to breathe without him. Deep inside, I feel that gaping chasm of loneliness and pain, like a pit that I'm standing over, about to topple in and drown in the dark, sticky depths of heartache.

No fucking way.

I shove red hair over one shoulder and move up the steps, finding Copeland sitting on the couch and reading a book. He looks to be near the end and he's bent over the pages like he's on a roller coaster.

"No fucking way!" he says as he snaps the cover closed and tosses the book aside. "No fucking way did it end like that."

I smile as I move into the living room and his turquoise eyes snap up to me. He looks a little chagrined at being caught talking to a book, but he smiles at me anyway.

"Did you like the show?" he asks, and I try not to think of Octavia's saccharine sweet smile when she asked me that same question.

"It was incredible," I tell him, moving around the end of the couch and sitting on the furthest cushion from him. "I love that, like *rat-a-tat-tat* thing that you do." I imitate the furious flurry of Cope's arms as he pounded away at his drums, sitting above his friends on a raised platform.

"Rat-a-tat-tat," he says with a curved smile that sets my heart aflutter. "I like it. Very descriptive." He affects a half bow from a sitting position and sits up straight to look at me, eyes warm and vibrant and brimming with intelligence.

I didn't get to see much of him—or any of them, really—today. After Muse invited me to stay on the bus, and Pax came out for coffee, the other boys got in a fight with Michael and I excused myself to the Bat Cave for a while. I went through the boxes that Muse collected and sorted things out, got together a bag of laundry and put it up front with the boys'. Ransom told me someone would come and take it and bring it back tomorrow. Then I looked up my father's obituary online and cried some more; Ransom ended up coming in and sitting quietly next to me, rubbing my back. He even stayed and watched several episodes of *Grace and Frankie* with me before it was time to prep for the concert.

"I don't know if you can tell, but I'm not very knowledgeable when it comes to music. The peak of my music career was during my fourth grade concert. I was playing a pink plastic recorder in the third row."

Cope laughs again, sitting back and draping himself in the corner of the couch, looking sexy as hell in a sweaty black tank and a pair of charcoal grey skinny jeans. It's clear he came right back here after the VIP meet and greet and flopped right down to finish his book.

"I'm sure you were brilliant," he says, his voice warm and companionable, totally dangerous. When Cope talks, it's like a siren's song. It's not the actual pitch and tone of his voice that makes him so scary, but the way he talks, holds his face, smiles. He acts like that boyfriend I've always wanted but never had. Sweet, thoughtful, but also dangerously sexy, good in bed, skilled with his hands and ... other things. "I bet the line for admission was," he lifts his hand and flicks it through the air in an arc, "out the door and down the block."

"Made you guys look like small potatoes," I say, raising my brows and thinking about the massive line camped outside the venue. It was there by the time I was finished with my conversation with Muse; I could see it from the window inside the Bat Cave. Guess Beauty in Lies has some pretty dedicated fans. "But anyway, you were great. Seriously."

"Thanks," he says, blinking slowly, his eyes so riveting I can hardly look away. They're like turquoise stones, fixed in a classically handsome face, very boy next door but edged up with the auburn faux hawk, the eyeliner, the cluster of necklaces around his throat. All of them are on black silk cords, different shapes of pewter charms scattered at the base of his throat. He's got a pair of black sweatbands on, too, and I just barely see star and heart tattoos sneaking out from underneath in vibrant swooshes of neon color, their individual shapes made up with musical notes. "We try to put on a good show, especially now that we're getting more popular. It's important to keep it all low-key, rock 'n' roll, you know?"

"I wanted to … talk to you each individually," I start, rubbing my hands over my bare knees and I'm hoping I'm not ruining the moment by bringing this up. I look into Copeland's face, but he's still smiling at me, touching his fingers to a stack of books sitting on the back of the couch. He taps his fingertips against them in a steady beat, like he's playing his drums still.

"About?" he asks as he stands up and grabs a beer from the fridge, lifting one up to me. "Want one?"

"Sure," I say, accepting it from his hand and trying not to make contact with his fingers. It happens anyway and like I expected, I get a little jolt, a thrill. What *is* it with these boys? Is it just because they're rockstars? Because they're attractive? Because I'm so sad inside? I have no idea.

Cope sits back down, still smiling, but not like Muse. Muse just smiles with his whole face, like he knows who he is and has already accepted it. Cope … looks like he's smiling the way the person he wants to be would smile, like he wishes he could be something more but isn't sure how to get there.

"Is this about the sex?" he asks and I feel a slight flush color my cheeks.

"I just wanted to explain—"

"No explanation necessary," he says as I try not to think about the things I said to him, to a complete freaking stranger. *"I want to come."* Wow. Just wow. "I enjoyed myself, didn't you?"

"Well, yeah, I …"

"Then no harm done," he says, sipping his beer, his arm muscles rippling with the simple movement. "If you liked it, then what does it matter?"

"I've never fucked four guys in one night before," I blurt and his brows go up. "Have you ever fucked four girls in one night?"

"Oh, hell no," he says with a laugh, putting one hand behind his head. "I don't think I could get it up fast enough to satisfy four girls in one night. You ladies are lucky; you can go as many times as you want." I put a hand to my mouth to stifle a chuckle as he sets his beer aside and leans forward to look at me. "Besides, I'm more of a one girl a night kind of a guy anyway."

"I've only ever slept with two guys before," I say and then flush a little brighter when I realize how that sounds. "Not … you know, at the same time. Or even in the same year."

"Wow," Copeland says with a whistle, sitting back and looking at me with interest. "So, in one night, you tripled your number? That's pretty impressive."

I smile tightly and feel my cheeks dimple.

"Yeah, I suppose." I glance down at my thighs and push the stretchy black fabric down. It refuses to budge, but at least I tried. I look back up at Copeland. "I never intended to sleep with anyone, let alone the whole band. I was just … really, really sad. The sex helped a lot. It made me forget."

"You won't find anyone judging you here," he says and I breathe out a small sigh of relief. It *is* still a little weird to sit and have a casual conversation with Cope though, not knowing a damn thing about him except for the way his cock felt between my thighs, the way he kissed me, the way his arms felt wrapped around my naked body. And then I fell asleep crying on his chest. Jesus. "And if you ever need another hug, I've got extras."

"Are you hitting me on? Or just being nice?" I ask, smiling and finishing off my beer. I get up on my knees on the couch as his smile twists up in the corner, the slightest hint of a smirk hovering there.

"Maybe a little bit of both?" he offers and without letting myself think too hard about it, I lean forward and let him wrap his arms around me, pulling me in against his chest.

All the breath rushes out of me in an instant as Cope squeezes me tight in his strong arms.

"You weren't kidding; you really *are* good at these."

"I've had to hug a lot of people through a lot of things," he says, and there's this melancholy sadness to his voice that's so at odds with his boy next door attitude that I lean back to stare into his eyes, my palms flat against my chest, my feet lifted and crossed at the ankles.

We look at each other for a long moment and the mood shifts, from this casual friend vibe to something else.

I let my eyes flutter closed and lean in, feeling Cope's mouth press up against mine, cutting the distance between us. He's a *damn* good kisser, like he's taken a master class on it. He keeps his arms wrapped tightly around me, making me feel safe, wanted. I know how dangerous it is to give into a guy like this —especially for a second time—but I can't seem to help myself.

Copeland likes to feel needed.

That's what it is, that's the feeling I'm recognizing in the delicate but insistent brush of his tongue, in the careful but confident touch of his hands. The advice, the hugs, the sex, it's all the same for him, dispensing something that's wanted, needed—and relishing it.

It's a little disappointing, knowing that this giddy feeling of being wanted by a boy is something else entirely, but I decide I'll just relish the relishing and enjoy myself. These two weeks that Muse has given me, these are mine, and Cope's touch, it does exactly what he wants it to do: it makes me feel better.

He slides his hands to my waist, holding me with his long fingers, tasting like cherry cola and smelling like fresh sweat and laundry soap. The mix of those three things makes me feel light-headed, makes my heart pitter-patter in a way it hasn't done since high school.

"I must be good at these," he murmurs against my mouth, "if this is what I get in return."

"Oh, this?" I joke softly, touching the pendants on his chest with my fingers, "this isn't for the hug; this is for the forty bucks you gave me at the gas station."

Cope laughs as I pull away, sliding down his body and going for the button on his charcoal skinny jeans. They're actually not denim like I thought at first, but something else. Twill, maybe? Anyway, they're soft beneath my fingertips as I open the button and tug the zipper down, suddenly reminded of Ransom and all his scars.

I push the thought away and focus on the man that's in front of me instead, freeing his cock from his pants and glancing up to catch his lids drooping and his breath sighing out with pleasure as I take him in my hand.

I'm aware even as I do this that it's not just Cope that has ulterior motives; I do, too.

My lips touch the side of his cock, hot and velvety in my palm, completely foreign in shape and size and texture. Now that I've seen four other guys to compare him against, Kevin was not very impressive in width, length, or appearance. God. How could I have wasted five years with that idiot?

Pushing those thoughts aside, I adjust myself to get more comfortable, putting one knee on the floor and leaving the other on the couch. I'm aware that my short as fuck dress just got even shorter and that the black thong I had to wear underneath it —my choices of underwear in those boxes were ridiculously limited—is exposing my bare ass to anyone that walks in that door.

But somehow, that thought's kind of exciting, too.

I curl my fingers around Cope's shaft and gently push his cock between my lips as he lets his head fall back and kneads my scalp with his fingers. I'm not very experienced at giving blow jobs, so I improvise, trying to take my cues from the way Cope moans, breathes, from the way he shifts around on the couch.

I'm so focused on trying to get this right that I don't hear the door to the bus open, don't hear the footsteps coming up behind me until I feel a pair of hands on my bare hips.

"Hey there, sweetheart," a soft syrupy voice says from behind me. Ransom. "What are you up to in here, baby doll?" His voice is thick with desire and his fingers burn hot trails against my skin as he touches me with a needy tentativeness that's clearly asking for an answer.

Without saying a word, I reach a hand back and pull my dress up a few more inches, exposing more of my ass to the warm air in the bus. My sex is completely liquid now, throbbing and hot, ready to be filled.

Cope's eyes open halfway and take in Ransom standing behind me, but he doesn't say anything, resting his right hand in my hair and arcing his hips towards my face, pushing his cock into my mouth. Now that Ransom's here, watching, I should probably feel more self-conscious. Instead, it turns me on to know that he's watching and I drop my inhibitions, slicking my tongue down the side of Cope's shaft, all the way to his balls. I tease the seam of his flesh down the center and then gently suck some of that soft skin into my mouth.

Ransom kneels behind me, bringing his flirty scent with him. He, too, smells like sweat from the show, but in a good way, like he's just come off of a really good workout. I can feel him moving behind me and my heart goes crazy, beating so fast I get that light-headed feeling again.

Um, is this really happening right now?

I've never had a threesome, never even really *thought* about having a threesome, let alone one with two guys I just met.

Fuck. Is this wrong?

I decide that I don't really care if it is, groaning against Cope's shaft as Ransom puts his hands on my hips and adjusts my position to give himself a better angle. When I feel the head of his cock pushing into me, I gasp and slick my fist up Copeland's shaft, hoping I'm not squeezing *too* hard. He groans and thrusts against my hand as I arch my back and feel one of Ransom's hands on my left shoulder. The other he puts on the hip that's propped against the side of the couch.

He starts to thrust and the air's knocked right out of me, the leather sofa refusing to give, making the sensation of his body inside of mine just that much sharper, deeper, harder. I take the sudden surge of pleasure out on Cope's cock, sucking it into my mouth, throwing all caution to the wind and swirling my tongue around the head, teasing each vein with wet kisses from my panting lips.

Vaguely, I think I hear someone cursing from the direction of the door, but I'm too wrapped up in sensations to care. I have a hot guy on either side of me and it's not just *twice* as hot, but like, three or four or five fucking times as hot.

"Suck him deep, honey. I want to watch," Ransom says, and

the sound of his voice alone almost kills me. I moan as I wrap a tight fist around Copeland's dick, pushing him into my throat as deep as I can get him and sucking until his fingers dig into my hair, into the leather of the couch, and he comes in my mouth. The taste of his come on the back of my tongue is salty but not unpleasant, and I swallow hard as I collapse against him and groan as Ransom fucks me hard.

My bones turn to jelly and without thinking, I curl my fingers around Copeland's, and he squeezes them back, laying there panting and watching us with gently parted lips. He doesn't even bother to fix his pants as my body moves against him, each one of Ransom's thrusts jostling us both.

My clit is literally pressed up tight to the couch, so there's no shortage of stimulation to push me over that edge, turn my body into an aching mess, and then break it into pieces as I listen to Ransom moaning behind me. I cry out as he rams into me, stirring my own pleasure into a frenzy. I come hard around him, taking him with me, making him curse as he spills himself into the condom, fingertips digging painfully into my shoulder and hip for a moment before he shudders and relaxes a little.

"Holy shit, baby doll," he whispers, moving away from me, leaving me feeling cold in the sudden absence of his warmth. I sit back and glance over my shoulder as Ransom stands and fixes his black jeans. My body feels tingly all over and strangely alive, excited, needy, wanting for more.

I stand up on shaky legs and stumble, falling into Cope's arms again. He doesn't seem to mind, wrapping me up and holding me against him. I can hear his heart thundering a million miles an hour.

"You guys do … this kind of thing a lot?" I whisper, curious but also scared to hear the answer.

"No," Cope says as Ransom sits down on the chair across from us to catch his breath. "Never."

I can't believe how much that answer pleases me.

CHAPTER TWENTY-FOUR

Michael

What a serious fucking mistake.

An awful goddamn mistake.

I slam the door to the shower room and flick the lock, hitting my fist against the faucet and letting cold water stream down from the ceiling and drench me like a rainstorm—clothing and all. I was *not* prepared to walk onto my bus and find those assholes engaged in a sweaty, groaning threesome.

I slick my fingers through my wet hair and lean my back against the tiled wall, sliding to the floor in my jeans, boots and t-shirt. At least I had the foresight to take my goddamn jacket off.

"Shit," I whisper as icy water trickles across my heated skin, washing away the sweat of the show but doing absolutely nothing to fuck with my libido. I'm so goddamn horny, I feel like my cock's about to snap off. "Shit," I repeat, kicking off my boots and letting them bounce into the dry half of the tiled room. This whole bus was custom, put together by the record label as a signing bonus for the band and it's just … like fucking posh. If I jammed my hand against the drain and plugged it up, this whole room would flood, turning it into a bath for two … or more.

I run my hands over my face and curse again, stripping off my other boot and my socks.

Burnished auburn waves falling across a pale white neck, a dancing line of freckles across those smooth shoulders, generous curves swathed in black.

"This is fucking ridiculous," I murmur as I curl my shaking

hands around the wet denim covering my knees. I haven't had sex in *months*. No, more than months. Like a goddamn year almost. A year. A year. A fucking *year.* That's probably why I'm so wound up; it has nothing to do with that girl. Could've been any groupie on her knees like that and I would've flipped.

I tear my shirt over my head and toss it aside in a wet heap, unbuttoning my jeans and gritting my teeth at the intensity of the cold wet spray of the showerhead on my cock.

"Jesus fucking Christ," I groan as I slide my hand down my shaft and grip hard enough to hurt. Doesn't help. All it makes me do is fantasize about driving my cock into the tight band of heat between that fucking girl's legs, shoving Ransom out of the way and taking his place behind her.

I groan and twist my hand in a corkscrew motion, reaching the other up and shoving the faucet in the opposite direction, until hot water replaces the cold, steaming against my aching flesh. Closing my eyes, I can almost imagine that the wet heat drenching my shaft belongs to Lilith, that she's soaking me in her desire, lubing me up to fuck her harder.

With another growl of frustration, I get up on my knees and grab the handheld shower head from the hook on the wall, shoving the faucet over so that water comes out of both—the one in my hand and the one on the ceiling.

I lay back on the floor and use the spray to tease myself, changing the setting on the showerhead to this angry pulse that matches my mood. *"I just broke up with my boyfriend of five years and honestly, even though it broke my heart, it was also kind of a relief."* The sound of her voice inside my head *infuriates* me, and I press the water's raging spray up against the underside of my shaft, groaning and thrusting my hips toward the sensation.

What's even worse, when I try to imagine Vanessa—tall, thin, modelesque Vanessa—I can practically *feel* the blood draining from my cock. I'm pissed at her; she's pissed at me. All we do is fight and yet, I can't get up the courage to do anything about it. I keep telling myself that when I actually see her in person, everything will be good again, like it was before. *When you were cheating on her, you mean?*

145

I take my dick in my hand again, hating myself for what I'm doing but unable to stop. This isn't cheating, right? Just thinking of the curvy redhead with her too small dress and her bright red heels and the giant burger she could barely hold between her long fingered hands … and I'm blowing my load *hard,* a small scream tearing from my throat that I hope to *God* nobody else can hear.

But then, we are on a fucking bus.

I finish cleaning up in the shower and wrap a towel around my hips, heading to my bunk and opening the small drawer underneath where I keep sweats and extra tees. There's a trailer in our entourage that has the rest of my clothes—everyone's clothes actually—since there isn't room to store an entire rockstar's wardrobe worth of crap anywhere on this bus. When we need something, we either go get it ourselves or have a roadie bring it over for us.

Once I'm dressed and letting myself back into the kitchen, I stumble on another fight. *Another* fucking fight. Over the same girl.

I'm about to go goddamn mental here.

"Well, I've changed my bloody mind," Paxton growls, inches away from Ransom's face. The two of them look like they're about to go batshit on each other. "I don't *want* her here," he snarls, pointing at Lilith. To her credit, the girl's curled on the couch in Copeland's arms looking like she doesn't give a shit about Paxton and his angry yelling.

I can't tell if it's all a facade or if she just doesn't let crap like that bother her. I watch her, towel drying my shoulder length hair as my eyes rove over that same stupid dress, tight and clingy in all the wrong places. *But oh so right to look at.* Fuck.

I tear my eyes away, trying not to think about Muse telling me her father just died, that she has nowhere to go, that she has no family. How is any of that my problem?

"What the fuck is going on in here?"

Both Pax and Ransom turn to look at me, Muse standing off to the side with his arms crossed over his chest, Cope looking pissed as fuck but too cozied up to Lilith to bother to get off the damn couch.

"He barreled in here shouting and screaming and obviously fucking drunk off his ass," Ransom whispers, his voice dark as shadows within shadows, like what happens when night turns to something darker. When he's like this, it's not that hard to imagine that he killed somebody. "But if he doesn't back up and shut the hell up here soon, I'm going to get angry."

Ransom pauses to light a cigarette, the flicker of the lighter brightening up the inside of his hood for a moment.

"You are properly fucking mental, you are," Pax slurs, still wearing his suit, covered in sweat and swaying like crazy. He even has a bottle clutched in one hand, sloshing amber liquid across the wood floor. "Getting attached to some bitch you don't even know. Didn't you learn your lesson with Chloe? With Kortney?"

"I don't want to talk about Chloe and Kortney," Ransom says slowly, his voice coiling dark and wicked in the room.

I move forward; this shit is about to come to a boiling point.

"Pax," I say as he stumbles away from Ransom, cursing and throwing open the fridge door like he knows what he's looking for inside the fluorescent depths. "Why don't you take a little break and have some water?"

"Get the hell away from me," he says and then he throws the full bottle of brandy into the sink where it cracks into pieces and splashes across the counter. "I don't *like* her," he insists, throwing his hand out to point at Lilith. "She's always bloody crying. I wanted to bring one of those girls from the meet and greet back here, but you know what? There's a weeping woman on my bus and who the hell wants to see any of that?"

"You need to go lie down," I say, gritting my teeth, even though I know I should probably be using this moment to my advantage, teaming up with Pax and kicking Lilith off the bus.

"I don't *need* to lie down," he shouts at me, throwing my hand off when I try to take his arm. Pax grabs a beer from the fridge, and I watch with pursed lips as he struggles to get the top off. "I'm fucking fine. More than fine. I'll have another drink and then I'll find myself a real groupie, one that doesn't start crying when I fuck her."

"It's okay to be sad," Lilith says, and I look back to see her standing up in front of the couch, looking at Pax less like he's a drunken idiot and more like she feels sorry for him. "There's nothing wrong with crying."

"So you say only because you're always bloody doing it," Pax says as he finally gets the top off his beer and turns to stare at her. He points at her with the drink, spilling more liquid across the floor. "Something's not right with you. It's just not. And I don't care to find out what that is."

"There is something wrong with me," she says, reaching up and running her fingers through her red hair. Looking at her now, I feel a warm stirring inside of me, this primal feeling that makes me want to storm across the bus, grab her and fuck her over the kitchen counter.

I need to call Vanessa. I need to deal with this shit, and then call her *now.*

"But there's also something wrong with you, Pax. You're really sad." She pauses and closes her eyes for a moment. "No, not just sad, but miserable."

"Are you a shrink then?" he asks, slugging back some beer, dropping his grey eyes to glare into her green ones. "You're an expert on me and my problems?"

"Just one broken person looking at another as he scatters his pieces across the floor," she states firmly, crossing her arms over her chest. She exchanges a glance with Muse and he smiles. Apparently this is enough to *really* get Pax going.

"Don't look at him," he says. "Don't fucking look at him. This isn't between you and him; this is between you and me. I had you first." Pax points to himself with a tattooed finger and looks like he's about three seconds from falling over. "I fucked you first."

He drops the beer on the floor and then takes a long, slow breath.

"Bleeding hell," he mumbles and then he's scrambling into the bathroom and leaning over the toilet, not even bothering to shut the damn door.

"I'll get him," I growl, feeling like I should break Pax's neck. If he'd come up here just a little less drunk, maybe we could've reasoned with the other guys. Now I'll have to spend hours keeping him from puking everywhere and dying from alcohol poisoning. Vanessa's going to be *pissed* when I don't call to check in.

"I've got him," Lilith says and I'm not the only one that blinks stupidly at her as she kicks off her red heels and leaves them next to our living room couch. Somehow, I like that, seeing a woman's shoes mixed in with Ransom's boots and Cope's blue Chucks.

I scowl.

What a stupid fucking thought.

"You don't even know Pax," I snap at her as she ties her hair back with a band she pulls out of her bra. I hate that my eyes track the movement of her fingers between her breasts.

"No, but I know what it's like to feel the way he feels. I lost my sister, too."

"That was four years ago," I snap and Lilith smiles sadly, tightly in my direction, her green eyes sparkling with emotion.

"I lost my sister five and a half years ago; the hurt never stops. If you bottle it up, the way Pax clearly does, it starts to poison you from the inside out."

Without waiting for permission, she breezes past me, smelling like roses and shampoo ... *my* shampoo. Out of all the shampoo she could've chosen from the glass cabinet in the bathroom, she picked mine.

I want to scream.

I look at Cope's scowling face, Muse's frown, Ransom's quiet rage, and then I jerk my cell from my pants pocket and storm down the steps of the bus, through the brisk cool air, so embroiled in my thoughts that I can't even admire snowcapped mountains in the distance, topped with evergreen trees and starlight.

"Hey babe," Vanessa says sleepily, "I thought you were gonna call me like an hour or two ago."

I check the time, but it's just after eleven; making it ten back home. What the fuck is she doing asleep?

"Things got weird with Pax," I say and she mumbles something incoherent. "What are you up to?"

I pad across the cold ground in bare feet and lean against the side of the bus, listening to the murmur of people in the parking lot, the distant sound of music. I used to live for that shit, for the night after a show, all the drugs and the fucking and the drinking. Then one night I almost OD'd and Vanessa ended up finding out about everything after I was released from the hospital. And then she told me she was pregnant and that changed my entire world. Of course, she lost the baby in a miscarriage anyway, but I told myself that night in the hospital that I'd make it right. And I have, for two fucking years I've been a damn saint.

Of course, it's been almost a full year since we've seen each other; she had some exchange student bullshit she was doing with the university, moving to Japan for a year to teach English or something, and the band's been working on the new album and all the fucking touring …

"What's new?" she asks, sounding annoyed, like it's all me that put this distance between us, like she didn't sign up for her Japan trip the same day we lost our baby. Still, I feel like a piece of shit for masturbating to thoughts of Lilith. What the fuck is wrong with me? "Aren't these fucking tours always like this, full of bullshit and drama?"

I grit my teeth and shove wet hair away from my forehead. But she's right, and she has a point. Touring is where I cheated on her, where I almost killed myself with too much crystal. She has a right to hate it.

"You texted earlier, said you had some news. Please tell me it's good news?" I ask and she pauses. I can almost hear her smiling when she next speaks.

"Do you miss me?" she asks, and I sigh. We get in huge fucking fights about this shit all the time. She'll ask me a hundred times on one phone call if I miss her and I'll tell her I do, over and over and over again. Doesn't matter. Even though I've quit doing drugs, barely drink, haven't touched another girl since that night, it doesn't seem to matter to Vanessa. I wonder if I'll be paying for my mistakes the rest of our lives.

"Of course I do."

"Good," she says, surprising the shit out of me. "Because I'm coming to see you."

"What?" I ask, snapping to attention, feeling this weird surge of emotion inside of me. Joy, frustration, excitement ... fear. But we've been fighting so much lately, this could be the answer to all our problems. I'm sure one night in bed with Vanessa and I'll forget all about Lilith Goode.

"Next week, when you guys play Atlanta. My dad has some sort of business trip he needs to make, and he has tons of extra miles. Oh, and I'm bringing Tim with me, too." Vanessa squeals and I frown. Fuck. She's bringing my older brother with her?

"Why?" I ask because even though he's always been good to me, our relationship is strained as hell. He blames me for stealing his childhood after our parents died. It was either eighteen year old Timothy stand up and take responsibility for a ten year old or the state would. I think he's hated me ever since.

"Why not, silly? Don't you miss your brother."

I light a cigarette and decide it's best not to say anything to that. Still, I'm surprised Tim's agreed to even come on this trip. I never much thought he and Vanessa liked each other.

"We'll be staying in a hotel for the night, so you don't have to make room on the couch like last time," she says, and I can practically hear her lip curling. She woke to the sound of Pax screwing a groupie with the Bat Cave door open.

"I can stay with you," I tell her, excited at a whole night of uninterrupted fucking. *A year. A whole damn year.* I almost feel like I can breathe a sigh of relief.

"I don't think Dad would like that much," she tells me and I roll my eyes.

"You're twenty-six years old, Vanessa," I say, but it doesn't matter. Her dad funds everything she does; she won't do a damn thing to make him mad. "Just make sure you clear up some time to hang with me on the bus?"

"Feeling extra horny tonight?" she asks and I smile as I smoke my cigarette. What I did in the shower didn't even seem to touch the well of longing inside of me and already my cock is as hard as fucking diamond.

"Let me get in my bunk and we can video chat," I purr, hoping I don't sound guilty as fuck. I *feel* guilty as fuck, even though I know I shouldn't. I try not to think about why that is.

"Later," Vanessa says suddenly. "I've got a call on the other line. I think it's Dad."

And then she hangs up on me.

I glance around for a minute, stick my phone back in my pocket and then spit on my palm, sliding my hand inside my sweats and curling my fingers around my cock.

I try to think of Vanessa as I rub a quick one out against the side of the bus ... but really all I can think about is Lilith.

I wake up to that familiar jostling sensation, the wheels of the bus turning beneath the floor, making the bed quiver and rock as I sit up and run both hands down my face. Last night was a *long* fucking night. Pax was sick five times before he'd thrown up enough to down a glass of water and fall asleep. I kept waking him up to drink more, gave him a few ibuprofen so hopefully his hangover wouldn't sting as badly the next morning.

At some point after I'd dragged Pax onto the bed in back, Ransom appeared and curled up next to me, like he didn't even care that Pax was sleeping in there, too. Between his nightmares and worrying that Paxton might have alcohol poisoning, I hardly got any sleep.

"Hey."

I glance up suddenly and find Paxton staring down at me, clean and freshly showered, his dirty blonde hair hanging across his brow. He's shirtless and beautiful, his tattoos gleaming with tiny droplets of liquid, his voice soft.

"Hey," I respond, glancing quickly over at Ransom and finding him fast asleep next to me, curled on his side and swimming in his black hoodie. I look back at Pax, his shoulder leaning against the door, his wicked sexy curve of a mouth set in a slight frown.

"I was a right proper fucking twat last night," he tells me and I smile slightly. "Truth be told, I have a hard time remembering what happened between the meet and greet and you rubbing my back while I threw up."

I study him, slouching in the lazy darkness of the bus, a pair of grey sweatpants slung low on his hips. It's the first time I've seen him in anything but a suit. Without the sharp crispness of a starched collar and the glitter of expensive cuff links, he doesn't look like such a wicked asshole, just like a lost, damaged boy.

You're going to get yourself into trouble with this one, I think, but then, I've spent my whole life holding back and avoiding trouble. For the next two weeks, I'm leaping off the cliff with my wings spread wide and I'm not going think myself into a corner; I'm going to fly.

"You said you didn't like me and tried to kick me off the bus."

Pax snorts and nods his head briskly, like that's about what he expected.

"Yeah, well," he starts, lighting up a cigarette and watching me through a thin haze of white smoke. "I can't very well kick off a girl who wipes my sweaty face with a cold cloth and brings me a dozen glasses of water to drink, now can I?"

"It's only for two weeks," I say and Pax shrugs loosely, his shoulders and arms blanketed in a sea of tattoos. The only bare spaces I can see besides his face are his palms. His ink literally dips down inside his sweats, covers his neck, his fingers.

"Suppose I can live with that," he says, looking me over like he's never seen me before. "Is it true what you said last night?"

I cock an eyebrow because I can't remember all the things I said last night. Between Ransom and Pax, I spilled my heart out a dozen times over, but I was sure neither of them were awake enough to process any of it.

"Which part?" I ask quietly as he holds out a tattooed hand and uses the other to smoke his cigarette.

"The part about your sister," he says as I reach up and take it, letting him pull me out of the bed and onto my feet. I'm not wearing the sweatpants right now, just the shirt and … nothing underneath it. I only have two pairs of panties left and they're both in fairly questionable shape. The shirt I've got on is long enough to cover all my sexy parts, but still …

"I lost my sister," I reply because I'm not sure how much he heard last night. Pax holds my fingers in his and pulls me down the hall and into the kitchen. Looks like we're the only ones up. A quick glance at the clock on the wall to my left shows that it's about a quarter til eight.

"She was murdered?" Pax asks, shutting the door to the hall and pouring us both cups of coffee. He hands one to me and I take it gratefully, letting the familiar smell soothe the small burst of anxiety blooming in my chest.

"She was," I reply, sipping my drink and then holding it back out to him. "I'll love you forever if you give me some more sugar and cream."

Paxton glances back at me, his cigarette stuck between his pretty lips, and raises a brow.

Without saying a word, he pours some cream into my cup and then uses his sexy tattooed fingers to drop two sugar cubes in after it. He takes his cigarette in his other hand and exhales, giving me a spoon to stir with.

"Sugar," he says a few seconds later, leaning in and pressing a coffee and tobacco kiss against my mouth. "And if you want cream …"

"Whoa, whoa, whoa," I say, even though my heart is beating in rapid-fire bursts, and my lips are tingling. "You can't tell me how much you hate me at night and then try to … whatever in the morning."

"No?" Pax asks, tossing his cig in a black glass ashtray and turning to face me fully, leaving his coffee on the counter behind him. "Why not? You fancy me, don't you?"

I make a point to stir my coffee before I answer him, staring into the swirling liquid instead of at his face. Because, really, it *is* a beautiful face.

"I'm not going to fuck someone that doesn't like me," I say and Pax snorts. I continue to ignore him, focusing on the coffee, trying my best not to grin like an idiot when I think of last night. I had a threesome. A *threesome.* My very first. By the end of this tour, I'd have upped the ante to a *sixsome,* but at the time I had no idea that was going to happen.

"Why not?" he asks, stepping forward and causing me to step back. I drop my spoon in my mug and hold it tight to my belly, enjoying the warmth seeping through the cotton t-shirt.

"Because at the very least I demand apathetic neutral," I say, looking back up into his grey eyes. They're less tempest-tossed today, more silver, almost shimmering. Pax is staring at me like I've suddenly become interesting to him.

"How about interested casual?" he asks as he temporarily gives up and rescues his coffee from the counter, curling his hands around it, the dark tree line and the night sky tattooed in minute detail across his fingers and knuckles. "I mean, you'll be here for two weeks yet. We may as well shag."

"We may as well *shag*?" I ask with a laugh and then Paxton does something that surprises the hell out of me.

"I'm sorry about your dad," he says, and then all of a sudden I'm shaking again. This tour, these men, it's all so glittery and magical and surreal. Death, cancer, loneliness. That stuff seems so far away from here.

I glance sharply away from Paxton and stare at the shiny dark grain surface of the door leading down the hallway. It blurs in my vision for a second and I gasp when Paxton's fingers curl around my chin and drag my face back to his.

"It's a lie, you know," he says as I stare at him, at the wild shimmer of his eyes.

"What is?"

"*Harper B.,*" he says, "my song."

I take a deep breath and back away again, until my ass is pressed firmly against the counter on the opposite side of the kitchen. Obviously, we're on a bus, so it's not like the move puts that much space between us.

I lift the mug to my lips and drink.

"Which part?" I ask finally, because I can tell Pax wants—maybe even needs—to tell somebody this. *"When you see another lonely traveler walking the same sad, strange path you almost fell off before ... it's only right to see if you can guide them down a different road."* Muse's words ring in my head as I stare at the man standing in front of me, angry and bitter and practically falling apart at the seams. Those perfectly put together suits of his, that wicked smirk, his swagger onstage ... it's bullshit. All of it, down to the shine on his ridiculously expensive loafers.

"The crying part," he says, surprising me a little. He's so focused on the outward expression of grief, like if he can just keep staring that part of the equation in the face, he won't have to feel the other half, the internal struggle, the battle between angels and demons that takes place deep inside your own soul.

"That's why you ran away," I say. It's not a question. And as much as I'd like to wring Paxton's neck for leaving me tied up like that, I understand—at least a little. Grief makes people do crazy things, things like shack up with five hot guys and sleep with almost every single one of them.

I drink some more coffee to keep my expression neutral.

"You're so …" Paxton gestures at me with one hand, holds his coffee with the other. "*Bare.*"

I glance down sharply to see if my shirt's ridden up, but it hasn't. He must be speaking metaphorically then. I look up at his face.

"You wear your emotions all over your fucking face." He points two fingers at the steel grey color of his eyes. "You looked *right* at me while we were screwing and you started sobbing. I've never seen a girl look so … fucking *naked* before."

I smile, but it's a sad one.

"You haven't cried over your sister, not once?"

"No."

Another sip of coffee.

"I see."

"I'm guessing you did? Probably bawled bloody buckets," he murmurs, drinking his own coffee and watching me with an exacting expression, like he's determined to keep pushing until he sees me open up even further. I get it now, Paxton's interest in me. In my grief, he sees his own. Mine's … messy and loud and intense and his is quiet, contained, and covered up.

"Some guy was stalking her on campus," I say as I tap my fingernails with the chipped polish against the side of the mug. I think I saw some polish in one of the boxes; I should try to find it and paint my nails. Maybe something as mundane as that will help me come back to reality a little? "She reported him, but nothing ever came of it. Not until he surprised her at her car after a late night study session and shot her six times in the chest."

My stomach roils as I think of the leaked crime scene photos and suddenly I just want to puke.

I shut my eyes tight and feel myself falling into that old well of pain and frustration and anger, but then I hear the hall door slide open and glance up.

It's Ransom, sweaty and shaking, cloaked in his hoodie and smiling this nightmarishly sad smile.

"Morning, sweet thing," he says in that easy, soft voice of his. The sound of it breaks my concentration on the past and I smile. Based on his expression, I'm assuming another nightmare woke him up. I feel almost guilty that I wasn't in there. I mean, I know I just met the guy and it's not my responsibility to take care of him, but ... for some weird reason, I want to.

"Morning," I respond as Paxton makes this angry sound in the back of his throat. *God, what is it with these two?* I wonder as Ransom glances at Pax and they exchange glares laced with old hatred. Their rage is deep-seated and painful to bear witness to, especially with them having to live and work in such close quarters like this.

"I hope I'm not fucking your sleep up too much, honey," Ransom says, dragging his gaze from Pax to look back at me. His dark eyes take in the long pale lines of my legs with interest. I color a little, thinking of last night, of having sex with him and Copeland on the couch. And then wondering what I was thinking wearing this shirt with no underwear, like I know these guys at all. I'm too comfortable here; this should be weird.

Only it's kind of ... not.

"You'd drive anyone completely mental after a few nights," Pax says, but Ransom ignores him, getting his own cup of coffee. He's so completely dark and adorable in his hoodie and black sweats. They've got grinning white skulls all over them and several tears in the side seams. What the hell does he do in those things?

"Like you weren't thrashing and groaning in your sleep,"

Ransom mumbles, turning and focusing his sleepy bedroom eyes on me again.

"I was pissed out of my skull," Pax says, taking his coffee to the couch and draping his entire tattoo covered body across the leather. To say he looks anything but delicious in that position would be a lie. "'S not like I do that every night." He smiles, and the expression is back to being ice cold and cruel. "Though I suppose I can't blame you. If I murdered someone, I'd probably have nightmares, too."

My eyes flick back to Ransom, watching as he goes completely still. But damn, he's got a leash on that rage because all he does is look at me and sigh softly.

"I stabbed the man that raped and killed my mother," he whispers, voice even lower than usual and without its gentle coating of sensuality.

"Stabbed a hundred and fourteen times," Pax says loudly and I swear, I could slap him.

"He raped her," Ransom says, knuckles white as he grips the cup, "he killed her. For no fucking reason." His voice raises up several notches, but he doesn't move from his spot in the kitchen.

"Pax, no more," I say because I can see Ransom winding up inside, darkness coiling and getting ready to strike. *He killed somebody?* I glance at him out of the corner of my eye, but he's not looking at me anymore. He's staring at Paxton.

"Why? You don't want to hear about the other people he killed?" Pax asks casually, clearly using Ransom's pain as a shield for his own.

"Leave her out of this, Pax. She's got nothing to do with our sick, fucked-up pasts."

"That why do you like her so much? Want to make her your next victim ... ah, I mean *girlfriend.*"

"Why would I do that?" Ransom growls, voice trembling with suppressed rage. "If I make her my girlfriend, you'll just fuck her to teach me a lesson like you did with Kortney."

"Guess it's better that all I did was fuck Korney, yeah? Because you *killed* Chloe." Pax's voice catches sharply and his silver eyes lock onto mine. He wants me to hear this, is practically desperate for it. "And baby Harper B." The words break on his lips as he drops his coffee mug to the ground and lets it roll across the floor, spilling milky coffee everywhere.

"I did not kill Chloe and Harper," Ransom rasps, the words fading to smoke as they fall from his lips. "Chloe was drunk; she crashed and killed them both."

"If you hadn't fucked everything up that night, I would've been there!" he shouts, standing up, his feet in the puddle next to the couch. "If you hadn't moved in on Chloe, if you hadn't come over to fight with me that night, it wouldn't have happened. You may as well have been behind the wheel."

Paxton rakes his fingers through his hair.

"Fuck!"

He storms across the floor, leaving watery footprints, shoving past me and making me spill my own coffee as he shoves his way into the hall and slams the door behind him.

"Jesus," Ransom says, shaking so hard he, too, sloshes coffee across the floor. His dark eyes are shifting, lids quivering, mouth trembling.

"Are you okay?" I ask, but Ransom obviously *isn't* okay.

"Chloe and I were in love," he whispers, turning and dropping his cup into the sink. It cracks right in half as Ransom slides to the floor and puts his forehead against his knees. "I didn't kill Chloe and Harper."

I set my mug aside and move over to Ransom, kneeling down next to him and putting my arms around him. It might seem that a hug from a stranger shouldn't be able to do any good, but I remember how wonderful it felt when Copeland put his arms around me backstage. That simple gesture kept me from falling to pieces. Maybe I can do the same for Ransom?

I squeeze him tight, not even caring that my shirt's ridden up and my bare ass is exposed.

When I try to push his hood back, he grabs my wrist in tight fingers and shoves my hand away. I wonder if I should give him some space and start to stand up, but he tugs me into his lap and curls his body around mine.

"You smell like roses and soap, baby girl," he whispers quietly and I almost smile. But I feel too sad for him. Why the fuck would Pax do that, bring those things up all of a sudden? Then again, maybe it's not all of a sudden, maybe this is partially my fault? Pax practically said as much. Something about me, about my grief, is stirring the pot on this bus.

"You smell like violets," I tell him and he lifts his head just enough to show me that *he,* at least, has no problem crying. Tears track down Ransom's cheeks, the one on the left sliding crookedly down his face as it gets caught in the faint mark of his faded scar.

"It's my mother's perfume, darling, the same brand she's used since I was a baby, the same bottle she used the day before she died."

"Oh, Ransom," I say and I feel my own eyes tear up as he buries his face in my neck. He's so gentle and wonderful, but his darkness goes deep, to places I hope I never have to see. Not that I haven't thought about it though, about killing the guy that killed my sister. But looking at what that blood has done to Ransom's hands, I'm not sure I could handle it.

"This happens all the time," he whispers, like he can somehow read my thoughts. "This stuff with Pax; it isn't just you. But I think he likes having a new audience for it." There's a long pause and then he lifts his face to mine again, expression shadowed by his hood. "Are you scared of me now, sweetheart?"

"Should I be?" I ask, raising my eyebrows.

"No," Ransom says seriously, looking into my eyes with this deep, wounded longing. God, after two days with this guy, I don't want to leave his side. I'll be a mess after two weeks. "But I did kill that guy. I did stab him over a hundred times. I stabbed him until he was dead and then I kept stabbing." He pauses and glances away, toward the wall. "I almost died that day, too."

"The scars," I whisper and he nods, putting his forehead against mine for several long minutes until the hall door opens again.

"Holy shit."

It's Muse.

I glance over my shoulder and he smiles softly at me.

"I better clean this up," he says, without asking for an explanation.

I like him just that much more for that.

"Something happen with Pax this morning?" I ask Ransom, but he barely looks at me, crouching like a vampire in the corner of the sofa. Lilith's curled up against him, a blanket draped over her quiet form. I watch her sleeping face for a moment, thinking of the tears streaming from her eyes as she lay on my chest.

Damn, what the hell happened last night? One second we were talking and then she was sucking me off and then Ransom was just there … We don't have threesomes on this bus. Like, *ever.* Not once. But it was hot and I'm starting to wonder why not. Lilith's got a sweet spirit; she deserves to have two guys taking care of her like that.

I pop a piece of jerky in my mouth and watch the two of them snuggling up like that, wondering if I'm jealous at all. I kind of like this girl, you know. And maybe I am a *little* jealous, but Ransom's my buddy and I've never been able to do a damn thing for him. He looks pretty content with this girl on his lap.

"Chloe?"

"Chloe, Harper … that piece of rotten dick cheese."

I frown as I move over and sit on the opposite end of the couch. Rotten dick cheese, that would be the man that killed Ran's mom. If Pax is pulling that out again, shit's getting real on this bus.

I sigh and grab my book from the arm of the sofa. I don't open it yet, just let my fingers filter through the pages. I fucking love romance novels. Erotic novels. Whatever you want to call anything fictional that has women and lovers and fucking and relationships. I feel like if every man on the planet sat down and just read a few of these, he'd understand the female side of the species so much better.

"Pax is pulling out all the stops then?" I ask and Ran nods, flipping through shows on Netflix like he actually cares to watch something. I've seen him do this for hours though, browse shows and never watch a single one of them. "What a fucking asshole."

I watch Ran for a moment, trying to remember the perpetually smiling guy with the wicked smirk. He could get any girl. Seriously, more than Pax or Michael. Everyone wanted to be around Ran—backstage, at after-parties, at the club, even at school. He was nice, but he had this slick, dangerous edge that no woman could resist.

Now ... fuck. He sits drenched in hoodies and smokes cigarettes and picks up groupies to *sleep* with, not for sex— although he always has sex with them because it's what they expect—but just to have someone by his side when he wakes up sweating and shaking with nightmarish memories. Most of the time they run the fuck off of this bus after his first fit of the night and straight into an NDA that our manager shoves down their throats. I wonder if she's hit Lilith with one yet?

I play with the bracelets on my wrist for a moment and look at Lilith again.

God.

If I was ever into having another girlfriend, I'd want one that looked like her. She's curvy and sexy and classically beautifully all at the same time. I run my finger up one of her bare feet and she gasps in her sleep, pink lips parting.

I smile and glance up to find Ransom watching me.

He looks away for a moment and goes back to his Netflix surfing, and I crack open some new ménage à trois book that I'd ordered but hadn't opened yet. After last night, I'm interested to see what lies between these pages.

I pull jerky from the bag on my lap with one hand and use the other to crack the cover of my new book, wondering if I'd still like these things if my mother hadn't flooded our house with them. Books with happy women with wonderful men, those were the only things that made her happy. Them, and me.

"Octavia just called and completely bitched me out," Muse whispers when he comes into the room and pauses, gazing down at Lilith with an inscrutable expression on his face.

The way he looked at her, it was like he'd fallen in love from their very first moment together ...

I scrub my hand through my hair and try not to think in book lingo. Happens sometimes, though. Books—even erotic ones ... *especially* erotic ones—are simply reflections of the human soul. Sometimes they're silly and sometimes they're exaggerated, but it's through that enhancement of the world that we can see both its beauty and its flaws.

"What for?" I ask, finding my left hand absently abandoning the jerky and sliding back to Lilith's foot. She makes another cute, little sound but goes on sleeping as I look up at Derek, his silver and black hair fucked-up and swirling around his head like he's in a Japanese visual kei band or something.

"Lilith was supposed to stop by her trailer and sign an NDA last night, but she didn't show."

"Ah," I say, feeling bad because for whatever reason, I just don't like Octavia. She's one of a few women in this world that I haven't liked without good reason. She's too much a puppet for the record label ... and way too into Paxton. I think she crosses professional boundaries sometimes. "That would be my fault."

"And mine," Ransom says as Muse raises his brows.

"Oh, come on, like Michael didn't tell you," I say as I scan the first line of my new book.

Soul mates ... an old concept, a new twist. I'm in love with two men; they're in love with each other; they're both in love with me. I won't let the world tear us apart.

I close the cover and look up, meeting Muse's hazel eyes behind his thick rimmed glasses.

"We had a threesome," I say with a smile and he laughs.

"No," he says, but he doesn't sound convinced.

"Yep," I confirm, giving in and dropping both of my hands to Lilith's foot. It feels good to touch her, rub her skin with my thumbs, make her moan in her sleep. "Me, Lilith, Ransom."

"Did you like it?" Muse asks, which is totally a weird Muse-like thing to ask.

"I did," Lilith says, waking up with a yawn. She stretches her arms above her head and the blanket accidentally slides off onto the floor, flashing the creamy white curve of her ass to all three of us.

"Well, I like *that,*" Muse says as Lilith laughs and tries to grab the blanket back from the floor. He snatches it up first and wraps it over his shoulders as she tugs her shirt down and sits up, tucking her knees to her chest and covering it all up with the tee. "Here." He holds a corner of the blanket out. "You can have it back."

"I don't want it now," she tells him haughtily, some of the sadness in her eyes fading away behind a sheen of amusement. I watch her face and then grunt when Muse drops down to sit between us, wedging himself onto the narrow couch. "So you hear the word threesome and come running, huh?"

"I'm intrigued," Muse says, as blatant and forward as always. He gets himself into serious trouble sometimes. I study him as he leans in towards Lilith, like he knows her, like they're not complete strangers. "I've always wanted to have group sex, but it's never really happened."

"Figures that'd be a dream of yours," Ransom whispers from inside his hoodie. When he reaches up and pushes it back off his hair, I know his mood's improving.

"Wouldn't you rather have group sex with a bunch of girls?" Lilith asks and Muse shrugs, seeing how close he can get his face to her lips before she stops him. She doesn't and they end up kissing. It looks a little forced at first, like neither of them is really sure where to go with this … but then it's like a flip's been switched.

His body relaxes; her body relaxes.

Whether it was pheromones, hormones, whether it was the bud of love in the making, when the two of them touched each other, it was as if the world stood still. Old wounds scabbed, healed, faded away. When their mouths touched, it was grief that was the unwelcome enemy in the room, their happiness held prisoner by it no longer.

I breathe out long and slow, watching Lilith touch her pale fingers to Muse's face. The way she touches him, I wonder if she knows how alone he is in the world. My mom might be … messed up, and I might've lost people in other ways, but Muse is —and always has been—alone.

I stand up to leave, give them some privacy, and Lilith grabs my t-shirt.

"Stay," she says between kisses, giving me pause. Her fingers stay curled in my shirt as she relaxes back into Ransom's lap, still kissing Muse, his hands pushing her shirt up her legs as she stretches them out, spreads them and lets him lay between them.

"Shit," I say as Ran looks down and watches the action taking place in his lap, like he's not sure what to do with it.

"Here," Lilith says, pushing Muse back a few inches and reaching up to grab Ran's chin. She pulls his face down to hers and starts kissing him next.

My heart's thundering, and my book's still clutched in my left hand, but all I can do is stand there and stare with parted lips and dilated pupils. My whole fucking life I've lived just to please women. First, my mom and grandma in one way. Then my girlfriends in another. And then random girls, any girls, whoever I can find for the night. It's interesting to see someone else shoulder the responsibility for once.

Lilith breaks away from Ransom and rearranges herself, turning over so that Muse is behind her. When she takes her shirt off and tosses it aside, I feel my entire body go white-hot. My cock's so hard it hurts and my hands are clenched into fists. Without even realizing it, I've dropped my book on the floor.

"I'm not …" Lilith starts, pushing red hair behind her ear. "This is completely new territory for me. This may take some … maneuvering." Her cheeks turn as red as her beautiful hair and I smile.

"So you do get embarrassed," I say as she grabs Ransom by the legs and encourages him to face her.

"Sometimes," Lilith says and then pauses, crossing her arms over her breasts for a moment as she looks at Ran, over her shoulder at Muse, at me. Her green eyes are bright and curious. "I've lived my whole life one way, questioning and wondering and thinking and planning. I just want to fucking do things and see what happens. If you guys are okay with this … I really like the three of you."

She shrugs her shoulders, and keeps watching me, like somehow I'm the lynchpin that might hold this idea together or tear it apart.

"This isn't a threesome," I say and Lilith smiles.

"No, it's a foursome."

We stare at each other for a few more seconds and then I tear the white tank I'm wearing off and toss it aside. What the hell, right? If this is what Lilith wants, why not give it a shot? It's just sex; sex is supposed to make people feel good. It's supposed to make them fucking happy.

"Just tell me what to do," I say as Ransom reaches over the back of the couch and slides open the drawer on the small side table. There are condoms in there; there are condoms fucking everywhere on this bus.

He passes some out to Muse and me and then pauses, taking a deep breath and then pulling his hoodie off. My mouth parts in shock because the number of girls that Ran takes his shirt and hoodie off for number less than fucking one.

As in, I haven't seen him show his chest to anyone but us since Kortney cheated on him with Pax.

"Should we move into the bedroom?" Muse asks as he takes his shirt off and leans in toward Lilith, putting his mouth to her neck and kissing her with such slow sensuality that I'm almost jealous. A sensual foursome, huh? When I think of foursomes, I think of porn and god, I fucking hate porn. But then I close my eyes and scan through my mental reading list. No, I've read some good foursomes.

It's all about the woman, about making her feel worshipped and loved and wanted.

It's what I live for, after all.

If I were to maybe sit down and psychoanalyze my reasons why, I'd probably uncover some pretty fucked-up shit, but I won't go there, not today. This isn't about me; this is about

Lilith.

Kneeling down next to the couch, I press a kiss to her knee and watch her body shiver under my touch. Smiling, I kiss my way up her thigh, fingertips trailing behind me as Muse takes care of her neck and Ran sits up to slide his hands over her breasts. When he sucks her nipple into his mouth, Lilith goes limp, Muse's arm around her waist the only thing keeping her upright.

The bus hits a small bump and jostles us all around, but we don't pay it any attention. My eyes drift up to Lilith's face, find her lids half-closed and her mouth parted in ecstasy.

Gently, I tug her knee toward me and she shifts, sitting back on the couch with her legs spread for me while Muse and Ransom sit on either side. Sliding my palms up the insides of her smooth thighs, I curl my fingers under Lilith's ass and drag her hips forward a few inches, giving myself the best possible view of her glistening pink pussy.

My fingertip traces around the champagne shape of red hair as I press a firm, demanding kiss to her inner thigh. Muse and Ran each have one of her breasts in their hands. Right now she's making out with Muse while Ransom slides his tongue up the side of her throat, nibbles on her ear. Keeping my eyes on her face, I drop my mouth to her sex, kiss my way down to her opening and then slide my tongue back up.

The moans falling from her lips get softer, more needy, as I slick my tongue in a circle around her clit and Muse breaks away from her mouth to kiss her breasts. When she starts to make out with Ransom, I dip a single finger into her scorching wetness, gasping at the vibrancy of her heat, the way she thrusts up against my fucking hand.

God, this is gonna be good.

Lilith, she still tastes like rain, even down here. Fresh, wet, but kind of sad, too, like a grey sky drenching the dry earth. It's needed, but most people prefer the sun. Not me. It's not that I *want* her to be upset, just that it's nice to be needed. Lilith clearly needs this, all of it. She wants all three of us, needs all three of us, that's how deep her pain is. And somehow, she found her way to this bus full of sad, lonely, people that Pax collected for his band. It's no coincidence that so many guys with such awful backstories ended up here.

Lilith adjusts her legs, putting them on either of my shoulders, encouraging me to kiss her deeper between the thighs, bury my face in her warmth. Her fingers knead my scalp, hips bucking gently against my mouth and fingers. With Muse's and Ransom's help, I bring Lilith to a shuddering, sweating orgasm on our leather couch.

My jeans feel so damn tight and uncomfortable that when I stand up, I shove them down my hips and kick them aside, sweating and running my hand over my mouth, the sweet taste of Lilith still clinging to my lips.

"Let me grab some lube," Muse says, totally and completely comfortable with this whole scenario. He leans over and digs around in the side table closest to him as I take his place, kissing down the smooth curve of Lilith's spine as Ran leans back and she lays across him, kissing his mouth.

"Give it to me," I tell him when he turns back around with a small bottle of lube in his hand. I check the label and then hand it back. "That's water based. Get me a one with a silicone base."

"Oh, picky, are we?" he asks, but he does what I say and gives me a different brand. I don't bother to explain—water based lube does *not* work for anal play. Yet another fact I learned from reading romance-erotica novels. To be honest, this is kind of my first time in this arena. Lonely groupies just want to be fucked; they usually don't care to experiment or play around much.

I open the cap and squeeze a generous amount onto my fingers as Muse watches hungrily, pupils dilated as he watches Lilith and Ran feel each other up, hands everywhere, mouths tasting each other with frenzied passion.

"Go get on the couch arm," I tell him quietly, feeling like the conductor for the entire operation. I kind of like that, too. As nice as I want to be, as much as I want to make people feel good, I also have this wildly intense need to be in charge. "Put one knee up, leave the other on the floor."

Muse wrinkles his dark brows for a moment and then gets

his *aha* expression on his face, snapping his fingers at me and pausing to squat down on the floor next to Lilith. Gently, he steals her mouth away from Ransom and kisses her tenderly, moving his lips along her jaw to her ear. She blushes and he grins, standing up to unbutton his jeans.

Meanwhile, something's been happening beneath me and I glance down to find Lilith helping Ransom find her opening, pushing her hips back until he's sheathed inside of her cunt. I adjust myself—group sex takes a lot of fucking adjusting—so that I'm straddling Ran's legs, Lilith's ass pressed up close to my pelvis.

My cock is rock solid, pre-cum beading at the tip, but I can't rush this. I want this to feel good for her, not hurt her. My eyes take in the sight of her pussy sliding up and down Ran's shift, the bright pink heat squeezing tight, holding him inside. I run my tongue along my lower lip and close my eyes for a moment.

"Oh yeah, honey, right there," Ran whispers as I take Lilith's left hip in my hand, curling my fingers around the contours of her pelvic bone. She groans and lifts her lips from Ran's mouth, raising her head up towards Muse as he leans his knee on the arm of the sofa and frees his cock from his sweatpants, putting him at just the right height for a blow job. With one hand on the base of his shaft and the other curled in Lilith's red hair, he guides her lips to the head of his dick. Muse's head falls back with a groan as Lilith takes him in deep, sucking him around groans of pleasure.

My own cock quivers and aches, desperate to be inside of her, but I hold back, slipping that one single lubed finger inside Lilith's ass and gritting my teeth against the tight band of flesh. As she moves against Ransom, I can feel his cock on the other side of a very thin wall, feel him thrusting his pelvis up and burying himself in her heat. Holy shit.

I move my finger in and out, slow and easy, increasing my rhythm only when I'm sure she's relaxed enough to handle it. Then I switch to two, and then three fingers. Lilith gyrates her hips with wild abandon, sucking Muse's cock, dragging throaty rasps from Ran's throat.

I can't take it anymore.

I snatch a condom from my pocket, slide it down the aching flesh of my cock and then make sure there's plenty of lube for us both. The head of my dick pushes inside slowly, so fucking slowly. I can't go any faster because with Ransom inside her too, it's the tightest I've ever felt a woman before.

"Jesus," I whisper because my heart is pounding and my hands are shaking. For a second there, I'm afraid I won't be able to do this, that I'll come right now and blow the whole experience to shit. But then I push my cock in the rest of the way and feel the tightness of her ass close around the base of my shaft like a cock ring, trapping the blood in my dick.

Ransom's still thrusting from beneath and with each movement, I can feel him sliding against that wall, teasing me through the veil of Lilith's flesh. I'm not into guys, but holy crap, that feels amazing. I stay there for a moment, letting Ran's and Lilith's movements work me up into a frenzy. When I glance up, I find Muse watching me, his fingers still buried in Lilith's hair, his hazel eyes half-shrouded and hazy with lust.

Then I start to fuck, grabbing hold of Lilith's hips and pumping mine with deep, long strokes, keeping my cock sheathed tight inside of her, listening to Ran grunt and buck beneath us. This time it's me teasing him, slicking Lilith's pale white skin with sweat as she curls her fingers around Ran's shoulders and lets Muse fuck her perfect pink lips.

The sounds she makes are nothing short of ecstasy; I'm not sure if I've ever heard a woman make sounds quite like that.

I close my eyes, my skin achy and hot, my balls tight, my entire body this ball of energy that craves more of whatever this is, this twisted ball of four fucked-up souls. We might just be bodies in motion, but there's something more here. I can *feel* it.

The sex was good—it was great, actually—but it wasn't their be-all, end-all. No, it was their outlet. Whatever they did, however kinky, dark, twisted, or different, it was all just an expression of their love, a way to get as close as possible, to keep the blackness inside their souls at bay for another night, another day. No, the touching, joining, rubbing of their bodies wasn't the answer to all their problems, but it was the symptom of their solution.

I blink past the swirl of literary porn inside my head and drive myself into Lilith harder, deeper, rocking the couch and everyone on it with each thrust. A single movement of my hips drives my cock into Lilith, slides her pussy along Ran's shaft, pushes Muse deeper into her throat. I control the entire thing, moving us in this strange, wild rhythm that shouldn't work but totally does.

It's Lilith that comes first, before all of us, screaming and arching her back, her lips temporarily falling off Muse's shaft as she digs her nails into Ran's shoulders and shudders around me and him both, squeezing us with her body. It's intense and long, but I keep moving through it, even as she tries to collapse, holding her up by tightening my fingers on her hips.

As soon as she recovers a little, Lilith sits back up and wraps a hand around Muse, pulling him back to her mouth, squeezing the base of his dick as she swirls her tongue along the underside, teases the sensitive spot just beneath the head.

I enjoy watching that, moving faster and harder, feeling my pulse race inside my head, my skin tightening as an orgasm builds up quick and desperate inside of me. Muse comes next, both hands on the back of Lilith's head as he makes these wild sounds low in his throat, making Ran buck and thrash beneath us. I realize he's coming, too, and hold a steady pace, sweat dripping off my chin onto Lilith's perfect round ass. Once I drop my gaze down to the joining of our bodies, I can't look away, watching her take both Ran and me, soothe away some of that darkness in our souls with the beauty of her own pain.

"Fuck, sweetheart," Ran gasps, shaking and quivering again as Muse stumbles away and collapses into one of the swivel chairs. But Lilith and me ... we're not done.

Carefully and quickly, I pull out and toss my condom into the trash, putting a new one on and pulling the sweaty crying girl into my lap. Because she is crying again, and that's okay. She can cry as much as she wants.

I swipe a tear away with my thumb as I pull her onto my shaft, filling the space where Ransom just was and curling my arms around her waist as she rides me. Those hunter green eyes finally meet mine, searching and tearing through me, asking me what secrets I have to uncover, making me actually want to spill them all.

It's her next orgasm that finally gets me, her body grasping tight, her face pressed into my neck, hot lips against my pulse. Her bare breasts smashed up to my chest, I groan and we both end up screaming a little, making so much damn noise that Michael comes storming out of the hall to stare at us.

The look in his eyes … it's pure hunger.

CHAPTER TWENTY-SEVEN

Lying on my back on the couch, I use a stylus to sketch something out on the screen of my phone. It's nowhere near the level of technology I'd need to create something awesome—and it's certainly *not* my mother's oil paints and old-fashioned stretched canvas—but I'm creating and it feels awesome.

I feel awesome.

My body feels free and lightweight and deliciously sore in ways I never could've even dreamed of.

I just fucked three guys. At the same time.

And it was … oh my God. I felt like a queen, like I was being worshipped and wanted, but also like I was taking care of my subjects, holding all three of them inside of me at the same time, keeping them safe and warm.

I roll onto my side and feel my cheeks flushing a little.

Cope is curled in the chair across from me, a book on his lap, this strangely peaceful expression on his face. As if he can feel me looking at him, he lifts those turquoise eyes of his and then smiles.

"What are you drawing?" he asks, but even if I'm ready to share my body with these guys, I'm not ready to share my art. I tuck my phone close to my chest and make a face that I hope looks coy and sexy instead of nervous and closed off. I *really* like these guys, but I *just* met them and already I'm drawing parallels, making connections, dreading the end of a two week period I just started.

Not good.

"Wouldn't you like to know?" I ask him, keeping my feet well away from Pax as he sits on the opposite end of the couch and does something on his phone. Every once in a while, he looks at me like he wants to say something but can't figure out how to phrase it. Or maybe he's just looking at my ass? Last night, the roadies dropped off the clean laundry, and I found my bag sitting near the door after our foursome. Thankfully there were clean panties and a pair of floral shorts that I put on to feel cheerful.

Dad is dead. Cancer ate Dad from the inside out. Some stupid multiplying cells stole my daddy away.

I swallow hard and sit up.

"I used to think I was going to be an artist when I grew up," I say with a strange sense of self-deprecation. It's not that I don't believe in myself anymore, it's just … life hurts and it's so stupidly practical that even though it's beautiful, it can be agonizing at times. Life is like a rose, stunning to look at but covered in thorns, and it pops those beautiful floating balloons of dreams one by one until there's nothing left.

"When you grew up?" Cope asks with an interesting half-smile, looking at me like something huge just happened between us. And maybe it did? I mean, I guess it could've just been raunchy sex, but … no, it wasn't about the sex. It was something more. I *know* it was. "You said you were twenty-one, right? You're just a baby."

"A baby?" I ask and he laughs, raising two red brows at me. They're almost the exact shade of my own. We definitely have some shared genetic heritage, Cope and me.

"Okay, wrong word. But still, you have plenty of time left to grow up and do whatever you want."

"How old are you?" I ask, sweeping gently tangled hair over one shoulder. I should probably shower properly. After our foursome, all I did was rinse. My eyes drift over to the kitchen, to Michael talking on the phone as he prepares himself some frozen thing from the fridge. His voice is low and angry, and I wonder if he's talking to his girlfriend again.

"Twenty-nine," Cope says, drawing my attention back to him, to those stunning eyes of his. I could stare at those all day and never get tired of looking at them. "I'm the oldest one on this bus."

"Fucking ancient," Pax mutters from his end of the couch. Still, he doesn't bother to look up from his phone screen.

"Ransom is twenty-five; Michael and Pax are twenty-six, and Derek is twenty-one."

"Seriously?" I ask, glancing at the hall door as Muse emerges dressed in a sleeveless silver hoodie and charcoal grey pants tucked into black boots. He sees me looking and smiles sharply. It's that look again, the one that says this is someone he who gets what he wants ... but maybe only because he's never allowed himself to want the wrong things, difficult things. It makes me sad for him. "You're the youngest? If someone had made me guess, I would've said *you* were the oldest."

"Because of all my wrinkles?" Muse asks, his silver and black hair teased into an impressive mohawk, this curved arc that travels down the center of his head. The hair on either side of his scalp is dark and buzzed short, showing off a black cuff wrapped around the upper lobe of his right ear.

"You're so ... practical and put together. You brought me my shoes; you had my car towed; Muse, you made me a sandwich." He laughs and I smile, feeling this easy intimacy between us that I just know is going to get me into trouble. Being around these guys at the peak of my despair, revealing my darkness to strangers because there was no one else, letting the tightly coiled control I had on my sexuality unravel—all at the same time—is tricking me into feeling safe and comfortable here.

This isn't home though; this is transition.

I suck in a deep breath and look down at my drawing. It's an erotic twist of bodies. But instead of drawing a foursome, something that could've been explained away by the day's events, I drew a ... sixsome? Is there such a thing? Do people even do that?

"I learned young that life's a hell of a lot easier if you think logistics first, passion later."

Really, that's a terrible thing to say, but he doesn't seem bothered by it, so I keep my mouth shut. I want to tell him that I tried that route, too, and it brought me here.

I keep sketching on the screen as Ran finally reappears from the hallway, putting all six of us in the living room/kitchen area. Not that that's surprising. No, I figure this'll happen a lot throughout my time here on this bus. After all, there's not really anywhere else to go except the bunks—which are hardly even big enough to sleep in—and the bathroom. I figure they probably use the Bat Cave to get some space from each other, but it looks like even Michael and Pax are going to respect my temporary use of the room. Nobody's gone in there since we got up this morning.

"Since there's no show tonight, you guys want to go out and party? I know this killer club that serves all their drinks in silver skulls." Muse sits down on the other swivel chair and puts his boot up on the coffee table, accidentally knocking my pink leather purse to the floor. "Crap, sorry," he says, leaning down to scoop up the fallen contents.

I don't pay much attention, sketching erotic expressions on the figures in my drawing for a moment until I notice that Muse has paused with a piece of paper in his hand.

It's the negative test results from my last STD panel.

I make a sharp sound in my throat and he startles, dropping the page on the floor and lifting up his palms in surrender.

"I'm sorry, Lilith," he whispers suddenly. "I caught some of the text on the page by accident. I shouldn't have looked at it."

I scoot off the couch and kneel down next to Muse, pushing lipstick tubes and sunglasses and mints back into my purse. My hands are shaking as I go about it, and then suddenly his hands are on my wrists.

"Hey, there's nothing to be ashamed about," he says, leaning in to press his mouth against my ear as Cope stares down at us in confusion. "A few days ago, just before we left Seattle to drive to Phoenix, we all got tested, too. All five of us."

He leans back and smiles as I blink in surprise.

"Seriously?"

"Yep." There's a long pause as he glances away and then this wicked sexy look crosses his features and he glances back at me. "Come with me for a second," he tells me, pulling me to my feet. It's in that moment that I really can see his age written across his face. He looks young and excited as he pulls me down the hall and into the Bat Cave, pausing to yank out a drawer on the bottom of the bed. Inside, there's a set of manila envelopes that he hands over to me—removing one at the last second and tossing it into the drawer.

It has a sticker with the name *Michael Luxe* printed across it.

Derek notices me looking and rushes to explain as I clutch the rest of the envelopes.

"He's clean, too," he says, confusing me a little until I open the top folder—the one with his name on it—and find a set of results similar to the ones he just discovered in my purse, "but I figure since he's not sleeping with you, I shouldn't show you his results. I mean, you have a right to look at the rest of them."

I go through the folders one by one, looking at the date, the names, the results. All four of the boys I've slept with, all negative, all from a couple of days ago.

"We were so busy that nobody got a chance to, you know, fuck these up before we met you."

I glance up suddenly, meeting his hazel eyes and noticing that they look blue right now, flecked with green and gold. So beautiful.

"You mean … I'm the only person you've slept with since you got these results?"

"Yeah," Muse says, raising his dark brows, the four piercings above his left brow winking in a flash of sunlight as the bus jostles and the curtains flap open for a split second. He leans his shoulder in the doorway and smiles. "You're clean; we're all clean."

I bite my lower lip and feel this weird prickly sensation take over my body. My first boyfriend and I used condoms the two times we had sex; Kevin and I basically never did. But then look where that got me. Trusting Kevin could've cost me everything.

But then … the thought of doing what we did today, but without condoms?

My skin thrills at the idea of having all of that warm, bare skin inside of me.

"How do you know? About the other guys, I mean? How can you be sure?"

Muse smiles and reaches out, tucking hair behind my ear. When he touches me like that, I want to tell him everything about Kevin and ... the cheating and all that, but how gross is that? Maybe he won't want to touch me if he knows? Maybe he'll find me as disgusting as I found myself that night?

God.

My eyes close as bad memories sweep over me. Do you know what it's like to find out that you've got a *disease* because your boyfriend doesn't love you, doesn't even *respect* you enough to tell you that he wants to sleep with other people, break up, hell, even that he's unhappy with your relationship? I had bumps on my arms, and I felt dizzy and weak, and why? Because Kevin was sticking his dick into any poor girl he could schmooze into bed. And I don't blame any of them—I blame *him.*

I open my eyes and find Muse watching me curiously.

"I saw the Nexplanon on your sheet," he says softly and I flush. "That's the little, like, stick thing they put in your arm, right?"

I nod and turn my left arm over, taking Muse's hand and pressing his fingertips to the match size little bump inside my arm. It's a three year hormonal birth control implant that I had put in last year. And awfully convenient now that I find myself ... in this situation.

"Most guys have never heard of Nexplanon—or have any clue that this kind of birth control exists at all."

"Yeah, well, then they're idiots. How can you be a sexually active adult and not know what kinds of birth control are on the market?"

"And this is why I thought there was no way you could be twenty-one," I say and he smiles again as I clutch the manila envelopes to my chest and feel my heart racing beneath the paper.

"I got emancipated at fifteen. I had to learn how to take care of myself early on." He pauses, like he wants to say more but isn't sure he's ready. I don't blame him. An awkward silence follows. "Anyway, no pressure, but I just thought you should know the option was there."

I swallow hard.

"If I … agree to this," I start, meeting his eyes when he looks up at me. "You'll all have to agree to be exclusive with me while I'm here. The second somebody sleeps with another girl …"

"Let's talk to Ransom and Cope together," he says and then pauses, licking his bottom lip for a second. "You'll have to talk to Pax."

"Talk to Pax about what?" he asks, appearing like a silver eyed ghost in the hall behind Muse.

As soon as he sees the envelopes, his face crinkles into a frown.

"The bloody fuck are those?" he snaps, shouldering Muse to the side and snatching the papers from my hand. The look he throws his friend is downright fucking terrifying. "Who gave you the right to flash this shite all over the damn place?"

"He saw my results," I blurt before this can escalate into a fight. Pax likes to pick them with his friends, that much is painfully obvious. It makes him feel better, I think, directing all of the negative energy in the room, like he's in control. I used to do that, too, with Yasmine and Mom, before they died. "They were in my purse. Muse saw them and thought …"

I trail off as Pax gives me a wary look and then tosses the papers to the floor. They flutter like birds for a moment before coming to rest in various spots on the glossy dark wood beneath our feet.

"Let me see," he says, face unreadable. "You looked at mine; it's only fair that I get to see yours."

"Fine."

I dig in the pocket of my shorts, where I stashed the results, holding them out to Pax and watching as he takes them in his tattooed fingers. He reads them carefully, eyes scanning everything.

"What's a Nex-whatever-the-fuck?" he snaps, looking up at me.

"Birth control," I explain, turning my arm over and doing

181

the same thing with his fingers that I did with Muse's. I want there to be complete honesty, right here, right now. I've lived with lies for ar too long. Lies from Kevin, even lies from my dad. *How could he not have told me he was that sick? Why would he deny us what little time we had left together?*

"That's fucking weird," Pax says, but then his mouth curves into a dangerous smile as he drops his arm by his side.

"Did you sleep with one of those girls?" I ask, looking up and into his face. "When you got drunk the other night?"

He snorts at me and lights up a cigarette. I think Pax smokes because he likes to always appear that he's got something fucking important to do. He parks the cig between his lips and traces his palm down the royal blue tie he's got on. Yes, he's wearing another perfect suit. This time, his cuff links are silver vintage microphones.

"Never got the chance, now did I? My manager was breathing down my neck, and then there was this weepy little girl on my bus," he says, making this horribly sexy pouty mouth as he leans in close to me. "So no, love, I didn't sleep with any of them. How fucking fortuitous are we both then?" he asks with a flourish of his tattooed fingers.

"If ... you want to fuck me without a condom, then you—"

"Demand at least apathetic neutral, yeah, I remember."

I smile, despite myself. The fact that Pax and I are both just assuming we'll fuck each other again is ... interesting. Neither of us even bothers to ask.

"If you want to do this, you can't sleep with any other girls while I'm here. As soon as you do, it's over." I take a deep breath and look him straight in the face. I know he's a bad boy and a rockstar and all that, but I won't take shit in this arena, not ever again. "My last boyfriend lied to me, cheated on me, and he made me sick," I whisper, feeling suddenly nauseous.

Pax raises his eyebrows and Muse makes a soft, sad sound under his breath.

"Luckily it was completely curable and I caught it early, but I won't let anyone ever do that to me again. It's the worst kind of violation there is, and I'm lucky that it wasn't something worse. I can't take that chance. Please respect me on this. If you want to … fuck somebody else, just tell me you did and don't lie about it. Then that'll be the end of … this."

I gesture randomly at the fallen pages.

The thought of any of these four screwing another girl while I'm around makes me sick, but what right do I have to demand their exclusivity? I slept with all of them one after the other on night one. But in this, at least, I have a valid reason, an excuse. I try not to feel so damn pleased about it.

"Look at you," Pax whispers, touching his fingers to my hair, "roped yourself an entire rock band. And I thought you said you *weren't* a groupie."

He smiles and takes a step back, disappearing down the hall and leaving me to look up at Muse, my heart pounding frantically in my throat.

Groupie.

See, there's that word again.

Lilith Goode, the one and only groupie for Beauty in Lies.

I'm disturbed by how much I like the way that sounds.

CHAPTER TWENTY-EIGHT

Lilith

LILITH GOODE

As soon as the bus comes to a stop, there's a sharp knock on the door and Pax is opening it to Octavia's angry face. The second she sees him, some of that ire melts away and she blushes, but then her gaze connects with mine and I feel this sick churning in my stomach.

She hates me and I haven't done a damn thing to deserve it.

"May I come in?" she asks Pax and he shrugs.

"Sure, what about? We're getting ready to go out."

Octavia pauses as she ascends the last step and looks over at him.

"I see," she says, and that's that. I guess the record label can't really control what the boys do in their spare time, now can it? I cross my arms over my new dress. Well, new in a sense. I made it out of the baggy Beauty in Lies t-shirt that Muse gave me. It was so long that I just sort of got inspired by it, using my time on the bus to let my creative juices flow ... among other juices.

The dirty joke inside my own head makes me smile and Octavia turns a funny pink color.

"You agreed to stop by my trailer and sign a non-disclosure agreement," she all but barks at me, her sweet voice tinny with anger as she takes in my outfit. In one of the boxes Muse rescued for me, I had a small portable sewing machine that I whipped out, taking in the waist of the dress, cutting out the armholes all the way down to the natural curve of my hips. Since I got my clean laundry back, I happened to have a pale pink lacy bra that I put on underneath. When I move, the sides of it show in the massive armholes.

The way the boys looked at me when I put it on—even Michael—I think I did a pretty good job. And it felt *amazing* to work with my hands again—to sketch, to sew. I just love to create, I guess.

"Oh," I say, my mouth popping open as I remember our conversation backstage. I'd meant to head over there after I stopped by the bus, but then Cope and Ransom and I …

"Yeah, *oh*," Octavia says, her pert nose lifted in the air, her hair the color of dirty dishwater bouncing in its usual ponytail as she turns to look at Paxton, cheeks coloring again. "I *really* need her to sign an NDA, honey."

Honey.

The way she says it and the way Ransom says it could not be anymore different. He says it with this gentle sort of sincerity while Octavia just sounds desperate. I try not to hit her with a serious case of internalized misogyny, but I can't seem to help myself. She's being such a bitch.

Pax looks down at her with his sexy grey graze and then pans his expression over to me. We lock eyes and he gives me a wicked smirk.

"Nah, Lilith's alright then, aren't you, Lilith?"

"Um, yeah," I say because signing an NDA sounds so formal and weird. My connection to these guys is so organic and strange and new. I don't really want to sign anything that promises I'll keep my mouth shut. I shouldn't have to. "I'm not sure I'm comfortable signing something I don't really understand."

"She's not a media hound," Pax says, and I find myself flushing with pleasure to hear him defending me against his manager. It's weird because we really don't know each other at all, but even with his anger problems and his cold indifference, he sees at least some of what I see.

"It's not up to you or me," Octavia says softly, laying her fingers against his hand and looking between the two of us with this awful awareness dawning in her features. "If she's going to ride on the bus, she has to sign an NDA."

185

Octavia produces a document from the folder tucked under her arm and thrusts it in my direction like it's a weapon.

"You can't spend another night on this bus unless you sign this and give it back to me."

"Back off, Octavia."

I glance over my shoulder to find Ransom in a black sleeveless hoodie with, of course, the hood thrown up, his dark chocolate hair spilling across his forehead, brown eyes rimmed in black. He's smoking a cigarette and glaring at his manager.

"You don't have to be so rude about it, okay?" he continues, his legs encased in white skinny jeans speckled with holes and tears that look genuine. On the front of his hoodie, a giant skull grins back at me with an evil mouth, wicked and sharp. "Leave the paper on the counter and we'll deal with it when we get back."

"She can't sleep here without signing it," Octavia repeats, looking from Pax to Ran to me with a curious expression on her face. "These aren't even my rules. This bus belongs to the label and the label has rules."

"Fine," I snap, taking the pen from Octavia's fingers and throwing back the top pages of the agreement to scribble my name. "There. Done."

"Thank you," she clips sharply, snatching the paperwork and shoving it back into the envelope. Octavia looks at Pax again, but he's staring at Ransom like he wants to start shit. Ran notices it, too, and gets stiff, exchanging a charged glare with his ... friend? I guess they're not really friends at all, but it seems like they used to be, once upon a time. "Pax," Octavia says, but he's too focused on Ransom to really pay her much attention.

"Well done," Pax drawls in his thick British accent, "can we bloody go now? I'm so sick of this fucking bus, I could puke."

He turns away from Octavia and descends the steps without waiting for the rest of us.

I'm nervous as hell and totally out of my element—I never went out much except to dinner and bars with Kevin—so this is kind of a new experience for me. I think I look good, too, not much like a girl who's dad died just a few days before.

Groupie

My heart clenches painfully, but I breathe past the pain, reaching up to touch the silken red strands of my hair. It's clean, brushed until it shone, and hanging halfway down my back. My makeup is dark and intense: black around the eyes, lids covered in glitter, a bright pop of red at my mouth. My arms are drenched in bracelets—including my mother's charm bracelet. I never take it off. *Never.* Not even to shower.

"Everyone ready?" Muse asks as he steps out of the hallway with Michael and Cope at his heels. Michael's gaze catches on mine and I smile, trying not to notice how beautiful his violet eyes are, how his tattoos peek out the neckline of his black tank, or how his leather jacket emphasizes the strong cut of his shoulders and arms.

He doesn't smile back, but he doesn't scowl at me or say anything rude either, so I guess we're moving in the right direction.

"Ready, baby?" Ransom asks me, his gaze so intense that when I meet it, I can feel him inside of me all over again. I can't *wait* to feel him bare, can't wait for him to come inside of me … I swallow back the thought and smile, refusing to let residual sadness leak into my expression. It's not so difficult to ignore it here, getting ready to go out with a group of sexy rockstars. I feel like I'm living in a book or a movie, like I've left my real life to live on Mars.

"Ready," I say, letting him link an arm through mine, his clean clothes reeking of violets. I smile as we descend the steps and pause next to Paxton. I stand between the two boys like a shield, wishing I knew a little bit more about their history but not yet ready to outright ask about it.

"We've got a hired car for the night," Pax says, smoking his cigarette as the other three boys cluster around us. Standing amongst them all—several inches shorter than the shortest one —I feel safe and protected, like I'm among friends. Even though we're going out in a strange city—I've never been anywhere but Gloversville, New York City a handful of times with my dad or Kevin, and Phoenix—I feel confident that there's nothing for me to worry about tonight. "They're meeting us at the gates."

C. M. Stunich

He gestures through a cluster of trailers and buses toward a set of black metal gates on wheels. To our left, the venue stands tall and imposing against the night sky, quiet until tomorrow evening. All around us though, there's activity. Roadies hopping down from trucks towing trailers, the other bands spilling from their buses. Some of my boys—because that's how I was going to start thinking of them all (even Michael eventually) in the future, as *mine*—raise their hands and exchange pleasant greetings with the other musicians.

But they don't invite any of them to go with us.

We hit the gates and they open automatically on a sleek black limo with a fucking driver standing by the open door.

Holy fuck.

I've been a limo two times in my life—both of them during prom, junior and senior.

I remember Dad pressing a gentle kiss to my forehead as I ducked inside the white limo Kev had hired, his eyes shining with pride, his lips telling me how beautiful I looked that night.

I choke on tears for a moment and cover my mouth with my palm.

"How are we all this evening?" the driver asks politely as Paxton ignores him and slides inside the car.

"Wonderful, thanks," Muse says, stopping and checking something on his phone. He flashes the screen to the man. "We might bar hop a little, but we're starting at the Silver Skull. You know it?"

"Yes, sir," the man says as Muse puts his phone back in his pocket and waits for Ransom and me to crawl in next.

My shirt-dress is so short, my thighs brush against the buttery leather when I sit down and gasp at the sensation.

"Oh, that's nice," I say, curling my fingertips into the fabric as Pax laughs at me and fills a pair of champagne glasses with a bottle he rescues from an ice bucket. I'm beyond pleased when he hands one to me.

"Not used to the finer things in life, love?" he asks, like maybe he is. I wonder about Pax, where he comes from, what his parents are like. Maybe if I knew, I could understand why he's so angry all the time? His sister's death didn't help obviously, but there's something else inside him that's bleeding and festering, too.

"My dad was a mechanic, and my mom was an artist, so no." I laugh and lean back into the leather as the other boys climb in and the driver shuts the door. "These seats are to die for."

I cross my black booties at the ankles and lace my fingers together behind my head, listening to the slight drone of pop music in the background. It should be rock, shouldn't it? I open my eyes and spot the controls for the stereo underneath the window connecting us to the driver's side of the car. I crawl over Paxton's lap to get to it and he grabs me around the waist, spilling champagne on the sumptuous buttery seats.

"Where the fuck do you think you're going?" he asks me, heating the air in the small space up substantially. Our eyes lock and I take a sip of my champagne.

"To turn up the music," I say and he relaxes his grip on me slightly, giving me just enough slack to crank up the volume. I finish off my champagne as Muse pours glasses for everybody else, passing them out as I sway with the music.

Dad is dead, this ugly little voice inside of me whispers.

I ignore it and grab the champagne bottle, swigging a giant mouthful as Pax chuckles low and deep. And then I let myself move with the song and don't give a fuck that the rest of them are staring at me. I need to … shake myself out a little.

Muse reaches out to take my hand and pulls me into his lap instead, dancing with me as best we can in the enclosed space as Cope smiles and Michael stares with violet eyes.

"You like to dance, Cutie?" Derek asks me and I shrug.

"I don't know. Honestly, I have no clue. Kevin never took me dancing and I never really made any friends in Phoenix, so I had nobody to go out with. Mostly I just went to these boring business functions he attended with his dad. When I danced at those, though, I sucked at it."

"Kevin?" Cope asks with interest, sitting between Muse and Michael. Ran's on the other side and Pax is next to him. They seem to be on-again, off-again with their fighting, so I keep a close eye on them.

"Kevin's my ex," I say with a sick churning in my gut. He

actually texted me today, a few hours after the whole no-condom conversation. *Sorry about your dad.* That's literally all it said. After knowing my dad almost his whole life, after dating me for five years, that's the only thing he had to say. I'd rather not have received anything from him at all. "He's a fucking lying, cheating, womanizing piece of shit asshole," I say and most of the boys laugh.

"Did he fuck your best friend?" Pax asks casually and I turn my head to see Ransom gritting his teeth in anger. The moment gets tense for a second, but stops when Michael's phone rings and he curses under his breath. "Fucking Vanessa *again*," Pax growls as I lean against Muse. "She calls like fifty fucking times a day."

"I've counted," Cope says casually. "It was *fifty-four* today."

"Lay off," Michael says, but he sounds exhausted when he answers. "Hey, Van, what's up?" A pause. "Yeah, we're going out to some place called the Silver Skull." Another pause and his mouth creases into a deep frown. "Vanessa."

The way he says her name, like a warning, makes me cringe a little. I don't know a lot about their relationship, but when those three syllables roll off of his tongue, I see the end of that relationship flashing before my eyes.

Michael's violet gaze meets mine and I glance away, down, toward the sparkling sea of tattoos I can see peeking above his neckline. Black, blue, and purple flames are inked up and over his shoulders and halfway up his throat, emphasizing the unique color of his eyes. His dark hair is razored in layers, feathered and falling almost to his shoulders.

I wonder what it'd be like to run my fingers through it?

I shiver and glance away. No fucking way in hell I'll ever be the other woman. I mean, ultimately, the responsibility in an affair lies with the person in the relationship, but with how much Kevin hurt me, I couldn't knowingly do that to somebody else.

"Vanessa." Her name again, another warning. I remember Pax saying something about Michael having cheated on this poor girl before and I get the chills down my spine. If Vanessa was willing to forgive him after that, she either really loves

Michael or she just doesn't know how to let go. I know both feelings—intimately. "I have to go; we're almost there. I'll call you later," he snaps, his voice low and angry. "I'm *not* going to fuck anybody. I've been celibate for a goddamn year waiting for you for fuck's sake. I messed up before; I won't make that mistake again."

Michael hangs up the phone, turns it off and throws it against the wall where it bounces harmfully off the detailed black leather panels attached beneath the driver's window.

"We done with that shit for tonight?" Pax asks as the car rolls to a stop and he raises a blonde brow at his friend.

"We're done," Michael promises, opening the door before the driver can get to it and stepping out into the icy cold Minnesota evening. As soon as the breeze sweeps in and kisses all my bare flesh with icy lips, I know I'm completely underdressed.

"Don't worry, darling," Ran says, putting a hand on my bare knee and raising his dark brows. "You won't be outside long enough to need a coat."

I smile and turn towards Cope, taking his hand and letting him help me out of the limo. On the street side of the sidewalk, small hills of dirty snow sit, collecting the small fresh flakes from above. But the awful weather doesn't stop the line for the Silver Skull from traveling all the way down the long city block and around the corner.

I blink in surprise at the gathered crowd as Cope leads me along behind Michael, straight to one of two bouncers manning the door. Above us, a silver arch made entirely of metal skulls frames the entrance; the sign with the club's name hanging beneath it in block purple letters glows the same color as Michael's eyes.

I'm so overwhelmed by the whole scene, by the people leaning against the wall watching us with curious expressions, that I don't even think about how we're going to get in. I guess I just assume we'll be waiting in line with everyone else, but that's just because I'm not used to hanging out with rock stars.

The crowd before me is dressed to the nines, in costumes, in leather and lace and velvet and masks, high heels and long dark coats. More than a few of them notice my boys and cover their mouths with their hands, point and call out, cheering Beauty in Lies from the side of the black and brown building. Some of them raise their phones and start recording us, but they don't get long because Cope's pulling me into the building, through the door on the opposite side of the velvet rope.

There's a coatroom with pulsing lights in the floor and an attendant dressed in a top hat, but we breeze right through and into the main part of the club.

I can see now why, even with the snow, I wouldn't need a coat.

Inside the Silver Skull, it's wicked hot, sweat already collecting on my brow as Copeland weaves us expertly through the gathered revelers, past women dressed in ball gowns, like cigarette girls, like vampires.

"What kind of club is this?" I shout when Cope pulls me close to his side and slips in between two other couples standing next to the bar. When he looks back at me, his turquoise eyes shimmer and then lift up, looking over the heads of the throbbing crowd toward a stage in the far corner.

I follow his gaze and feel my mouth drop open when I see the show. Men and women with black X's taped over their nipples, with whips and high-high heels and paddles are engaged in some light BDSM, seemingly oblivious to the sea of faces below.

My attention snaps back to Cope and even though I can hardly hear his laugh, I see him shaking with a deep chuckle.

"If you like what you see," he whispers in my ear, drawing goose bumps up on my neck, "they have rooms in the back where you can pay dominatrices to show you a good time."

"Seriously?" I ask, leaning back, intrigued and shocked both at the same time. It's not that any of this stuff really bothers me, just that I've never been a part of anything even remotely in this realm.

"Sure," Cope yells as he flags the bartender down and passes over his credit card, "just ask Ransom."

As if on cue, Ran squeezes in beside me, his muscular arms slicked with sweat. I find my fingers curling around them,

192

tracing the hardness of his biceps before I can stop myself. He looks down at me with a wicked sad smile, bleeding his pain into an atmosphere already filled with it. In a room this crowded, this full of people, I shouldn't be able to taste loneliness in the air, but I do. That's not to say that *everyone* here is desperately seeking human connections, but a lot are.

Or maybe I'm just projecting?

"You ... like BDSM?" I say and Ran shrugs his broad shoulders a little. "You paid people for sex?" I ask and his smile changes a little as he drops his dark eyes to mine and accepts a drink from Cope over my shoulder. He passes one into my hand next. I have no idea what it is but turquoise colored sugar frosts the rim and the drink itself is frosty and cool and absolutely laden with alcohol. Plus, just like Muse said—it's served in a silver skull.

"I've never paid for sex, honey," he says as he glances over at the stage and then back at me. "BDSM can be sexual, but it doesn't have to be. For a lot of people, it's not sexual at all." Ran looks down into his drink for a moment and then back up at me. There's a conversation here, but this isn't really the place to have it.

I turn around and lean my elbows against the bar, watching the crowd gyrate and thump and thrash. The music seems to be alternating between EDM or dubstep beats and hard, thrash-y metal tunes, but the DJ in the corner is talented and it all blends seamlessly.

"Hey." It's Pax.

He leans in and puts his mouth to my ear.

"I got bottle service, love. Let's pay too much and see how many women we can get that want to sleep with us." He takes my wrist, the one with my mother's charm bracelet, and starts pulling me through the crowd again. I follow after, unsure if Cope or Ran will follow, not sure what happened to Muse or Michael.

But then I see them together, sitting at a table in a second room, just off the main portion of the club. The silver surface of the table is shiny and shaped like a skull, but there are plenty of chairs clustered around it, hidden behind a black velvet rope that looks very official.

"I bloody hate bottle service," Pax laughs as he takes a seat and very promptly pulls me into his lap. I get these dark butterflies in my stomach as he wraps his arm around my waist. Somehow, that conversation in the bus today is leading to a lot of casual touching. Even more than the sex, this feels heavenly, this easy skin on skin contact that pleads familiarity. I wish so deeply in that moment that I *really* knew these boys, that they were my friends, that I could hang out with them all the time, that I never had to give them back.

I place my own hand across Pax's and lean back against his chest.

"It's a fucking joke, a trick for middle-aged techie losers that can't get laid to lure young girls into their webs." He grabs the drink from my hand and downs the rest in a single swallow. I trace my freshly painted fingernail down his tattooed throat as he sets the glass aside and smiles his cold, cruel smile at me.

"Who wants to sit down in a club anyway?" Muse asks, his hazel eyes sparkling as he takes in the smaller but more densely packed crowd in this section of the club. On the wall to my right, an old black and white horror movie plays, but nobody's watching it.

Ran and Cope appear a moment later, more drinks in their hands. They pass another one to me—something bright green and currently smoking with dry ice—and pause at the edge of the table. They could not look anymore different, Ran in his hoodie with his glittering black eyes and Cope in a pair of those expensive and admittedly sexy jeans that he likes, draped in black corded necklaces and bracelets. Cope's red hair is styled in its usual faux hawk and his turquoise eyes are lined with black. He's like the punk rock version of the boy next door in his loose white *Dracula* tank, a half dozen leather belts wrapped around his hips, each with a different fantastical buckle, and a pair of red skate shoes on his feet.

Ran's wearing scuffed black combat boots with his torn white skinny jeans and sleeveless hoodie, his scar vibrantly visible in the strange half-light of the club, the black and grey tattoos that stretch down both arms a stark contrast to the vibrancy of the ones on the back of Cope's wrists.

To me, they're both beautiful in completely different ways.

I wiggle on Pax's laps, the fabric of his expensive slacks slick and foreign feeling against the backs of my thighs. Dressed in that dark eggplant suit jacket and grey button-up, I feel like he must be sweating buckets, but when I glance over my shoulder at him, he looks cool and calm as usual.

"Dance with me?" Muse asks, finishing up his drink and smiling tightly at the scantily clad waitress as she walks by with swaying hips and teases her fingertips down his arm. He starts moving into the crowd before I get a chance to respond, drawing me along in his wake. I suck down as much of my drink as I can, trying to get a decent buzz going, and skip down three steps into the thick of the crowd.

Muse grabs me before I can lose my nerve, dragging me into the fray, into a bouncy, sweaty mass of bodies, his hands curling possessively around my hips. His mohawk is styled outrageously today, in a way that emphasizes the ombre effect of his black to silver hair and the short dark buzz on either side. He's wearing the glittering black cuff on his earlobe again, a perfect match to the black piercings above his brow and the tattoos on his right arm.

He's also not wearing a shirt under his leather zip-up hoodie, the hard muscles of his chest and tummy slick with sweat. That's where I put my palms as we dance in the outrageously dressed crowd. To me, the boys all look like glittering rockstar statues, like demigods just barely connected to their human roots, but in here, they're some of the most casually dressed people.

For some reason, I find that funny and start laughing as Muse twirls me and I come back around, reaching up and slicking a hand along the length of his mohawk. I get a sexy smile in response as I drop my palms back to his tummy. His black jeans are so low-slung that the waistband of his boxer briefs is visible, advertising the brand *Andrew Christian* in white across the black elastic. I curl my fingers around the dark denim of his pants and get a little thrill inside my belly when my fingertips graze across the bulge of Derek's cock.

"Maybe you should borrow one of Cope's belts?" I shout as I stand on my tiptoes and press my lips to Muse's ear. He laughs, but he doesn't stop dancing, swirling me around the room, his hands traveling all over my body, touching every part of me but the parts I *really* want.

"I want to see what's in the back rooms," I shout after a few songs and Muse grins, turning me around by the shoulders and pushing me back towards Ransom. As I go, I see Michael dancing with some girls near the wall where the movie's being projected. I watch him for a second, but all he's doing is dancing. When the girl closest to him gets a little hands-y, he gently removes her fingers from his jeans and twirls her in a circle.

Pax is on the other side of the crowd with Cope, laughing with a group of guys dressed like priests. Seriously, five dudes dressed like priests with colored hair, piercings, and tattoos. Muse steers me past them all and grabs Ran by the arm; it's just so fucking loud in here that it's easier to snatch people by the hand than it is to talk to them.

Without a word passing between us, we find our way down a dark, narrow hallway crammed with people. Men and women in outfits each more outrageous than the last kiss and fondle each other in all variety of combinations—men and men, women and women, groups and couples—and we ignore them all, finding ourselves in a circular room with several doors and hallways leading off of it.

"Ransom Riggs," says a man with more piercings in his face than I have fingers and toes, "Derek Muser, I just want to say that I'm a huge fan of Beauty in Lies. I have tickets to the show tomorrow and VIP passes for the meet and greet." There's a breathless pause as he glances at me with interest, sandwiched between the two men, and then flicks his gaze between the two musicians. "If you'll sign my boots, I'll get you in wherever you want for free."

He hands over a silver Sharpie and Ransom takes it, bending down and scribbling his name across the toes of the man's boots. Muse does the same and then they both stand up.

"We just want to watch tonight," Ransom says, putting his

arm around me and pressing the most deliciously decadent kiss against my hair. Even with all these people and the smell of sweat and cologne and perfume, I can taste the flirty scent of violets on the back of my tongue. "Muse and I have a new girlfriend and we don't want to share."

"Sure thing," the guy says as my cheeks color and the word *girlfriend* gets stuck in my head on a loop. Obviously, Ran just said that to make things easier—who wants to explain a situation as unique as ours to a stranger anyway—but I can't help myself. I get both excited and terrified at the same time. I just escaped being a girlfriend after five straight years, but ... the idea of being Ransom's or Muse's—Ransom *and* Muse's—girlfriend fills me with jittery excitement.

The man with the piercings leads us down the hall and opens a door, stepping back so we can squeeze inside. It's much cooler back here than it is in the front of the club, and strangely empty. Music still pumps into the small dark room, but the only people here are us.

"This room's technically out of order for the night, but everything's clean and it's got the best view in the house."

Piercing Guy smiles at us and raises his metal studded brows before bowing out and disappearing.

I take a second to look around, heart beating frantically, that strange otherworldly feeling creeping over me again. Like, where the fuck am I? I smile softly as I try to imagine Kevin in a place like this. It'd never happen; he'd call all these people freaks and leave with his face that ugly purple-red color it gets when he's angry.

"What exactly goes on in here?" I whisper as I step up to the window and put my palms against the glass. On the other side, a whole story below us, there's a room dressed in black and gold and silver, with chains and tables, benches, contraptions I have literally no name for. A woman in leather has a man on a leash and she's leading him around the carpeted floor on his hands and knees.

"All sorts of play," Muse says, standing next to me, his unzipped leather hoodie drifting down the shoulder with the bats, flashing me delicious swaths of skin. "As long as it's consensual, it happens." He pauses and glances over at Ransom, watching as his friend pushes his hood back. "What do you do in places like this?"

Ransom shrugs his broad shoulders, watching the action below with glittering black eyes. But when he looks over at me, they darken even further with hunger and I feel my pussy bloom with wetness.

"Most anything short of sex," he admits as he reaches out a hand and traces a finger down my arm. "Just enough of whatever to make me feel something other than the usual, sweetheart."

"And what's the usual?" I ask as music thrashes the room from the speakers in the corners of the ceiling. Ran and I are staring hard at each other, this electric feeling in the air between us. He could seriously be the other half of my soul's pain and that scares me. A *lot.* The way we process heartache and hurt, it's the same. The exact same.

"Gaping emptiness and regret," he says as I drop my hand and curl my fingers through his, glancing back down through the window at the two story room room beyond it. The man and his mistress—sorry, I don't know the official terms—have paused their walk so she can spank him with a pink leather paddle.

"Can you tell me about Kortney and Chloe?" I ask tentatively and Ran sighs, running his hand down his face. His brunette hair is mussed up and sexy from his hoodie and I reach up a hand to ruffle it with my fingers.

"Do you want me to leave?" Muse asks softly, but Ran shakes his head.

While I wait for him to speak, I take in the rest of the room: there's a king size bed with red velvet blankets and black leather pillows, chains hanging from the headboard and footboard. To the right of that, there's a whole wall of random instruments— whips, paddles, feather dusters, ropes. The walls themselves are covered in some thick textured burgundy wallpaper with black roses on it. There's even a small fridge next to a counter with a sink.

"Is sex not allowed in here?" I ask as I turn back to the

window and watch the man on his knees continue his leashed walk.

"It's allowed, honey," Ran says as he lifts his face to look at me, curving that hot dangerous mouth of his into a sad smile. "It's just not something I was ever interested in."

I imagine him looking at me standing here in what I thought was an edgy shirt-dress feeling totally out of my element and loving it, and I picture his lips adding, *"Until now."*

I press my own lips together, feeling the slick shiny slide of the lipstick and gloss I slathered across my mouth.

"That woman," I start, touching my fingertips to the glass, "she works here?"

"The Dom," Ransom says, his voice as soft as silk, dripping with innuendo, audible somehow even with the music pouring into the room, "and the man is the sub. Maybe they're a couple? Maybe they just rented the room?"

"It's okay for us to watch this?" I ask as the man climbs to his feet and the woman attaches him to a big black X hooked to the wall, latching his wrists and ankles to the device.

"That's a St. Andrew's Cross," Ransom explains idly, tilting his head to the side and tucking his hands in the front pocket of his hoodie, "and if they didn't want us to watch, we wouldn't be in here. Don't worry, doll baby."

"Doll baby," I whisper with a faint smile, giving him a look that he returns with a slight smile. "That's a new one."

"Stick around long enough and you'll hear some real crazy ones," Muse says from beside me, drawing my attention back to him. While Ran's finally removed his hood, Muse has pushed his up, squashing his mohawk a little, silver and black strands of hair sticking out the front. "What did you use to call Kortney? Crazy Legs?"

Ran makes this disgusted sound in his throat, putting his forehead against the glass.

I turn to look back at him and happen to catch the 'Dom' literally tearing the shiny black briefs off her subject, his cock bouncing out and making me squeal.

"Oh my god!" I shout as I turn around and put my back to the glass, breathing heavily. "You said there was no sex involved!"

Both Ransom and Muse laugh at me as I put a hand to my chest and try not to act like the complete prude that I am ... was? Must be was because I just had a fucking *foursome* in the living room of a rock star's tour bus. My sexual revolution has arrived apparently.

"I said that *I* didn't have sex here, darling," he reminds me, putting his hands on my shoulders and trying to turn me around. I close my eyes as he does, wrapping his body around mine from behind, holding me against the big warm expanse of his chest. My heart flutters and my cunt feels hot and desperate, but I don't open my eyes. "Don't tell me you have a problem with *cock* all of a sudden? Because that'd be a shame."

"Just strangers' cocks," I blurt and then feel slightly uncomfortable. This is only my fourth night hanging out with these guys; they're almost as strange and foreign to me as that man and his Dom down there. But that's not how it *feels;* it feels like I know them already. Pain speaks to pain and all that, and they saw me at my lowest ... are *still* seeing me at my lowest because I haven't recovered yet. I think I'm still in denial, like there's no fucking way this tour won't end with my dad smiling at me from our porch in New York, standing there with his arms out and welcoming me home.

I have no home to go back to.

I feel stupid for a second, standing here in some club partying while my dad's body gets burnt to a crisp and my stepmom throws away decades of memories without my getting any say in the matter. And then there's all the practical stuff, like how I still only have two hundred bucks and no job and no apartment and my car's all the way back in Phoenix.

I take a deep breath and close my eyes for a moment.

When I open them, I catch Muse's gaze and find him smiling at me, leaning his now bare shoulder against the glass as the leather hoodie hangs casually off his elbow.

"Or maybe just that guy's cock?" I joke as I catch sight of the Dom slapping her sub's erect shaft with a purple and black whip. Even though the man's blindfolded and gagged, I can see his body ripple with ecstasy. "He's not really my type, you

200

know."

"What is your type then, honey?" Ran whispers as he slides his hands down the front of my dress and I gasp, clenching my thighs together when his fingers curl beneath the hem. The touch of his fingertips on my bare skin is almost too much, this vibrant heat pouring through him and into me. My eyes flick up and meet Muse's, sending another shock of rampant excitement arcing through me.

"You fucking twats."

Both Ransom and I jump when Pax opens the door and steps into the room, his shirt unbuttoned and his tie hanging loose around his neck. He kicks it closed behind him and tears the aubergine silk off, crumpling it up and shoving it in the pocket on his jacket.

"What the hell are you languishing back here for? The real party's up front."

Pax saunters over to the window and parks his tattooed hands in his pockets.

"Well, well," he tsks as he studies the couple in the room below, glancing over at the three of us, "now I see. Come to pay homage to your voyeuristic tendencies, Ran?"

"Don't start," Ran growls, still holding me possessively against his chest.

Pax ignores him, turning around and walking over to the wall with all the paddles and ropes hanging off it. He takes down a red leather flogger in his hands and snaps it tight between them. I try to tell myself that the sight doesn't turn me on at all ... but it kind of does.

"You're in here with all these lovely things and you haven't touched any of them?" Pax asks, turning around, smirking with that perfect sharp mouth of his. "Come 'ere, Lilith," he says and even though he sounds cold and cruel, I want to go to him.

"She wants to know about Korney," Ran says and Pax sighs like he's completely put out by the whole thing. Also, he's very clearly drunk.

"It's not a particularly interesting story," Pax says, climbing on the bed and patting it with his palm. "But if you come over here, I'll tell it to you. I want to spank that perfect white little ass of yours and see it turn red." He winks at me, and even though he's acting playful and nonchalant, there's heat in his expression when he looks at me.

"Fuck off, Paxton," Ran whispers, letting go of me and turning toward the bed like he's ready for yet another confrontation with Pax. "Why don't you just tell her how you fucked by girlfriend to get back at me for something I didn't do?"

"Oh? Is that how you see it?" Pax asks nonchalantly as Muse tucks his fingers into his pockets and looks between the two men. "Well, you seduced the girl I'd been in love with since I was sixteen—"

"I never slept with Chloe," Ran says tiredly, like this is a line he's repeated hundreds—maybe even thousands—of times. "We fell for each other, that's it. Nothing happened. We weren't going to do anything until she'd broken up with Pax," he says, looking at me now, wanting and pleading with his eyes for me to believe him. I feel like Ran needs someone on his side ... but so does Pax.

I cross my arms over my chest and listen to the thumping bass beat trill through the floor and up through the heels of my black boots.

"Yeah? I'm supposed to believe that shite am I? Six years together and she breaks up with me because she *fancies* you? What a load of bullshit."

"I never fucked her!" Ran yells, raising his voice for the first time since I met him. He tosses his hood up and glares daggers at Pax. "At some point, you're just going to have to accept that *you* fucked up, sweetheart."

It takes me a second to realize he's still talking to Pax. And he called him sweetheart. It'd be cute if the two of them weren't so fucking tragic.

"But you won't, will you? Because if you do, you'll have to accept that Chloe and Harper died in an *accident*, that you have no right to make me the enemy anymore. And *then* you'll have to accept that you kicked me when I was down for no goddamn good reason at all."

"You fucked my girlfriend; I fucked yours. At least Kortney

didn't die afterwards."

Pax cocks up a knee and slaps the leather whip against the velvet blanket covering the bed.

"Maybe if you come over here, I'll spank you, too, Ran? I wouldn't mind beating the shit out of you with one of these things."

"Go to hell, Paxton," Ransom says quietly, turning and heading for the door. He throws it open in Cope's surprised face and then takes a small step back. "What?"

"Just wanted to see what you guys were up to," he says and then spots the couple through the window, raising both brows in surprise. "Ah."

"Don't you read about this shit all the time?" Pax drawls as Cope steps in and closes the door behind him. Pax reclines back into the sea of leather pillows, laying the whip across his lap. "There's a whole drawer of this shit in the Bat Cave, isn't there?"

Cope just smiles and doesn't say anything, his eyes alighting on mine for a moment before he refocuses back on the action below.

"We should get out of here soon. Saw a couple paps in the crowd," he says and I raise my eyebrows, pretending I don't notice Pax watching me and playing with the leather tails of the flogger.

"Paps?" I ask as Ran leans against the wall and lets his hood cover his face.

"Paparazzi," Cope says, smiling bemusedly as he lets his attention drift from the view of the room below, back to me, and then over at Pax. "You guys playing around in here without me?" he asks and I get this shivery little thrill racing down my spine.

"We just came to watch," Ran whispers from inside his hood, but Pax's laughter cuts through the sound.

"If Lilith would get her lily white ass over here, we could get started."

"Who says I'm even into this stuff?" I ask, studying Ran, exchanging a look with Muse. He knows Ransom better than I do. Is he going to have another breakdown? I know if I had someone like Pax on my ass all the time, I'd probably be hiding inside my hood, too.

"Your hard nipples, dilated pupils, and the way you keep licking your damn lips, that's who."

Pax slides off the edge of the bed and grabs me around the wrist, pulling me toward him, and wrapping a hand in my hair. When he kisses me, he tastes like brandy again, like he did that first night. It should turn me off considering he was such a damn jerk then, but even when he's being cruel, I can see his pain. Stupid as it sounds, I want to comfort him, drown all of those feelings until they float away and leave him in peace.

"Well the gang's all here, right?" Pax whispers when he breaks my kiss and challenges someone over my shoulder with a steely eyed glare. Only person that could be is Ransom. "You've got all four of us in thrall right now. Might as well use us then?"

"I wouldn't trust you to top someone on a good day," Ran growls from over my shoulder, making me shiver. "You're too fucking awful."

"Oh, rubbish," Pax says, making me gasp when he shoves up the fabric of my shirt-dress. "I don't want to play any of your stupid little dominance games. I just want to fuck Lilith—and smack her ass with this whip."

I gasp when he hits me on the back of the thighs with the leather flail. It's barely a brush, but the sensation turns my knees to jelly. Holy crap. Suddenly I'm very much aware of the situation, of the fact that I *do* have all four men in a private room full of … toys.

"How long do we have this room for?" I ask, pushing Paxton away slightly and glancing back at Ransom, trying to get a read on his expression.

"Long enough," he says, voice still low and then he reaches out and takes the whip from Pax's fingers, making his friend's blonde brows raise up.

"Hold on a sec," I say as I take a small step back and look between them, grab a quick glance back at Muse and Cope. They're hanging back, watching the situation with interest. Both of them have strange, almost wry smiles on their faces when they exchange a look. "What's the hurry then?" I ask, taking the whip back from Ran and lifting a hand to his face.

Gently, I push the hood back and press my mouth softly to his, just a peck before I pull away and do the same to Pax, sliding the whip across his cheek before I kiss him, too. It's like kissing night and day, two halves of the same cycle. Ran tastes like kindness with a healthy dose of anger simmering underneath, while Pax tastes like cruelty over pain.

It's a lot to take in.

I kiss Ran again, deeper this time, sliding my tongue against his, loving the feel of his hand sliding up my back. Pax makes a sound and I switch back to him, letting that wicked sharp mouth take over mine. And then when I pull back, I take him with me, drawing us together in a three-way kiss, just mouths and tongues and heat.

I can feel my body responding to the hot warmth on either side of me, the rigid cocks pressed up against me, the sounds emanating from each guy's throat. They might be pissed off at each other—might even hate each other—but right now, they both want me and that gives them some common ground.

I pull back and take the whip with me, dropping down to my knees between them.

"Don't stop," I plead as I look up and pop the buttons on Ran's skinny jeans, on Pax's aubergine slacks. "You stop, I stop," I say as they stare at each other and Pax makes a face.

"Oh, what the fuck. I want my cock sucked," he says with a shrug, putting a tattooed hand on the back of Ran's neck and kissing him like he's still kissing me. Ransom goes completely stiff, so I go down on him first to relax him, freeing his hard shaft from his jeans and sliding my mouth over the head. My other hand finds Pax inside his slacks and frees him, too. I take a brief moment to slick my tongue over Paxton's cock so I have plenty of lube to work with and start pumping him with my hand.

Stuck between cruel and kind right now. That's where I am. And it's a beautiful fucking place to be. When I glance up, I can see Ran and Pax kissing, and although there's a definite tension there, they don't stop.

So I keep my promise and keep going, switching my mouth to Pax, using my hand on Ran.

When I glance back to look for Cope and Muse, I find them lying on the bed. Cope's leaning into the pillows with his hand in his jeans and Muse is lying on his stomach, watching us.

"That's a serious feat, Cutie," he whispers and then he rolls onto his back and puts his hand under the elastic waistband of his boxer briefs. Just knowing that I've got *four* fucking guys hanging on everything that I do makes me feel like a goddamn princess … or a queen. They all want to fuck me; they all want to please me.

Ending up at the concert, it doesn't feel like an accident right now. It feels like fucking fate.

I work Pax and Ran until I feel fingers curl in my hair. Surprisingly, it's Ransom, not Paxton, getting my attention, making me look at him.

"On the bed," he rasps and then lets go of my hair, stepping back from Pax and me with a small, rough sounding sigh. "I can't take this anymore."

"Is my mouth too much for you?" Pax quips, stepping back and joining Cope and Muse up on the velvet blankets. "Apparently I have the same effect on men that I have on women. Thank you for being the first bloke I ever fucking kissed," Pax says with a cruel laugh, grabbing me before I can decide what to do next. He throws me over his lap and steals the whip from my hand. "I did what you wanted. Now you'll do what I want," he growls out, tugging down my black panties. "Knickers *off*," he demands and I shiver as I feel fingers sliding the lingerie down my legs.

It's Cope.

He meets my eyes for a moment and then tosses the ball of black lace aside just before I feel the sharp sting of the leather flogger on my ass. I can see it, too, making the round, white curve of my ass jiggle with the motion. A sharp gasp escapes my lips and then a giggle.

"Not hard enough?" Pax drawls, not at all put off by my laughter as I turn my head back around and drop my forehead to the bed. I'm draped over his lap, his knees up, the whip cracking and connecting with my skin again. This time it's a little harder and not quite as funny.

"Oh," I gasp as he smacks me again and I try not to squirm in his suit covered lap. I think about that supposed drawer full of toys in the Bat Cave and I get *really* excited. I mean, I already got to witness firsthand the toy that Ran used on me. What else is in there? "That feels ... really good." My lips part as I feel fingertips sliding up the insides of my thighs. "Harder," I say and then bite down on the blanket as the whip stings my skin again and brings goose bumps up all over my body.

And then suddenly there are just all these ideas in my head, all of these things that I never knew I wanted to do until now.

These two weeks are going to go by *fast*.

Pax curls his fingers in my hair and lifts my head up, leaning in to press his mouth to my ear.

"Tell me you want my bare cock first," he whispers and I go completely stiff. I'm both exhilarated and terrified at the idea of doing it without a condom. But I won't let Kevin scar me for life. I saw the boys' results; they saw mine. We're completely safe right now.

I take a deep breath.

"I don't care who's first," I whisper and Pax lifts me up like I weigh nothing, tucking my bare ass in his lap as he holds me and leans against the sea of pillows.

"Well I do," he tells me with a smirk, running his tongue up my throat. "Get on your knees."

"Who put you in charge?" Ran growls, drawing my attention back to the other boys. He's still cloaked in his sleeveless hoodie, but the hood's pulled down for once. Muse is lying on his side with his leather zip-up hoodie open, exposing his bare chest and tummy and the few bat tattoos that drift over his left pec while Cope's lying next to Pax and me, fingering the whip and watching us curiously.

"Lilith did," Pax says matter-of-factly, meeting my gaze with his grey eyes and waiting for me to say something in response. "Didn't you, Lil?"

It's the first time any of the boys uses less than my full name; I like it. It sounds familiar, like I actually belong here with these guys.

"Prove Ran wrong, Pax," I whisper in his ear, feeling his hands tighten around my waist, "prove that you can be in charge without being cruel." To me, it's as clear as day why Paxton acts the way he acts. He misses his sister, yes, but he misses Chloe, too. *A lot.* "Make me feel good, Pax," I say, a little louder, the sound of wild drums pummeling us through the speakers. "But you have to make *them* feel good, too. That's my challenge."

"Is it then?" Pax asks, reaching up to pull his loose tie out of his pocket and smirking wickedly again. It's not as cold this time though. There's some heat to his expression now. "Challenge accepted," he growls and then he wraps the purple tie around my eyes, the silk sliding against my shuttered lids, the sensation making me shake with adrenaline. "Like I said, on your fucking knees, *Lilith Tempest Goode.*"

Feeling my way off Pax's lap, I face the end of the bed, the sound of my breath seemingly louder in the sudden darkness, my fingers curled in the blankets.

"Boys, pick your poison," Pax says authoritatively, proving that even if this is just a game, he really *is* the one that's in charge of this band. "Something off the wall."

I gasp and bite my lower lip.

"You're okay, honey?" Ransom asks, his gentle fingers on my chin. Somehow, I can tell it's him from the touch alone.

"More than okay," I whisper and feel the bed jostle beneath me, my heart racing like crazy in my chest, feeling ridiculously exposed in this position, all dressed up but missing my panties, my cunt exposed to the pulsing warm air of the club dungeon.

"Like I said," Pax tells me, his warm body suddenly pressed up tight against my ass. I can feel his cock slicking up my cunt, teasing the exposed wetness of my folds. "If you want me to stop, just say it. I'm not into this kinky shit the way Ransom is."

"Go to hell, Pax," he whispers, but then there's another jostling motion and Pax puts some more space between us.

All the places he just touched feel cold now, making me feel even more exposed all of a sudden.

I'm putting a ton of fucking trust into these guys and it's

scaring the shit out of me. I don't know them at all. And now *they* know that there's nobody in this world that cares about me, that knows where I am or would give a crap if I disappeared.

My heart starts to thunder in a different way, but I force myself to take several, deep slow breaths. I'm being ridiculous; these guys are famous rockstars. They're probably worth millions and besides, I've looked into each one of their gazes and seen something of myself in them. There's no way they'd do anything horrible to me. No, I trust them.

But don't you dare try this shit at home.

My life is … mine to risk.

I make a small sound and then feel the hard press of a paddle caressing my ass.

"Ready?" Pax asks and I nod.

The paddle disappears and then with a rush of air, it's back, cracking against my skin, making my body tingle and flush. It feels like all the blood in my body is rushing back to meet it, kissing the sharp sting of the leather paddle.

I bite my lip and drop my head, curling my fingers into the blankets, taking low, deep breaths. Ransom said this kind of stuff wasn't sexual for him … but it is for me. At least right now, with these four men in this room, it is.

With each smack of the paddle, I feel myself getting wetter, more desperate. I want to feel Pax fuck with me his bare cock, come inside of me, claim me so I don't feel so guilty claiming him right back.

I assume it's him that's in charge of the spanking, but maybe not? I can't see anything, can only hear the sound of my own breath, the smack of the paddle, and the dubstep coming from the main part of the club. Whoever's in charge, they seem to know exactly how far to take it before I ask them to stop, putting aside the paddle and caressing my stinging cheeks with soft, gentle fingers.

No, there's no way that's Paxton.

My throat gets tight with excitement as I realize I'm not exactly sure *who* is going to fuck me right now—something that would normally be a terrifying prospect but these are my boys, my *men*. At least that's what they'll become. For me, they'll be my night stars and I'll be their moon. It just wouldn't be night without all of us there to shimmer and shine.

"Oh God," I moan as I feel fingers curve around my hips, feel the hard press of something at my opening. I arch my back, lift my hips up and groan as one of my boys pushes inside of me with a hard, cruel thrust.

Now *that* really is Paxton.

The warmth of his body filling mine is overwhelming, making me cry out, shudder around him. I hear him curse and give my tender ass a slap with his palm.

"Slow down there, Miss Lily," he says, hitting me with another nickname. I lift my fingers up almost imploringly and find them catching on a crisp denim waistband, sliding down and finding a cock already slicked up with lube, fingers wrapped around it.

I think it's Cope, but I'm not a hundred percent sure.

Grabbing his waistband again, I tug him toward me, encourage him to slip the hard velvety length of his shaft between my lips. My hand drops back to the bed and I open my throat, letting him in as deep as I can, groaning softly as he buries his fingers in my hair.

Maybe I should feel like I'm being used, but I don't. I feel like I'm being worshipped. Something about the monsoon of grief inside of me has washed away all my boundaries, stripped down my walls, torn me apart and left me aching and empty and open and wanting. One man couldn't satisfy me. No, all five years I was with Kevin there was something missing. And maybe that was just him, maybe *he* was just lacking. But now I've got four guys looking at me like I'm something special and I'm going to take advantage of that.

When I feel Pax tensing up behind me, I push back into him, heart thumping and listen to the sharp sound of his orgasm tearing from his throat as he spills himself into me. And my only regret is that I can't see his face as he does it.

"Bloody hell," he murmurs and then there's this horrible emptiness as he pulls away and the bed creaks beneath us. The boys don't let me regret or want for long though. Fingers knead my scalp as I suck the cock between my lips and somebody else

—the gentle fingers again—pushes up my dress and exposes my bare back.

There's a little spot of sudden warmth on my spine for a moment.

"Tell us if that's too hot, honey," Ran says and I realize that those gentle fingers are his. Pax might be 'in charge' but Ran is watching over me. The shaft between my lips slides back for a moment, giving me a chance to speak.

"Don't stop," I murmur because like this, with all of these people and all of these things happening to me, there's no room to feel sad or insecure or lonely. In here, like this, I feel like I might never be lonely again.

"You like this, doll baby?" Ran asks as more bright spots of warmth drip down my back. I think it's candle wax.

"Yes," I breathe and then the boy in front of me is backing up and moving away. I start to reach out to him when somebody else takes my hand, curling their fingers in mine and dropping their mouth down to kiss me. That controlled need … the smoky smell of incense. Derek? He kisses me for long moments as the wax drips down my back and then gets replaced with gentle fingers, kneading and massaging my skin, fingertips digging into my muscles and making me feel like I might collapse.

Those same hands keep me from falling forward, curving around my hips and pulling me back against a hard warm pelvis. It must be Ran, it has to be, but I don't really care. These four guys, I want them all.

I relax into his touch as he presses the head of his shaft to my sex, pushing inside so slow I almost want to scream. It's like he's *trying* to be the exact opposite of Paxton. I distract myself with what's happening in front of me, the warm lips of the man kissing me pulling away and being replaced with his cock.

I take it eagerly into my mouth as the man behind me starts to thrust with these long, deep aching strokes that stir up everything inside of me. His shaft feels hot, almost scorchingly so, and I forget all about that little twinge of anxiety at having these guys bare inside of me.

211

As Ran's thrusting and I'm teasing Muse with my tongue, I feel a tickling softness against my stinging ass cheeks. Somebody's teasing me with a feather and the contrasting sensation of that gentle softness against my sore skin ... it makes me crazy.

My hips lift up and press against Ran, encouraging him to move faster and deeper as I increase my intensity on Muse's shaft, sucking and licking him without restraint.

"Holy crap, Cutie," he says, giving himself away, and I'd smile if ... you know.

Ran adjusts himself, pulling me back onto his lap so I'm sitting more or less on my knees, encouraging me to take over the motion of our bodies and freeing up my hands to play with Muse's balls. Someone else—must be Cope because the touch isn't cruel enough—slips their hands inside the large arm holes of my dress and frees one of my breasts from my bra, pushing the excess fabric out of his way so he can press his mouth against me, tongue slicking across my nipple, lips scorching.

Pax does the same on the other side and like the gentle feather and the stinging paddle, the two boys couldn't be anymore different.

"Fuck," Cope whispers from beside me and I can hear the strain in his voice. My left hand seeks him out again, just like I did before, finding the denim of his pants, drifting down to his cock. He lifts up on his knees, giving me better access to his shaft, moving his mouth to my ear, my throat, giving me goose bumps all over my body. I work him with a slow, twisting motion, turning my fist clockwise around the base of his cock and drinking his groans in like fine wine.

Ransom's the next to come, giving into the tight heat of my body with this ragged cry that almost drags me over the edge with him.

But I'm not done yet.

I want to please *all* of my boys.

I pull away from Muse and shove the blindfold over my head, blinking at the hazy atmosphere of sex and the heavy lidded hazel eyes of the man in front of me.

"Muse and Cope," I say, focusing my attention on them,

eager to show them that Ran and Pax aren't the only stars of this particular show.

I climb off of Ransom as he collapses into the pillows and throws his hood up over his head, Pax watching the three of us as I guide Cope onto his back and straddle him.

He's wearing this adorably sweet but sexually strained little smile as I guide him to my opening and watch his expression shift from desperate to devastated. It feels so fucking good; neither of us is going to last long.

"Muse," I whisper as he comes up behind me, kissing my neck, brushing my hair over my shoulder as I ride his friend. He produces a small bottle of lube from his pocket, warming me up from behind with a single slick finger, then two, just like Cope did. "I'm ready," I promise him and he obliges my new carnal obsession, putting his cock to my ass and pushing inside to share my body with Copeland.

The sensation overwhelms me, sending shivers through every inch of my body, taking all my breath away. I feel like I don't dare take another, like there's not enough room inside of me for it. My lids flutter as pleasure takes over my entire body, invades my bones, digs into my muscles. The two cocks rub this thin wall between my ass and my pussy, this bundle of nerve endings I didn't even know I had.

My fingertips dig into Cope's hard chest as sweat drips down the side of my face, a droplet spattering against the pair of heart tattoos on his left pec. Our eyes meet and I feel that same surge of emotion I felt in the gas station, this overwhelming need to cave in and tell him everything. Everything. Everything.

Then my breath catches so sharply my lungs hurt and a powerful orgasm tears right through me, so vivid and vibrant that color flickers behind my tightly shuttered lids. My lips part with a breathless gasp and I collapse onto Cope's chest, sighing as his arms go around me I realize my own orgasm stole one from him and Muse both.

"Jesus Christ," Ran says as a rush of cool air sweeps into the room and I glance over my shoulder to find Michael standing in the door staring at us. He has Pierced Guy's keys in his hand and a frown plastered on his face.

His violet eyes are murder when they look at the five of us.

"What the hell? We go out to party and you guys come back here to *fuck*?" he snarls, his gaze focused mostly on me. With a scowl, Michael steps inside and closes the door behind him, his leather jacket draped over one elbow, exposing his tattoos and a pair of sumptuously sculpted arms. "Put your dicks away and let's go. Too many paps here now to relax."

"Jealous, are we, Mikey?" Pax asks, standing up from the bed and buttoning up his slacks. "I would be, if I were chained to a monster like Vanessa."

"Eat shit, Pax," Michael says, looking briefly at his friend before turning his glare back to me. "Get up," he repeats, pupils dilated, skin flushed. Whether it's from dancing or because of what he sees in that dungeon room, I'm not sure. "Follow me and I'll show you what a real night out looks like."

He turns and leaves the room, slamming the heavy wooden door behind him.

CHAPTER TWENTY-NINE

Ransom

RANSOM RIGGS

The next morning, I wake up to a knee in my back and reach over to slap Muse away from me.

"You're fucking stabbing me in the goddamn spine," I mumble in a dazed half-sleep, sitting up slightly and staring at the gathered collection of assholes on the bed around me. Well, the assholes and Lilith. My friends look like ugly demons when they sleep; Lilith looks like an angel.

Her pink bloom of a mouth draws my thumb, encouraging me to press the whorls of my fingertip against her bottom lip. She sighs gently in her sleep, lashes pressed to her pale cheeks, red hair splayed out across the black silk pillows in a purple-red curtain.

Ah, I really like her.

A lot.

But I have terrible taste in women, so maybe that shouldn't count for anything?

I look back over at my friends. Muse is behind me; Cope is next to Lilith; Pax and Michael are several careful inches apart on the far side of the bed. This wouldn't be the first time we all got drunk and passed out in here—it's the biggest, nicest, most comfortable spot in the entire bus—but it's the first time we've all crashed here with a girl between us.

I sit up against the headboard and try to remember something beyond the dungeon room at the Silver Skull. It's all a goddamn blur. I think we hit two more clubs. Three? I remember having drinks at a small quiet bar, the air hazy with

C. M. Stunich

smoke.

And then ... I'm completely fucking nude, so more sex I presume?

I think.

God, we need to change these fucking sheets.

I crawl out of the blankets and slide off the end of the bed, searching for my hoodie in the sea of clothes on the floor. When I can't find it, I give up and head to my bunk, open the small drawer underneath and fish out a fresh Beauty in Lies hoodie and some sweats with a faux tear in one leg, a battered skeletal leg showing through. I like the idea of these pants, like part of me's been ripped away and everyone can see my horrid insides peeking through.

I move into the living room and start some coffee, trying to decide if I had any nightmares last night. If I did, I can't remember them.

"Can you bloody believe we made out last night?" Paxton asks from behind me, appearing in ... fucking nothing, his dick already half-hard as he leans over me and steals the coffee pot from my hands.

I grit my teeth at him, but he ignores me, pouring a cup, dashing creamer into it and lifting it to his lips as I tug my hood over my hair and glare at him.

"No, not really," I say as I pour my own coffee and try not to look at him. I have a hard time looking at Pax nowadays—and not just because I don't particularly want to see his dick. He was the first real guy friend I ever had, this pompous rich asshole from England trying to navigate the seedier side of Seattle. I took him under my wing and we've been together ever since, since I was fifteen and he was sixteen.

Ten years of friendship, half of them wonderful and the other half ... fucking heartbreaking.

But neither of us will quit and walk away, so here we are. There must still be something here to save, right?

"You kiss like you don't expect to live through tomorrow," Pax says mildly, giving me pause, drawing my gaze up to his grey eyes and his perfectly combed and styled hair. So, he got up and didn't bother to take the time to put pants on, but he did

216

his hair? Figures. But his words are, well, fuck, I don't know what to make of them.

"Sometimes I pray that I won't, honey," I whisper and my hands start to shake. My cup starts to slip from my fingers and Pax catches it from the bottom, setting it gently on the counter in front of me. I miss my mom so damn bad in that moment that I could puke. I imagine her sitting at the breakfast nook in our kitchen, sipping coffee from her favorite floral mug.

And then I imagine her waking up to some strange guy in her room, feeling him violate her, kill her, steal her away from me.

My head gets dizzy and I lean against the wall on my right as Pax walks away and leaves me alone in the kitchen. He's only gone for a moment, but when he comes back, he steps right up to me and pulls the hood from my hair.

"Your mum?" he asks as I turn my head slowly to look at him, noticing that he's put on some grey sweats.

"I can't even remember her without remembering how she died," I whisper, trying not think of the police reports, of Mom's panties around her ankles and her body lying in a pool of blood. He raped her. He killed her. Raped her and killed her.

Killed her, killed her, killed her.

And I killed him.

I stabbed him a hundred and fourteen times. Over and over and over again. And I just couldn't stab him enough. When that bastard died, I was as heartbroken as I was when I found out my mom was gone. Because if he was dead, he couldn't suffer anymore. And I wanted that. I craved it.

I feel myself start to slip away, the world around me blurring into shapes and colors instead of objects and things … and then I hear Pax sigh.

"Fucking hell, Ran," he says and then he's hugging me.

He hugs me.

Paxton Blackwell *hugs* me.

"Your mouth tastes like ash and heartache, Ran," he says, giving me a long, tight squeeze that snaps my brain back to the bus, to the steaming cup of coffee in front of me, to the light streaming in above the kitchen window. "Don't kiss me with it again until you get that shite cleaned up, okay?"

"Okay," I whisper and then we both pause at the sound of soft footsteps behind us.

Pax lets go of me and I glance back to find Lilith in Cope's *Dracula* tank and a pair of Muse's sweats. She slips out of the hallway and closes the door softly behind her. When her eyes search us both out, she smiles at what she sees.

"Good morning," she says as I look back at her, my eyes catching on the vibrant green of her gaze, the faint blush of hardened nipples I can see beneath the shirt's thin fabric.

"Good morning, sweetheart," I say, passing over my coffee and enjoying the brush of our fingers when she takes it.

"Thanks," she says, nodding at Paxton. He smiles sharply at her, but he doesn't say anything. I think we both need a minute to process what just happened. God. I hope this isn't a fluke, some hungover remnant of what we used to have. Losing Mom and not having Pax around to help me through it was like torture.

The night Chloe and Harper died ... it was like he died right along with them.

"What time's the show tonight?" Lilith asks, eyes sparkling.

Before I can question myself, I step forward and kiss her coffee tainted lips.

"Nine," I whisper, "but the doors open at eight. We'll be busy most of the day today."

Lilith nods as I take a step back, watching her and imagining that beautiful body laid out in front of me, dripping hot massage oil from the black metal candle down her curved spine. Her cunt was warm and slick, a million times better bare than with a condom. I never want to use a condom with this girl again.

"I should probably try to ... make some plans," she says, her voice dropping slightly as she glances away from Pax and me, sipping her coffee and letting her face crumple up with pain. I don't think she even realizes it, but there it is, pulling down the corners of her beautiful mouth. "I have two hundred bucks cash and a car from 1977." She flicks her gaze back to us and makes herself smile. "People have done more with less."

"What's your passion, baby?" I ask as she moves over to sit

on the couch, her bare breasts showing through the giant armholes on the side of the tank top. Jesus. I glance over at Pax and see I'm not the only one that's noticed. We exchange a look, me and him, and it's the most companionable look we've shared in four years.

"My passion?" Lilith echoes, glancing up and staring between the two of us for a moment. "I'm not sure. Art, I think. I like making things."

"Then you're in the right place, baby girl," I whisper as I pour myself another cup of coffee and join her on the couch, sitting so close that she has to adjust herself and drape her left leg over my right. "We're all artists here. What do you like to make besides sexy shirt-dresses?"

Lilith smiles and the expression makes her cheeks dimple, makes the scattering of freckles on her nose stand out. I want to kiss each and every one of them.

"I like to paint," she says tentatively, and I remember her drawing yesterday on her phone, using a stylus to trace out a design that she didn't show to anyone. "Digitally or with oils. I guess it doesn't really matter. I just like to see something beautiful come from nothing."

"What kind of stuff do you like to paint?" I ask as Pax sits down in one of the swivel chairs and for once in his fucking life, has the decency to say nothing at all.

"Life," she says, her cheeks reddening slightly. I wonder if she's thinking of last night, of being blindfolded and surrounded by the four of us. Not a single one of us could take our eyes off of her, not even for a second. She has magnetism, this girl does. And she's nothing at all like Chloe or Kortney, not even close. They were similar to each other, pretty and elusive and fully aware that they held all the cards in life. Neither of them was particularly artistic although they were both smart. Chloe wanted to be a plastic surgeon ... Kortney ended up marrying some guy back in Seattle and having a son. I think she's a housewife now. I don't particularly care.

"Anyway, painting isn't exactly an easy or lucrative trade as far as making a living goes. I'll have to find something else. I have my high school diploma but not much else. I took a few classes at the community college ..." Lilith trails off with a small sigh, her shoulders sagging a little. I want nothing more in that moment than to see her succeed at something. "I'm trying to decide if I should move back to New York. Even though my dad's gone, I know the people in Gloversville. Then again, my car's already in Phoenix, so I guess I could go back there, beg for my waitressing job back."

"You sound like you're discussing funeral arrangements," Paxton says and Lilith's head snaps up.

"I *wish* I were discussing funeral arrangements," she whispers, her skin getting tight, face going pale. "My wicked stepmother isn't having one for my dad. If she has her way, I doubt he'll even get his name inscribed in the Goode family mausoleum. *That* is where he should be, with his parents, with my sister. I could've scattered my mom's ashes there so they could all be together again. I guess I still can ..."

Lilith rakes her fingers through her hair. I see her eyes going glassy, fading, her spirit drooping below the floor, diving straight to hell. I was literally just there, so I get it. I feel her pain. I want to pull her close and mix it with mine, press my face to her hair and breathe in her scent.

So I do.

I take her coffee away, set both our mugs on the side table, and then drag her into my lap.

"Oh," she says as she settles against me, staring into my face. I wonder what she thinks about last night, about the sex, or maybe how I called her my girlfriend to that guy at the club. My girlfriend. Muse's girlfriend. Both. That's what I said. But can we even do that? I don't know the answer to that question.

"*You* could ask for his name to be inscribed yourself," I say, thinking of my mom's grave back in Seattle, that rain drenched plot of earth shaded by a handsome red cedar tree. The first night she was buried there, I slept on it until the caretaker came and woke me up in a pool of wet moonlight. "Then sprinkle his ashes there with your mom's."

"Assuming Susan really does give them to me like she promised," Lilith whispers, leaning into me, letting me use her for comfort as much as she's using me. "I hate her."

"You should try not to, sweet thing," I whisper, feeling an answering call of rage inside of her. She should let it out before it breaks her the way it broke me. "Hate like that will destroy you."

"That it will," Pax says and when I glance up, I see him looking straight at me and I wonder for a second there if the expression on his face … is the beginning of an apology.

After the show that night, Michael catches up to me outside the venue and pulls me aside. His fingers are slick with sweat when he grabs onto my bicep and drags me over to the front of the bus. I'm slightly annoyed; all I want right now is to see Lilith. After our little coffee chat on the couch, she got dressed in his sexy as fuck green dress and skipped out on the rest of us. I have no idea where she went, but I didn't catch sight of her before or during the show so she must be up to something.

I'm ridiculously interested in what she's been doing.

"What do you want?" I ask, my hands shaking from adrenaline as I light up a cigarette and raise my brows in question. Michael looks awful. I figure it's because he was the drunkest out of all of us last night, waking up only when he absolutely had to to get ready for the show. While he was scrambling to wash his face and get eyeliner on his lids, he was having a screaming argument with Vanessa over speakerphone.

"Did I have sex with Lilith last night?" he asks and I blink suddenly at him.

"What?"

"Did I have sex with her?" he asks, raking his fingers through his dark hair and looking like he wants to kill something or somebody. A few of the roadies rolling equipment past give us both a wide berth.

"Um." I take a drag on my cigarette and look at him, standing there in a purple t-shirt with a flock of black bats across the front. The color looks good with his tattoos—they're all in these cool, dark jewel tones. Royal purple, navy blue, hunter green, svelte black. "I was drunk as fuck, Michael. I have no idea."

"Shit, shit, shit," he says, spinning in a tight circle, looking up at the sky with this disgusted expression plastered on his face, like he hates himself almost as much as Vanessa does. Because the way she talks to him, she must hate him. I get it—I was cheated on, too. It fucking *hurts* like hell. It's hard to explain how deep something like that cuts into your soul. If I ever got bored with my girl and wanted to move on, I'd break up with her *before* I fucked somebody else. Even it's only ten minutes before. Jesus. How hard is that?

"Do you ... *want* to have sex with Lilith?" I ask, feeling a tiny spark of jealousy. Kind of ridiculous considering I've been sharing her with three other guys since the beginning, but there it is.

"No."

The way he pauses and turns that violet glare of his on me tells me that he's most definitely lying. We stare at each other for a moment before he pushes past me and storms up the steps to the bus, shoving the door open and spilling some bouncy pop music into the air.

I follow after him and shove him out of the way when he blocks the door, catching sight of Lilith in a white apron, dancing and grooving to the song, those generous hips of hers rocking with the beat. The music's so loud she doesn't realize we're standing there watching her.

"Jesus Christ," Michael says as I grab onto the doorframe to keep myself upright.

When Lilith turns away to grab something off the counter, apron strings trailing behind her, I see that she's wearing, like, *nothing* underneath but a bra and panties.

"Move," I growl and push Michael out of my way, moving across the wood floor and pausing at the edge of the counter. When Lilith turns around, she screams and nearly drops the baking sheet full of rolls clutched in her mittened hands.

"Oh my God!" she gasps and then flushes red from chin to forehead. "I thought ... is the show over already?"

"It's over, honey," I say as she glances around for a place to set the tray and ends up balancing it over the sink. I notice then that the counters are covered with cooking utensils, a stack of plates, a giant wooden bowl brimming with green salad leaves and vibrant red tomato chunks. "It's over," I whisper as she reaches back, trying to tie up her apron, like that'll provide any coverage for the colorful turquoise lingerie draped over her pale skin.

Putting my hands gently on her shoulders, I turn her around and slide the apron strings through my fingers, putting my mouth to her ear.

"What are you doing, doll face?" I whisper before placing a kiss to her neck and tying the apron in a neat little bow. What I really want to say ask is, 'Why am I falling for you so quickly?'. I must be crazy.

"I was about to get dressed up, but I was afraid of overcooking the rolls …"

"You look dressed up to me, baby," I whisper as she turns back around and sweeps a few loose strands of her mahogany-red hair from her face. The rest is up in this flirty ponytail that sways when she moves.

I am fucking mesmerized.

"Hey," Michael says, moving up next to me, his stance aggressive and forward, shoulders taut, face locked in a frown. But when Lilith turns to face him, flushing slightly when she realizes he saw her dancing in her lingerie, too, he softens up considerably and sighs. "Can I ask you a question?"

"Of course," Lilith says, sucking her glossed up lower lip between her teeth. "But first, maybe I should get dressed?"

"You can do whatever you want," Michael says, not unkindly, as he tucks his fingers into the pockets of his black skinny jeans. "I'll go tuck myself in my bunk with some headphones and you guys can … do whatever it is that the five of you do."

"You don't have to do that," Lilith says, sounding slightly disappointed. "I was hoping you'd join us for dinner? I made bread from scratch. Oh, and these ridiculous mac 'n' cheese BLT things that my dad was in love with … I made them every

Sunday after church for years." Her voice trails off and her eyes get glassy for a second.

"Did we have sex last night?" Michael asks and surprisingly, Lilith's blush actually seems to fade a little. She blinks in surprise for a second and then smiles.

"No," she says with a small laugh. "*You* all might've been blackout drunk, but I remember what we did."

"What *did* we do?" I ask and she gives me this scorching look that drums up memories of sweaty naked bodies and wet, wet heat. I shiver slightly.

"You're sure?" Michael asks and Lilith nods, looking him straight in the face.

"You collapsed on the edge of the bed and feel asleep. Honestly, I guess I was pretty fucking drunk because we shouldn't have … done anything with you around like that."

"I was passed out," he whispers and then runs his hand through his hair again. This time, he actually smiles at her. "I don't care what you guys do if I don't have to see it."

"Wow," Cope says when he climbs the steps to the bus and smells the rich velvety scents of cheese and bacon, fresh bread and warm butter. My heart flutters a little because this whole scene—minus the lingerie—reminds me of my mother.

I breathe out low and deep as Cope comes to stand beside me and smiles.

"You cooked us dinner?" he asks and Lilith smiles back.

"Don't get too excited: this is partially me being selfish. My mom and dad went to the same church my whole life and if any member of the congregation passed away, they had this big potluck in the Sunday school building …" She pauses and takes a breath that looks an awful lot like the one I just took.

I want to fucking *marry* her.

And I've known her, like, five days.

"This is my dad's funereal potluck party," she says, squaring her shoulders. "His celebration of life dinner." She pauses as Pax and Muse join us on the bus next and take in the scene with a similar expression to the one I must've been wearing when I walked in here: surprise, excitement, heat. "Let me get dressed," she says suddenly, turning and giving us one last look

225

at that gorgeous ass wrapped in lace.

"Damn it, I missed the show?" Pax asks, wrinkling his nose at the pop music and surveying the food on the counters. Sometimes, Cope cooks but otherwise, it's takeout, the occasional restaurant or bar food. This is … nice. Totally unexpected, too.

"I don't think so," I say when Lilith reappears, her red hair shimmering down her back, this floor-length red dress sparkling on her curvy frame. "I think the second act is about to start."

"It was my prom dress," she says with a slight cringe, like she has no idea how fucking hot she looks in it. "But at least it still fits, right? I don't have a lot of clothes with me …"

"I could give you some money to shop with," Muse offers and I kick myself for not thinking of it. Muse always fucking thinks of everything. I smoke my cigarette and then pause to reach up and throw my hood back.

"I can't take your money," Lilith says with a shake of her head, the beaded fabric of her dress swishing as she walks, pulling a couple glass pans from the fridge that are full of macaroni and cheese.

"Who bought all of this stuff?" Muse asks, hazel eyes sparkling as he takes in Lilith's glittering form. All of that femininity breaking up the masculine on our bus is fucking refreshing as hell. I'd forgotten what it was like to have a girlfriend. I mean, not that all girls cook or whatever, but there's just this … aura that women have that I like. Or maybe I'm just imagining it because I'm straight as hell? I have no clue.

"I did," Lilith states proudly, putting her shoulders back as she takes a knife and starts cutting the cold mac 'n' cheese into squares. "I made some iced tea and lemonade, too, if you're thirsty."

"Vodka and lemonade," Pax says, licking his lower lip and watching Lilith like he's considering throwing her over the counter and fucking her. "That's what I'm having. Should I mix you a drink, Miss Lilith Tempest Goode?"

"I'd love that," she says, smiling at him in a way I haven't seen a girl do since Chloe died. Oh, girls *smile* at Paxton all the time. But not like that. Like they see something other than the music or the money or the suit.

"If you bought all of this," Muse continues, completely unperturbed by her avoidance of the subject, "then how much money do you have left?"

"It's ..." Lilith starts, but I can see the tense set of her shoulders as she greases up a pan and drops the first block of cold mac 'n' cheese into it. "I wanted to do this for my dad. For you guys. You've been great to me."

"Really?" Pax asks as he grabs a bottle of vodka from under the cabinet. "If that's what you think then people haven't been treating you right, Miss Lily. All we've done is fuck you."

"It's more than that," she says as she adds several more blocks of mac 'n' cheese to the pan, flipping them over when they brown and transferring them to a plate. "And anyway, two hundred dollars is nothing. I'd rather celebrate my dad with it here and now than use it to scrape by later. I'll figure it out. I think I'll sell my car."

Lilith keeps cooking the food while Muse digs in his pocket, pulls out his wallet and removes a wad of cash. When she isn't looking, he grabs her pink purse off one of the swivel chairs and shoves it in the side pocket, smiling at me when he catches me looking.

I don't say anything.

"If you guys want to sit down, I can bring you your food."

"Let me help," Cope says, stepping up next to her at the stove. "What can I do?"

He looks completely at home in the kitchen, even in his torn jeans and vintage band t-shirt. Cope's used to helping out like this. He practically raised himself. Both his mom and his grandmother had severe mental issues—anxiety, depression, loads of other shit—and he had to take care of all three of them. He's just lucky he doesn't seem to have inherited any of it. He did tell me once that he'll never have kids, just on the off chance they might get the wrong combination of genes from him.

That fucking sucks.

My mom was ... she was everything to me. Cope, *he* was everything for his mom. Even now, she treats him like the husband she never had. She cuddles him inappropriately—like *way* inappropriately—and takes his money and doesn't do shit for herself. It's weird and totally fucked-up. I know he hates it, even if he won't admit it. And I've known Copeland since I was twelve and he was sixteen; he was my 'mentor' sent from the high school to my middle school.

"Maybe butter the bread?" Lilith asks, gesturing over her shoulder with the spatula. "But be careful; the rolls might be hot."

Cope nods, reaching up to ruffle his hair with his fingers, messing up his careful faux hawk until his red hair's just mussed up and laying across his forehead. He washes his hands in the sink, shakes them out and dries them on a black dish towel. When he notices me watching, he smiles and raises his eyebrows.

"Want to show Lilith that we're not complete slobs? We do actually have a proper tablecloth and some fucking candles in here somewhere."

"Do you now?" she asks with a smile as she dishes up the hot squares of macaroni and layers them with bacon. "I've been snooping all over this place today and I haven't found them. Are these hidden away like the chairs?"

"Like the sex toys under the Bat Cave bed," Pax says with a cruel laugh, handing Lilith a glass with lemonade and vodka in it.

"I'll show you," I say, moving over to the couch and kneeling down, reaching underneath it for the small silver handle. In a space as tight as this, there's shit hidden everywhere. We could probably hide drugs here and survive a DEA raid.

Yanking the drawer open, I find the promised tablecloth and a few white pillar candles with a metal holder. Honestly, I think this shit's been in here since I was dating Kortney three fucking years ago. This is the same bus we used then and even though the entire interior was overhauled shortly after I broke up with her—including new leather on the couch—the stuff in this drawer's remain untouched. See what I mean? Even a remodel couldn't uncover these fossils.

I stare at the shit for a long time and then yank out the

tablecloth, sending a flutter of floral napkins scattering like a flock of birds.

As soon as I see them, I feel like I'm about to puke.

"Jesus," Muse whispers, bending down and gathering them up as I sit there and shake like the pathetically useless piece of shit that I am. "Ransom," he says, trying to get my attention. I ignore him, staring at the napkins with wide eyes.

My mom gave me these napkins. She said even bachelor boys should have nice napkins, just in case they meet a nice girl. Because nice girls need nice dinners. She taught me how to fold them into shapes—bow ties, fans, pinwheels, hearts.

I sit back on my ass with one of the napkins in my hand, just staring at it and wondering if it, too, smells like violets or if it's just the perfume I spray on all my clothes.

Muse throws the tablecloth and candles on the couch, shoving the drawer closed and gathering up the rest of the napkins. They're white with tiny purple flowers—fucking *violets*—all over them. My mom was raped and killed on a violet bedspread that looked just like this.

"Ransom," Muse says carefully, getting on his knees in front of me and trying to catch my attention. I jerk my hood up over my face and close my eyes tight against the rush of feeling. It's not like this shit happens everyday; it doesn't. But something about Lilith, about her own grief for her father, it's bringing mine rushing up to the surface.

"Ran?" Lilith asks, using my nickname. I like that, her acting familiar with me when she doesn't know me for shit. I'm just this weird, scarred up, fucked-up guy with a dead mom and blood on his hands. I wish I'd died that night, from all the times that piece of shit stabbed *me* before *he* died.

I should've bled to death in that alley.

I would've probably if Copeland hadn't followed me that night and found me lying there next to a dumpster, next to a corpse.

Lilith climbs onto the couch, past Muse and straight over to me, sliding her arms around my neck and pulling my head between her knees, curving her body around mine. Like I said, doesn't know me for shit. Gets me completely.

"I know they're ugly napkins," she whispers, smelling like butter and garlic, "but we can make them work. I promise."

A small laugh claws its way out of my throat as I reach up a hand and curl my fingers around one of hers, squeezing tight. Her warmth, her smell, her touch, it all takes me away from that edge, just like Paxton's embrace did this morning. Maybe I need to stop investing in one-night groupies and start investing in real relationships again? Because this is nice.

Nice.

Nice girl, nice napkins.

I lift up the white and purple cloth and tuck it into Lilith's fingers.

CHAPTER THIRTY-ONE

Muse

DEREK "MUSE" MUSER

After Ran's breakdown, he clings to Lilith's side like they're a couple, but I don't much mind. When he gets like that, all sick in the face and far away, I want to crawl inside his hood and die right along with him. His grief is all consuming, like a wave. I can *feel* it in my chest.

"That dinner was fucking *awesome,*" I tell Lilith, glancing over at her in that shimmery red dress of hers, curled up between Ran and me. "Mac 'n' cheese BLTs. I didn't even know that was a thing."

"It's a recipe I learned from one of my mom's friends. Cook up the mac, cool it in the fridge, fry it up, and voila, you've got yourself some seriously delicious fucking 'bread'. I mean, who *doesn't* like the idea of bacon, cheese and butter all squashed together like that?"

"Hey," I ask as her fingers run through the dark brunette strands of Ransom's hair. "He asleep?"

Lilith pauses for a moment, leaning forward, her own red hair dangling in front of her face as she examines my friend.

"Yeah," she says with a long a sigh. "Yeah, I think he is."

I breathe out my own sigh of relief in the darkness, the bus dim and jostling as we drive toward Chicago, a movie flickering on the wall-mounted flat-screen to my left. It's situated just beneath the wall of windows that leads into the front of the bus where the driver sits. The curtains are drawn now, so nobody can see in here. Probably a good thing because I saw Octavia watching Lilith when she left the bus earlier today and *damn,* she's got it out for her.

Must be the Pax thing. Everybody knows Octavia's in love with him. Except for, you know, maybe Pax himself?

"Thank God," I say as Lilith leans her head against my shoulder and I get this hot, achy thrill down my fucking arm. Damn. I like her just as much like this as I did when she was on her knees and sucking my cock last night. Maybe more.

I put an arm around her shoulders just to see if she'll let me do it.

She does.

I smile.

"Derek?" she asks and I shiver again. I love my nickname— Muse is a seriously cool name, right?—but I like hearing my real name pass her shiny pink lips, too. Not sure why. Muse is a way better fucking name than Derek, but something about the way she says it makes it sound special. "Why were you emancipated at fifteen?"

"Well," I say as I tease a few silky strands of Lilith's hair with my bat covered fingers, "that's a very interesting story, but ..." She turns her head to look up at me, meeting my hazel eyes with her green ones. Across from me, Pax sits in one of the leather chairs fucking with his phone and pretending not to be paying attention to us. Michael sits in the next one over, the only person in this room actually watching the movie. And Cope, of course, sits on the other side of Ransom reading another damn romance novel.

This one has four half-naked guys on the cover and one girl.

I think I kind of know where he's coming from with that one.

But I have no fucking clue what my friends are doing with this girl. Me, I actually like her. I have no idea how the rest of this tour will go, but if I feel anything like I do right now—like I want to know more, more, more about her—then I'm buying her a plane ticket and taking her to Dublin with me. If she wants to go, that is.

"It's not important," I finish finally. Because it's not. My past is ... I've let it go cold. I don't hold onto it like Ran and Pax and Michael do. I just ... don't want to fucking think about it. Sweat starts to bead on my lower back and I know for damn sure that I'm lying to myself, but I can't help it. I just want to get as far away from all of that as I can. "Tell me something about you. Besides making homemade bread—which is a serious fucking feat by the way—what occupies your time? Are you a bookworm like Cope?"

He pauses to glance up at me and makes a face, but then his attention gets caught on Lilith and Ran and he smiles sadly. I wait until he refocuses back on the page. Even from here, I can very distinctly read the word *cock* about a thousand times. Hmm. So long as the word *moist* is absent from that page, maybe I could get into a romance novel or two?

I shake my head with a small smirk on my lips.

"Video games? Movies? Do you like building model airplanes?"

"Besides art," Lilith starts, looking down at Ran when he stirs. I get tense when I think another nightmare's coming on, but he's just adjusting himself, curling around the girl in the red dress with a gentle sigh. Well, shit. Look at that. Barely a week in and she's taming Ransom's demons. "I don't know." There's a long pause and she makes this sad, tight little smile. "I make a really good girlfriend," she says, cringing a little. "I know that's not exactly a hobby, but it's true. I'm a damn good fucking partner. I clean shit, and I cook, and I run hot bubble baths. I pay bills and organize junk drawers and tile bathroom walls."

She pauses and sighs again, this sad, weary sound that makes me wish I could pull her closer. But there's no way in hell that I'm disturbing Ransom, so I make myself be happy with what I've got, my arm wrapped around those beautiful shoulders of hers.

"I've been using all of that as an excuse not to learn anything about myself since I turned fifteen. That's why I wanted to know about your emancipation. Fifteen was when my mom died and I started dating this guy named Kevin Peregrine and I stopped caring what I liked or wanted or needed. I got over all of that grief by focusing on what *Kevin* wanted or needed. That, I'm damn good at it. I can tell what people need and get a sense of why." She plays with Ran's hair again and I feel suddenly guilty. Is that what she's doing here? Babysitting us? I don't want that.

"At fifteen, I learned to shut my emotions off and read everyone else's. I learned to feel what they were feeling so I didn't have to accept what *I* was feeling. So I'm good at that stuff, too. Like you said, all the practical shit."

"I noticed," she says, looking back up at me and smiling. "I went to grab some Chap Stick from my purse and found five hundred bucks shoved in the side pocket." There's a long pause. "I respect you and I'm not too proud, so I'm keeping it. But you didn't have to do that, you know. That's not why I bought this food or made this dinner. I just wanted to eat some good food with some good people and know that if my dad were watching me, that he'd be happy with what he saw."

She pauses, smiles, grins a little.

"I just hope he wasn't watching me *last night.*" Her grin flickers, fades, that beautiful mouth settling into a sad, thin line. But I can tell it's not about the sex or the drinking or the wild dancing. She just misses him. A lot. And she hasn't processed it yet. I dragged her in here on this bus with the four of us and got her entangled in something that I'm sure neither of us understands yet.

As nice as this is, all this stuff that's happening between the five of us, it's still a clusterfuck.

See, practicality. That's my drug of choice. How can one girl be with four guys?

At some point, shit's going to come crashing down. That's why I'm thinking ahead. And right now, I'm thinking that I'd like her to be my girlfriend. But I'm also definitely *not* a hopeless romantic. I want to keep talking, hanging out, fucking, until we get to New York. Then I'll decide, ask her, see what she wants to do.

I tug a black afghan off the back of the couch and toss it over us—me, Lilith, Ransom, Cope.

"You want some tea?" I ask and Lilith's smile flickers back across her mouth for a minute.

"That'd be great," she says as I ease myself out from under her and she settles into the empty space, nestling her head on one of the decorative red pillows with the band's logo printed on them.

I move into the kitchen and start the teapot, cleaning up the dishes while I wait for the water to warm, scrubbing the counters until they gleam. At first I think Lilith's going to fall right asleep, but then she starts talking to me about all sorts of random things—her junior prom, her best friend from high school, the cat she left behind in Phoenix.

When I make our tea and squeeze back in beside her, she puts her head in my lap and we talk for hours.

By the time we fall asleep, drifting off with whispered memories still trailing from our lips, we're already in Chicago.

CHAPTER THIRTY-TWO

A knock at the front door wakes me up, but I ignore the sound, rolling onto my side and finding myself wrapped around a hard warm body. *Kevin?* I think because who else would be in my apartment at this hour? But then I remember that Kevin fucked anyone and everyone he could get his hands on and gave me a goddamn STD and I snap to with a sharp gasp, flicking my eyes open to the curved ceiling of Beauty in Lies' tour bus.

I assume at first that it's Ransom I'm sleeping with, but then I glance up and find Paxton's tattooed chest moving in a slow, easy rhythm. Rolling toward the door, I find Ransom in his hoodie padding toward it in bare feet.

"Octavia?" he asks with a yawn, stepping back to let his manager come up the steps. "You're up early. Did you want a cup of coffee?"

"No, thank you," she says crisply as I wonder when and how I traded out Muse and Ransom for Paxton. Cope was here for a while, too. Come to think of it, Michael was still sitting in one of the swivel chairs when I passed out. Huh.

I lay there for a moment, enjoying the sound of Pax's heart beating beneath my ear. It's proof he really is human, even with his perfect suits and his sharp smiles. But then I think of him putting his arms around Ransom and I know he's not as big of an asshole as he pretends to be.

"I was actually hoping to speak with Paxton ..." she says, trailing off as she spots me lying on his bare chest, his button-up undone and crumpled on either side of his sleeping body.

The look in Octavia's brown eyes is one of complete shock.

"Want me to wake him up?" I ask, forcing myself up into a sitting position between his legs, trying to put a little space between us. I glance down and find his grey eyes cracking open to stare at me.

"I'm awake," Pax groans, but he doesn't bother to keep his eyes open. He closes them again and lays his arm across his face. "What is it?"

"I …" Octavia stutters and then just stops talking, like she has no idea what to make of me. I guess she was under the impression that I was here with … Muse? Cope, maybe? Ransom? I guess she just definitely didn't see me with Paxton.

And she doesn't like that. At fucking *all*.

"Are you free for breakfast?" she asks finally, puffing her chest up with courage and laying into me with a steely defiance that I meet with a sympathetic smile. She's in love with Pax; I'm fucking him. I'm not sure what there is to say in all of that.

"Breakfast? For what? Because I'm not doing that *Parade for Paxton* bullshit again."

"No, the label's attorneys decided it was too big of a liability after the first night. We won't be doing that again."

"Oh, great," Pax says, dropping his arm off the side of his couch and opening his eyes again. He sits up and ruffles his hair with his fingers. "They decided it's too damn dangerous *after* I go and do it. Like I said, what a bunch of shite. It was a stupid idea anyway. What bloody twat came up with that one?"

"It was me," Octavia says, her cheeks flushing bright. She covers up her embarrassment by reaching up and adjusting her ponytail. She's not wearing her usual black t-shirt and jeans. This morning, she's got on a cute little black wool peacoat buttoned to the throat, a red scarf, and a pair of black leggings tucked into boots.

Uh-oh.

I scramble up to my knees and peek out the window above the couch, shoving aside the black curtains and finding … snow.

It's snowing in Chicago.

And I have literally *nothing* appropriate to wear.

"Well, it was a dumb idea," Pax says, completely

unapologetic as he reaches over and drags me into his lap. I start to protest because this whole interaction with Octavia is making me feel slightly off, but then I glance at the gorgeous stormy grey of Pax's eyes and I'm completely done for. "If it's not for business, I'll pass on breakfast."

"Okay," Octavia says, but when I try to turn and look at her, Pax touches the side of my face and leans in to press his mouth to mine. "Don't forget that we have an early show tonight—doors open at *six*."

Vaguely, I recognize the sound of her boots pounding down the metal steps, the front door closing, the lock flicking into place. But Paxton's slanting his mouth over mine, slicking his tongue between my lips, tasting me with heady, desperate *want*.

"Wait, wait," I whisper, pulling away slightly and watching as a smirk crawls across his face. "Do you have a thing with Octavia?"

"Octavia?" he asks and then laughs—and not in a nice way. "That corporate lapdog? Fuck no."

"I think she really likes you," I say and Pax pauses like he's never even bothered to consider that. But then he just shrugs and leans over the arm of the couch to dig in the side table. Other than condoms and lubricant, I guess the band also keeps cigarettes in there. As far as I can tell, Cope's the only one that doesn't smoke at all.

"Well, I don't much fancy her, I can tell you that," Pax says as he lights up and I grab the black afghan, curving it around my shoulders and smiling at Ransom as he brings me a cup of coffee without my even having to ask.

"You've never slept with her?" I ask and Paxton laughs again, shaking his head like the idea's deplorable to him. "Why not? She's pretty enough."

"You *want* me to shag her, Miss Lily?" Pax asks as I turn toward him and tuck my back against the arm of the couch. The way he looks at me before he stands up and goes into the kitchen for coffee is ... hard to decipher.

"No," I say because even though I'm fucking four of these guys, the thought of any of them with another girl makes me feel ... oddly possessive.

238

"Guess we're in bloody agreement then, aren't we?" he jokes as he moves into the perfectly clean kitchen and pours himself a mug.

I feel terrible; I should never have let Muse clean up last night. Or at the very least, I should've helped him out a little. I wanted to honor Dad with a good meal, but I also wanted to take care of the boys for a night. I'm not the only who's suffered here, who's lived through some seriously messed up stuff. Just *thinking* of that look on Ransom's face when he found his mother's napkins makes me feel so sick inside that I want to start crying and never stop.

"Morning," Michael says, stepping out of the hallway dressed in a pair of dark navy jeans tucked into thick black boots, and a long winter coat. Somebody's prepped and ready for the snow. "Vanessa wants some Chicago souvenirs and I need to get some sort of present anyway since she's meeting us in Atlanta—"

"She's meeting us in fucking Atlanta?!" Pax asks, whirling on his friend. "What the fuck, Mikey?"

"Yeah, her and Tim," Michael says, and I'm completely lost in the conversation. I have no idea who Tim is. *Vanessa's coming to Atlanta?* Interesting. I guess I'll finally get to meet the girl that holds the heart to Beauty in Lies' lead guitarist.

"Tim is Michael's older brother," Ran whispers in my ear before he sits down on the couch and takes my feet into his lap. "He raised Michael from age ten and up."

"And you didn't think to say anything until now? Well, that's just lovely. I can't wait to see that bitch again," Pax drawls in his sexy as hell British accent, giving Michael this cold, hard glare that matches the weather outside.

"You don't have to see much of her; she's staying in a hotel."

"Well thank the bloody gods for that. It's been, what, a year since you fucked anyone—including her? I don't even want to *hear* the repercussions of that mess."

"Guess you wouldn't considering you'd never get over the gap in our skill levels. Once you'd seen me fuck, it'd be hard for you to ever kid yourself that women were actually pleased with what you have to offer."

C. M. Stunich

"Sure thing, you bollocking prick," Pax says as he alternates between smoking and drinking his coffee. "Go on then, get out of here and go buy some *Made in China* t-shirt thats say *Chicago* on the front. Vanessa always did like cheap crap. She's dating you, isn't she?"

"Eat shit, Pax," Michael says, but he smiles a truly excited smile and glances over at me. "I fucking doubt you were wearing snow boots and wool in Phoenix," he says and I blink a few times in surprise as Michael comes over to stand next to me, smelling like that pomegranate spice shampoo I've been using from the boys' bathroom.

His violet eyes take me in with a completely different regard this morning than they did the last few days. I guess just knowing he'll get to see—and most definitely *fuck*—his girlfriend in a few days has improved his mood considerably.

"I want to apologize," he says, but I can't quite figure out what he's apologizing for. "For being a dick to you. I know you're not out to get me. I'm just … a little wound up."

"Try a *lot* wound up," Pax murmurs and I stifle a laugh as Michael runs his tongue across his lower lip and throws a glare back in Paxton's direction.

When he looks back at me though, he makes himself smile again.

"I thought you might want to come with me to shop? It'd be nice to have a woman's opinion on this gift thing, and I thought maybe I could get you a coat and boots to make up for being a complete asshole."

"That gift better not be a *ring*," Pax says as he sets his coffee on the counter and disappears down the hallway, scooting out of the way to let Muse pass by.

"You're heading out?" he asks as he pauses next to Michael and looks between me and him. "Because if so, I'd love to go with you guys. I want to buy Lilith some clothes."

"You don't have to do that," I say, but Muse just shrugs, looking young and sexy in a white hoodie layered underneath that leather zip-up sweatshirt from the other night. His silver-black hair is already styled, and he's even got on some eyeliner.

I feel a little ridiculous sitting in my old prom dress,

shedding glitter and tiny glass beads everywhere.

"If you're going, I'd like to go, too," he says with another shrug, smiling at me and putting his tattooed hand in his pants pocket. "A coat and boots sounds nice, but aren't you like, seriously low on underwear? The roadies don't do laundry as often as you'd think." His smile gets a little dirty and I feel myself running my tongue over my lower lip, unconsciously returning the flirtation. "And let's be honest: we haven't exactly been kind to your poor underwear."

"Mr. Practical again," I say as I reluctantly pull my feet from Ran's lap and put them on the heated floors. *Oh, that feels nice.* Not as nice as the press of Ransom's rough thumb against my arch, but still amazing. "I guess I can't go another week with the three pairs I have."

"Hey, I was considering being completely impractical and buying you a lacy teddy and some garter belts, too. Maybe a pleather nurse outfit? A schoolgirl uniform?"

I laugh as I stand up, finishing the last gulp of coffee in my cup.

"I'll go," I say as I rinse my mug out at the sink. "But I'm not letting you guys buy me anything. I can purchase my own underwear, thank you very much."

CHAPTER THIRTY-THREE

Lilith

LILITH GOODE

The boys bundle me up and we head into the city, leaving the venue tucked away in a suburb of Chicago. In the snow and the traffic, it takes our hired car over an hour and a half to get to this eight story mall at the base of an enormous skyscraper.

When I first moved to Phoenix, the sheer volume of people in the city overwhelmed me to a point where Kevin had to really work to get me to leave the apartment. I mean, Gloversville, NY has a population of less than sixteen thousand people while the Phoenix metro area is in the millions mark. But I adapted, even if I never really *liked* the lonely anonymity of a crowd.

Still, the sheer number of people inside the Water Tower Place shopping mall is almost staggering. I stick myself between Muse and Michael and follow along. Michael has some app on his phone that gives directions around the mall and shows him where all the shops are. I'm more than happy to be a backseat driver on this one.

"Are you guys going to get recognized in here?" I ask Muse as I look up at him, at the four black piercings above his brow, at his black and silver mohawk. It's styled conservatively today, but there's just *something* about him that says *rockstar.* I can't decide if it's the eyeliner, the careful but confident smile, or the black boots with the white skulls all over them. Maybe all of the above?

"Possibly," Muse says as Michael steers us toward a jewelry store and my heart starts to thunder in my chest. *"That gift better not be a* ring.*"* Would Pax have even brought that up if it

242

wasn't a possibility? As I watch Michael pause at the store's threshold and narrow his eyes on the glass cases and the slickly dressed salespeople, I feel myself wishing I could get to know him like I'm getting to know the other guys. And it's not just because I'm a crazy slut that needs to add another dude to her harem. He just … I don't know. There's more to him than meets the eye. "But our security team will take care of it if anything gets out of control."

"Security team?" I ask as Muse turns me around by the shoulders and points out a woman sitting on a nearby bench, a man window-shopping a few storefronts away. "You have bodyguards?"

Muse laughs and shrugs his shoulders.

"Yeah, the record label makes us take them out with us, but sometimes I forget they're even around. They have their own car and they don't talk to us unless shit goes down." Muse tucks his fingers into his black and white pinstriped skinny jeans and watches the male guard for a moment before turning his attention back to me. "It's not like anybody's trying to shoot at us or anything," he says with a small smile. "At least, nobody has yet."

"Were they at the club with us, too?" I ask as Muse and I turn back around and find Michael standing in the exact same spot, rubbing one tattooed hand down an equally tattooed arm. He started sweating in the car ride over and chucked his coat. Now that I'm standing in here, wrapped up in my only coat—the rest either got stolen or left in my damaged car—I wish I'd left mine, too. It's *stifling*.

"They were," Muse says as he smiles at a pair of giggling girls and gives them a wave. I can't tell if they just think he's hot or if they recognize him from the band. Then, of course, I see that the girl on the right is wearing a *Beauty in Lies* t-shirt. Wow. I keep forgetting how popular these guys are.

And I'm fucking them all. Well, except for Michael.

I smile as we approach the guitarist in question, looking like your typical hot as hell but totally dickish metalcore prick. My sister used to date guys like this; I was never into them. Until now, I guess.

C. M. Stunich

"What's wrong?" I ask as Michael narrows his violet eyes on the salespeople, keeping them all safely at bay. I notice a few of the girls—and one of the guys—checking him out. I can't blame them; Michael looks damn good today. His body is tight and muscular, but he's not bulky. He's tall and lean and his hair is razored and dark as night, a startling contrast to the soft color of his eyes. His face is hard and masculine, and he's just dripping with well-placed tattoos. All the shapes and colors blend together in this seamless line from one hand, up and across his shoulders and chest, and down to his other hand. In the blue band tee he's wearing, a lot of them are invisible, but I remember them. That first night, looking up and seeing him in the shadows of the Bat Cave's doorway, I felt my heart skip several beats.

Vanessa is a lucky girl.

"You don't have to get her jewelry, you know," I say as he turns his attention back to me and Muse. Well, mostly to me. He stares into my eyes and makes my heart do that same skittering, stopping thing again. I pretend not to notice, pulling the black knit cap off my head and shaking my long hair out of its loose knot.

Michael watches it cascade down my back and glances away suddenly.

"Vanessa's old fashioned; she'll want jewelry," he says matter-of-factly, but not at all like he's excited about it. I remember his good mood from the bus and feel my lips turn down slightly. Maybe the whole idea of getting her a gift is stressing him out?

"If she loves you, she won't care what you get her as long as you put some thought into it." I try not to think of Kevin, but I don't have any other real relationship to compare it to. My first boyfriend was nice, but we were so young and we only dated for three months before he moved away. Still, I remember this one time he picked me flowers on his way to school. Stuff like that totally counts, you know.

"Right. You've *definitely* not met Vanessa then," Muse says with a small laugh, drawing Michael's ire in his direction. "What? It's just ... Lilith wouldn't say that if she'd met the girl."

244

"I cheated on her, Muse," Michael says blatantly. "While she was *pregnant.* She has a right to be angry."

"Sure, but at some point she has to stop punishing you and move on or else she should break up with your ass. Besides, you didn't *know* she was pregnant."

I stand there and listen to them argue, but the word *pregnant* gets caught in my mind on a loop.

"You have a kid?" I ask and Michael shakes his head.

"She miscarried pretty early," he says and then he moves into the store and stares at the sea of shiny jewels like he's never seen anything like them in his life. Or maybe like they could grow legs, break out of the glass, and glom onto his face, suck the life right out of him. Yeah, that's more or less what he looks like right now. "What about a bracelet?"

"A bracelet?" I ask as I step up beside him and think about the last bracelet Kevin bought me. It was beautiful, ridiculously expensive. He tore it off my wrist when we broke up. I saw one of his new girlfriends wearing it once when I came to get the last box of my stuff out of our apartment—the apartment that I painted and tiled and replaced the bedroom carpet in.

I'm such an idiot.

"Definitely not a bracelet," I say as I sigh and Michael reaches up a hand, giving my shoulder a squeeze.

"You are tense as *fuck,*" he tells me and I blink sharply up at him as he gives me a weird look. "What the hell are my friends doing to you? When I was having as much sex as you are, I could barely stand up I was so relaxed. My body was like fucking jelly. The *only* part of me that was hard was my dick."

A laugh bursts out of my throat and I clamp a hand across my lips as Muse slides a finger along the gold rim of the cases, moving in a circle around the room and pausing next to a case on the far side, squinting and leaning in to examine the jewelry.

"I'm just thinking about my ex," I respond honestly and Michael wrinkles up his face.

"Pax told me about him," he says and then sighs, letting go of my shoulder. "The cheater, right?" I make a face and he shakes his head. "Don't worry about being politically correct with me. I know that what I did was fucked-up. Your ex, he's a royal fucking asshole. I'm one, too, so I get to say that."

"Well, thank you for that," I say as I breathe out a long sigh, studying the curve of Michael's lower lip. It's full and pouty when it's not curled up in an angry scowl. "So, tell me, how long have you and Vanessa been together?"

"Five years," Michael says and I feel my mouth twitch a little.

Five years. That's how long Kevin and I lasted; I wish someone would've helped me cut that cord sooner.

"Five years," I repeat as I walk slowly and reach up to unzip my white leather jacket. I layered one of Ransom's black hoodies underneath, partially because of the snow but mostly because I wanted to smell violets while I was out shopping today. "Tell me what you love about her," I say, and I'm not just asking because I want to help him pick out the right gift. I truly, sincerely want to know; my curiosity's gotten the better of me.

"What I love about her?" he echoes, like I've asked a question that's virtually impossible to answer. I glance back at him, at the tightness of his navy blue band t-shirt, the words *Beauty in Lies* stamped across the front in big, block capital letters. Underneath, there's a sketch of that convertible with the five stick figures inside of it, the same drawing I saw projected on the curtain at the show.

"Yeah. Tell me why you'd pick Vanessa over any other girl."

I stop walking and watch him expectantly as I slip my jacket down my shoulders and then shrug out of the hoodie, putting both items in the crook of my elbow.

"I love that she has the power to forgive," he says, and I smile. But Michael doesn't. In fact, he looks pissed off when he tears his gaze from the brightly lit cases to stare at me.

"I like that," I say as I mull his words over in my head. The power to forgive. I wish I could say I had that, too, but when I think about what Kevin did to me ... What's even worse is the way he handled it. I was upset; I was crying. I'd just been diagnosed with a disease that *he* gave me and yet he had the audacity to treat me like I was the one who'd done something wrong.

No, I'm not ready to forgive Kevin. Maybe someday I'll be

as strong as Vanessa, but not now.

"My mom and dad got married way too early, but somehow they made it work," I tell Michael, saying the words but not really *feeling* them. How could I? Could I really stand here in this busy, crowded mall with all these breathing, laughing, smiling people and think about my dead parents? All of this life, all around me, and the dead cling to my heart like ghosts. "On their five year anniversary, my dad bought my mom a charm bracelet with a rhodonite crystal on it, in the shape of a tear drop."

I look up and make my mouth smile, even though inside I'm dying a little bit.

I lift my left wrist and jingle the charm bracelet around, touching the splotchy pink and black gemstone with a finger.

"Rhodonite stands for love and forgiveness," I explain as Michael walks over to me and wraps his fingers around the pale skin of my forearm, gently pulling on my arm until I extend my wrist toward him. "Some people also believe it helps heal emotional wounds and scars. My dad said he chosen it for her because he wanted to make the clear distinction that this would be the last teardrop he'd ever give her."

Michael smooths his thumb over the pulse point in my wrist, using his other hand to gently turn the bracelet and study the other charms hanging from it. I've collected a lot of them since Mom died. In fact, the *only* ones she ever added to the bracelet were little birthstones—one for me and one for Yasmine.

It makes me sick that out of the four people this bracelet used to represent, I'm the only one left alive.

My eyes well with tears, but I blink them back as Michael lets go of my wrist and I spin back to the jewelry case, rubbing and tugging at my tear ducts with my middle fingers and trying to keep the moisture in my eyes from running down my face.

"You could get her a teardrop necklace," I suggest in a slight sniffle as Michael steps up next to me. "As a promise that you'll never make her cry again. Or maybe just something out of rhodonite?" I point out a shiny heart wrapped in silver leaves. "That's rhodonite right there. It's a unique stone; I'm surprised they even sell it here."

"Are you okay?" he asks in a quiet voice. "Do you want to grab a shake or something?"

"I want to help you pick the perfect gift," I say on the end of a long sigh, dropping my arms by my sides and dropping my coat and hoodie to the floor on accident. Michael and I both bend down at the same time to pick them up and almost bump our heads together. When I glance up, I see him looking right at me, his lips just a few careful inches away.

"He must've been a real romantic, your dad," he whispers. "I wish I had some of that in me."

Michael gathers up my hoodie and jacket, but he drapes them over his own arm instead of handing them back to me.

"Romance isn't about jewelry, Michael," I say as I nod my chin at the coat and sweater. "It's about meaningful gestures." We look at each other for a long time, long enough that I know something could happen between us if either of us let it.

Neither of us will.

I rise to my feet and glance over to find Muse watching the two of us with a strange smile on his face.

"Did you pick something out yet?" he asks as I brush off the knees of my white leggings and glance over at Michael.

He glances inside the case one more time and then flicks his violet eyes over to mine, stealing my breath away. He doesn't look so mean or angry in that moment. Just … hopeful. His smile, when he does give it, is heartbreakingly beautiful.

"Is it okay if I have a few minutes alone to think?"

"Sure thing," Muse says, curling his fingers around mine and drawing my attention back to his face. "Lilith and I still need to pick out some underwear."

He drags me away from the jewelry store, and I squeeze his hand tight, trying to cool the sudden aching in my heart. There are so many painful emotions fighting for supremacy in there that I feel sick. There's the fresh bloody red hurt of Dad's passing, the old scabbed wounds of Mom's cancer and Yasmine's murder, the dark purple bruise of Kevin's betrayal. And something else, too. I have no idea what that is. But it aches and sloshes and burns my insides when I walk.

God.

Maybe I shouldn't have told Michael that story? I feel exposed and open now, like maybe some of my pain is dripping in a red trail behind me as I walk, just this bright ruby sparkling of blood from all of my emotional wounds.

When he catches up to us, he's got a shiny black bag held loosely at his side and a decidedly *romantic* smile on his face. I smile back at him when he glances over at me. And he didn't think he had it in him … I wonder what he picked out for her or if he'll show it to me?

"Where to next?" he asks as Muse pauses outside a women's lingerie store and points a finger at the gold and taupe striped walls inside.

"Panties?" he asks with a slight smirk.

"Or a *coat*," Michael says, pointing over his shoulder at a different shop. He's still holding my leather motorcycle jacket and Ran's hoodie for me. He makes no effort or sign that he wants to give them back. "It's fucking snowing outside."

"Oh come on, *under*wear is so much more fun that *outer*wear," Muse says with a sigh, like he already knows he'll give into whatever Michael wants. He gestures with the tattooed bats at his friend. "Whatever. Let's just get this over with so he's not scowling and bitching at us the whole time."

"Which I will fucking do if I don't get my way," Michael says, leading the way into the shop as I shrug my shoulders at Muse and we exchange an amused look.

"See how he is? Aren't you glad he's not a part of our, uh, ménage à cinq?"

"Ménage à cinq?" I ask, our hands still laced as we walk into the store behind Michael.

"You know, like a ménage à trois but with five people instead of three?" Muse winks at me and starts helping me navigate rack after rack after rack of beautiful—and *expensive* —clothing. He seems dead set on making me pick a few things out.

I try to resist at first, but eventually figure that it's just easier to give in and try a bunch of stuff on. Anyway, if buying me new clothes will make him happy then where's the harm in it? It doesn't feel like he's trying to patronize me or pay me off or make me his whore. Nothing at all as sinister as any of that. My pride demands that I turn him down, but my heart refuses.

Honestly, it feels like I'm on a date with my boyfriend.

"Muse and I have a new girlfriend ..."

Ransom's words ring in my head as I slip out of my clothes and pull on a tight green sequin minidress that my dad would've absolutely hated. Oh God, he could barely get past that red glimmering bodycon dress I wore to prom, and *it* didn't plunge between my breasts like this one does.

But Dad isn't here. *I* am. I'm partying with rockstars and hell, the boys always look so damn good, wouldn't it be nice if I felt good, too?

"Hey, Muse, can you zip this up for me?" I ask, peeping out the curtain and finding only Michael waiting for me outside the dressing room. "Where's Muse?" I ask as Michael's eyes lift up and catch sight of me in the dress.

"Holy shit," he says and I feel my cheeks warm with the unspoken compliment. "With that red hair and those eyes, you should wear green every-fucking-day."

"Thanks," I say as Michael ruffles up his dark hair and glances over his shoulder.

"Muse slipped away to grab something. Knowing him, it's probably inappropriate as fuck, and probably a gift for you." He smiles tightly and steps forward. "Need some help?"

"Um, yeah, that'd be great."

I turn around and sweep some hair over my shoulder, completely conscious of my bare back, the straps of my bra.

"So what'd you end up picking out for Vanessa?" I ask casually, desperate to know for whatever silly reason. I can't even *believe* I'm acting like I've got some stupid crush on Michael Luxe. I have the other *four* musicians in his band. Can't I just leave it at that? What the hell is wrong with me? And the guy has a damn girlfriend that he's buying expensive jewelry for.

Besides, whatever he is now, however faithful he's been to Vanessa since his indiscretions, he's still a cheater. And I could never get involved with a cheater again—especially not one who, you know, *cheats* on his girlfriend to be with me. Gross.

250

But then his warm fingers brush my spine and fire shoots through me, stealing my breath away in a vibrant blaze of heat. With slow purposeful intent, Michael drags the zipper up my back, scattering the butterflies in my stomach, making me wonder how the hell I'm going to stay standing up if he keeps touching me.

"There," he says, releasing me at the brink of my own annihilation. I glance accusingly over my shoulder, but if his eyes are heavy-lidded and his sexy lips parted, he acts like he doesn't give a fuck. "All zipped up. God. I forgot how much I loved helping a woman get dressed."

"You don't prefer to get her undressed?" I ask and as soon as I do, I regret it. Our eyes meet and my sex clenches tight; sweat pools on my throat and lower back. Sexual tension stretches tight between us, explaining away all of the anger and the stress of the last few days.

Michael didn't want me on the bus because ... he's attracted to me?

Maybe?

I swallow hard and he licks his lower lip. He's flirting, but I don't think he means to do it.

"Yeah, well, let's just say that a year of celibacy is a year too long. I can't wait to see Vanessa." He smiles wickedly at me, like we're sharing some sort of dark, delicious little secret.

"What do you think of the dress?" I ask, just to get him to look at something other than my face.

What a mistake.

Having Michael Luxe examine the long, pale lines of my legs, the tight pull of the dress across my hips and breasts ... that's a beautiful sort of agony.

"You look perfect in it," he says and then his smile gets even darker as he reaches out and traces a single finger over my hip. "Although you want might want to size up. You are curvy as hell, Lil."

Lil.

He has no right to call me Lil. But I want him to keep doing it.

I reach up and adjust the tags hanging from the inch wide

strap on my shoulder, peering down at the three figure price tag and feeling my eyes widen. My turn to curse.

"Fuck. There's no way I'm letting Muse buy me this," I laugh as I drop the tags, wanting to break whatever the hell this moment is with Michael. "The last time I got a dress this expensive, Kevin was buying me some hideous black frock to wear to one of his dad's corporate lawyer parties."

"How expensive was that dress compared to this one?" Michael asks, his voice a little breathy. I tell myself not to look down, not to examine his navy jeans for ... that. I look up and our eyes lock again.

"Um, half as?" I say and then gasp as Michael reaches over and snaps the tags off the front of the dress.

His smile is ... well, it's not romantic anymore.

"Tell the boys they can thank me later for this one," he says and then steps back, dropping the curtain into place and leaving me completely ... breathless.

CHAPTER THIRTY-FOUR

Michael

I took the flirting with Lilith too far.

I know that, and I feel like such an awful fucking shit for it. I try to call Vanessa in the car on the way back to the venue, but she can't or won't answer. Doesn't matter. Three more nights until I get to see her, kiss her, fuck her. Once I do, Lilith won't even be a blip on my radar.

Right.

I'll just look right past her curvy naked form draped all over my bus for the next week and a half, ignore the moans escaping from her lips as my friends fuck her and I wish like hell that *I* was fucking her, too.

Jesus.

Why did I buy her that damn dress? That skintight fucking green dress that turns her hair to fire and brings out the color in her eyes?

Goddamn it, I am fucking losing *it.*

Must be all the sex hormones, just chemicals and shit backed up and screwing with my brain. I mean, I've been masturbating like five times a day for the last week, but it doesn't seem to help. It's hard to feel satisfied with a bottle of lube and my own five fingers when the guys are having these wild orgies in the back rooms of nightclubs and shit.

I lean against the wall and pretend I don't notice Paxton and Lilith making out three careful feet away from me. His hands are all over that old Hollywood body of hers, tracing those curves with arduous reverence, cupping her ass and dragging that green dress up several terrifying inches.

Fuck.

I rub my hands down my face. I really don't want to go onstage with a hard-on, but if they keep this shit up …

My hands fall to my sides and I catch sight of our manager, Octavia, watching the two of them kiss and fondle each other. The expression on that thin pixie face of hers is nothing short of murderous, and the way she's looking at Lilith … I would not put it past Octavia to stir up some imaginary trouble for her in the future.

The old brick wall behind my back and the shiny polished wood floor beneath my feet reverberate with sound, shaking me up, turning my blood into this frothy mess of emotion. I *need* to see Vanessa. And I need to stop obsessing about some strange girl that none of us knows a damn thing about. For all we know she could be some undercover reporter or something.

But that hurt in her eyes when she talked about her father … nobody can fake that level of emotion. It's been sixteen years since my parents died, and I still think about them all the damn time.

I make a point to keep my attention off of Pax and Lilith and study the crew backstage. During our last tour, we had a bunch of gossipy assholes on staff. This time, the label's really buckled down and I have yet to see anyone act less than professional. Sure, they still party and smoke pot and fuck, but the gossip and the drama is at a minimum. Of course, everyone's curious about the new girl, the girl that's sleeping on our bus, that's been kissed and fondled and teased by every member of our band except for me.

"Thanks again for the dress," Lilith says, surprising me. I manage not to show it and glance casually in her direction, my body reacting instantly to the swollen redness of her lips, her dilated pupils and the dark eyeshadow around her glittering gaze. She's so ethereally beautiful in that moment that for a second there I question if she's even human. Maybe she's a succubus come to steal the souls of the boys on my bus? Considering her name, that would make some sort of sense.

"You're welcome," I say as she leans against the wall next to me. Whether by accident or design, our arms brush and desire coils tight and hard inside of me. *I'm sorry, Vanessa,* I think, but I can't control my thoughts, just my actions.

I scoot a few careful inches away—even though it fucking kills me.

God, I need to get laid.

"Where'd Pax go?"

With great fucking effort, I tear my gaze away from Lilith and close my eyes against the smoky backstage haze. Pax says everyone here looks like a card-carrying member of the dark faerie court, like at any moment they might shed their beautiful glamours and morph into something hideous. Sometimes, I even believe that.

"Your manager said she needed him."

I smile meanly, my eyes still closed.

"I'll bet she did."

"She really likes him, doesn't she?"

"Guess so."

There are several long moments where neither of us talks. The kick drum shakes the ground beneath my feet and the aching melancholy of the lead singer's voice tears into me, giving me the jitters, making me excited to get onstage in I way I haven't felt for a long time.

Or hell, maybe that's Lilith that's doing that? This isn't the first time I've felt another band's music inside of me, listened to them pour their hearts out onstage. The only factor in this equation that's been changed is this girl, this Mary Sue that I shouldn't like but do anyway.

I think I kind of want to get up there and show off.

"That's for the advice in the jewelry store," I tell her as I crack my eyes open and drop my gaze down to Lilith's face. She's studying the action backstage with a novice's gleam in her eye, but a practical set to her lips that says she knows this life isn't all glitter and drugs and sex. There's not a single guy on our bus that hasn't had it hard, that hasn't hated his life so damn much that he's wanted to die. That's what makes Beauty in Lies so fucking good. We play our music with pain. "I never did tell you what I picked out, did I?"

"You don't have to tell me if you don't want to," she says, pushing away from the wall, her dress reflecting back stray shafts of light from the stage as she moves. "My mom didn't reveal that story about my dad until she was on her death bed. Some memories are just too precious to share."

"Why did you tell me then?" I ask, digging my fingertips into the bricks behind me, looking for some way to ground myself. "If it was such a big secret?"

"My parents are both dead," she says as her eyes get this far away look that I recognize so damn well. In the mirror, in my friends' faces. Maybe *that's* why they like this girl so much? Misery loves company—especially when that misery's born from the same monster. Lil's monster looks awfully familiar. "One is ash; the other is about to be. All they are now is their stories, their secrets. At this point in time, I'm the only one that knows them. If something were to happen to me, everything they were would die along with me."

She smiles and reaches up to squeeze my arm.

"Now you know, too. It makes me feel better, thinking that there's somebody else out there carrying around the secret of the rhodonite tear." She points to her jingling charm bracelet and laughs a little. The sound is forced and tight, but it stirs some warm, primal bullshit in my belly. Like I have *any* claim on this girl whatsoever. This feeling alone is reason enough to stay away from her; I feel like I'm betraying Vanessa with my *thoughts.*

When the fuck did I let myself get beaten so damn low?

Vanessa and I *really* need to have a talk about our relationship.

Lilith watches me for a moment, her eyes big and green, lashes long and dark. I'm not sure if they're natural or not. Do redheads have red eyelashes? I have no fucking clue.

"Michael, it's showtime," Octavia says, popping up and putting a hand on my arm. She throws Lilith a tight smile that's about as inviting as a bucketful of rusty nails and moves away, giving us one last second to be alone.

"Do you think some pasts are so dark they overshadow the future no matter what you do?" I ask, and I have no idea where that question comes from.

"Is that what you think?" Lilith asks, looking up at me with a curious smile, red tendrils of hair falling across her pale forehead. Without thinking, I reach out to brush them away, letting the atmosphere of the evening get to me. With all the glitter and the sex and the smoke, everything feels sensual and desperate, like this is my last night on earth.

If it were, I'd probably choose to spend it with Lilith; I want to know what that sad mouth tastes like, what that curvy body feels like beneath mine in bed.

"Maybe."

"Then we're both fucked I guess."

She tries not to smile when she says it, but I can tell she doesn't believe that at all.

Her confidence … somehow makes me feel a hell of a lot better about my own life.

CHAPTER THIRTY-FIVE

Lilith

Beauty in Lies takes the stage behind that same long white curtain I saw at the first show, the animated sequence projected across it making the Chicago crowd shout and cheer as colorful confetti fills the air like red and pink rain.

I lift my face to it with a smile, letting little bits of paper stick to my sweaty skin as I curl my fingers around the bar of the metal divider in front of me. My body leans toward the stage like a flower fighting to kiss the sun as I listen to a voiceover introduce the band to the city. People push against me, their bodies stacked tight, tense and giddy with excitement.

At this particular venue, I'm not allowed to stand in front of the divider with the roadies—it's security staff only—so when their backs were all turned, I snuck behind them and climbed the fence to stand in the crowd. The people waiting there were surprisingly excited about it, cheering me on and letting me cut in front of them.

A sense of camaraderie settles over the massive room as the curtain slides up and away, revealing the now familiar silhouettes of my boys—and Michael, of course—as Pax makes his way to the front of the stage and I feel my mouth tingling with the memory of his kiss. Honestly, I was surprised he wanted to kiss me in public, in front of all the tour staff, the venue staff, his glaring manager. But if Pax wants to keep whatever relationship he has with me secret, he doesn't act like it.

I try to imagine what the public would think if they found

258

out that I was fucking four of the five members of the band. Would they think less of the boys? Would they think less of *me*? I decide then and there that I don't give a shit. This is my body and my life and when I'm with them—*any* of them—I don't feel the gaping darkness of my own mortality, the inevitability of my loneliness, the wrenching ache of my father's demise.

"Hello, hello, Chicago," Pax says, dressed in a charcoal grey suit with a white shirt and a red tie. His cuff links are pairs of silver drumsticks that I can't quite make out from where I'm standing. No, from here, they're just these two spots of glimmering metal on a man that's all polished perfection and easy, cold grace. "We're Beauty in Lies from Seattle, Washington. My name is Paxton Blackwell, and this"—he pauses to lick his lips and pull the mic off the stand—"this is *Me in Ruins*."

"On the count of three," shouts a drunk brunette standing next to me. "One, two, three. WE LOVE SEATTLE!"

Her friends shout and cheer with her as I laugh and the crowd goes nuts as Pax stalks to the edge of the stage and wraps his tattooed hands around the mic, whispering the first few lines of the song without any accompanying music.

"I was up; you were down. We weren't making a sound." Pax points up and down along with the lyrics, and Michael starts strumming his purple guitar. "I'd have killed and died for you. Don't be cruel; I always played by the rules."

Cope starts drumming and the room around me erupts into chaos: people shouting and pumping their fists, cheering and jostling me with their movements.

"*WHY. DID. YOU. BETRAY ... !*" Pax growls, his voice deep and dark and completely chilling. My skin prickles with goose bumps as he drags the last note out and tilts his head back, dirty blonde hair gleaming in the purple haze of light that covers the stage. "*Betray and destroy and ruin me? YOU OBLITERATED MY CHANCES OF BEING HAPPY!*"

Pax lets go with a wordless animalistic scream while Ransom picks up the backup growls.

"*THERE'S NO MORE CHANCE OF BEING ME!*"

"*YOU DESTROYED EVERYTHING THAT I COULD BE!*"

Pax shouts, taking over again, slamming his foot against the stage, rocking out to his friends' music as the crowd forms a mosh pit just a few people away from me. They spin and whirl and kick and fight, spiking my adrenaline, making me wonder if I should join them or be afraid of them.

"There's just no way to recover it, that friendship we built. You ruined it, burned it and made it wilt. Somehow you worked your way to the deepest part of me. Were you curious to see me bleed?"

"WHY. DID. YOU. BETRAY ... betray and destroy and ruin me?" Ransom sings, his fingers wrapped around his black bass, his hoodie up and his eyes shadowed and dark. He stands relatively still, sweat dripping down his face as he sings into a mic stand, leaving the rest of the show up to Muse, Pax, and Michael.

Michael.

Ugh. I try not to look at him, but his words backstage have gotten stuck in my head.

"Do you think some pasts are so dark they overshadow the future no matter what you do?"

I had no idea how to respond to that. The moment felt so heavy and important and then it was just ... past and I wasn't sure if I'd made things better or worse. Clearly, he's not my responsibility, but there's so much regret and self-hate inside of him. Seeing him punish himself like that, I almost *want* to talk to Kevin, offer up my forgiveness. But there's no way in hell Kev's as aware of his own failures as Michael is.

"There's just no way to replace, the things you stole from me in that race. That crash and burn deserves more than just my spurn because you shackled me to this pain. And you, you're the only one to blame."

"WHY. DID. YOU. BETRAY ... betray and destroy and ruin me?"

My mouth parts, my sweaty hands slick as they curl around the metal divider. The drunk Seattle girls from next to me flick their hair in my face as they thrash in time with Muse and Michael. The two guitarists turn and put their feet up on the dais where Cope sits, worshipping him as he pummels his kick drum, grips his sticks in tight fingers, his short red hair stuck to his sweaty forehead.

"*WHY. DID. YOU—*" Pax starts, lifting his mic out over the crowd.

"*BETRAY!*" we all scream back. "*Betray and destroy and ruin me!*"

"That's the bloody spirit," Pax shouts with a laugh, taking the mic back to his sweaty mouth and breathing hard into it. "There's the spirit." But something about the way he says that sounds disingenuous. I'd have to be an idiot not to realize that this song is about Ransom and Chloe. Maybe Pax isn't feeling the hate as strongly tonight? I hope so. If there's one thing I want to accomplish before I leave that bus, it's getting Pax and Ransom to make up. The night of the car crash, they both lost each other as well as Chloe, as Harper.

It's so fucking sad.

The audience screams in the sudden silence as Michael strums one last note from his guitar and Pax slips his mic into its stand. Roadies appear as confetti explodes from the machines— little white hearts this time—and push Pax's piano in place. He slips onto the bench as Michael switches his purple instrument out for a green one and Muse trades in a red guitar for a red and black striped one.

Ransom and Cope wait patiently as Pax takes a sip of water and adjusts his fingers on the keys.

"You like power ballads?" he asks into the mic and the girl next to me bares her breasts at the stage, laughing. My cheeks flush with color and laughter and the excitement of being so wrong in such a right way. That's what rock 'n' roll is, I think, why people like it so much. It's everything you've been told *not* to do surfacing in a way that feels too goddamn good to resist.

I close my eyes as Pax starts playing the piano.

"*I live for the soft sound of your breathing. Sleep so I can dream of our first meeting. Without you my heart would simply stop beating.*"

Copeland starts drumming, soft and easy in the background of Pax's powerful vocals. I notice Michael's eyes are closed during this part of the song, making me wonder if there's something special about this particular track. Did he write it? Is it for Vanessa?

"When our lips come together, I find myself drowning in love's painful splendor. Each kiss we share"—Pax cuts off as the other members of the band start strumming their instruments, low, strong notes that reverberate through the crowd, sending us all swaying gently where moments before there was rippling rage—*"is an event I hold onto forever."*

Pax presses his hands into the keys as Michael picks up the sound with his guitar, moving to the front of the stage where a row of four benches are set up. He climbs onto one and uses his tattooed fingers to make love to his instrument, all of the anger in his face falling away as his he guides the crowd with soft, lilting sounds that pick at the chords of my own heart.

Oh God.

I was so wrong. If the way he looks right now is even a small reflection of the way he feels for Vanessa, then I'm a complete idiot. He must *really* love her.

Michael opens his violet eyes and rakes them over the crowd, smiling when he finds me standing there like an idiot, tears on my cheeks. I brush them off and decide there's no way he can see them from up there.

"I won't spend a single night away and I won't forget a single day. Because, baby, I'd never find another way, not a single other thing that could weave my life together with such beautiful pain."

Michael's guitar playing amps up into this heavy, driving metal riff, cutting into Pax's piano playing. And then they all just stop for a second. When they start playing again, it's with that same thrash-y riff on Michael's guitar and Pax is standing up from the piano, snatching up the mic and taking it with him.

Muse, Ransom, and Pax join their friend up on the benches and start playing hard, sweat dripping down their hands, off the sides of their faces, lighting the crowd up into a heavy frenzy again. I'm new to this scene, but even I can feel it, can understand why all these people would flock here to listen to this.

It's … fucking magnificent.

My fist pumps in the air as the venue bounces and cheers their way through several more songs—some of them bouncy, some of them angry—all of them catchy as hell. Long after I leave this bus and this tour, I know I'll be humming these songs under my breath.

After the last song, the crowd shouts for an encore and they get it, throwing shirts and hats and water bottles into the air as they jam and trash and flail. The air smells like sweat and beer, but the mood is jubilant, and the cheering that follows the final song is deafening.

"And that's it, Chicago!" Pax says as Cope chucks his sticks into the crowd, and the other boys throw their guitar picks. "We're Beauty in Lies, and we're calling it a fucking night."

He puts the mic in the stand and bends low, taking a bow and rising to his full height to wave at the shouting, raging fans. Muse waves, too, vigorously and excitedly, and between the two of them, they get the people so riled up that they start to push toward the front of the room. I feel like my breath's being squeezed out of me, my body crushed between the crowd and the metal divider.

I figure what the hell, and throw a leg over, finding myself grabbed by one of the security guards and hauled back like a rowdy fangirl.

"Alright, out the side door," he barks, putting me on my feet and herding me towards the fire exit on the left side of the room.

"Wait, wait," I shout as he half-drags me toward the door, his hands completely rough and his manner beyond rude. A few other people climb the dividers, too, and get the same treatment, but none of them have backstage passes on, do they? "I'm with the band," I say as I struggle and the guy laughs.

"Sure you are," he says, opening the door and pushing me out into the cold before I can get out another word. The metal door slams shut behind him and locks.

"Jesus," some teenage kid barks as he comes flying out the door next and slams into me. I almost topple over in my heels, but manage to catch myself on the wall as he stumbles past. "Beauty in Lies!" he screams, raising his fists in the air as a few more young guys get thrown out.

I'm the only woman that gets tossed out like trash.

My heart is beating like crazy as I clutch my backstage pass and wonder what I should do. Run around to the front and try to get back in? That seems like the only option. My heart starts to thunder as I realize I'm standing out here with no ID, no phone, no money, and only a very tentative connection to this tour.

Holy shit.

Holy fucking shit.

For the first time in days, I get this sense of teetering on the edge, a realization of exactly how little I really have in this world.

"Hey, babe, you want to come party with us?" one of the teenagers asks, reeking of stale sweat and pot. I give him a tight smile and try to act like I've got my shit together.

"No, thanks," I say as I take in the dark alley and wonder which way I'm supposed to go. I didn't exactly come in the front doors with everybody else; I'm completely disoriented and turned around right now.

"You sure? You look like you're ready to party," the guy says, grabbing my wrist in tight fingers and tugging me toward him. Without thinking, I knee him hard in the balls and he collapses to the garbage strewn pavement of the alley. "What the fuck?" he snarls, glancing up at me with rage burning in his eyes. "You fucking *bitch.*"

I stare down at him, debating how dangerous I think this guy really is. Do I run down the alley? Or do I wait for him to leave? Surely there are security cameras out here, right? Somebody must be able to see what's going on.

The door opens again and I step aside, expecting another person to come tumbling through it.

"Lilith?"

It's Michael.

He steps out and squints into the darkness of the alley, the bright lights of the venue falling across the ground near my feet.

"Jesus, is that Michael Luxe?" the angry kid asks as I feel this huge surge of relief and throw my arms around Michael's neck. As soon as my skin makes contact with his, heat surges through me in a violent wave, knocking my breath away, liquefying that hot, sweet spot between my thighs. He smells like that spicy shampoo I've been borrowing, like fresh sweat, and his body's trembling from the adrenaline of the show.

I'm so fucking *relieved* to see Michael that without thinking, I kiss him. *Hard.*

And oh my god. Oh my god. Oh my god.

As soon as our mouths touch, I lose it. A groan slips unbidden from my lips and I curl my fingers in his t-shirt. His arms encircle me almost automatically and for just the tiniest fraction of a second, he kisses me back.

I have never been kissed the way Michael Luxe kisses.

His lips say the sweetest things while the firm press of his body against mine growls nothing but sinful betrayal. His cock is hard against my stomach and his hands are almost painfully rough on my back, my ass. He yanks me against him, kisses me like a fairytale prince ... and then gets angry, almost mean.

My back slams into the wall as Michael's kisses get fervent, wild. He's so aggressive about it that he actually makes my lip bleed.

"Fuck!" he shouts suddenly, pushing back from me, stumbling like he's been kicked. "Fuck, fuck, fuck. No, no, no."

"Michael, I'm sorry," I say, putting a hand over my mouth and trying to feel awful about what I've just done. I didn't mean to kiss him. I didn't. I wouldn't ... I'd never do to another woman what Kevin did to me. "I'm sorry, Michael."

"Aren't you Michael Luxe? Can I get your autograph?" the angry kid asks as Michael whirls on him and gives him this *look* that sends the kid and his friends stumbling back. "Never mind, man. Enjoy your night."

When Michael looks back at me, he's clearly *pissed.* Whether at me or at himself, I'm not sure.

"I'm sorry," I say again but he's not looking at me. He pounds his fist on the door a few times and one of the men in *Security* t-shirts opens it. Michael puts his arm along the door and holds it for me, panting heavily, the slightest shine of red blood on his lower lip. "Michael ..."

"Inside, please, Lilith," he says as I squeeze past him, being very careful not to touch.

"Are you okay?" I ask as he drops the door and lets it slam shut, reaching down to take my wrist and shuddering when his sweaty fingers curl around my equally sweaty skin.

"I'm fine," he says, dragging me past the rest of the security guards and milling fans, keeping his hold on me down the backstage stairs and through the crowd, out another door that leads to the back where the buses are parked. Michael doesn't let go of me until we run into Ransom. "You almost lost her tonight," he barks, still not looking at me. "If she's your guys' …. fucking girlfriend or whatever, you should let the crew know so this doesn't happen again."

He shoves past Ran and up the stairs of the bus. Even from all the way out here, the sound of the bathroom door slamming is loud and jarring.

"What happened, honey?" Ran asks, pausing and looking into my eyes for a moment. He wrinkles his brow, reaches up and rubs his thumb against my lower lip, lowering his hand and examining the red shimmer of my blood against his thumb with a frown.

I wish I had an answer to that question.

CHAPTER THIRTY-SIX

Lilith

I splash my face with cool water from the kitchen sink and feel this tight, awful clenching sensation inside. Guilt. That's what that is. I just knowingly kissed another girl's long-term boyfriend and now my lower lip is throbbing with the memory. How can I just walk around with this tender mouth and not imagine what it'd be like to take things further?

"Baby girl, what happened?" Ransom asks, rubbing my back as I stay bent over the sink for a moment and try to soothe my sore lip with cold water. It helps the physical ache, but it does nothing for the fury inside my heart, nothing for the heated pulse between my thighs.

"I kissed Michael," I blurt when I spin around, sweeping my hair back over my shoulders and waiting in terrified agony to see the expression on Ransom's face. He stares back at me with surprise and blinks those heavy-lidded bedroom eyes of his.

"Michael?" he repeats, like maybe he thinks he's misheard me. My heart thunders with anxiety and my stomach twists with trepidation. I have no fucking idea how to define the relationship I have with Ransom, with Pax, with Muse, with Cope. But I know that what I just did was wrong on so many levels. "But Vanessa—"

"Damn shit, Vanessa," Michael says from behind me, making me jump when he appears with his hair wet and dripping from the bathroom. His indigo eyes are sparkling with anger, but his lower lip is just as swollen and full as my own. "We need to have a conversation," he says but then he looks up

267

at Ransom. "Lil got thrown out of the venue tonight. How the fuck is she supposed to get back in if something happens?"

"Jesus," Ran breathes as Michael grabs his leather jacket off the back of one of the swivel chairs and ... throws it over my shoulders.

"Let's talk outside," he says, lighting up a cigarette as I tuck myself into the leather and shampoo scent of his jacket. He waits for me at the door as I glance back at Ransom and try to read the strange expression on his face.

"Are you angry?" I whisper, because I am. I'm angry with myself on so many levels.

"Angry?" Ransom asks in his syrupy bedroom voice. "Why? Michael's one of us."

"Michael is fucking *not* one of you," Michael growls, grabbing my wrist in a surprisingly gentle grip. "*Michael* has a fucking girlfriend."

He pulls me down the bus steps and around the back, near the whirring generators and a couple of young roadies smoking pot. They scatter when they see us and Michael frowns, taking several drags on his cigarette before he looks over at me.

"That was fucked," he says, lifting his chin at me, "what you did. You shouldn't have kissed me like that."

"I know," I whisper, glancing down at the black heels that Muse bought me. They're covered in these small, decorative silver spikes and they look fucking badass. With the green shimmery dress, the new black leather bands on my left wrist and the makeup, I feel like maybe I actually do look like a rockstar's girlfriend—if that's even what I am. I've known the boys for a week; maybe I am just a groupie?

"You made a mistake," Michael says with a long exhale, dropping his cigarette to the wet ground, "but so did I. And I'm sorry. I shouldn't have kissed you back." I look past him, towards the crest of snow that lines the edge of the lot. It really is cold out here and I end up actually slipping Michael's jacket on properly to ward off the icy chill in the air. "Now I have to call Vanessa and tell her what happened. That sucks."

Michael sighs again and when I glance back up at him, he's looking across the icy parking lot with a strange, frustrated expression on his face.

"First time in a year that I've even remotely come close to falling off the wagon. But goddamn, she's going to kill me." He pauses again and finally glances in my direction. "There's just something about you, I guess. Clearly I'm not the only one that sees it."

I have to smile at that, but Michael doesn't smile back.

"She's meeting us in Atlanta?" I ask and Michael nods. "Early?" Another nod. "What if I talked to her with you? Explained the situation? That it was my fault. Would that help?"

His laugh is harsh and critical, but I don't think he means to be cruel.

"Seeing the gorgeous girl that I just couldn't help but kiss back in person? I don't think so."

"How is she going to *not* see me?" I ask as I hear Paxton's laughter echoing across the lot. "Either you're going to have to lie about who I am, or you're going to tell the whole truth and she'll know it's me anyway. Humanizing the situation, hearing me apologize, that's probably better than having to tell her over the phone, don't you think?"

"You're the one that got cheated on," Michael says with another sigh. Just watching sound flutter across his lips brings the memory of our kiss racing to the forefront of my mind. I want to kiss him again. So bad. So, so fucking bad. "You tell me."

"Don't call her and fuck up your visit. Once she sees you in person, she'll know how you really feel." *I saw it in your face onstage tonight,* I think but I keep that thought to myself. "We'll tell her together and I'll apologize personally."

Michael gives me a dubious look, but after a moment, he nods again.

"Okay, Lil," he says, and I like that he's still decided to call me that. Makes me smile again. "But that can *never* happen again, do you understand? If you kiss me, I'll … I'm too fucking into you to resist."

"I won't," I tell him and even though it *kills* me, I add, "I promise."

The thought of never kissing the swollen beauty of that mouth again makes me feel sad inside, but then Muse comes around the corner with his silver mohawk styled low and soft, the hood of his red sweatshirt thrown up over it. He neglected to wear a shirt again today—not even onstage—and holy crap. That combo of low slung pants, hooded sweatshirt, and no top? It makes my heart thump and beat in the craziest rhythm.

"Ransom told me what happened," he says, holding out his arms and giving me a quickie hug. The leather of Michael's jacket rustles as I breathe in the smoky scent of Muse's hoodie. He smells like Earl Grey tea today. "But I can't figure out exactly what the fuck those idiots were thinking. I showed your picture around, talked to the staff. It must've been one of the venue's security guys."

"No, it was definitely one of ours," Michael says and I get this little foreboding chill down my spine. For whatever reason, Octavia's hateful expression flashes across my thoughts, and I have to fight hard to push it away. Why would Beauty in Lies' manager try to sabotage me like that? I'm not the first girl she's seen Paxton Blackwell with and it's doubtful I'll be the last.

"Huh," Muse says as he lets go of me and reaches up to rub at his forehead. A quirky smile teases across his mouth as he looks between Michael and me. "So you guys finally kissed, huh?"

"Finally?" Michael snaps, giving his rhythm guitarist a bitchy look. "What the hell does that mean?"

"I'm sorry, Derek," I say, drawing Muse's hazel eyes back over to me. "We never talked about Michael being a part of our agreement. And it's fucked-up of me to ask you guys to be exclusive if I'm not."

Muse stares at me for several long moments and then nods briskly.

"Right. If we're going to keep this thing in our circle, let's just do that. Michael is … well, if he's with Vanessa, then he's not with us. And since we're not using condoms, we have to be pretty damn clear about how all of this works."

I nod again, feeling my cheeks flame with embarrassment. But it's not the sex stuff that's embarrassing to me, it's

270

everything else. For a second there, *I* feel like the cheater and it's awful. I can't even imagine how Kevin was able to put on airs with me when he was the one that got caught dicking around. I can still remember the evil twist of his smirk, the way he tore the diamond bracelet from my wrist.

Just the memory is enough to make me shiver.

"If you two like each other," Muse starts with a strange sigh, "then we should talk about that."

"There's nothing to talk about," Michael says, not unkindly.

"Well, it's either Vanessa or Lilith," Muse says softly, looking at me. I return his stare and have no idea what to say in response. What I do know for certain is that I don't want to be responsible for breaking Michael and Vanessa up. I won't do it. If they're meant to break up, then something else will have to be that catalyst.

At the time, I felt almost sick at the idea of losing Michael— not that I ever really *had* him in the first place. But I wanted him. Good thing that for once, fate was on *my* side. She'd been a bit of a fickle bitch lately, so it was no surprise that I didn't expect it.

Lil and her five rockstars.

Because I *would* have five of them.

They were always meant to be mine.

"But this isn't like an open relationship sort of thing," Muse continues, snapping me out of my daze. "The five of us ... we have a different kind of bond. Normally, I wouldn't even *dream* of sharing a girl with anyone else. But we're ... Beauty in Lies," he ends softly, looking down at the ground in front of my feet. "Nice shoes, by the way." When he looks back up at me, he's grinning.

"There aren't any other guys that I could ever want," I promise him, letting him fold me back into his arms again. I know we only have about nine days left in our arrangement, but it feels more permanent than that. I tell myself not to fall into that trap, but like an idiot, I don't listen to my own instincts.

"Good. Because I think four or five, those sound like pretty healthy numbers to me. Don't you think?" I laugh and pull away, giving Muse a playful slap on the shoulder. I also notice that Michael's watching us, and that he hasn't exactly answered Muse's question. *Vanessa or Lilith.* I almost don't want him to answer.

"We have a ton of extra time tonight," Michael says, putting his hands in his pockets, "but I am partied the fuck out from Minneapolis. You want to grab the guys and we'll go to dinner somewhere?"

"Somewhere fancy?" Muse asks with a boyish grin. "With fucking steak and cloth napkins and waiters that look at us like we're hoodlums?"

"What do you think, Lil?" Michael asks me, his anger bleeding out and fleeing into the darkness of night. I feel a huge surge of relief that he's willing to drop the subject. If nothing else, I'd like us to be friends. If the other boys like Michael so much, there's no doubt in my mind that he's got a good heart.

"I think that sounds like fucking heaven," I respond honestly.

So, for the first time in my life—but not the last—I get taken out to a nice dinner by not one, not two, but *five* strapping young men.

Let's just say this: it was the best date I've ever been on.

And the sex afterwards?

Even if Michael wasn't a part of it, that night in the Bat Cave was easily one of the best nights of my life.

No family, no apartment, no job … but four passionate, skillful lovers?

It might not make everything in my life better, but I was starting to feel okay. Really fucking okay. And at that point in my life, that's all I could really ask for.

CHAPTER THIRTY-SEVEN

Lilith

LILITH GOODE

The boys and I sleep together in the Bat Cave again—well, all of us but Michael obviously.

When I wake up, I'm wrapped in Cope's arms, my head pressed tight to his chest. I don't feel the bus moving, so I get up and peek out the curtains. We're definitely not in Chicago anymore, and I can see the other trailers and buses parked nearby. St. Louis, then. Rain drives against the pavement as I squint and try to make out any distinctive city landmarks. Can I see the Gateway Arch from here?

My charm bracelet jingles as I flop back onto the bed between Copeland and Ransom.

It's the only thing I'm wearing.

I lean back into the pillows and rub my thighs and calves together, luxuriate in the silky feel of the sheets and the soreness in my core. It's a good kind of soreness, a carnal memory like my tender lips, a reminder that I was with someone and they cared, that we connected, that we touched.

There are two sleeping men on either side of me, not cuddling together exactly, but not terrified of each other's bodies either. I don't think any of them are bisexual, but they don't exactly shy away from accidental—or even purposeful—contact when they're fucking me.

I love it.

Right now, laying here like this, I get that worshipped queenly feeling again. And my sex drive is in fucking high gear right now. I don't know if it's because I'm just realizing how many years I wasted with Kevin, or if the grief inside of me has just washed all of my inhibitions away along with my tears, but I can't seem to get enough. Honestly, each one of these guys is a damn good lover in his own right … but I'm not sure that one man could satisfy me with the way I'm feeling right now.

"Let me take you out tonight," Cope whispers, drawing my attention over to his sleep drenched face. I scoot close to him and drape a strand of my hair across his, comparing the color. My hair has this purple-y sheen to it while his is more of a rich red-brown.

Cope's turquoise eyes watch me and his gentle mouth quirks into a smile.

"Let's go dancing."

"Dancing?" I ask as he pulls me into him, tilting my chin up with his fingertips and kissing me like I'm his real girlfriend, his partner, the love of his life. He kissed me like that my first night on the bus, so I imagine it's just something he does. But damn, it feels good. I wonder about him as he kisses me, tucks me close to his body and slips a knee between my thighs.

In the past few days, I've learned a hell of a lot about Ransom and Paxton, why they are the way they are.

Cope is a bit of a mystery to me.

"Do you want to dance with me, Lilith?" he whispers against my lips, the touch of his hand trailing down my side making me arch my body into his. Cope is naked, too. It wouldn't take much maneuvering for us to come together, his bare cock sheathed inside of my wetness. As soon as I have that thought, I feel my cheeks flush guiltily.

Last night, before we went to the steakhouse, I slipped into my room to change and peeked inside the drawer with the manila envelopes. I looked at Michael's test results and felt this stupid giddy thrill when I found out that he was clean, too.

God. What is *wrong* with me?

"I want to dance," I say, gasping as Cope rolls on top of me and curls his fingers through my own. His short red hair is mussy and cute right now and his eyes are sleepy and tender. He has this way about him that makes me feel like I should spill all my secrets, my worries, just get them out there and trust in him to make them all better. "But I'm no good at it," I whisper as he kisses the side of my neck, trails his hot mouth down to my breasts.

When he lets go of my hands, I tangle them in his short hair, wondering how I ever confused his and Muse's hairstyles. Cope's hair is short but not buzzed, and slightly longer on top. When he styles it up into a mohawk or a faux hawk or whatever you want to call it, it makes this sexy little crest along the top of his scalp that blends in with the hair on either side. Muse's hair is buzzed and dyed black along the sides, and his black to silver ombre hair on the top is probably three times as long as Cope's, maybe more. I've seen him style his mohawk into a gentle curve, into spikes, into a tall gelled crest.

I muss up Cope's hair as he disappears beneath the black blankets and puts his mouth between my thighs, tasting and kissing my sex with such gentle movements that I almost want to cry. It feels so good that it's almost *too* good. I curl my fingers into the sheets to keep from pressing his head down, fighting to breathe through swirls of easy pleasure that turn my tense body back into mush.

By the time he slides back up and mounts me, I'm completely and utterly enthralled with him, wondering how he could possibly be so loving, so gentle, to a complete stranger. What if I *really* were his girlfriend? How much love and care would he show me then?

My toes curl into the sheets as I bury my face against Cope's shoulder, knead the firm curves of his ass with my fingers and try not to moan so loud that I wake everyone else up. The sheer exquisiteness of his bare body inside of mine is too much to take, especially when his moans get rougher, less polished, more broken. Inside of the rocker boy next door persona, is a man that's desperate to let it all out.

I feel like I *have* to hear his story. I just fucking *have* to.

"God, Lily," he says, taking up one of my nicknames right then and there as he comes inside of me, satisfying some base biological impulse that makes me so giddy that I come, too. My body tightens around his, squeezes and pulses, drags a few rough sounds from his throat as he collapses and we spend a few minutes catching our breath together. "So, dancing," he whispers against my ear and I shiver.

He rolls off of me and I turn on my side, squeezing my thighs tight. I should get up and clean up, but I don't want to leave the comforting darkness of the cave yet. It's too peaceful back here, with all of these warm, breathing bodies and Cope's gently smiling face. But I guess it doesn't matter so much. After last night, these sheets are *toast.*

I hope the boys have a lot of extras on hand.

"I'll go dancing," I say and he quirks his smile to the side. "Hey, do you guys happen to have extra sheets? Now that we're not using condoms ..." I start and he laughs. I smack him in the arm. "There are *four* of you. Sex is messy with just me and one dude. But *four.* Four?!"

"We have lots of extras," he says as Ransom stirs behind him. We both pause, but he falls right back asleep. "They're in a hidden drawer around here somewhere. It's usually Muse that changes them—whether he's slept in the bed or not. I bet we could find them if we searched."

"You guys must go through a lot of sheets and blankets," I say and then blush. Now that we're talking about *other* girls with my boys, I get embarrassed. Or maybe that hot flush I feel is jealousy? "I mean, if you have to change them every single night. They must fade and go threadbare pretty fast." Before Cope can answer, something comes to mind and I bite my lower lip. "And what about the toys?" I point up towards the headboard and its many mysterious drawers that I have yet to peruse. "Those don't get ... reused, do they?"

Cope laughs again, this time so loudly that he wakes Paxton up.

"What fucking time is it?" he mumbles, his accent thick and adorable with sleep. I glance over my shoulder and find him snatching his phone off the headboard shelf.

"We throw those away after every use."

"Isn't that kind of an expensive hobby?" I ask, looking back at Cope. He just shrugs and sits upright, the colorful tattoos on his forearms dancing as he rubs at his face.

"Now that you're here, we can just wash them, right? Save

ourselves some money."

I start to smile at Cope's joke—and the implied sentiment behind it—when Paxton starts cursing under his breath.

"Jesus Christ," he growls, the anger in his voice making me jump. I glance over my shoulder again, but he's not looking at us. His grey eyes are focused on his phone. Before I can ask if he's okay, he's dialing somebody up and climbing out of bed, yanking on a pair of sweats that I don't think are even his. "Yeah, what?" he snaps at the person on the other end of the line, shoving the Bat Cave's door open and disappearing down the hall.

"What's that about?" I ask as I glance back at Cope. His face is pinched and he tilts his head to the side as he swings his eyes over to mine.

"Pax's parents probably," he says, and there's a whole other fucking story buried in his words that makes me curious. I want to know everything there is to know about these boys. And I only have nine days left to do it. That terrifies me.

"What about your parents?" I ask and notice Cope's face shift into this sad but resigned sort of expression.

"My mom's still around," he says mildly, looking down at the blankets draped across his legs. "But she's not well." My heart skips and I feel sick inside. My dad wasn't well. He wasn't well and he fucking *died.* He died, he died, he died, and I wasn't fucking there.

I squeeze my eyes shut tight and feel Cope take me into his arms, pull me into his lap and hug me tight. He really is good at hugs, damn it. Within a few minutes, my panic's receded enough that I can think clearly.

"What's she sick with?" I ask, hoping I'm not overstepping any boundaries. I might be naked in this guy's lap with his come inside of me, but I don't know him at all. Not at fucking all.

"All sorts of stuff," he explains on the end of a long sigh. "She has severe anxiety, depression. Most days she has a hard time even getting out of bed. And then sometimes, when she does, she has these awful panic attacks where her whole body locks up and she has to go to the hospital."

"Damn," I whisper, unsure how else to respond to that. "Your dad?"

"He couldn't take it, so he left when I was really young and started a new family down the street. When I was a kid I used to sit on the lawn and watch him play with his new sons."

"Are you … serious?" I ask, wondering how the hell Cope can discuss something so awful with such a straight face. My dad might be gone now, but I knew—I'll always know—how much he fucking loved me. I will *always* have that. To know that my dad didn't care? That he couldn't bother to walk down the street and see me? That, I can't imagine.

When I look up and see Cope's expression, I try to change the subject.

"You're such a nice guy," I say and his lips twitch, "giving random girls at gas stations money and all that. Why don't you have a girlfriend?"

"I've had girlfriends," he says with a careful sort of neutrality. I decide not to press the matter any further. Everyone on this bus is steeped in tragedy—including me. If Cope wanted to talk about his, he'd elaborate. I'm about to cajole him into going out for breakfast when he surprises me and keeps talking. "I grew up with my grandma, too. But she had the same problems as Mom. That's why I'm never having kids; I got lucky enough not to inherit whatever's wrong with them. But it feels like my genes are tainted. That's one of the reasons I don't have a girlfriend. A lot of girls want their own biological kids, and that's something I won't give them."

"I'm sorry, Cope," I say because it seems like an appropriate response, but he just smiles at me and exhales sharply.

"This conversation sucks," he says with a smile, fingering my charm bracelet and examining my sister's birthstone. It's a diamond for April. In fact, her birthday's just a few short weeks away. Dad and I used to celebrate with ice cream cake and a marathon of Yasmine's favorite movies.

The thought of watching those movies alone makes me want to throw up.

"This conversation *does* suck," I say with a laugh, shaking the thoughts from my head as I look up at Cope. "Do you want to get something to eat and like, go to a bookstore or something?"

This time, when he laughs, it's completely genuine.

"Food and books," he says as he kisses the side of my face and makes my toes curl again. "You already know me so damn well. Let's get dressed and you can tell me all about you."

Paxton picks out this hilarious bodice ripper and throws it at me, laughing as I fumble to catch it without wrinkling the pages. I give him a look as he manages to attract the attention of every person in the store with his inappropriate commentary.

"You see the tagline on that shite? *He destroyed me with his heaving love.* What the bloody hell is *heaving* love? And who wants to be destroyed by some heaving bloke anyway?"

I turn the book around and examine the cover.

"I've read this one," I say as he rolls his grey eyes at me and Lilith smiles. "I gave it five stars," I tell her, passing over the book and bending low to examine the bottom shelves. A lot of people don't know this, but publishers pay extra to have their books put on higher shelves, so that they're at eye level with customers. That usually means all the hidden gems are hiding on the bottom.

"Why don't you get a Kindle or something?" Lilith asks, but not like she's judging, just curious. I like that. It's hard to find a person in this world that isn't judgmental as hell.

"Tactile experience," I say, even though I know eBooks would make a lot more sense considering my situation. Our band spends a lot of time on the road, on planes, in hotels. Space is sort of at a premium for me. I should rightfully give up the random stacks of books around the bus, the mess of pages and ink stuffed into my bunk. But I can't. I won't. "It's not like I *don't* read eBooks. Indie authors are my favorite, but ..." I tug an erotica novel off the shelf and flip it over to read the back. "I get sick of digital everything. Don't you miss CDs? DVDs? I just want to touch what I'm consuming for once."

"Miss Lily's a bit young for CDs and DVDs, Cope, you old bastard," Pax says as he parks himself next to me and squats down to read over my shoulder. He scoffs under his breath, but I smile and take the book along with me. The first lines read, *When you fall in love, you disregard logic. Because logic and love are two sides of the same coin. Together, they make a beautiful sort of currency, but you can never look them both in the face at the same time.*

I like that.

"Hey, I'm not completely unsentimental. I still have my mom's vinyl records—" Lilith starts and then pales suddenly, glancing away from me sharply. "I mean, I *had* her records. They got stolen from my car."

"If it'll help, I have some limited edition Beauty in Lies vinyl back on the bus. We could sign one for you and start your collection all over again," I say, hoping my joke's not so far off the mark that I scare the poor girl.

At least she's smiling when she glances back at me and holds up a book.

"I think I found one, Cope. Please tell me this is a five star."

"That," I say, pointing at the tattooed rockstars on the cover, "is one that I haven't read."

"Oh! Like a needle in a haystack then?" she asks and I laugh, wishing I could spend all day smelling ink and paper and drinking overpriced coffee with this girl. I haven't had this much fun with a woman in a long time. And what I really like is that we started off our relationship with hard shit, with pain, with tears. Before anything happens—*if* anything happens—at least she has some idea of the awful shit I have to deal with.

I'll probably be taking care of my mom for the rest of her life —and she's only fifty. That, and I'll never have biological kids. *Never.* I realize that my mom and grandma are messed up because of genetics *and* the horrible trauma they both experienced in their life. Still, no kids for me.

I have a lot more I want to tell Lilith, but how do you segue into stories about your grandpa beating the shit out of you, coming into your house and fucking your messed up grandma when she's in the middle of a panic attack? You just don't tell people that shit without seeing the way they look at you get all twisted and distant.

And anyway, who wants to date someone that comes from that sort of fucked-up genetic pool? I feel like my blood is tainted and poisoned, but I try to make up for it. Because if there's one thing I know how to do, it's how to take care of people, of women, how to protect them from the world. That's what I've been doing my whole life, protecting my mom and grandma—or trying to anyway. I had to wait until I was thirteen before I could fight my grandpa back and win. He never did come back to the house after that.

"Like a needle in a haystack," I agree with a smile, pushing past the pain, letting it settle into the background. I'm twenty-nine years old; I'm resigned to it at this point in my life. Lilith is young and all of her pain is fresh and dark and sad. All I want to do is take care of her, make her feel better, hold her close. "Pick as many as you want, and I'll get them for you. Maybe we could read together later?"

"There are paps outside," Ransom says, curling around the end of the bookshelf like a shadow, his face twisted in a dark frown. He stares out at me and Lilith from inside his hoodie and sighs. "Fucking goddamn paps," he whispers, voice low and thick with carefully leashed anger. Poor fucking Ransom. He used to be such a happy kid. I remember when I got assigned to be his mentor, back when I was a sophomore and he was a seventh grader. He was bouncy and fun and wild. Now ... I wouldn't exactly use any of those terms to describe him. "The store manager asked them to leave, but they're hovering around out there still. They already drove Muse and Michael into hiding at the café next door."

"Got it," I say as Lilith puts another book on top of my own, a big, thick fantasy novel this time.

"I could use a distraction from another world," she says, looking up at me with her long lashes and big green eyes. Before I can stop myself, I lean down and press a searing kiss to her mouth.

It's only meant to last an instant, but Lilith lets out this small sound of surprised pleasure and pushes into me, squeezing the small stack of books between us. She's wearing one of the outfits that Muse bought her—this tight pink t-shirt with a flock of black bats silhouetted across the front, a pair of low-slung jeans, and grey boots. Her body is so curvy and exaggerated in all the right places that even though the clothes are new, even though they fit, she just falls all the hell out of them.

I set the books in my hand aside and pull her fully into my arms, pressing her body against one of the towering black bookcases and trying not to fantasize about fucking her there. Wouldn't the paparazzi just *love* to film that?

Still, I can't seem to stop my hands from roaming over Lilith's body as she wraps her arms around my neck and leans into me. I'm taller by several inches, but it doesn't matter because the way we fit together feels destined, easy, almost perfect.

I know in my heart that meeting this girl was just a random coincidence and that in the end, it'll probably amount to nothing, but for now, it feels really, really fucking good.

"Goddamn it." It's Ransom, his voice a low uneasy growl. "Fucking paparazzi," he warns as I pull back from Lilith just in time to avoid getting a photo snapped of us in mid osculation. That is, in the act of tonguing the shit out of this strange girl that I really like for no apparent reason whatsoever. Because she cries a lot? Because she's sad? Because I want to save her, fix her, make her smile? I think I have a problem here.

"Is this your girlfriend, Mr. Park?" the guy asks, taking several more shots before one of our security guards appears from the self-help section to escort him back a few steps. I notice him zooming in on my crotch—and the hard bulge beneath the denim—and smile.

"Maybe," I say as Lilith grabs the stack of books I abandoned and clutches them against her chest with a secretive sort of smile, "or maybe I just *really* like to read?"

CHAPTER THIRTY-NINE

Lilith

This time, when I head over to the venue with the boys to watch the show, I decide to stay backstage. The last thing I need is a repeat of last night's fiasco—although I wouldn't mind another wild, flirtatious kiss with Michael …

No.

No, I *would* in fact mind that. He hasn't said anything else to me since last night, so as far as I know, everything is still okay with Vanessa. I'll keep my end of the bargain, too, and talk to her with him, tell her what happened. I meant it when I said I don't want to be the one responsible for them breaking up. That would put too much pressure on whatever this attraction is between us.

So I make myself watch the show from the safety of the curtain and enjoy getting a behind the scenes view that nobody else has, a little taste of the action from close up. Is it wrong that knowing what each guy in the band tastes like somehow makes the show that much more exciting?

Maybe I really am a fucking groupie?

I cheer and sing and clap with the rest of the venue, but when the boys finish up and file offstage, I'm waiting for them.

"You guys were fucking great tonight," I tell Cope, kissing him first and then moving onto Muse, Ransom, and then Pax. He's the only one that's greedy about it, grabbing me and squeezing me tight against his sweaty front, his shirt unbuttoned and his tie already missing, chucked into the needy hands of the crowd.

"We bloody were, weren't we?" he asks, slinging an arm around my shoulder and leading the charge through the backstage area. With his other hand, he manages to slide a pack of smokes from his pocket, extract one *and* light up, all without letting go of my waist. Impressive. "Fucking *brilliant.*"

The boys and I head out the door and over to the bus, only to find a gaggle of well-dressed girls waiting outside. They glitter and sparkle in tall heels, tight dresses, their makeup flawless and their hair even better.

I feel instantly self-conscious, even though I know I shouldn't be. There's a reason that I'm here with these boys at this point in my life. There's something more between us than just sex—and that's pain. Maybe some of these girls have it, I don't know, but right now, the connection is between me and the guys. I know that at the very least, they'll ride this thing out with me. Whether they get tired of our arrangement or not, I can't see any of them—even Pax—letting me go before the end of the tour.

"What the fuck?" Pax asks, getting this seriously ticked off expression on his face. He manages to smooth it away before any of the women notices us. "Pardon me, ladies," he says, not even bothering to stop. He just pushes his way forward, straight through them and toward the door. Most of them try to talk to him, some of them even touch him, but he ignores them, dragging me up the stairs and inside.

"I told Octavia no girls for a while," Muse says as the rest of the boys file in and he closes the door behind us. "I know she knew what I meant by that," he adds with a sigh, pulling the curtains over the kitchen sink closed and running a hand along the buzzed hair on the right side of his head. "Either she forgot or ..."

"She's too fucking obsessed with Pax to resist punishing Lilith," Michael snarls. "Jesus. You want me to talk to her for you?"

"I want you to fire her," Pax says as he lets go of my waist and grabs a beer from the fridge. "Would she let them in here if Vanessa were here? No, she damn well wouldn't. She never let groupies in when Chloe and Kortney were around either."

C. M. Stunich

There's this tenseness that springs to life at the mention of those two girls, but it fades quickly when I kick off my heels and sigh at the sheer pleasure of being flat-footed again.

"It's okay," I tell them, loving this ridiculous amount of protectiveness that they're showing me. It's adorable and honestly, flattering as hell. Who wouldn't want five guys fawning over their emotional well-being like that? "I don't mind —as long as you don't bring any of them onto the bus." I smile when I say that, but I'm dead serious. If they want to fuck other girls, they can do it elsewhere—and they can say goodbye to sleeping with me, even with a condom. I know it sounds selfish to impose that rule considering *I'm* fucking four of them at the same time, but that's just the way it is. That's how I want it right now.

Besides, I haven't left a single one of them wanting for sex since I got here. Apparently I have a healthy enough sex drive to keep them all happy.

"It's not okay with me," Pax says as he stabs his cigarette out in an ashtray and turns his grey eyes in my direction. "Feels like a threat. Or at the very least, a serious sign of disrespect. Octavia's being a right git. Either that or she's gone completely mental."

"You guys are going dancing, right?" Muse asks, looking between Cope and me with a slight smile.

I blink at him and suddenly feel a little guilty. Is that okay? Is it fair for Cope and me to head out on a private date while the others stay behind? I mean why *shouldn't* they bring one of those girls up on the bus to hang out with? It would be completely fair.

But I wouldn't like it. Not at all.

"Yeah," I say as Cope pauses beside me and smiles. I flush a little because it's the same smile he gave me when we started reading the same book together this afternoon, after we got back from our breakfast/shopping outing. Three sentences in and the main character is already having gratuitous sex with some guy she just met and Cope is casting me these flirty glances across the couch. "If that's okay with you guys?"

"It's fine with me, baby girl," Ransom whispers in that

lusciously dark voice of his, pausing next to me to kiss me on the forehead. "I'll shower and watch a movie while I wait for you." He breathes against my scalp, stirring my hair, making me shiver. "Have fun, okay?"

"You know what's *not* alright," Pax continues, glancing at his phone and frowning. He's been doing that all day. Cope said something about his parents, but I wasn't sure how to broach the subject and ask—or even if I *should* broach the subject and ask. "Bringing groupies all the way back here when she knows damn well that we're not interested in them. I'm going to fucking talk to her—right now."

Pax's words thrill me, even though I know I'm letting a lot—too much—of my current happiness ride on what these guys think and feel about me. But finding self-worth at this point seems impossible; I'm too buried in grief. Drowning in it. Together, these boys make up the tightly lashed logs of my life raft. Lose one and I might sink.

I really need to get my shit together, I think as I realize that for a week, I've done literally nothing but hang out with them. Tomorrow, I'll post an ad and try to sell the Matador—even though it was my mom's car when she was growing up. It's time to let it go and see if I can get some cash to start a fresh life. After all, these guys, these new clothes, this bus, it's all part of a fairytale. One day, the clock really will chime midnight and the whole thing will turn into a fucking pumpkin.

"Please don't fire her, Pax. Do you remember what our last manager was like?" Muse asks as he follows along behind his friend and tosses an apologetic smile over his shoulder. "I'm going with him," he adds and then there's the sound of excited voices and the distinct scent of perfume before the door slams closed behind him.

"You guys go ahead," Michael says, watching me with his beautiful eyes. "And have fun. Don't worry about any of this."

I stare back at him, but I can't read the expression on his face. I wish I could decipher it somehow, get inside his head and see what he's thinking about when he looks at me. Hopefully nothing, right? I mean, one of the things I find attractive about him is that he's faithful to his girlfriend. But thoughts can't be helped, I guess, and maybe deep down I'm hoping that just one or two of the ones in his head are about me.

"I won't," I promise as Cope holds out a hand and helps me step back into my heels. As soon as his fingers touch mine, I forget about Michael for a moment and meet those brightly colored blue-green eyes of his. Now that I've had a glimpse into his past, he makes more sense to me. That boy next door act isn't really an act at all; it's a backlash against the shitty men he's known in his life. It's a natural response for him to want to reach out to women, show some fucking kindness and respect.

It does make me wonder though if there's anything specifically about *me* that he likes or if it's all just a part of his routine.

Still, I wouldn't trade going dancing with him for anything in the world right now.

"Ready?" he asks, and I nod, following him outside and down the steps. The girls are still there, but they look slightly less than enthused at this point. One of them even glares at me as we move past.

"Bitch," she whispers under her breath, but I ignore her. I don't want to compete with other women for a man's affection. Either he wants to give it to me or he doesn't. I refuse to let thoughts of Michael invade my brain and push that notion aside.

"Do you know where we're going tonight?" I ask Cope as he leads me out toward the edge of the lot and a pair of gates. This particular venue has a giant brick wall around the parking area, lending it an unusual amount of privacy for a place smack-dab near the city center.

"I have some ideas," he says, his hair still styled up into a messy faux hawk, a slight tracing of eyeliner around his beautiful eyes. His white Beauty in Lies tank is stuck to his body with sweat, but I like it because it gives this feral edge to his kind face. He looks gorgeous but flawed right now, the boy next door in black sweatbands and ripped jeans, shiny red Docs and several spiked belts with a white and black bandana tied around one that he uses onstage to wipe sweat from his forehead.

It's sexy as hell.

"But," Cope adds as he shows his badge to one of the security guards and they let us out of the gate, "I will take you wherever you want to go, Lily." He pauses as a yellow cab pulls up and opens the door to let me in. "Is it okay if I call you Lily?"

"You can call me whatever I want," I say as I slide in and he climbs in next to me.

A proper date. With a rockstar.

I pinch my arm as he shuts the door and gives the driver an address in the city.

Thankfully, my pinch hurts and I don't wake up.

I'm afraid that when I do, all of this fairy dust and dark magic will have tainted me, and the real world—the pumpkin and the wicked stepmother and the dead dad—all of it will come crashing down around me and there'll be no prince around to save me then.

CHAPTER FORTY

Lilith

Cope takes me out dancing, just like he promised.

And he doesn't just drag me to a bunch of crowded nightclubs. He seems to have done his research because the first place he picks is this adorable little brick building that serves drinks and bar food ... and dance lessons.

While the night is still young, I learn to dance the Charleston with Copeland. Well, *he* learns to dance the Charleston, taking to it like a duck to water. Me, I mostly just fumble around and try not to die laughing when the instructor corrects my form for the hundredth time.

"I told you I wasn't much of a dancer," I tell him as he helps me out of the car and under a black umbrella when we get back to the venue. I've got a paper cup of coffee in my hands, a gentle buzz from all the alcohol I drank tonight, and a smile plastered across my face. After our dance lesson, we hit a few clubs, but since nobody dances the Charleston anymore, we went back to the first place and rocked out to music from the 1920s.

"You were great," Cope says with a mysterious sort of smile hovering on his lips. "Even if you managed to somehow kick me in the balls while you were dancing." I snort and almost spill coffee everywhere, rainwater spattering my feet and ankles, making me feel a little silly for wearing peep toes in the rain.

"My only regret is that I didn't have a flapper dress to wear," I say as Copeland opens the door to the bus and shields me with the umbrella while I climb inside. I head up the steps and finish off the last of my coffee, setting the empty cup on the counter as I survey the sleeping boys in the living room.

Ran and Muse are asleep on opposite sides of the couch, both of them curled over the arm at their end, a muted movie playing on the flat-screen. I watch Ransom's face for any sign that he's having—or has already had—nightmares, but he looks peaceful enough right now. He did say that he didn't like to sleep alone; I guess with Derek a few feet away from him, he's not alone right now.

"Come on," Cope says, taking my hand in his, curling his warm fingers through mine and sending that excited little thrill through me. We've spent all night touching, dancing, kissing each other and still, when his hand finds mine I'm nervous all over again. Butterflies tease the inside of my belly as he pulls me past the bathrooms—someone is in there showering—and down the hall.

When we pass Michael's bunk, I see his arm sticking out of the curtain, the soft easy cadence of his breathing letting me know that he's asleep, too.

Cope opens the door to the Bat Cave and I step inside, climbing up on the bed and kicking my heels off onto the floor. He does the same, shedding his shoes and tossing aside the three belts he had wrapped around his hips. I watch him as he undresses part of the way and crawls over to me.

I roll onto my back, my feet facing the headboard, my own head pointed toward the bedroom door and try not to gasp when Cope pushes my new little black dress—another gift from Muse —up my thighs. His hands are warm and calloused from his drumsticks, gently caressing my leg as he kisses his way down the inner part of my thigh, my knee, my calf. He even kisses the aching arch of my foot, sore from dancing in the silver peep toe pumps.

The whole night's been like foreplay, Cope's hands holding my body, pulling me close, his mouth never too far from mine. I know my core is slick and wet and ready, but I don't rush him, enjoying his easy, practiced touch. This is a man that's made love to a lot of women yet clearly has taken his time to get to know their bodies. Maybe he asks a lot of questions?

"Just tell me what you like, what you want," he whispers as he massages my sore foot with his thumbs, drawing these deep, sensual groans from my throat. There is *nothing* in this world so fucking exquisite as having your feet massaged after wearing heels all night. Hell, it almost makes the torture of wearing the damn things worth it in and of itself.

"I have no idea," I whisper back, because I don't. Sexually, I don't really know myself at all. I spent too much time worrying about Kevin and what he might want. Cope pauses and sets my foot down on the bed, tearing his white tank off and coming to lay next to me on his side. His fingers skim across the waistband of my new silver panties, just as glittery and sparkling as my shoes.

"Like I said before, I'm down for pretty much anything," Cope says with an understanding smile. "No judgment, I swear."

"My ex-boyfriend," I start, hating that I'm bringing up Kevin yet again, "didn't really do much for me. If I wanted to come, I pretty much got myself off." Just *thinking* about having sex with that man makes me sick. One of those awful times he climbed into bed with me after a late night at the office—or more likely a late night out fucking some random girl—and mounted me in his rough, clumsy, amateurish way, he was giving me a disease. A fucking disease.

I close my eyes and put a hand over my mouth to keep from being sick.

No, no, fucking *no*. I can't let Kevin ruin another second of my life.

"I'm sorry," I say with a deep breath as I drop my hand and Cope sits up so he can look down at my face. "I'm ruining this."

His smile is understanding and completely adorable.

"You're not ruining anything," he promises, pushing my dress up a little further and leaning down to press several kisses along the waistband of my panties. "If it's too much pressure, you can let me take over. I told you: orgasms are my specialty." His smile is sharp and gleaming with mischief when he glances up at me.

"Okay," I whisper back, heart pounding, wishing I was

experienced enough to tell him what I want, not even knowing if I could do that if I really tried. It's like I'm learning to have sex all over again from scratch, like I came onto this bus a virgin or something.

"Then let's start with a cock ring," Copeland says, moving to the headboard and tugging open one of the drawers. He pulls out a small purple-black ring and a bottle of lube, coming back to lie next to me. "This is a fancy one," he says as he sets the lube aside and stretches the ring over his fingers. It looks hard at first, but when I reach out to touch it, the material is soft and smooth. I think it's silicone. "But they all work pretty much the same."

One end of the ring is thicker than the other, and there are several buttons there that are just as soft to the touch as the rest of it. Cope runs his thumb over these and presses one down, making the ring vibrate in his hand.

"You know what a cock ring's for, right?" he asks and I try not to sound like a complete idiot.

"It ... stimulates the clit?" I say, feeling like a student with a teacher—a very, very sexy teacher with a rock-hard bulge in his jeans.

"It does," Cope says, his eyes piercing in the darkness, his smile losing a little of its mischief, filling with heat instead, "but it also helps keep blood in the penis, engorging an erection, making it last longer. And for me, it increases sensitivity."

He leans over me, pressing a kiss to my lips that's a lot less gentle than before. It's almost ... commanding. Copeland is a nice guy, and he's nowhere near as aggressive as Pax, but he also likes to be in charge. I can feel that in the way he kisses me, presses my body into the mattress, slides the vibrating ring between my thighs.

I gasp with surprise when he presses it against the outside of my panties, teasing me with slow, easy rubbing motions that massage all the best parts of me. I know my underwear is already soaked, too, so he must be able to feel that, the proof of my arousal.

My lower lip is still sore from Michael's kiss and the sensation of Cope sucking it between his teeth almost breaks me in half with desire. He teases the fine line of pleasure and pain, kissing and licking and tormenting my mouth the same way he tortures my clit with the ring in his hand.

I can feel the tickling sensation of wetness running between my ass cheeks onto the bed. That's how fucking wet I am and it's driving me crazy. Cope must take some sort of cue from my face or my kisses because he moves away and settles himself between my thighs, taking my panties off and tossing them aside. I get excited when I think he's going to put the ring on and enter me, but he doesn't. Instead he drops low and slips the cock ring into his mouth.

"What are you doing?" I ask, but then any chance I had of iterating a single other word is blown to bits when he puts his now vibrating tongue against my bare heat. My hands clench into the bedspread and before I can stop it, an orgasm rolls right over me, tearing me apart as Cope takes hold of my hips and continues to tease and caress with the hot slick vibrations from his mouth.

My body bucks and thrashes enough that when the orgasm finally passes, I'm shaking and flushed from head to toe, completely embarrassed.

"Did you like that?" he asks, sliding the ring from his mouth when he glances up at me. His smile tells me he already knows the answer to that question, but when I just glare at him, he gets comfy and props himself up between my thighs. "Well?"

"You're going to make me say it, aren't you?" I ask as he grins and finally sits up, grabbing the bottle of lube and opening his jeans. His cock is curved and beautiful in the half-light, and I find myself squeezing my thighs together in anticipation as he squirts lube into his hand and slicks his palm down his shaft.

He pauses when he realizes I've stopped talking, and stares at me.

"I liked it," I whisper and Cope laughs, stretching the ring over his fingers.

"You're supposed to put these on when you're semi-hard," he says as he flicks his eyes back to mine, "but with you, there's no such thing. I'm always rock-fucking-hard."

"I thought you were supposed to be the nice one?" I whisper

as he slides the silicone ring down to the base of his shaft and smirks at me.

"Am I?" he asks and then he presses one of the buttons on the ring a few times until he gets the vibration he's looking for. I notice his eyes are already half-lidded with pleasure when he leans down over me. "Who told you what? They must've been lying." He kisses along the side of my jaw and finds my opening with the now vibrating head of his shaft. I almost lose myself and come again, just from the newness of the sensation. "If you want a nice guy, you should try Muse. I think I'm really just an asshole with mommy issues."

"I don't believe that at all," I whisper, sucking on the silver ring in the center of his bottom lip. Cope indulges me for a moment before taking over the kiss again, and I surrender happily to his touch. I don't really want to be in charge right now; I want to let go and not think about anything beyond this moment. "I think you've got a good heart."

"Maybe," Cope says and then he's pushing inside of me with his cock.

The groan that escapes my lips is damn near a scream, and I find myself tossing my head back, arching my body so drastically that I end up with my head hanging off the edge of the bed. Cope grabs me and holds me still, using his engorged shaft to pump into me. It really does feel bigger with the ring on, stretching me to my limit at the same time it vibrates every part of my core. With each thrust, the side of the ring with the buttons bumps my clit just right, teasing the hardened nub with pleasure that'd be too intense to take all at once. Instead, it's just a bit of a tease to match up to every one of Cope's forward thrusts.

With my head back like this, I can see all the way down the hall to the door that leads into the kitchen. The bathroom door on the right opens, letting out a burst of steam, and then there's a pair of legs in grey sweatpants, a pair of tattooed feet.

It's Paxton.

"Miss Lily," he says as he pads down the wood floor towards me and drops his towel near the end of the bed. "What's all this then?"

I can't speak, not with Cope fucking me the way he is, but I reach my hands out and grab Pax's sweatpants, pulling them down his hips. He never wears underwear, so his half-hard cock is free in an instant, getting harder by the second as he watches us.

He doesn't hesitate, not even for a second, sliding his hand down his shaft and then stepping forward to put the head of his cock between my lips. The way my head is tilted back, my throat is completely open, and I encourage him to push all the way in by dragging him forward by his pants.

"Fucking hell," he growls as I deep throat him, his body so intimately acquainted with my face. I'm literally staring at his balls as he starts to move inside of my mouth. For such a cruel asshole, Pax takes it fairly slow, listening to my cues, stopping when I dig my nails into his skin, thrusting harder when I groan around the fullness of his shaft.

With Pax as deep into my throat as he is, I have to completely relax, let my entire body succumb to the pleasure of having these two men inside of me. Normally, when I get close to coming, I tense up all my muscles. Not this time. The feeling coiling inside of me is completely different, this tingling rush of vibrant emotion that builds with each movement of Cope's hips.

The three of us find this perfect rhythm together, our bodies synced, pleasuring one another in the most intimate way. Pax comes first, groaning and fighting not to just fuck my mouth, but when he tries to pull away, I grab hold, encouraging him to stay for those last few thrusts. His seed fills my throat and then he's sliding out, leaving me to swallow and gasp at the frenzied motions of Cope's hips.

Seeing his friend come in my mouth must've revved him up because he goes fast and hard, driving me into the mattress, bringing me over the edge even before he gets there. I end up coming around him with these intense pulses of muscle, these squeezing, milking sensations that he somehow manages to resist.

"Fucking ring," he whispers as he pulls out and slides it off his slick shaft, tossing it aside and mounting me again before I can even recover a single breath. Cope fucks my sweaty, aching body, pulling me toward him so my head isn't hanging off the bed anymore. I wrap my arms around him and hold him close as he finishes with a low, deep groan, almost a sob of relief. "Holy shit," he whispers as he pulls away from me and invites me to sit up, join him in the nest of pillows near the headboard.

Pax is already there, and I end up sandwiched between the two men. Pax's body is still moist and warm from the shower, and Cope is hot and slick with sweat. I nestle between them, Cope's arm around my waist, his face pressed into my neck. Pax slides down and lays his head against my tummy.

Nobody says anything as I curl my fingers in the dark wet strands of his dirty blonde hair.

I try to think of something clever, but by the time I do, I can feel the soft breath of both men feathering against my body in sleep. A few minutes later, Ransom is pushing his way into the hallway and padding down the wood floors toward us. Without a word, he climbs into bed and lays horizontally, cradling his head against one of my calves.

"The nightmares," he whispers into the easy darkness of the room, "they're so much better when you're around, honey."

I don't think I've ever felt so wanted by anyone as I do in that moment.

CHAPTER FORTY-ONE

"Welcome to Nashville," a voice whispers in my ear, waking me out of a fogged dreamy stupor. A careful hand slides down my side and over my belly, tugging me close. "I made some tea— darjeeling this time. Want a cup?"

"Are you a tea connoisseur, Derek?" I ask as I roll toward him and find his hazel eyes hidden behind the thick dark frames of his glasses. I'm not sure when he joined us last night, but I'm glad he's here now, holding me close and gazing at me with bright interest and that enigmatic smile of his.

"Actually, yes," he says, his silver-black hair falling across his forehead and over one side of his shaved head. It's wet and warm from the shower, a single drop falling onto my lips as I look up at him. "When I got emancipated, my first job was working in this tea/magic shop in California."

"Magic shop?" I ask as Muse flashes a grin and sits up, pulling me along with him. I'm happy to go until I realize that I'm completely naked. I mean, it shouldn't be a big deal since I've been having sex with—and cuddling—these guys in the nude, but I pull on a pair of Muse's sweats and a shirt that I think actually belongs to Michael. Oops. I'm not sure how it ended up in the pile of clothes spilling from the Bat Cave floor into the hall, but there it is. It even smells like him, spicy and warm.

I start to change it when he swings his legs out of his bunk bed and notices me standing there. "I didn't realize ..." I trail off and drop the fabric as he averts his eyes and stretches his arms over his head.

"No big deal," he says, and then excuses himself to the bathroom.

"Magic shop?" I ask again as I meet Muse at the end of the hall and he lets us out into the cold, bright sunshine filling the kitchen. Glancing at the clock over the stove, I realize I've slept way past noon. I know that I was up late last night—really fucking late—but I don't like the idea of sleeping away my time here. I don't have much of it left.

"Yeah, like occult type stuff. We sold incense, organic herbs, special blend teas." Muse stops at the counter and grabs a steaming mug, handing it over to me and watching as I breathe in the sweet, easy scent of the tea. It's a little fruity with a gentle herbal smell that lingers on the back of my tongue. "Runes, tarot cards, how-to books on magic and past life regression." He pauses to take a sip of his own tea and closes his eyes in bliss. "The owner was this crazy old guy, but I guess I made some sort of impression on him because he insists on sending me care packages with tea and other random trinkets."

We move over to sit on the couch and Muse taps a pink and black book with his black painted fingernails. *Love Spells: an easy how-to guide for beginners.*

I bite my lip and try not to laugh, but Muse is already grinning.

"I know, right? I guess that's a sign that he thinks I need some help in the love department."

"Have you ever been in love?" I ask as he settles back in his purple zip-up sweater and black wifebeater. There's something casual and easy about Muse that I like. He's relaxed, and he doesn't try too hard. He's not trying to please anyone or make them happy; it's just something he does naturally by being himself.

"Nope," he says, not at all ashamed of that. "I've never really had time for it before."

I finally take a sip of my tea and feel my lips curl into a smile.

"This is really good," I say, lifting up the mug in salute. It has the band's logo on the side in purple cursive.

"Better than coffee?" he hazards and I chuckle.

"Maybe."

We sit there in companionable silence for several moments, studying each other. Now that I really look at him, I can't believe I thought he was the oldest of the bunch. He has this edgy boyish quality to his face that makes me wonder what he'll look like in a few years. I mean, he's handsome as hell already, but I could see his features hardening up just a bit, giving him a more distinguished look later on.

Of course, then I glance down at his chest and ab muscles beneath the fabric of his wifebeater and it's fairly obvious that there's not a lot of growing to be done down there. Muse is ... well, he's ripped.

"Have you?" he asks finally, drawing my attention back to his face. It's fun sitting here with him, drinking tea with bare feet and matching black sweatpants. I could do this everyday for the rest of my life and never get bored of it. "Been in love, I mean."

"I thought I was," I say as our eyes stay locked and we take turns lifting our mugs to our lips. "With my last boyfriend, Kevin. But ... maybe I was just scared to see what else was out there? He was around when my mom and sister died, and I guess I just sort of glommed onto him." I tap a red fingernail against the side of the mug. "Five years I dedicated myself to that guy, and he ..." I don't have to finish my story; I already told Muse what happened and I don't want to say it again. "Now that I think about it, maybe I've never been in love either?"

"Nothing wrong with that," Muse says, finishing his tea and setting it aside. He stands up and pads around the side of the couch in his bare feet. I notice that his toenails are painted black, too, and I smile. "We're only twenty-one," he says as he grabs a black guitar case, almost completely covered in different sized and shaped band stickers. I see *Beauty in Lies, Rivers of Concrete, Tipped by Tyrants*—the three bands from this tour—as well as a few others I don't recognize: *Indecency, Amatory Riot, Ice and Glass.* "We have plenty of time to fall in love."

He sets the case on the couch, clicks open the latch and pulls out a black acoustic guitar with white bats all over it.

"Do you want to hear a song?" he asks as I blink surprised eyes at him and set my tea in my lap, my fingers enjoying the warmth of the mug as I squeeze the ceramic with nervous hands.

"You sing?" I ask and Muse shrugs, sitting down in the swivel chair opposite me. I adjust my position to face him, curling my legs toward the guitar case and listening to the rapid thumping of my heart, the only sound besides the faint murmur of the shower behind the closed bathroom door.

"Not at a professional level, but it helps to write music if you can at least carry a passable tune. My passion," Muse says, tapping the guitar with a loving hand, "is this baby right here."

He starts to strum the strings with his fingers, forgoing a pick. The sound is softer, warmer than I expected—especially coming from such an edgy instrument in the lap of such an edgy looking musician. The notes are sad but hopeful, accompanied by the gentle tapping of his bare foot against the wood floor.

"*If I had a first choice, love would be my last. My heart would always stay whole, my own secret stash.*" Muse's voice is rougher than Pax's, not as practiced, but it's beautiful anyway, especially when he closes his eyes, his silver hair fanning across his forehead, the tattooed bats on his fingers dancing across the strings of his guitar. "*If I let all of the hope go, would I be happy? Would I be? Would I be? If I took you in my heart, would you make me bleed? The love I've always let go, the truth I'm afraid I'll never know. If I let you in, could you show me how? Could you though? Could you though?*" Muse carries the notes low and easy, doesn't try to show off by hitting notes he knows he can't reach. And oh god, the way he plays that guitar … it's no wonder Paxton recruited him for his band. If it's pain he was looking for, Derek Muser has it in spades. "*Ooh, could you show me how to be happy? Could I be? Could I be?*"

His voice trails off and his fingers tell the rest of the story, strumming and plucking and teasing emotion from the gorgeous black instrument clutched in his hands. He looks just as comfortable holding that guitar as he did his cup of tea.

"*Ooh, tell me this is a night I won't regret. That I won't lose it all on this one bet. Ooh, could I be happy? Should I be? Should I be?*" he finishes, glancing up at me through the thick lenses of his glasses. Muse ends the song with a few high, sweet notes and then smiles. "So that's that," he says, like he didn't just serenade me with a soft sad song that brought tears to the edges of my eyes.

I set my tea aside and stand up as he puts the guitar down and lets me hug him tight, sit in his lap and squeeze him the way he deserves to be squeezed.

"Does it have a name, that song?" I ask, my face pressed into his purple sweater, the sweet scents of incense and tea making all that much more sense now that I know where they come from. I like the idea of Muse getting care packages from somewhere. It shows that somebody's thinking about him. That's always nice, to have somebody in this world care not just whether you live or die, but if you're happy. I glance at the *Love Spell* book.

"Nah, it's not even finished yet," he says, but there must be *some* reason he decided to play it for me, so I hug him a little harder.

"It's beautiful," I say, leaning back and looking into his eyes.

Our mouths meet just a few seconds later and when he reaches up to take his glasses away, I put a hand on his wrist to stop him. His tongue parts my lips and warms my body from the inside out, burning me up with heat and want and desire. I don't know *anything* about Muse when compared to the other guys on this tour—even Michael—but I can't make him tell me. I just have to coax and wait, to be patient.

But I'm afraid that if I'm too patient, I might not learn anything about him at all.

His kisses get more fervent, his hands sliding up the back of my shirt. I stand up and let my sweats fall around my ankles, stepping out of them as Muse shoves his own down and pulls me onto his lap. Our bodies join in slick, sweet agony and I ride him until the sounds coming from his throat are barely distinguishable from the sad but hopeful notes of his nameless song.

CHAPTER FORTY-TWO

"I like her," I say mildly as we mill around backstage waiting for our set.

"We all like her, you fucking twat. Why the hell else would she still be hanging around here if we didn't?" Pax says as he smokes a cigarette and ignores the glares coming from the venue's manager. He's not supposed to smoke in here, but he's doing it anyway; he's not the only one.

"No, I mean, I *really* like her," I say, wondering how Lilith's doing up in the balcony, if she's wishing she was down here instead of all the way up there. "I think I might ask her to be my girlfriend."

"Are you bloody fucking kidding me?" Pax snaps, casting a steely eyed glare in my direction. "You just fucking met her."

"So what? It's been a week, and I still like her. We have about a week to go until we head to Montréal. I saw a passport in her purse when it spilled the other day, and if everything keeps going well, I'm going to ask her to come with us. But I figure I should talk to Octavia now and see if there's anything else I need to make sure Lilith's okay to fly with us."

"You want Lilith to be your girlfriend, honey?" Ransom asks softly, drawing my attention over to him in his usual black hoodie.

"I think so. I mean, I know it's still early, but international travel gets tricky and there's only a week to go. It'd be easier to make arrangements now and cancel them later. Besides, why not? She has nowhere else to go and she seems happy with us.

Why not take her along for the ride if she wants to go?"

"You can't ask her to be your bloody girlfriend," Pax mumbles as he smokes his cigarette and shakes his head like I've completely lost my mind. But I haven't. My lonely traveler's met another lonely traveler, and he likes the company. Lilith has nobody; I have nobody. We could be each other's somebodies. I like the idea of that. And not just that. I like the shape of her smile, her curves, the way she talks about her family and her art, how she raves about strawberries like she's the fruit's damn lobbyist.

"Why can't I?" I ask, stuffing my fingers into the front pockets of my charcoal grey military jacket. I'm wearing it unbuttoned over a white wife beater, my mohawk spiked up into a wild crest. "What's it to you?"

"Because I'm not fucking finished with her yet, that's what," Pax snaps and I raise my eyebrows. He continues to smoke his cigarette like that's that, subject closed. I glance over at Ransom and Cope, noticing that Michael's staring at his phone, acting like he's completely checked out of the conversation. But that's a lie. I can see little beads of sweat on his forehead. If he was smart, he'd break up with Vanessa and spend a night with Lilith instead.

Which, I know, is a totally weird thing to say about a girl I'm thinking of asking to be my girlfriend. But it's not that I actually mind the arrangement that we have right now; I just don't want it to end in New York.

"What do you think?" I ask Cope as he drums his long fingers on the black matte wall behind him. He just took Lilith dancing last night, out on a proper date which he *never* does with groupies. But if any of the other guys have intentions, they best fucking tell them to me. I'm not going to let this girl slip from my fingers because nobody else wants to have a messy conversation with me. No, sorry, but my past is so fucked-up that just *thinking* about it chokes the life out of me. I see a possible future with Lilith and I'm not letting go without at least seeing where that might take me.

"I like her, too," Cope says, but his voice is completely shutdown and unreadable.

God.

How fucking annoying.

"So you want to date her, too?" I ask and he tosses me this glare that makes me smile. "I see. So that's how it is then. Ransom?"

He scrubs both hands down his face.

"Yeah. Yes. I want her to stay for a while."

"Okay then," I say, adjusting my stance, putting my hands in my back pockets instead and rocking back and forth in my slip-on checkered Vans. "So it's not that any of you mind her staying, just that you don't want *me* to ask her on my own behalf. This is an invitation issued by the whole band?"

"There's still a week to go in the States," Pax says, throwing his cigarette to the ground and crushing it out with his expensive loafers. "You might hate her by the end of it—or get tired of sharing."

"Maybe," I say, even as I feel sorry for the spoiled brat. Pax has had hard shit in his life, yes, but he's not used to having to deal with practicalities. That's always been taken care of for him. Even now, he knows that if the band falls apart, he's got his rich family back in England. I think they're even distant royalty or something. "But what if she needs a visa or something? You can't just decide last minute to rocket someone around the world. Arrangements need to be made, Pax."

"Whatever," he drawls and I roll my eyes dramatically.

Jesus.

Didn't expect this to turn into a goddamn production.

"I'll talk to Octavia tonight, after the show. If we decide we don't want her to come with us, no harm, no foul. But at least this way, we have options."

"You're smart as hell, Muse," Ransom whispers, lighting up his own cigarette. "You always think of every little thing."

I smile but Ransom doesn't smile back. He knows what it cost to me to learn to be like this, all the things I went through, saw, felt, suffered. I blink a couple of times to push the emotions back. I don't want to feel them, process them, understand them. I just want to let them all go and study Ransom's wary but desperate expression, Cope's stricken look of resigned disappointment mixed with unwanted hope, Paxton's false mask of rage covering up some real jealousy. Michael, too, texts Vanessa and pretends to be excited about seeing her tomorrow, but he's not. That relationship died a long, long time ago and I think they both know it. I wish either one of them would realize that and be brave enough to let this toxicity in their lives *go*.

"We're up next," Octavia says, her face drawn and blank. It'd have to be, after that row she had with Paxton last night. He almost fired her on the spot, but I managed to calm him down. If we fire her, the label will just send somebody else, maybe even somebody worse. Our last manager was a militant prick. "You guys ready?"

"We're ready," I say, but I'm the only one that bothers to answer her.

We take the stage a few minutes later, walking out behind the long white curtain, listening to the voiceover and the sound of confetti being blasted across the crowd. I pick up my red guitar and hoist the strap over my head, knowing that when I play tonight, I won't be playing for the crowd. I'll be playing for a single redheaded girl in the back, a girl who has so much heart that she cries at a half-finished song and tries to comfort other people in the midst of her own grief.

I *might* regret taking Lilith along on the *world* portion of our little tour, but I don't think so.

No, no matter what happens, having her with us on this bus has given me a brief reprieve from my loneliness and that, that's worth whatever price I have to pay to get it.

CHAPTER FORTY-THREE

Lilith

Michael is a bundle of nerves as we pack up quickly after the show and load onto the buses. It's not a long drive from Nashville to Atlanta, but the venue the boys played at tonight is having another show tomorrow and those bands are rolling their buses in later; there's not enough room for everyone in the back lot so we're heading out this evening instead of early the next morning.

Apparently this is something that was planned in advance because Michael's already got a date to meet Vanessa for an early breakfast.

"This is perfect, Mikey," Pax says as he loosens his tie and drapes it around his neck. "You can break up with her when we get there and then after the show, the six of us will go out and party without that fucking ball and chain dragging you into the cement. What say you, mate?"

"Shut the fuck *up*," Michael groans, leaning back in one of the swivel chairs and putting his boots on the coffee table. He's draped a cold rag over his eyes, moving it briefly to glare at Paxton. "Why are you so dead set on me breaking up with her? What's it to you?"

"She's an awful cunt, that's what," Pax says, glancing over at me as he removes his cuff links with a slow, careful intent that bathes my body in desperate heat. "Pardon my French, love, but it's true. Wait until you meet this girl and you'll see what I mean." He grins at me and moves over to the couch, taking my hand and pressing his cuff links into my palm. I look down and see that they're a pair of broken hearts. "Nothing at all like you."

"Lay off, Pax," Michael says, putting the rag back over his eyes. "I'm already stressed-out enough as it is."

"Because you hate the bitch," Pax supplies as he stands up and I lean my body into Ransom's, his violet tinted scent surrounding me like a fragrant hug.

"Shouldn't you be at least a *little* excited to see her?" Muse asks from his spot near the stove, pouring steaming water over a little silver strainer filled with loose leaf tea. "I mean, isn't that the whole point of dating someone? They make your chest tight, your heart beat, your—"

"And you've had how many *actual* girlfriends in your life, *Derek*?" Michael snaps, neglecting to move from his reclined position, white rag still firmly in place.

"None, but I'm telling you that if I looked forward to seeing my girlfriend for the first time in a year with literal dread and angst, I'd reconsider our relationship."

Michael makes a frustrated sound in his throat, but he doesn't respond to Muse's statement.

I fondle the cuff links in my palm and glance over at Copeland, noticing that he's acting strangely quiet tonight, eyes glassy and slightly far away. There it is, the first time I've really seen it so bare in his face: loss. That's fucking *grief* burning with an awful cold fire behind his turquoise eyes. I've seen him look sad, resigned, distant, but not devastated, not like this.

As if he notices my attention on him, Cope blinks and forces a smile.

"When I was dating Cara," he says and the room goes completely quiet, "I couldn't wait to see her. If it was a day, an hour, even just a few minutes, I was always happy to see her face."

"Yeah, well, you didn't cheat on Cara," Michael says, blatantly laying his sins out there for everyone to see. "I did. I gave Vanessa a legitimate reason to act the way she does. Fuck off."

"You never much liked her anyway," Pax says as Muse comes over to the couch and hands both me and Cope mugs of tea. Cope looks surprised, but he takes it in his hands with a sad smile.

Cara.

I haven't heard anyone mention Cara before. I wonder what that's about? Like Muse's entire history, this part of Copeland's is a complete mystery to me. He sucks on the silver ring in the center of his bottom lip for a moment and then takes a sip of his drink. I do the same and find myself overwhelmed with floral notes and the fragrant scent of roses.

"Shit, that's good," I whisper but the conversation is stuck on Vanessa and doesn't seem to be going anywhere. I notice Muse pushing his glasses up his face and smiling at me though. At least he heard me.

"Let's be frank here, shall we?"

"Are you ever anything *but* frank, Pax?" Michael asks caustically.

"The reason—the *only* fucking reason—that you're still 'with' Vanessa is because she had a miscarriage. That's it. Only reason. You feel bad for knocking her up and cheating on her. Be sorry about it and move the fuck on."

Michael finally snaps, and tears the rag off his face, chucking it at Pax. It hits him in the leg and falls to the floor with a wet plop.

"I'm done with this goddamn conversation," he says, kicking to his feet and storming past his friend down the hallway. There's this moment where he pauses, and I hear him walking back in this direction. Then he disappears into the bathroom and slams the door.

A small smile teases my mouth. I think he was on his way into the Bat Cave, remembered I was staying there and backtracked. I appreciate the respect.

"Do you all hate Vanessa that much?" I ask and feel Ransom shrug behind me.

"She and Michael just … don't really go together is all, honey."

"Go together?" Pax snorts, shrugging out of his jacket and tossing it over Michael's abandoned chair. "They don't belong in the same state. Just watch: I predict a blow-up by the end of breakfast. Maybe he just wants to fuck her? Hell if there's any other reason for him to see her. And I can't even *believe* she's bringing Tim with her. Has she gone completely mental then?"

"Tim's ... Michael's brother, right?" I clarify and feel Ransom sighing behind me.

"Yeah, older by eight years," Muse explains as he brings his own cup of tea over to the living room and sits down in the chair next to Pax's. "Michael's parents died in an accident when he was ten and Tim was eighteen. Basically, Tim resents Michael for having to raise him. They don't get along *at* fucking all."

Ah. Now I remember Ransom telling me that same story in Chicago. Shit.

"The fact that Vanessa would even think to bring Tim with her shows how little she knows or cares about Michael," Cope adds on the end of a long sigh, ruffling his red hair with his long fingers. He looks away, takes another sip of his tea, and then grabs for a book. When he cracks it open in his lap, I notice that his eyes are glassy again. He's not even reading the words as he sits there and stares at the page.

Fuck. Now I need to know everything about this Cara person.

I swear, I think I'm addicted to these boys' pain. And not because I want them to suffer, but because I want to save them from it. I want to bandage their wounds and staunch the bleeding of their hearts when what I really should be doing is that same thing for myself.

But my grief, my wounds, they feel like they'll never heal. Maybe by taking the pain of the men around me onto my shoulders, I can pretend my own doesn't exist?

I miss you Daddy.

I shut that thought down *quick.* I still have a week to be Cinderella, and I'll be damned if I'll give up my glass slipper early.

I toy with the rhodonite tear on my charm bracelet and try to banish the butterflies from my belly. How stupid for me to get all worked up over the fact that Michael's actually going to have sex with his fucking *girlfriend.* I have no claim on him.

And yet ... I can't banish the feeling of his mouth pressing hot and hard against mine, the torrid glaze of his hands across my body. Unconsciously, I reach up to press a finger against my lower lip.

"Anyway, fuck him," Pax says as he drapes himself languorously into the leather chair across from me, his eyes hooded and his expression wicked, like a cat who's got the cream. Hell, even the way he moves reminds me of a spoiled house cat. Smooth and easy, wanting for nothing, fully and completely aware of its own beauty. "So what if Michael wants to make an ass out of himself and be miserable? We don't have to share in his misery."

I take a few scalding sips of tea and raise my eyebrows at him.

"So … watch a movie then? That's what you're asking, right?"

"Oh, a *movie,*" Pax drawls in that lazy way of his. "A bloody *movie.* Make it a porn and you've got a deal."

"We can do more with Lilith than just fuck her, sweetheart," Ransom says, curling his arms around my body and breathing against the side of my neck. My heart thrills and flutters and this awful surge of affection just crashes over me. I want to throw my tea aside, turn in his arms and burrow against him, hold him tight, call him mine.

I want Ransom Riggs as more than just a … fuck buddy. Or a friend.

But then, I want the other three boys—*four* boys—in the same way.

Why does it feel like I'm falling in love five times over when I've just met these guys?

I force myself to keep sipping my drink, wondering if I'm just one of those people that can't separate sex from love. What if this was all just some huge mistake? Am I setting myself up for heartbreak here?

"Thank you, Ransom," I say with a teasing smile. "Do you have the remote?"

Pax sighs and reclines back in his chair, kicking his loafers off and putting his black socked feet up on the coffee table. Muse—practical as always—gets up to dim the lights while

Ransom supplies me with a sleek black remote.

"What kind of movies do you all like?" I ask, genuinely curious. Kevin would only watch war movies and football, that was it. Thinking on him now, I'm really struggling to come up with a reason why I ever thought I loved him. Hell, I didn't even *like* the guy.

"Muse watches cartoons, don't you, Muse?" Pax snorts derisively.

"I watch Japanese anime sometimes, sure. Hentai, too," he says with a wild smirk and when I don't seem to be getting the joke, he leans forward, dark glasses slipping down his nose. "That's animated *porn*," he says, popping the 'P' sound off the end of his tongue. He should look—and sound—like a complete nerd for saying that, but he's not wearing a shirt and his muscles are long and lean, his body still slightly damp with sweat from the show.

Why doesn't he ever wear a shirt?!

"But I also like comedies, action movies, anything superhero related," he adds, still smiling at me. There's this secretive little twinkle in his eyes that I noticed from the first moment he took the stage tonight. The way he held his guitar, the way he thrashed and flailed and played, Muse is definitely up to something.

And I think that something has to do with me, the way he's looking at me now.

"I like horror movies," Cope says, surprising me as he glances up from his book with his usual soft smile firmly in place.

"Not romance?" I ask and he shakes his head.

"No, romance in books is … amazing. In movies, it's too shallow. Besides, the sex usually gets left out. Either that or it's just full-on porn."

"Ask him how many times he saw those *Fifty-Shades-of-Whatever* movies in theaters?" Pax asks, smirking again. "Ask him."

"Those are different," Cope says as he leans back on the couch and crosses his arms over his chest, challenging his friend with a friendly stare. "And ask him how many times he came with me."

"Please, soft-core porn for housewives. Boring," Pax says, putting his hands behind his blonde head and staring at me with eyes the color of a silver sky after a good rain, still grey but bright, full of promise. Despite his picking, he's in a good mood tonight. "Give me a full throttle action flick any day. Something with a fucking plot, an explosion, and a beautiful girl."

"So basically James Bond?" I ask, but he just keeps smirking at me as I turn the TV on and start browsing for a movie to watch. "Ran?"

He thinks for a long moment, cuddling me in a way that comes damn close to bringing tears to my eyes. God, human contact is something I never realized I'd miss so much until it was gone. I broke up with Kevin, had no friends, no family in Phoenix. I haven't been touched like this for six months. It makes the world seem brighter, gentler, more hopeful.

"Anything with a happy ending. I don't care how the movie goes so long as it ends on a high note. I usually read spoilers before I watch anything. I can't take that awful sinking disappointment when things go to shit at the end."

I hand him my tea to set on the side table and make myself comfortable in his lap, the two of us reclining back against the arm of the couch, our feet pointed towards Cope. When he starts absently massaging my foot, I have to pinch my arm again to make sure I haven't died and gone to heaven.

At least Dad would be there, pops into my head before I can stop it and I grit my teeth.

"And you, Lilith?" Muse asks, still watching me, studying me with his gold-grey eyes. "What do you like to watch?"

"Besides strange blokes getting their cocks slapped by a woman in leather knickers," Pax inserts, and I ignore him.

"I'm open for pretty much anything," I say and then realize how that sounds, groaning and burying my face in Ransom's hoodie, his warm chuckling vibrating up through his chest.

"Yes, well," Pax says as he gets up and comes over to kneel down next to us. "So am I."

For a second, I think he's going to kiss me, but he doesn't.

He kisses *Ransom* instead, making the other man go completely rigid beneath me—just not in that one place where he should. Pax pulls away before anything else can happen and sits back in his chair, crossing his arms over his chest like he's just made the first move and expects us all to follow.

What a dirty trick.

Seeing the two of them kiss … makes me much less interested in watching a movie.

"Dick," I whisper, but I know Pax can see me smiling, can see my hard nipples through the thin white fabric of my tank top. I scroll through dozens of movies before I decide on one that I think they'll all like. As soon as I press play, Paxton make this disappointed sound in his throat and Muse chuckles.

"I'll make popcorn," he says, pulling out a yellow and white popcorn popper, pouring kernels in with a clattering metallic sound and turning the machine on. By the time the credits are done rolling, we're passing around a giant metal bowl of popcorn slathered in butter and salt. Muse even slices up some strawberries and tosses them with sugar and Cool Whip, making me wish he were my fucking husband. I could marry his face off for that.

Dad would've liked Muse, I think as I blink away sudden tears. That's the way with grief, insistent and needy, clinging to your soul with greedy hands. Sometimes, like an unruly child, it'll take a brief nap. But when it wakes up again, it comes at you with all of its previous vigor and then some.

"The fuck is this about anyway?" Pax asks, gesturing at the movie and making me smile.

Dad definitely would not have liked Paxton Blackwell.

Somehow, the thought is soothing, knowing that even though Dad is gone, he still lives on through me. His likes, his dislikes, all the things he taught me, they're all still here, coiled protectively beneath my heart.

"You'll just have to watch and see," I say coyly and for about an hour, the five of us sit there together and watch, eating popcorn, throwing out occasional commentary, chatting idly.

It's just about thirty seconds into the first sex scene of the film that things start to change.

I swear, I can *feel* the air getting charged with sex as the couple on-screen gets naked—all the best parts hidden beneath sheets, of course—but touching, kissing, fucking each other so sensually that we don't need to see everything to know what's going on.

I shift my body and feel Ransom's hard cock inside his black pajama pants.

When I turn and glance over my shoulder at him, I find his eyes glittering, his lips slightly parted. Me, I've been wet and wanting since Paxton kissed Ransom, so it's not a difficult transition for me to make, watching the movie one minute and turning around to straddle Ran the next.

Without a single word, he pushes his pants down and I slip out of my baggy pj bottoms—these old oversized gym shorts I used to wear to paint in. When I stand up, they fall right to the floor, no panties underneath.

Putting my hands on Ransom's sweatshirt covered shoulders, I lower myself onto his bare cock, our eyes locked, his own hands curling around my hips. As the couple on the screen behind me moans and rolls together in a tangle of sheets, I ride the darkest, twisted, most hauntingly beautiful man I've ever met in my life.

He sucks my nipples through my thin white tank, layering one torrid sensation on top of the next. His shaft is wide and warm, taking over me, spreading my hips and stealing my breath. I keep my movements slow but steady, careful to keep my clit from rubbing against his pelvis. No, I don't want to come yet. I have other plans.

I work Ransom with expert arcs of my hips, letting my body tell me what to do, favoring instinct over experience. And when he finally comes, this rough gasp tearing from his throat, pushing me down into his lap, spilling his seed inside, I get this primal feeling of satisfaction. Triumph, almost.

And then I stand up.

Before Ran can even catch his breath, I'm climbing onto Cope's lap and sucking his lip ring into my mouth. I kiss him, but only briefly. What I'm doing right now, this isn't about kissing or foreplay; this is about claiming, owning, pleasing.

Making these guys—my boys—feel good makes me feel good.

Is that so wrong?

Besides, my grief is squalling and loud tonight and this, this is the *perfect* distraction.

I unbutton Cope's black skinny jeans and free his curved shaft, straddling him and not caring that I'm making a mess, that I still have Ransom all over me. I lock eyes with Cope the way I did with Ran and take him inside of me. His moan is one of relief, of letting go, and I see that even bringing that girl, Cara, up for a second tore him apart inside.

I try to make the pain a little better for both of us, riding him with the same easy rhythm, keeping myself from toppling over the edge. It's hard, the way my body's thrumming and pulsing, wild with pleasure, giddy with the animalistic simplicity of this act.

I'm a woman and I want sex, lots of it. And I want these men, all of them.

Somehow, it feels liberating, wild, but also like it was meant to be.

Mine, I think as I dig my fingers into Cope's red hair and listen to the shuddering release of his orgasm, the exquisiteness of feeling him come while he's buried inside of me.

"Jesus fucking Christ," Pax murmurs, but he doesn't get up. No, he knows I'll make my way over there.

I swing myself off of Cope, his fingers trailing along my hips as I tear myself away from his warmth and tear my tank top over my head, Muse's hands taking hold of my waist and pulling me to him. He's already shoved his sweats down in eagerness, the quivering warmth of his cock already slick with lube. A bottle sits on the table between the chairs, and I smile as I sheathe him inside of my dripping warmth. If the boys are bothered at the idea of sharing me like this, they don't act like it.

Muse settles his hands on my ass, each touch of his body against mine like torture. I want to let go and feel my orgasm annihilate my thoughts, tear through me and leave me with an easy, relaxed after-sex glow. But not yet. Not yet. Not yet.

I breathe out slow, controlling the rush of pleasure as I rock myself against Muse's pelvis, clamp down around his eager shaft and milk him with my body. It's so … naughty that it feels almost wrong. Which, of course, only makes it feel more right. I tried to do the expected, 'normal' thing my whole life and it did nothing for me, got me nowhere. Maybe I was never destined for that kind of path? Maybe I need to forge my own path?

First, I claim my sexuality.

Next, it's time to make a plan for my life.

I take Muse's face in my hands, stare at his hazel eyes through his glasses and fuck him with my swollen pussy until his resolve cracks and his mouth parts with a final groan, giving up what Cope and Ran already gave me, making me feel just that much more complete.

Of course, even at the time I knew that it would take more than just my boys to save me from my pain, more than just me to save them from their own, but together we could fill the holes in each other's hearts, stop the bleeding long enough to recover, to open our eyes and realize that *anything* is possible if you believe, want, and try hard enough.

"Oh, Lilith," Muse whispers against my breasts just before I pull away. I give him a kiss on the forehead and move over to Paxton.

I knew I had to save him for last. He's too fucking alpha to just let me go like the others.

"Get the fuck over here," he growls, grabbing my wrist and pulling me into his chair with him. Like with Muse, his cock is already free, already slick from the wild pumping of his hand. I straddle him, guide his shaft inside of me and let out my own growl of frustration. I'm so worked up that I have to really work not to come right away. "You're such a naughty girl, Lilith Tempest Goode," he whispers in my ear, his voice rough with sex, with angry passion.

Paxton lets me ride him for several minutes, his grey eyes locked with my green ones. But then he gives up and slides both our bodies to the ground, pinning me against the heated wood floor with his weight, holding my wrists above my head. Paxton moves inside of me with harsh, angry thrusts, slamming our pelvises together as the others watch, panting and trying to catch their breath. They watch as Pax drives their come inside of me before spilling his own with a ragged, breathless sound.

It's the sudden flash of affection on his cruel face that makes me come, too, squeezing and tightening around him as I raise my hips and let out a shout, not bothering to hold anything back in here with these men. No, it feels too good to be bare in front of them.

As I tilt my head back and watch flashes of white pleasure explode in front of my eyes, I catch sight of a pair of bare feet, a hand wrapped around a cock.

It's Michael, watching us from the hallway.

But by the time Pax has caught his breath and is ready to let me up, I glance over my shoulder and find … nothing but darkness.

I tell myself I imagined the whole thing, but … I don't think I did.

Oh, Michael.

"Hey."

A warm hand caresses my shoulder and I lean my cheek against it, thrilling at the touch.

"Lilith," the voice whispers again, giving me a small shake. I press a gentle kiss to the man's knuckles, disturbed by how foreign they feel when all of my instincts say that this hand should be as familiar to me as my own.

I crack my eyelids and find Michael leaning over me, a tight frown on his face. He's shirtless and his hair's still damp from the shower. Part of me thrills at the sight, my body heating up, my thighs clenching tight, but then I remember what today is.

Atlanta. Vanessa. Michael must be up for his breakfast date.

"Yeah?" I ask sleepily, sitting up as he removes his hand, leaving this icy cool spot on my shoulder that aches for his touch with a strange sort of fierceness. "What's up?"

"I need you to do me a favor," he says, still frowning, violet eyes flicking to the side like he can barely look at me. That's when I remember last night, catching sight of him in the hallway with his cock in his hand. Did I imagine that? I'm still not sure. What I *am* sure of is that I fucked four guys, one after the other, like some kind of wildcat in heat.

And it felt *great.*

I *was* a wildcat, and those were my males, seeking their pleasure in me. And I took from them everything I fucking wanted.

My cheeks flush a little and I lift my hands up to cover my

face.

Yeah ... I think I'm going a little bit crazy in here. Maybe I need to get off this bus more? I promise myself that I'll at least go out and shop later, get some more raw ingredients so I can cook up a nice dinner. Michael could even invite his brother and Vanessa if he wanted.

Or maybe that's just me wanting them to spend time together where I can see them because ... because my wildcat is territorial and *hungry.* I groan low under my breath as Michael drags my hand away, the place where his fingers curl around my wrist burning with pleasure.

"Can you come to breakfast with me?" he asks and my heart goes nuts, pounding in my chest and ringing between my ears. He wants to tell her about the kiss *now*? At their first meeting? "Bring one of your boyfriends," he adds, pausing dramatically. "Well, except for Pax. You can't bring him."

Michael gets up and pads away before I can respond.

"I'll go," Copeland says groggily, sitting up slowly next to me. The blankets fall around his bare body, making the wild pounding in my chest even worse. He glances over at me, turquoise eyes dark in the shadows of the Bat Cave. The other three boys sleep on peacefully around us.

"Okay," I say with a smile, remembering the genuine smile on his face when he watched me try—and mostly fail—to dance the Charleston at our impromptu lesson. "Let's see what this is about, shall we?"

Cope and I climb out of bed, pulling on pj's and finding Michael already dressed when we enter the kitchen.

"What the fuck are you two doing?" he says, raking a hand through the dark, wet strands of his hair. "Get dressed. We have to meet Tim and Vanessa in fifteen minutes."

"What do you need us for?" Cope asks, but Michael just rolls his eyes and pinches the bridge of his nose like he can't be bothered to explain.

"Can you just do this for me?" he snaps, pacing frantically, dressed in a purple button-up with most of the buttons undone, a leather jacket, and a pair of dark jeans. He's wearing leather combat boots that are completely free of scuffs as well as a fine dash of liner around his eyes. "Tim's going to be there and I just ... don't want to do this alone, okay?"

"Alright, alright," Cope says, blinking sleepy blue-green eyes at his friend. "We'll get dressed."

"Thank you," Michael snaps, but then he casts me this ... look. I can't interpret it, but he stops frowning so hard and takes a deep breath. "Thanks," he repeats, much more kindly this time.

I smile back and excuse myself to dig through the sea of shopping bags in Muse's bunk. Since the boys have been sleeping in the Bat Cave with me—or on the couch—every night, I've been using their beds for storage purposes.

I figure Vanessa's probably going to want to punch me after she hears that I kissed her boyfriend, so I dress like I might have to evade a fight. I choose some new pale pink skinny jeans, knee-high black boots with a slight heel, and a white Beauty in Lies t-shirt with black cursive writing. I borrow one of Cope's studded belts and put my hair in a long, loose braid down my back. Some makeup, a few pieces of jewelry, and I look kind of like the female version of Copeland—like a rockstar girl next door.

"Wow," he says with a sharp smile when he sees me come out of the hallway. "I like the outfit."

"Right back at you," I tell him with a grin, finally breaking through the thick crust of sleep and feeling awake, invigorated ... nervous as hell. I'm on this strange precipice, wishing Michael and Vanessa would break up, praying they won't. It's so silly. I need to stop trying to poach some chick's boyfriend and get over myself.

I study Cope, trying *not* to conjure up images of last night, of riding him into oblivion on the couch. I mean, not that it wasn't fantastic, but I want to meet Vanessa and Tim without droopy eyes and wet panties. I'm already finding that hard to do with Cope wearing tight red jeans tucked into high top black and white Chucks, a black Beauty in Lies tee that stretches across his muscular chest, and a sea of his usual belts. The silver ring in his lower lip winks at me when his smile turns into a grin.

"We look kind of like twins," he jokes, but I'm checking out his tight ass in his jeans and can't even come up with an appropriate response.

"Are you guys—" Michael starts as he reappears on the bus steps with a cigarette in his hand. "Jesus, really? Are you two already trying for that power couple look? Good god." But he sounds almost wistful as he bitches at us. "Did you borrow her jeans, Cope?"

"Hilarious," Copeland says as he takes my hand in his and leads me down the bus steps to the damp pavement. It's early, but the sun is peeking its head from the clouds and smiling at us.

It's going to be a good day, I think.

My intuition is only half right.

The day will start out good, become fucking *awful*, and then end with an agonizingly beautiful finale. But how could I possibly know that at the time?

Michael takes us to this big purple truck with black flames on the sides and I raise an eyebrow.

"Belongs to the label," he says as he unlocks the doors and we all climb up into the cab. I sit in the middle and try not to notice the sweat collecting on the side of Michael's face. He doesn't look like a guy that's about to see his brother and girlfriend for breakfast. He looks like he's on his way to an execution—*his* execution.

"Are you ... okay?" I ask as I get my first view of Atlanta, Georgia in the early morning sun. It's brisk and cold out, but the day is promising to be clear with its blue skies and white fluffy clouds. I'm not sure what part of the city we're in, but I see a glorious skyline with tall skyscrapers, one of which I recognize: the Bank of America Plaza. "That's the eighty-seventh tallest building in the world," I say, trying to fill the silence when it's clear that Michael's not interested in talking.

"Did Muse tell you that?" Cope asks slyly, leaning his elbow against the door and raising his red brows at me. He's shaped his faux hawk up into a sexy, spiky crest. I want to touch it, but I keep my hands to myself, not wanting to mess it up. I like the idea of parading my rockstar ... fuck buddy? boyfriend? ... around town and showing him off while he looks basically perfect.

"He did," I respond, just as slyly and Michael curses under his breath as his phone vibrates in his lap. Cope and I stare at him for a moment, but he ignores us. I look back at Copeland. "He also told me that the city of Atlanta has a gross domestic product of two hundred and seventy billion."

"That so?" Cope asks, his red brows rising all the way up to his matching red hair. "That is *fascinating*. Muse tell you that one, too? You know he just Googles that shit."

"I thought it was cool," I respond briskly, but I can't stop myself from smiling at him. I'm glad to see that he's not glassy-eyed and vacant like he was last night, after mentioning that girl, Cara. I decide I won't let myself be that way today either.

In a week, the buses will pull into New York City and I'll be just a few hours from home. I've decided: I'm going to see my family home one last time, whether Susan likes it or not. And like Ransom suggested, I'm going to speak to the cemetery staff and see about getting Dad's name chiseled into the mausoleum —even if there's nothing of his actual body or ashes to put there.

So if I need to be sad, if I need to cry, if I need to curl up in a ball and sleep, I'm going to push it aside for the time being. I'm going to enjoy this moment with Cope and try to eke out as much happiness as I can while I've got the opportunity.

"Oh, it's totally cool," Cope says, leaning over and kissing me with such a tender level of care that I start to believe this is more than just a fantasy between us. Ugh. I knew Cope was one of the dangerous ones; I was right. He makes me feel too wanted, too cared for. "Tell me more about gross domestic products, Lilith," he says against my lips with a smile.

"Would you two lay off for a second?" Michael growls as he huffs out a deep breath, the spicy pomegranate smell of his shampoo filling the space inside the cab. "I think the place is right up here."

"Oh!" I say as we pass by a sign for the Atlanta Botanical Gardens. "I saw an ad for that online last night. I'd love to go. We've been to all these amazing cities and I haven't seen much in the way of landmarks."

"We've been keeping you too busy," Cope says with a flirtatious lilt to his voice. "I promise you that this next week, we'll see some shit. Pick something and we'll do it, whatever you want."

"Fucking finally," Michael curses before I get a chance to respond, snatching a parking space on the side of a tree lined street with old brick buildings and several small restaurants and coffee shops that I can see from here. Most of them are already busy.

He unlocks the doors and climbs out, leaving Cope and me to scramble after him.

"Dude, he is fucking *losing* it," Copeland whispers as he grabs my hand and we take advantage of the lull in traffic to cross the street behind Michael.

"Maybe he's just excited to see her?" I hazard and Cope tosses me a dubious look.

"Yeah, maybe," he says, but he sounds skeptical.

We enter the café behind Michael, finding ourselves in the ultimate hipster retreat—colorful murals on the walls and ceiling, exposed ductwork, trippy modern art pieces on the walls. The crowd is young, the vibe relaxed. Well, everyone except for Michael.

He pauses a moment to look around as I take in the sweet heady scent of maple syrup and the richly vibrant smell of freshly brewed coffee. My stomach grumbles appreciatively as Michael finds what he's looking for and starts off toward a table near the windows.

It's hard to see the people sitting there until we get a little closer and the woman stands up with a blindingly white smile on her long, thin face. My heart starts to pound dramatically, my mouth goes dry, my throat tight. Why the fuck am I so damn nervous?

Cope squeezes my suddenly sweaty hand as I watch Michael's yearlong break from his girlfriend come to an abrupt and rather fizzling end.

"Hey," he says, opening his arms to her and giving her a lukewarm hug. She returns the gesture with an equal amount of enthusiasm and steps back to look at him.

"Hey yourself," she says, and even though she looks less than thrilled to see Michael himself, her eyes roam his body appreciatively. "I missed you, baby. Did you miss me?"

"Of course," he replies, giving her a tight peck on the lips. She presses forward with the kiss and before I know it, their tongues are tangled and he's pulling her into his arms for a proper hug. I watch his hands, try not to imagine them roaming across my body the other night, burning fire and want and need into my skin. *He made my lip bleed.*

Cope clears his throat and the couple pauses.

Vanessa—a leggy blonde with big brown eyes and a frighteningly perfect face—smiles around Michael at the pair of us.

"Hey Cope," she says and he smiles his usual, gentle smile.

"Vanessa," he replies, holding up his left hand to indicate me. He keeps his right entangled with my fingers. "This is my girlfriend, Lilith Goode."

Oh shit.

There it is again.

I feel my cheeks flame and all those emotions come bubbling to the surface again. Of course *girlfriend* is really the only way to describe me without going into lurid detail, but wow. Wow. Fuck.

"Lilith," Vanessa says, a little tightly as she glances at Michael. "You didn't tell me Cope had a new girlfriend," she says coyly, her laughter like tinkling bells when she chuckles. I try not to hate her—I *really* try—but it happens and then I end up hating myself for it. "It's nice to meet you, Lilian," she says and I feel my mouth purse into a slight frown.

"It's Lilith," Michael says as a man stands up from the table, his eyes the same strange violet color as his little brother's. *And this must be Tim*, I think as I watch the two men face off for a moment. "Timmy," Michael says carefully as Vanessa steps out of the way. The two of them embrace for a moment before he gestures back at us. "You remember Cope, of course, and this is his girlfriend *Lilith*." He gives Vanessa a look that she returns. "Lilith, this is my brother, Timothy Luxe."

"Nice to meet you," I say to both him and Vanessa, even though I only mean about half of that.

"Nice to meet you, too," he tells me as we take our seats and

Michael ends up sitting at the end of the table in a chair instead of in the booth next to his girlfriend. Tim takes what should be his spot next to the window and across from Cope. Lucky me, I get to face Vanessa dead-on.

"I didn't know you were bringing friends," Vanessa says with another one of those falsetto laughs. She reaches out to pat my hand with her long, tan fingers and manicured nails. "But we're glad to have the company, of course."

Sure you are, I think as I sip the coffee the waitress poured and wait to order.

Michael declines to acknowledge his girlfriend's statement and takes a huge gulp of his ice water, sweat running down the side of his throat. He's nervous, edgy, uncomfortable. I wonder if that's because he's gearing up to tell Vanessa about our kiss? I wonder if he'll also confess to watching us from the hallway last night ... But is watching cheating? I have no idea. Or hell, maybe I hallucinated the whole thing?

"So, what are our plans for today?" Vanessa oozes, reaching over and squeezing Michael's now bare bicep. He's shrugged out of his leather jacket and button-up into the black wifebeater underneath, leaving his tattooed arms exposed and beautiful in the morning light. Sitting this close to him, I see cats, owls, the moon, books, hourglasses, and stars, among other things. All of it jewel toned, finely detailed, beautiful.

"I figured after this, you and I could spend some alone time together?"

Vanessa laughs as my stomach clenches painfully.

Alone time. Sex. Of course that's what he wants after a year apart, some time to connect on a physical level. I shouldn't be surprised, but I am. I wanted ... No, I didn't want anything. Still, the idea of Michael fucking this tall, blonde, model of a girl makes me want to cry.

He rightfully belongs to her, but in my gut, he belongs to *me.*

"If you guys have any spare time after the show, I'm making dinner on the bus. I don't have a lot of space to work with, but I've got this idea for macaroni and cheese pizza that I thought I'd try. I had good luck with the last macaroni recipe."

Groupie

I may as well have sprouted tentacles and torn apart the restaurant in a rage for the way both Tim and Vanessa stare at me.

"Macaroni ... and cheese *pizza*?" she quips, her glossy pink lower lip dangling off her jaw. "I'm sorry, but that's ..." She laughs a little and Michael grits his teeth.

"Come on, Vanessa, lay off," he says, but she continues to chuckle anyway.

"No, I don't think we'll join you for *mac 'n' cheese pizza*," she says, biting the words off the end of her tongue. Looking at her now, I kind of wish I'd pushed harder and fucked her boyfriend. Then, you know, I feel guilty for thinking that, too. Women in this world have a way of hating on each other that makes me sad; I don't want to be one of those people. We have to stick together. "I think after a *year* apart from my man, he can take me out to a *nice* dinner—he owes me that much, at least."

"She was just trying to be sociable," Cope snaps, getting frustrated on my behalf. I almost smile. "Look, if you don't want us here, we can go somewhere else?"

"Oh, come on, Cope, *relax*," Vanessa says with a roll of her Bambi brown eyes. "I'm just playing. Lilian knows that, don't you, Lilian?"

"Fucking *Lilith*," Michael snaps and Vanessa's face goes dark.

"This is how you treat Vanessa on the day of your reunion, Mikey? Didn't I raise you better than that?" Tim asks blandly, his short black hair in a crew cut, his clothing disturbingly similar to something that Kevin might wear—a blue polo shirt, khakis, and brown loafers. God. This whole thing just gets worse by the second ...

"Do not call me fucking Mikey," Michael says with a deep breath, glancing over at me. Our eyes meet and for a second there, I think he's going to choose me. As silly and ridiculous and stupid as that sounds, that's what it feels like. But then he looks away again.

"So, what brings you to Atlanta?" I ask, trying to steer the table's conversation somewhere a little more pleasant, just to make Michael's day a bit easier.

"Oh, my daddy …" she starts and my heart breaks a little. As silly as it is to hear a grown woman say *daddy*, I want to say it, too. Daddy, daddy, daddy. My daddy is dead. Cancer *ate* him. It fucking ate him.

My hands start to shake and I squeeze Cope's hand harder under the table.

"My daddy," Vanessa continues, oblivious to my pain, "is in town for this law conference thing." She takes a sip of her water and waves her hand around as she talks. I notice Tim watching her with a sort of … affection that surprises me. It's familiar and intimate the way he studies her; Michael doesn't seem to notice. "It's this fancy gathering for corporate lawyers —only the best are invited."

My heart stutters and jumps for a second. What a coincidence. That sounds *exactly* like the type of event that Kevin's father lives for. One day, Kevin will join him, schmoozing around with his father, some beautiful girl on his arm. That girl was supposed to be me, and once upon a time, I really wanted it to be. Sitting here with Cope on one side and Michael on the other, it sounds like fucking *hell*.

"That's … exciting," I say as I try to make myself smile. "Are you coming to the show tonight?"

Vanessa gives me this look, like I'm fucking stupid.

"I've been to more than my fair share, thank you very much. I don't need to see another one anytime soon."

"You're not coming?" Michael asks incredulously. "This is all new material; I wrote a lot of this shit. I thought you came to see me play."

"I came to see *you*," Vanessa says with a sigh, pushing blonde hair back from her face when the waitress arrives to take our orders. There's a brief moment of reprieve as we take turns ordering, but as soon as that waitress walks away …

"I'd really like you to come to the show tonight," Michael says and Vanessa rolls her eyes.

"Michael, don't. Just don't, please? I haven't seen you in forever; I don't want to fight."

Michael's nostrils flare and he closes his eyes for a long

moment, putting his palms on the table and standing up.

"I need some air," he says before stalking away and out the front doors. I watch him through the window as he lights a cigarette and paces across the sidewalk, smoking.

"Maybe we should go and give you guys some space?" Cope suggests and Vanessa smiles this awful smile at him.

"Really? You'd do that? I just think we need to be alone, you know?" I glance at Tim, but his presence doesn't seem to bother Vanessa the way ours does. "Thanks, Cope," she says all sweet and high-pitched. I don't wait another second, tearing out of that booth and heading outside with my breath coming in short, shallow bursts.

I have no idea why I'm freaking out so much.

"Dude, come *on,*" Cope says when we get outside. "What are you doing with this girl?"

"I owe her, Cope," Michael says, voice strained. I notice he won't look at me. "I cheated on her and knocked her up, and then she lost the baby …"

"Michael, you shouldn't be with someone because you think you owe them. You should be with them because you love them," I say, wondering when or if he's really going to ask me to discuss our kiss with Vanessa.

He throws a nasty look at me, but doesn't say anything back, digging in his pocket for the truck keys and passing them to Cope.

"I'm assuming you guys are leaving?"

"I'm not sitting and stewing in her toxic, hostile bullshit, Michael. You shouldn't either," Cope says, crossing his arms over his chest and frowning.

"Fine. Just go then," he says, turning away and walking down the sidewalk in the direction opposite the truck. Cope and I watch him go for a minute and then turn to leave. As we walk, I happen to glance in the window and see Vanessa and Tim, leaning in close, eyes half-lidded. The way they're looking at each other …

Her hand sits on his knee; his smile is sly and inviting.

If I had to bet money, I'd say they were fucking.

"Crap," I whisper, but then Cope's pulling me across the

street and I just have no fucking clue what to say to Michael anyway. No fucking clue.

Cope unlocks the doors to the truck and helps me inside, giving me this apologetic sort of smile as he looks up at me.

"Can I take you somewhere else for breakfast?" he asks and then lets his smile morph into a small grin. "Or to the Botanical Gardens?"

"Either of those things sounds heavenly," I say as he closes my door for me and I take one last look out the back window toward the restaurant. Michael is walking back down the sidewalk, pausing to put out his cigarette and throw away the butt.

Vanessa … is kissing Tim.

My mouth drops open as Michael enters the restaurant and I watch him navigate the busy tables through the row of front windows. Just before he turns the corner toward the booth, Vanessa and Tim break apart and I watch as Michael's girlfriend tosses a beautiful smile his way.

Fuck.

Fuck, fuck, fuck.

What am I supposed to do with all of that?

CHAPTER FORTY-FIVE

Michael

MICHAEL LUXE

As if breakfast isn't bad enough, the day just gets worse and worse.

"You came all the way out here to *not* attend my show, to tell me I *can't* stay in your hotel room with you, to *refuse* to stay in the bus with me. So tell me, Van, why the fuck are you here?" I ask as we drive around the city in Tim's rental car. The two of us are sitting in the back while he drives.

I have to admit, his presence here fucking *sucks*. When did he become one of Vanessa's henchmen, defending her at every turn, chastising me, butting in on all of our conversations? Already today, we've been to an art museum, out to lunch, and to the fucking College Football Hall of Fame. All of it with Tim in tow, none of it fun. It's just been a nonstop bicker fest this whole damn time.

"We'll have plenty of time to spend together," she says, leaning over and kissing me on the mouth. I think she expects the move to silence me, but in reality … I feel nothing when she touches me, kisses me. I felt only dread when I turned the corner in that restaurant and saw her sitting there with my brother.

I try to rationalize all the negative feelings in my head by telling myself that I deserve this, all of it. It was *me* that fucked up this relationship, turned it toxic. So no matter what I'm feeling right now, I'll push through it. Besides, Vanessa might be annoying, but she's tall, leggy, blonde, *gorgeous*. She and Lilith are so different they may as well be night and day: tall and short, blonde and redheaded, thin and curvy, tan and pale.

I refuse to admit to myself that I like Lilith better.

Inside though, I know it's true.

"*Alone* time, Vanessa," I snap, gesturing at the back of my brother's head. His shoulders and neck are tense as hell, and I see his hands tightening around the steering wheel like he wants to punch me or something. God, seeing him does nothing but stir up resentment and rage in both of us. At this point our relationship's so damn toxic I feel like we should just call it quits.

But Tim *did* give up his youth to raise me. He did. I should be fucking grateful, right? Only all I am right now is angry. I feel like I'm always angry nowadays.

"Look," she starts with a long sigh, pushing her long, blonde hair over her shoulder. Vanessa adjusts her cleavage as I watch, trying to drum up *some* sexual feelings toward her. Like, if we can make it into bed together, everything will go back to normal, right? I mean, I am *pent*-fucking-up. That, and maybe I'm full of guilt, too. I still have to tell her about the kiss, and there's last night … *What the fuck was I thinking?* Maybe I was right: maybe my past *is* too dark to overcome? Maybe I'll never be able to commit to a woman the way I should, treat her fucking right, be anything but a goddamn bastard. "Let's go back to the hotel; Daddy's out at his convention thing right now, so he won't mind."

I purse my lips and feel my nostrils flare as I lean back and run my fingers through my hair. Somehow in the frenzy of the morning, I forgot to bring the bag from the jewelry store with me. Was that a Freudian slip or just coincidence? Anyway, I bought both the opal teardrop necklace and the rhodonite heart necklace, unsure which one I wanted to give Vanessa … and which one I wanted to give Lilith. I told myself I was just buying her something as a thank you. I mean, after that fucking story she told me? I had to.

Sitting here now, I don't feel stupid for buying Lilith a gift, I feel ridiculous for thinking Vanessa would appreciate something with that much sentiment.

"We can go back, have some drinks, swim in the pool," she

says, tugging on my arm and pouting her lips at me. "What do you say, Mikey?"

"Fine."

"Fine?" she snaps. "Wow, real enthusiastic. I'm glad I flew all the fucking way out here to see you on the anniversary of our baby's *death.*"

My heart breaks when she says that and my stomach turns over a dozen times. Jesus. I am a selfish fucking asshole.

I turn to Vanessa and reach out, taking her hand and curling my fingers around it. I rub my thumb across her knuckles and force myself to take several deep, slow breaths. She looks at me and I make myself to smile.

"I'm sorry," I say, that awful wave of guilt drowning me and any feelings I might have towards Lilith. Because honestly, I've spent the last few days thinking about breaking up with Vanessa for good. Like, Jesus, I realize how fucking *weird* this whole thing is with Lilith and my bandmates, but for the life of me I can't help wanting it. I came close last night, so damn close. When I came out of the bathroom and saw what I saw, I almost lost it completely. I couldn't stop thinking that I should be number fucking five, that she should climb off Paxton's lap and come sit on mine.

"Are you?" Vanessa asks haughtily, forcing me to breathe past the rush of anger.

"Yes, I'm sorry. I know how hard losing that baby was on you. That's why I'm trying to make it right. I was just want to spend some time together with just us is all." I glance back in Tim's direction and notice that he hasn't relaxed at all. If anything, he looks even more tense. He's been that way all goddamn day.

Vanessa smiles at me and then removes her hand from mine, taking out a compact to fix her makeup. We don't speak for the rest of the drive.

When we do get to the hotel, I take a moment to hang outside and smoke while Vanessa goes upstairs to change into her swimsuit. Tim follows her up to his own room which is fine by me since we have nothing more to say to each other than we did last time I saw him, a few months ago back home in Seattle.

When we're both in town, we have lunch occasionally, make small talk, but neither of us really cares about having any sort of intimate relationship.

"Fucking fuck," I growl, leaning my head back against the building and enjoying my cigarette. I think I'm on pack number two today; that's how goddamn stressful all of this is.

The sun beats down on my skin and even though the air is cold, the sunshine feels hot, searing my eyes through my closed lids. When my phone rings, I just assume it's Vanessa and answer without opening my eyes.

"What?"

There's a long pause before someone clears their throat on the other end.

"Michael, it's Lilith," she says tentatively and my eyes slide open, glancing at the unknown number on the screen. One of the boys must've given her my number which, surprisingly, I don't mind. Normally I am militant about that shit.

"Hey," I say softly and then sigh. "I'm sorry about breakfast."

"Not a big deal," she says in a rush, her words tumbling over each other. There's another long pause as I wait for her to continue. Clearly, she called me so she must have something she wants to say. "Michael, I … need to tell you something." There's a graveness to her voice that freaks me the fuck out.

I drop my cigarette to the ground and crush it out with my boot, adjusting my position so that I'm standing in the shade of a sprawling white oak tree, the leaves rustling softly in a gentle breeze.

"Lilith," I say slowly, my heart pounding as I try to drum up any number of awful situations that she might want to talk about. Like, did I actually fuck her that night I got blackout drunk? I can't remember a damn thing. That would be so fucking like me. I close my eyes again. *"What?"*

"I don't really know how to say this," she starts, like this is something she's been thinking about, debating on, all damn day.

"So just say it," I snap, but not because I'm mad at her, just because I'm frustrated with this whole situation. Honestly, I'd much rather be back on the bus with Lilith than standing here getting ready to borrow my brother's swim trunks so I can spend an awkward afternoon at the pool with Vanessa.

"Michael, I think ... I don't really know what's going on, but I feel like I should say something. If our positions were reversed, I'd want to know. I just want to say beforehand that I ... this isn't because of the kiss or anything."

"Jesus Christ, I'm already on pins and needles here. What is it?"

"When Cope and I were leaving the restaurant, I happened to glance back and saw Vanessa and Tim kissing."

My heart stops.

"*What?*" I ask, this surly, awful quality to my voice that I don't even feel like I'm in control of. It just comes out this scathing, angry sound and I can't stop it.

"They were flirting, touching, kissing. I didn't see too much of it, and honestly, I'm not sure what to make of the whole situation, but I just thought I should let you know. They were mouth to mouth ..."

"Are you fucking with me?" I ask, hating myself for being such a dick. "Is this a joke?"

"It's not a joke. I saw them kissing and I thought you deserved to know."

"Really? Is that what I deserve? You don't even fucking *know* me," I growl, taking my anger at Vanessa, at Tim, out on Lilith. It's not fair, not at all; I know that. It's not her that I'm mad at. "You know what, Lilith, just because you're alone and your life fucking sucks doesn't mean that I have to suffer along with you."

I hang up the phone in a rage, lighting another cigarette and pacing back and forth for several moments until I can calm myself down. The tree rustles its leaves like an angry murmur, chastising me for being such an asshole.

Tim and Vanessa? Really? Really?

No fucking way.

Just ... no.

I turn and head inside toward the elevator, languishing in my own stubborn doubt for thirteen floors until I end up knocking on Tim's door with a fist. He opens it, already dressed in a

swimsuit, Vanessa sitting on the edge of his bed in a gold bikini
…

"Finally," she says, tossing me a pair of black trunks when I step inside. "We've already ordered drinks to be delivered to the pool. I got you a long island."

"You know," I say as I finger the stretchy fabric in my hands and close my eyes against a surge of rage, "I was under the impression that this is where our alone time was going to start, so what the fuck is he still doing here?"

"Michael, don't," Vanessa says and even though it's *right* in fucking front of me, I don't believe it. I can't. I stayed celibate for a year for this woman. I took all her calls—ten, twenty, whatever times a day. I let her treat me like shit and call me names and make me feel like a fucking demon for what I did. So no, I won't accept it. I won't. She's cheating on me? With fucking Tim? I'm sorry, but I just can't accept that. "Stop being so weird. He's your *brother.* You guys need to spend more time together."

"Do we?" I ask as I open my eyes and look my older brother in the face. "Is that so? If that's the case then why did he kick me out of the house on my eighteenth birthday? Why did he ignore my calls and my texts when I asked him for help with my addiction? Why didn't he visit me in the hospital when I almost *died?*"

"Michael …" Tim starts and he almost sounds pleading, like maybe he really does want some kind of relationship with me. But, as usual, Vanessa butts in and stands up, crossing her arms over her flat chest.

"If you're going to be a fucking prick, then why don't you just *go?* Come back later when you've cooled down a little. I am tired of your shit. You've been nothing but a mopey asshole all damn day."

"You know what—" I start and I have to bite back the angry words that threaten to spill from my mouth. I wish I'd done that with Lilith, held myself back like this. God, I wish I'd saved this tiny scrap of self-control for her instead. "Maybe I fucking will? I have to get ready for the show anyway."

I snatch a key card off the table on my way out and kick the door open.

"I'll be back after the concert," I snap and then slam it shut behind me, storming down the hall, forgoing the elevator for the steps and forcing myself to walk down all thirteen flights. When I hit the lobby though, I stop, my eyes catching on a young blonde woman with a baby in her arms. The kid looks like she's a few months old, the age our child would've been if Vanessa and I had actually had him.

Fuck.

I run my fingers through my hair and lean against the wall next to a giant potted fern.

I can't run out on Vanessa like this; I just can't. I *have* to try. I owe this to her and really, I *am* being a fucking dick today.

Standing up, I pull my phone from my pocket and dial Lilith's number back as I climb the stairs again. With each step I take, my head gets cooler, calmer, and some of that volatile rage bleeds away. When she doesn't answer, I almost leave a message, telling her how sorry I am, how much I like her, how I wish I didn't owe my life to Vanessa.

Fuck.

I should've picked Lilith.

But then, I'm not good enough for her, am I? Some guy that can barely stay faithful for a single year. Besides, I've put Vanessa through enough shit, haven't I?

I tuck my phone away without leaving the message and continue up the carpeted staircase to the thirteenth floor, down a hallway with gold and white walls, and straight to Tim's door.

Using the key I grabbed, I let myself into the room.

And walk right in on my brother's bare ass pumping away at Vanessa.

She's moaning in wild ecstasy, her gold bikini top pushed down, her bottoms shoved to the side to make room for his cock. His swim trunks sag around his ankles as he fucks her with a passion I didn't even know the man was capable of.

I drop the key card to the floor.

"Jesus Christ!" Vanessa screams, covering up her breasts like I'm some goddamn stranger, some asshole that's broken into her room. I think she expects me to go into a rage, hit her, hit

Tim, I don't know, because she backs up off the bed and pushes her body into the corner.

"Really?" I ask, my stomach tight and twisted with betrayal. "Really? This is actually happening right now?"

"Michael …" Tim starts, fixing his shorts, running his palm over his short dark hair. "We came here together to tell you …"

Before I even register what I'm doing, I'm flying at him, punching him hard in the face and sending him stumbling back onto the bed while Vanessa screams horrible things at me.

"You brought this on *yourself*!" she yells as Tim and I struggle together and I manage to land a second punch to the familiar line of his jaw, a jaw we both share with our dead dad. I wonder what he'd think now, if he could see all of this bullshit? "You cheated on me, you asshole, so I cheated on you!"

"Yeah?" I ask as I step back and shake out my hand, looking at Vanessa's tan lithe body and long blonde hair. She's never looked as ugly to me as she does in that moment. "So this is all part of some elaborate revenge plot to get back at me?"

"We're in love," Tim says calmly, sitting up, his eye and jaw already beginning to swell. Blood drips down the front of his face and stains his pale white chest. "We have been for a long time now."

"You didn't think to tell me?" I yell at him instead because Vanessa … man, fuck her. I can't look at her right now.

"I didn't want to lose you," Tim snarls, but fuck if I believe that. He never gave a shit about me before, so why should he start caring now? He swipes his palm over his face as I rake my fingers through my hair. "Michael, I love you."

"Stop it, Tim," Vanessa says, coming around the bed with her bikini fixed back in place. She gets right in my face and shoves me hard. By the grace of god, I manage to control myself and just stand there glaring at her. "He doesn't deserve your sympathy. He doesn't deserve anything. The only person that Michael cares about is fucking Michael."

"Sure, yeah, that's why I stayed celibate for a fucking YEAR!" I shout back at her, my breathing coming in these huge, panting gasps. But even as I'm standing here arguing with Vanessa and Tim, all I can think about is how poorly I treated

Lilith.

Lilith.

I want to fucking see Lilith—*now.*

I should've broken up with Vanessa from the start, right at breakfast, like I've been longing to for days. I should've told her to eat shit and then leaned over and kissed Lilith right in front of her, like I've wanted to do since the first *second* that I saw her lying naked in the Bat Cave. No, before that when Pax pulled her up onstage at the concert in Phoenix. It should've been *me* that invited her onto the bus that night.

"Good for you, Mikey," Vanessa quips, propping a hand on her boney hip. "You kept it in your pants for a whole year. Bravo." She smiles wickedly at me and Tim stiffens in response.

"Don't," he whispers as Vanessa saunters up to me and puts her arms around my neck. I throw her off, but not hard enough to hurt her. No way am I going down that road.

"The baby," she says, putting her hands on my chest and leaning up to whisper in my ear, "I'm not sure if it was even *yours.*"

The implications of that statement ring sharply inside my skull.

"You've been fucking him for how long?" I ask, but Vanessa's clearly delivered the information she wanted to deliver, eyes sparkling in triumph.

"On and off for about two years," Tim says, looking me in the face with this strange eagerness that I've never seen before, like he's scared I really will walk away forever.

Good for him.

He's right.

That's *exactly* what I'm going to do.

"You two fucking *deserve* each other," I snap, and then I spin on my heel and slam the door behind me.

CHAPTER FORTY-SIX

"Lilith."

The sound of Michael's voice behind me makes my skin ripple in a horribly pleasant sort of way. I don't want to want him right now, but I do anyway. I stand stone-still as I listen to his footsteps climb the metal steps of the bus, the door closing softly behind him.

When I glance over my shoulder, I see him leaning against it.

"You're an asshole," I tell him, because it's the truth. I spent all day with the boys at the botanical gardens and all I could fucking think about was Michael and Vanessa, wondering if they were having sex, wondering if I should or shouldn't tell him what I saw.

But in the end, I knew that if someone had seen Kevin with another girl—even just kissing her—I'd have wanted them to tell me. Even if Michael cheated on her in the past, it doesn't give Vanessa the right to cheat on him. And with his brother? That's a low blow for sure.

"I know," he whispers, and his voice is ragged and broken like maybe he's been crying.

I turn fully around to watch him, still dressed in his purple button-up, the sleeves rolled to his elbows, all of the buttons undone by this point and flashing his black wifebeater. He tosses his leather jacket onto one of the swivel chairs and scrubs his hands down his face. Looking at him, I can't decide if he really did cry or if his emotions are just so heavy and morose

340

that they're making his voice crack.

"What you said to me …" I start, and then have to pause and close my eyes for a moment. "That was fucking awful, Michael." If I hadn't been sitting in Ransom's lap when he said it, I might've cried, might've let that awful hurt into the fragile cracks of my psyche. But he was angry and he was sad and in the end, he didn't mean it. I know that. He owes me a goddamn apology though.

Before I can say anything else, he's already giving it, glancing up at me with indigo eyes, his face tight with hurt and pain and betrayal.

"I'm so sorry, Lil," he says as he stands up straight and moves into the kitchen, pausing next to me as I peruse a recipe on my phone, trying to make a list of ingredients that I'll need for that horrible, disgusting pizza idea of mine. At this point, I'm so sick of Vanessa that I just want to make it in the hopes that it'll act as a repellant and keep her off this bus. "As soon as you said it, I knew it was true. Hell, I knew it was true from the moment we left that restaurant this morning. Vanessa didn't want to hang out with me; she wanted to fucking sightsee with Tim."

He pauses and lets out a long sigh, examining me in the new shirt-dress I sewed after breakfast, before we went to the gardens. It's pale pink, with crisscrossed black laces up either side, leaving two bare lines of body that I cover with a nude slip. In the right lights and at the right angles, it looks like I'm completely naked underneath.

"Fuck," Michael says as he studies my tall black heels with the pink bats on them. "You're all dressed up, aren't you?"

"I want to see the show tonight," I say because although I might not want to go *every* single night, nine times out of ten I'll be there, even if it's just for moral support. Although at this point every show's still exciting, new, different. I'm not saying it *can't* get old, just that it's not there yet. "But first I need to grab a few things from the store …"

"I really am sorry," Michael repeats, standing awkwardly by my side, watching me as I pretend to care about the recipe in my hand. "I should never have taken my anger out on you like that.

I just … you came in here like a whirlwind, and I didn't know what to do. I'm attracted to you in a way I've never been attracted to anyone before. It fucking freaks me the hell out."

I almost smile at that, but I pretend to ignore him, scrolling with my thumb down the recipe website.

"I accept your apology," I tell him, glancing at the time and wondering why he's not scrambling to get ready for the show. The other boys left already, giving me just enough time to make a list, hit the grocery store that's two blocks down, and get back before their set. I just really want to cook dinner for everyone tonight, right here, on this bus.

I'm so fucking glad that Michael's here, too.

"But I'm still pissed off at you," I say, finally looking up and meeting his violet gaze. "Go get ready for the show and we can talk some more after."

He stares at me for a moment, purses his lips and breathes out, long and low.

"Can I give you something first?" he asks me. I nod tentatively, tucking my phone to my chest as he moves into the hallway and down to his bunk, emerging with the shiny black bag from the jeweler's.

My heart starts to pound furiously in my chest.

"I don't want a gift meant for another woman," I whisper and Michael smiles tightly.

"I know," he says, pulling out a pair of velvet boxes and handing them to me. "I realized too late that I wasn't shopping for Vanessa; I was shopping for you."

I crack the lids and in one, find an opal teardrop necklace on a silver chain. In the other, the rhodonite heart necklace with the silver leaves.

"Opal's my birthstone," I whisper, tilting the box in different directions so I can admire the shine on the pearlescent white gem. "How did you know that?"

"You said something about having a Halloween birthday to Muse that night, on our way into Chicago. I didn't even realize I'd picked your birthstone instead of Vanessa's until today."

"So why two necklaces?" I ask as I fight the urge to pull them both out and put them on. He has two boxes. So what?

That doesn't really mean they were meant for me.

"I was thinking one was for you, as another thank you for helping me out, and the other was for Vanessa. But … that heart? Made from the same gem your dad gave your mom? How the fuck was I supposed to give that to another woman? Lil, your birthstone, your fucking heart."

I set the boxes aside and run my tongue across my lower lip. I pick my phone back up off the counter as a distraction and find that it's dead. Whatever. I know what I need to buy at the store. I close my eyes and try to focus on that mental list instead of on Michael and his dumb apology and his stupid necklaces.

"You've been an asshole since I got on this bus," I whisper and he doesn't protest. When I open my eyes, he's still staring at me. His face is … cracked and broken, all of his most tender parts exposed. I want to ignore him, turn him away, but I can't. I just can't. "What would've been different about today if Vanessa *hadn't* been cheating on you?"

"I wanted to break up with her," he says, and the cadence of his voice, the softness of his tone leads me to believe him. It could all be bullshit, definitely, but … I don't think so. "For days. For *months,* actually. I knew our relationship was toxic, that I didn't love her anymore. But hell, I thought I owed her for the things I'd done. I was trying to be responsible for once in my life and make plans, think about a future, about marriage, kids. I felt like I owed all of that to Vanessa for the way I treated her, for the baby we lost … the baby that might not have been mine," he adds with gritted teeth, glancing away toward the door.

It opens up a second later and Octavia's standing there, panting heavily. Her eyes, when they meet mine, are *furious,* as if Michael being late is somehow my fucking fault.

"Mr. Luxe," she says, trying to pretend to be sweet, failing miserably. Her ponytail bounces as she comes up the steps in her usual black tee and jeans, glaring daggers at me. "We need you in the venue *now.*"

"I'll be right there," he growls back at her. Octavia looks for a moment like she might protest, but then she catches the feral glint in Michael's eye and clenches her jaw tight.

"Fifteen minutes, please," she barks and then retreats back the way she came, letting the door slam behind her.

"Did you fuck Vanessa today?" I ask, almost too scared to hear the answer to that.

"No."

Relief surges through me, but I refuse to show it.

"What do you want from me?" I ask Michael as he takes a step closer and hovers his fingertips down my arms, igniting that same fire I felt the night I kissed him.

"I'm not sure," he answers honestly, meeting my gaze when I look up at him, "but for now … I want to kiss you without restraint."

He puts his hands on my arms and I drop my phone to the floor, not giving a shit whether it cracks or breaks. I don't have anybody to call; everybody I want to talk to at this point in my life is right here. Since I gave him my promise before that *I* wouldn't kiss *him,* I wait for him to do it to me.

Michael's fingers sear my aching flesh as he curls them around my biceps and pulls me a step closer, dropping his mouth to mine with this sharp, rough sound of relief. As soon as our lips touch, fire streaks through me like a shooting star, burning up the last of my inhibitions. Michael and I need to talk more and he needs to tell me what happened after I called him, but first … I need to make this right.

I need to claim the last of my boys.

My tongue slides between Michael's lips as I throw my arms around his neck. As soon as I do that, he lets go completely and kisses me hard and fast, making me bleed again, making me not give a crap that I am. The pain blends with the pleasure as he shoves me back into the cabinets and then lifts me up onto the counter with his fingers digging into my ass.

He hasn't had sex in a year … and I can *feel* that, all of that pent-up want and desire, that basic need. I want to fulfill that here, now, have him desperate and wild inside of me.

Michael shoves my dress up, pushing my panties aside as he undoes the button on his jeans with a rapid swiftness borne of desperation. As soon as his cock is free, he's shoving it into my slick wetness with this agonizing groan of pleasure and relief.

344

I cling to him, my arms around his neck as he fucks me into the side of the counter with hard, violent thrusts, his need for sex as rapacious and angry as his initial rejection of me. I wrap my legs around him, pull him close, take him in and soothe away some of that pain. The sounds he makes as he drives into me are nothing short of animalistic, bestial and primal and satisfyingly awful. I feel bad for him, for what he went through today, but that wildcat part of me is triumphant.

I got him.

He's mine.

And since Vanessa is a cheating bitch … I don't feel at all guilty about it.

Michael's grunts get deeper, more languid, almost sleepy and then he's coming so hard that his whole body trembles, muscles quivering, fingers bruising my ass as he buries himself balls deep into me. His reaction is so violent and base that it triggers something in me, too, and I find my orgasm with him, wrapping around him, claiming him.

First woman he's had in a year.

And I like that. A lot.

"Fucking fuck," he says, still holding onto me, still trembling slightly. "Fucking fucker fuck."

"Eloquent," I murmur as he breathes out a long sigh of relief against my neck, but I'm smiling as I say it. *I got them; I did it; they're mine.* Thank god I had that grown-up talk with the boys the other night, when we went out for steak. Michael is one of them, so Michael is in. I think they all figured this would happen eventually.

"I don't want to do the fucking show," he growls, nuzzling into my neck, making goose bumps spring up all across my skin. "I just want to stay here and fuck you instead. Do you know how damn good that felt?"

"Because it's been a year?" I whisper and he laughs.

"Because it's you," he replies.

CHAPTER FORTY-SEVEN

I am seriously fucking glowing when I loop my VIP badge around my neck, tuck my ID and some cash behind it, and take off down the bus steps toward the gates of the venue. Muse and I walked down to this little grocery store earlier for snacks, and I forget to grab everything I needed for my recipe. At least now I know where to go and about how long it takes to get there.

I flash my badge to the woman at the gate and she lets me through, out into the cool Atlanta night with Michael's leather jacket slung over my shoulders. I can still smell him on me, that pomegranate spice of his shampoo, the almost untraceable scent of sex. I rinsed off, but still, I can *feel* him inside of me, grunting and thrusting and filling me.

I grin like an idiot, cutting off all thoughts of death and pain and loss. I just can't right now. This is *my* moment. Those boys … something about those goddamn boys … they called to me and I came. And here I am.

One week left.

It won't be enough, but at this point, I'll take what I can get.

I hurry down the sidewalk in my heels, wishing I'd changed before I left, but too damn giddy to care much about some aching arches.

When I come around the corner, my mouth drops open and I see the line for the concert stretching all the way down the block, a sea of glittering people in black band tees and tight jeans, leather vests and short skirts, spiked mohawks and outrageous piercings.

I have to walk past them to get to the market, but I don't mind. It makes for interesting people watching and besides, the band they've all come to see, Beauty in Lies, they're *mine*. I try to stop the basic, primal wildcat type thoughts, but I can't help it. And why am I even here doing this if not to enjoy it? So I give in and march past the crowd with my head held high and a smile on my face. They don't have to know that I just fucked the lead guitarist, but I do, and it feels fucking great.

Hell, maybe I *am* a groupie after all?

I'm about halfway down the block when I hear a familiar voice call out my name.

"Lilith?"

I stop right in my tracks, going completely still, feeling this awful chill course over my body and down my spine.

No. No, no, no. Not here, not tonight.

"Kevin?" I ask, this little quaver in my voice as I turn around and spot my ex standing against a brick wall in Atlanta, Georgia of all places. What. The. Fuck. "What are ..." I can't even make the words come out I'm so fucking shocked.

"What are you doing here?" he asks, wide-eyed, looking at me like he's never seen me before in his life. I just stare back at him, at his bland, lifeless brown eyes and mop of equally lifeless hair. It's all slicked back with pomade, like he thinks he looks cool, very 1920s or something. He looks like a complete ass.

"Me?" I ask him, standing there in Michael's jacket with my red hair hanging loose and blowing gently in the breeze, my body tingling with electricity, sweetly sore from Michael's cock, physically and emotionally satiated with the events of the day.

I reach up, my mother's charm bracelet jingling, and touch the pair of necklaces at my throat. Yes, I'm a total sap and I put both on. I want to feel wanted right now, need it. Because if the boys want me, then I'm not alone. And you know what? I *like* them, too. I actually really fucking like them as people, all of them—even asshole Michael has a good heart.

"I'm with the band," I say, and the words feel so goddamn good as I drop my fingers to my VIP badge and caress it lovingly. Kevin stares at it like he's in complete shock—and hopefully jealous as fuck that I got to meet his favorite band when he's never even seen them live before. "What are you doing here?" I return.

"With the band?" he asks, still staring at me like he's half-fascinated, half-terrified by what he sees. His eyes drop to my bat shoes, lift back up to my face. "How ... but you don't even like their music."

"Kevin, what are you doing here?" I repeat, lifting a hand up to indicate the city. "You're supposed to be in Phoenix."

"Shouldn't you be in New York?" he asks, but I can't let myself go there, not right now. I have Michael and Paxton and Copeland and Muse and Ransom. I don't need to think beyond that at the moment. My grief has had plenty of airtime this week.

"I have to go," I say, feeling this sense of dread creep over me, like if I stand here for too long, Kevin might give me yet another disease to match the first. I turn and start walking, praying he doesn't follow.

He does.

He catches up to me and grabs onto my arm with rough fingers.

I jerk away from him, but all he does is lift his palms up in apology.

"I'm sorry, Lilith," he says, and he sounds genuine enough, but I don't trust him for shit. I never will, not ever again. Kevin scrubs a hand over his freshly shaved face, down the front of his black Beauty in Lies t-shirt. It's sort of ironic to see him wearing my boys on his chest like that. "Look, I really don't want to miss the show, but there's still a half hour until doors open. You want to grab a coffee real quick or something? I saw a place just down the street."

I'm already opening my mouth to say *fuck no* when he keeps talking.

"I know you don't want to talk to me right now, but if we could just chat for a second ... I'm really sorry about your dad." I stare at him and I think about Michael and how the *one* thing —maybe the only thing—he said he loved about Vanessa was her power to forgive. And that, that is a mighty power. It is awesome in its fragility and its strength.

I could posses it here, right now. I could forgive Kevin, let the nightmare of him go, and move on with my fucking life.

So, even though deep, deep down I know what a monster he is, I suck in a deep breath and make myself smile.

"Okay," I say with a brisk nod, tucking some red hair behind my ear, "okay, one coffee."

CHAPTER FORTY-EIGHT

Lilith

"I can't believe we ran into each other here," Kevin says as he orders us coffees—without even asking me if I want one or anything else for that matter—and smiles like he didn't give me syphilis as a parting gift. "So ... I don't get it, you're with the band? You never even wanted to go to that concert in Phoenix and now you, what, work for them as a roadie or something?"

"Something like that," I say, leaning back in the seat and crossing my ankles, putting my hands together behind my head in my strength pose. I need to feel strong right now, desperately so. And besides, Kevin always hated it when I stood or sat like this, so it makes me want to do it more. "I'm traveling with them for the time being."

"You like a groupie or whatever?" he asks with a harsh laugh, pausing as the waitress sets two speckled mugs of cheap coffee in front of us. "Because, you know, you're not really dressed like a roadie."

"Kevin, why are you here in Atlanta? This seems like a really weird coincidence to me."

"Yeah, I know. I thought you were stalking me at first or something."

I wrinkle up my nose as he takes a sip of his drink and makes an ugly face. Kevin dumps seven of the little creamers from the bowl at the end of the table into his drink and doesn't bother to stir it. I don't even think he wants it anymore.

"Stalking you? Why the fuck would I stalk *you*?" I ask, not even bothering to address the groupie thing. Actually, I *want* him to know. I want him to know I'm fucking five guys that are kinder and smarter and hotter and more interesting than he is.

"I'm here with my dad for the 48th Annual Institute on Corporate Liability Conference," he says, like I care what any of that means. Clearly, it's that fucking corporate lawyer get-together that Vanessa's dad is attending. What a strange twist of fate that brought all of us into this city for the night. It seems ... destined. "I just can't believe ... are you really a roadie?"

"Kevin, I forgive you," I say, before he makes too big of an ass out of himself and blows this whole meeting. As soon as I say it, staring at him across the sticky surface of a diner table, I know that I made the right choice. I'm not pardoning him for his crimes, just letting my spirit know that we are now done with this guy, that he holds no emotional ties or connections to us.

"Forgive me?" he asks, blinking his thick eyelids in a slow, stupid way. "For what?"

"Um, for cheating on me, destroying my art, tearing the bracelet you gave me as a gift off my arm, giving me a serious disease, and just generally being an unapologetic asshole." He just stares at me as I talk and then ... he smiles.

"You've changed, Lil," he says, and I want to tear his tongue out of his face. Lil is not a word that he gets to call me. It doesn't belong to him. "What the hell's happened to you these last few months?"

"You mean other than losing the most important man in my life?" I snap and Kevin's smile gets a little wider. Gross. Does he really think I'm talking about him? "My *father*," I clarify, glancing around the mostly empty diner with its hanging red pendant lights, sticky floors, and bored waitresses. I worked in a place just like this back in Phoenix; every city has one or two or ten of these within its limits.

"Look, I know things between you and I got rough there for a while ..." Kevin leans over and curls his meaty hand around mine. His touch, it repulses me now. I slide my hand away from him, but he doesn't seem to realize how done I am with this meeting.

I forgave him.

That's it; that was on me.

I don't need him to accept or deny that request, to admit to his wrongdoings, to do anything at all for that matter. Honestly, as disturbing as it is that we could run into each other in a city eighteen hundred miles away from where we both live, I'm glad. I've seen him and now I'm done.

He's not really worth much more of my time.

"Do you want to get together after the show?" he asks with what he must think is a sexy debonair smile. "I'm staying at the Four Seasons."

I blink slowly at him several times before what he just said makes any sense.

"Are you … hitting on me?" I whisper incredulously. And then I laugh. I laugh until tears trace down my cheeks and I have to wipe them away with the leather sleeve of Michael's jacket. "Kevin, go fuck yourself," I snap, and then I'm standing up and storming out of the diner, feeling pretty goddamn good about myself.

I'd feel even better if he didn't jog to catch up with me a few seconds later, stepping in front of me and cutting off my view of the market just across the street.

"Move," I say, but he doesn't, his face taking on his hideous purple-red color in his rage.

Before I can stop him, he's reaching up and snatching my backstage pass from my neck, breaking the lanyard at the clasp and lifting it up and away from me.

"Kevin," I say, trembling with rage. "Give that to me. *Now.* Don't make me call the cops."

"Who the fuck do you think you are?" he snarls, looking down at me as I try to keep my calm. What I really want to do is beat the shit out of him. "You think you're different now that you're dressed up and fucking a bunch of roadies?"

"I'm not fucking roadies," I hiss at him, unable to help myself, "I'm fucking Beauty in Lies, your favorite goddamn band. I'm sleeping with all *five* of them."

Kevin's eyes get wide and his thick, square jaw clenches tight with anger and jealousy. All around us, crowds move towards the venue, desperate to get there and get inside in time to see the start of the show. Nobody bothers to stop and pay attention to a bickering couple standing in the shadows of a diner.

The streetlamps above our head cast orange glows across the pavement, highlighting the pockmarks in Kevin's face as a slight breeze blows my hair over my shoulder.

"I always knew you were a whore," he snarls, playing the total hypocrite. This is a guy that sleeps with any girl he can get his hands on, and he does it with complete reckless abandon and no regard for safety or the health and well-being of either himself or his partners.

I don't want to feel anymore hate in my heart, but in that moment … I kind of do.

"Give me my pass, please," I say, holding out my palm, trying to act like it's not that big of a deal that I get it back. But it is. My ID and money are in there, and if I lose that, I might get locked out of the venue like I did that night when Michael rescued me.

The thought sends an ugly chill down my spine.

"You think if you dress yourself up, stick some fancy dicks up your loose pussy, that you'll be something? You're nothing, Lilith. The best you can ever hope to be is a fucking sidekick. I know it; you know it; your dead fucking dad knew it."

"Give. Me. My. Pass," I growl, ready to tackle him.

He lowers his hand like he's going to give it to me and then takes a lighter out of the pocket on his jeans, lifting both items up over his head and flicking the silver wheel. Flame leaps to life and melts the corner of the plastic badge.

"Stop it!" I scream, throwing myself at him. He moves out of the way, but at least he stops burning the pass for a split second.

"You want this?" he asks, stepping back, grabbing the handle on a postal service dropbox. In a split second, he's shoved the badge in and closed the slot, dropping my VIP pass inside what's virtually an impenetrable fortress. It's a federal offense to even tamper with one of those mailboxes; there's no fucking way I'm getting that back.

"What the fuck?" I scream at him, feeling tears prick the

corners of my eyes as he pockets his lighter and smirk at me. But I won't let him have the privilege of seeing me cry. Fucker. I can work this out, no big deal. Right? "You're the worst kind of human garbage, Kevin Peregrine."

"Well, I guess we'll *really* see if you're with the band now, won't we, groupie bitch."

And then he turns on his heel and walks down the sidewalk like he doesn't have a care in the world. I briefly debate charging him, leaping on his back and letting my wildcat tear his throat out.

But I don't.

Because he's not worth it.

Not even close.

I square my shoulders, take a deep breath, and pull strength from the jacket wrapped around my shoulders. Time to walk back to the venue with my head held high.

I head back down the street, past the rapidly dwindling line, people streaming into the building with shouts of excitement and cheers of triumph. The revelry of the crowd is so intoxicating; I wish I were a part of it. But I have no ticket to get in, so I go around the back instead, trying to stay calm, be confident.

This is no big deal, right?

Muse talked to the staff; they know me now.

When I hit the back gates, I come up on a huge group of girls, giggling and laughing, flirting with the two male guards that have replaced the woman that was out here earlier. I don't recognize either of them.

"Excuse me," I say as I push through the crowd of glittering bodies and perfume, finding myself in front of a man with a bald head and a fierce frown. It looks like the girl closest to him is near to breaking it, hanging on his arm and laughing girlishly behind her hand. She actually has the audacity to glare at me as I approach them. "Hi, sorry, but my name is Lilith Goode and I'm actually with Beauty in Lies—"

Several of the girls snicker as I grit my teeth and take a deep breath. God, I know how stupid that sounds, but what else am I supposed to say?

"I'm with the band, too," the blonde next to me says as she tosses her hair and grins wildly.

"And me," says another girl with curly brown hair. They laugh, like this is all a joke, but it's not funny to me. The things

Kevin said … they don't matter, not really, but that doesn't mean they don't hurt. I just want to get back inside and grab a hug from Cope, a smile from Muse. I just want *in*.

"Look, I lost my VIP pass just now and—"

"I lost my VIP pass!" another girl crows, and then they're all yelling it. Half of them are drunk, I think. The other half are just desperate for a taste of the dark glitter they see sparkling from afar. They have no idea how much my boys have suffered. No clue. And this, this is *my* job, not theirs.

"Shut up!" I scream and something about the fervency of my tone lends credibility to my statement. I smooth some red hair back from my head and close my eyes for a moment, taking a deep breath and opening them back up to stare the bald man in his small, brown eyes. "I work for the tour; I was out grocery shopping and a man stole my badge. You must work for the venue?"

"We do," the bald guy says with a sigh. "We'll have to get someone on the tour staff to ID you …" He glances over his shoulder and we both pause when Octavia appears, walking hurriedly across the cement in her usual get-up—headset, ponytail, tablet and clipboard. "Excuse me!" the man shouts, waving her over.

I feel this massive surge of relief followed by … terror.

"This woman says she works for the tour … ?" the security guard asks as Octavia slips through the small door inset into the gate and stares at me with a horribly blank expression on her face. I stare right back at her, willing her to spout a blatant lie right to my face.

And then her mouth curves in a terrible smile and I know she's going to do it.

"She doesn't work for the tour," she says, pretending to glance at her clipboard. "In fact, she's been denied tickets for the last three shows because of a breaking and entering and stalking charge. Please escort her off the property."

"Are you fucking serious?" I snap, reaching out before I can stop myself and shoving her hard in the shoulders. Octavia stumbles back, but the look on her face is sheer joy, that same sort of ugly triumph I saw on Kevin's. The two of them would make a perfect couple.

"Alright, miss, that's enough," the bald guy says, stepping forward to grab my arm as the other girls scatter out of the way. I don't resist though. If I do, the other guy'll just grab me and then maybe they'll call the cops. I bet Octavia would say whatever she needed to get me arrested.

The security guard grabs hold of the sleeve of my leather jacket in a meaty hand and starts hustling me away, pausing for a moment when Octavia calls out to him.

"Just a second, please," she says as she moves toward me in her white sneakers and tight denim jeans. When she leans in, I can smell a sickly sweet floral perfume wafting about her smug face. "*You* are just a fucking groupie, Lilith. Another nameless face that the boys'll forget about in a few days. Do you understand that? You are *nothing* to them. I've seen them do this a hundred times with a hundred different girls. You think you're different because they all fuck you? You're nothing but a shareable sex doll."

Octavia pulls away about a split second before I decide what the hell and punch her right in the face. Her smirk as she turns away is one of the most infuriating expressions I've ever seen in my life—save the one Kevin was wearing earlier.

But her words … even though I try to brush them off, they sting like hell.

Bald Head takes me all the way across the street and deposits me in front of a small café with that deep-set frown plastered across his lips, turning away and meandering back to his post in front of the sea of shimmering groupie girls.

I stand there in wordless shock for several minutes before I get my head together and try walking around the venue, looking for a place to sneak in. But I'm not the only person with that idea in mind, and the security is tight as hell. There are cameras, guards, even barbed wire on parts of the fence.

When I try the front, I'm told very firmly that no, they will not get a message to anyone on the tour staff and can I kindly wait outside if I don't have a ticket.

I try in vain to spot *somebody* from the tour that I might recognize or that might recognize me, but all the people on this side of the show work for the venue, not the band.

I stalk back to the café across the street and try not to panic.

My ID is gone, along with all the cash I had on me. My badge is gone. My phone is dead and lying on the kitchen floor of the bus. I don't know any of the boys' numbers and I have no way to contact them, even if I borrow someone else's phone. If I leave a message on their Facebook page, they won't get it. I know for a fact that they don't check any of their social media pages themselves; Octavia does all of that.

As far as private internet contact, I don't know their emails, and I never thought to add them on any social media platforms. When Kev and I broke up, I deleted my Facebook page, my Twitter account, everything. I just didn't want to deal with any of it anymore. Even when I blocked him, I saw messages from his friends—people I thought were my friends, too—saying awful things about me.

I know my dad's Facebook login, but did I ever even tell the boys his name? Would they even think to check that?

Fuck.

Fuck.

Fuck, fuck, fuck, fuck, fuck.

I'm alone. I have nothing and nobody.

Nothing and fucking nobody.

A groupie and a whore and a bitch.

I sit down on the quiet sidewalk and sob.

CHAPTER FIFTY

Michael

I keep looking for Lilith while we wait for our set, but I don't see her anywhere. I figure she's still at the store, or working on her damn pizza and decide not to freak out.

But damn, I want to see her. I want to see her so fucking badly.

"You're still fucking glowing," Pax teases, the slightest hint of real jealousy in his voice as he looks me over. The first thing I did when I got back here was tell them all what happened between me and Lilith. I don't bother to talk about Vanessa or Tim. I can worry about that shit tomorrow. Tonight, I feel alive, exhilarated. My skin is humming and I just feel fan-fucking-tastic.

First sexual experience in a year and it was mind-blowing.

"So what if I am?" I ask, leaning against the wall and smoking my cigarette.

"It's just funny how fucking right I was," Pax continues and I narrow my eyes at him. But I'm too damn happy to actually be angry about anything, so I end up grinning like an asshole instead.

"You're sure she's alright, sweetheart?" Ransom asks me, pushing his hood back and tucking his hands in his pockets. "She said she'd meet us backstage before we went on."

I study him, study Muse, Cope, Pax. But none of them seem to care that I've joined in on their ... relationship with Lilith. In fact, they seem kind of relieved.

"She was on her way to some store she said you went to

earlier," I say as I think about her slipping my leather jacket on, pulling her red hair out of the collar and letting it tumble in ruby waves down her back. "I'm sure she'll be here."

But then Octavia's waving us forward and we're taking the stage behind the white curtain, hoisting instruments up, getting into position. When the curtain lifts, I look for that red hair or those bright green eyes in the crowd and I don't see anything that even remotely looks like Lilith.

Still, I'm fucking thrilled with the connection we made. It's bright enough that it casts a temporary shadow over the Vanessa-Tim thing, soothes some of that violent rapacious anger inside of me.

I decide to let my feelings out into the music, play like Lilith is watching, let her know how damn good she made me feel. She forgave me, accepted me, when she should've kicked me in the balls. Why? Maybe she sees something in me that I don't even see in myself?

My guitar pick eats at my strings like a demon, tears into the instrument and unleashes its fury on the unsuspecting crowd. Its cries vibrate through me, into the floor, out the speakers, across the theater and into the desperate fingers of the audience.

I'm in good form tonight, playing like I haven't played in years, like I actually fucking care what's happening in here. Pax, Muse, Cope, Ransom, they all feel it, too, and we put on one hell of a show. We trade our guitars out between songs by tossing them across the stage to waiting roadies; we revel in the confetti and we climb on the props to rock out as close to the crowd as we can get without drowning in their fervor.

Sweat pours down my skin as Pax belts out the lyrics to songs written in part or whole by each and every one of us. It's a group goddamn effort, all of this sound and heat, this performance.

By the time it's over, my heart is pounding so fast I can feel my pulse in my head, and I'm shoving past roadies into the darkness backstage, looking for a pair of green eyes and a headful of purple-red hair.

There's no Lilith, not anywhere.

What the fuck?"

"Octavia," Muse says, grabbing our manager on her way past. "Have you seen Lilith?"

Octavia blinks her brown eyes a few times and then frowns.

"When I went out front to speak with the venue manager, I saw her leave with a young man from the line." She pauses and shakes her head. "He had brown eyes, slicked back hair, a black t-shirt. I have no idea where they went. Now, if you'll excuse me ..."

She moves past Muse and disappears into the staff backstage, leaving me feeling completely and utterly baffled.

"A guy from the line?" Copeland asks, ruffling up his red hair and wiping sweat from his brow with a white bandana. "Who would she know out here?"

"This is bullshit," Pax says, shoving his way through roadies as he heads for the back door and outside into the cool Atlanta air. He makes his way straight to the bus with me on his heels and finds the door unlocked. "Miss Lily," he calls as he pounds up the steps and inside.

It's a small space, and it only takes a minute to comb through.

She's definitely *not* here.

I pick her phone up off the kitchen floor with a frown as the other boys join us inside the bus.

"She doesn't have her phone," I say, feeling like a complete asswad for not realizing it. But when she dropped it on the floor, I was in such a passionate frenzy that I wasn't thinking clearly. And then after, my brain was too clouded with sex to give it much thought. "Fuck."

"We need to spread out and search like hell," Muse says, dead fucking serious. "Somebody go back inside and start talking to the staff, see if anyone else saw her leave. I'll check the venue; maybe one of you can check around out here and in the other buses? Also, we should probably walk the sidewalk, see if we can spot her in any of the cafés or restaurants."

I feel so fucking stupid when I lift my face up from that phone and meet Pax's eyes.

When Lilith got thrown out of that venue in Chicago, I gave the boys a warning.

I guess I just didn't take it.

Fuck.

I climb down the bus steps and find Octavia first, grabbing her by the arm and making her look straight into my eyes.

"Have you seen Lilith since she left with that guy?" I ask seriously.

"No, I haven't," she responds cooly, and with that glint in her eye, the haughty lift to her chin, I know for sure that she's lying.

After my initial breakdown, I get it together and try to walk up and down the sidewalks, but there are people literally *everywhere,* shouting and screaming and dancing to music that's no longer being played. Obviously the show is over because the crowd pouring from the venue is massive and thumping and excited. Three thousand of them fill the streets, the restaurants, the cafés, the shops that are still open.

It's a clusterfuck of epic proportions.

I decide it's worth a shot to try to get close to the gates again, but the groupie wannabe crowd has tripled in size and even fighting my way to the outskirts is hard. I stand on my toes and try to catch a glimpse of any of the guys, but I don't see a damn thing.

Fuck.

I'll have to wait for the crowd to disperse a little.

I notice then that Bald Head is staring right at me and speaking into a radio, so I wait for a lull in the traffic and head back across the street. The view from here is shit, hidden behind the row of trees that demarcates the median in the center of the road as well as one giant oak that shields the stupid café from the view of anyone trying to peep at it from the opposite side of the street.

I pace in frustration for a while, hoping the crowd will die down, wishing I wasn't so stupidly stranded. My boys are *right* fucking there, and I can't get to them, can't talk to them, have no way of telling them where I am.

Unless Octavia was right and they really don't give a shit if you disappear.

With a growl of frustration, I shove my way into the café and sit down at a table near the front window, ordering a mocha from the waiter as a show of good faith.

They'll find me here; they will.

I might not have money to pay for this coffee, but it doesn't matter. One of the boys will show up and pay for it, no big deal. *So why are your hands shaking then?* I wonder as my tentatively built happiness starts to crumple.

I was already fragile, sitting on a precipice, trying *not* to think of my dad and his wicked wife, of my dead mother, my murdered sister, fucking *Kevin.* And yet, here I am, all alone. Even worse off than I was before because I'm trapped in a city I don't know, with zero dollars, with no car, no phone.

But no.

No.

They will fucking find me.

Like the prince with Cinderella's slipper, they'll find the right foot to put it on.

Because if they don't, I have no idea what I'm going to do.

CHAPTER FIFTY-TWO

Paxton

"I need you on the bus," Octavia says, gritting her teeth and pretending like she gives a shit that we can't find Lilith. "I'm sorry, but we're moving venues again tonight; you knew that. We can't sit around here and wait for one girl that's not even on the payroll. I'm sending the staff vehicles and the other buses ahead now, but we *really* need you guys on yours, Pax."

"Then stop bloody lying to us," I say and Octavia gets this tight facial expression, like I've offended her delicate sensibilities. "I know you know where she is, so spill it."

Michael thinks she's a damn liar, then I believe him. Besides, it doesn't exactly take a far stretch of the imagination to think that Octavia would want to get rid of Lilith.

I cross my arms over my chest and try to wait her out while my bandmates comb the local area. The girl's hair is the color of a fine Merlot; she should be easy to spot, even in a crowd. Right? But inside, I'm nervous. Who the hell is this bloke from the line? And where the fuck would she go other than here?

"Look, Pax," Octavia says softly, dropping her voice to this soft, flirty sound that literally does nothing for me. "She left with that man; that's all I can tell you. I'm sorry if she hasn't come back, but we have a contractual obligation to be off of this property in the next thirty minutes. Otherwise, the label gets hit with a huge fine and you'll all be in breech of contract. What's more important? Some groupie you met last week? Or your career? Think about it, okay?" she asks, moving away before I can come up with a witty response to that.

Fuck.

If Lilith left of her own accord, then that's one thing, but why the hell wouldn't she give us a heads-up? I don't believe it for a bloody second.

Gritting my teeth, I head out of the venue and down the block. Most of the crowd's gone by this point, but a few people recognize me and ask for signatures, pictures. I blow them off, dragging my single bodyguard along in my wake.

This is a huge venue, with several public and staff entrances. And there are shops and restaurants along every side. It feels like it shouldn't be so hard to find her, but really, it's like looking for a needle in a haystack.

But I know that if I have to, I'll fucking look all night.

I won't leave a crying, weeping girl alone in a strange city.

That's never fucking happening.

Several hours later, one of the waiters comes over to my table with a crooked grimace on his face.

"Miss, we're closing up. I need you to pay for that now, okay?"

I just stare up at him and then the tears start to fall, right into the full cup of coffee that I couldn't bring myself to drink. My hands shake a little as I put them in my lap. I'm trying not to freak-out here, but in a very short time period I've been stripped of everything, all of that wonderful glimmering insulation that the boys had put around me, as well as the basics: phone, money, transportation.

All sorts of feelings that I've been pressing down on are working their way to the surface.

I should be in New York, holding Dad's hand, smiling at him as I tell him everything's going to be okay, making sure he gets better, watching a healthy glow rise in his cheeks again.

"Miss?" the waiter asks again, his brown hair flopping onto his forehead as he leans slightly forward and looks closely at my face. "Are you okay?"

"I ... I don't have any money," I say and he lets out this long, audible sigh, glancing over his shoulder at a woman in slacks with the word *manager* scrawled across the top of her name tag. "I ... I was supposed to meet someone here and they never showed, so—"

"Look, just ... go. I'll pay for this out of my tip jar, okay? But you can't stay. You have to leave."

I push the cold coffee away and stand up, my dress too short, too revealing to stand outside in the rapidly cooling night air, the scent and sound of revelry fading away until there's nothing but the breeze and the rustling of the leaves on the tree in front of the café.

I move up toward the street, trying to get a view of the security gates on the other side, but the damn foliage in the median is blocking my way, so I make the decision to cross.

When I do, I wish that I hadn't.

Looking through the bars into the venue parking lot, I don't see anything. Anything. Not a single bus or trailer or car. Nothing. Even Beauty in Lies' bus is gone. Gone. Gone.

They fucking left me.

They left me.

Left me.

I stumble back and almost trip in my heels, a car horn blaring as I narrowly miss getting reamed by a blue Taurus. With a cry of frustration, I tear my shoes off and throw them at the black metal gates, sinking down next to a decorative wooden planter box with flowers in it.

The worst part of this whole thing is that ... all I want to do is call my dad to come and pick me up.

Tears stream down my cheeks as I curl up in Michael's coat and press the fingers of my left hand into the cement next to my bare legs. I'm shaking from the cold, stupidly wondering exactly *how* frigid it is out here. Low forties, maybe? That sounds about right.

I scrape my fingertips against the ground until they hurt, lifting up the slightly bloody prints and staring at the bits of loose rock and grit.

If Dad were still alive, I could find a phone to use and call him; I've had his number memorized since I was six. Even if he couldn't understand what I was doing down here, or afford a plane ticket to get me home, he would hop in a car and come to pick me up. He'd drive nonstop, all the way.

And now he's gone.

And I'm the idiot that trusted some guys I met a week ago.

If I couldn't trust Kevin after five years, or my stepmother after six, if I couldn't trust my dad to tell me the truth about how sick he was ... then why did I think this was going to work out?

I press my bloody fingers against the side of the planter box and close my eyes, letting the sadness and the cold just wash over me in a wave. Why fight it? It's there and waiting to take over every nook and cranny of my heart and soul.

Rough, ugly sobs break from my throat as I cry for all the people I've lost, the family I'll never see again, the life I've never been brave enough to live. Eventually, I'll have to pick myself up off of the cold cement and find a way to do just that. But for right now, I just cry. And cry. And cry.

Footsteps pound down the sidewalk, and I glance up suddenly, my heart soaring.

It's just some late night jogger streaming by in colorful workout clothes and disappearing around the corner, a flashing light strapped to his hip to warn cars that he's crazy enough to go running after some all day slog at work.

Fuck him.

I curl my knees as close to my body as I can and drape myself over them, red hair covering my face like a shield. *Hair the color of an October sunset,* Dad would say, brushing strands from my forehead and smiling. I almost smile back through the tears at the vividness with which I remember his face, but then I ...

"My mom's ashes," I breathe against my knees.

Her goddamn ashes are on that bus, driving south to Florida while I sit here and weep.

I feel myself get empty and cold all over again. How is this fair that I have to lose Mom again today, too? Part of me knows that I could probably get those ashes back from the boys—even if they thought I was dispensable enough to leave behind tonight. Surely they wouldn't be cruel like that? Not my boys. No way.

I realize I'm crying even harder now, but I can't make myself stop.

I just want to hug my fucking dad right now, hold the dry smoothness of my mother's hand, curl up in my sister's bed for the night. And I'll never get any of those things ever again. Not ever. I lift my head up and watch the black metal bars of the gates blur in my teared vision.

My family is gone, but I'm still here. Is that just life being cruel ... or am I the lucky one?

With every last ounce of strength that I have, I grab hold of the planter box and haul myself to my feet. If I thought I had enough willpower and determination inside of me to help those five broken men find some peace in their pain, surely I can do the same for myself?

My hands slide down my face, smearing all that careful makeup I put on for the show I didn't get to see, and I sit carefully on the edge of the planter box. The sound of the city murmurs with distant sirens and the occasional drunken shout, but right here, it's just me.

Lost, lonely girl with nobody and nothing.

But a lost, lonely girl that isn't ready to join her dad, her mom, her sister.

Lost, lonely girl that wants to live.

I'm about to stand up, recover my lost shoes, and walk down the sidewalk with tears streaming down my cheeks to find a police station or a women's shelter, somewhere I can spend the night without worrying about my safety. That's when I hear another set of footsteps.

"Lilith!"

It's Ransom Riggs—a *shouting* Ransom Riggs.

The boy who never speaks louder than a whisper is yelling my name.

I glance up and find him jogging down the sidewalk toward me in a hoodie and jeans. But his hood's pulled down and I can see the worry and fear etched into every feature of his face. Before I can even really register the fact that he's here, he's scooping me up in the scent of violets and hugging me tight against the soft cotton fabric of his sweatshirt.

"Ransom?" I whisper, because I feel like I must be hallucinating right now.

When he pulls back from me, I see that he's shaking like crazy.

"Where the fuck have you been, honey?" he blurts and at the

sound of the word *honey,* I break into tears again, letting him scoop me up in his trembling arms and squeeze me tight. "Jesus, we've all been freaking the fuck out, baby girl. Were you here all this time?"

"I …" I start, but there's only one thing I can say right now. "I miss my dad," I whisper and then the sobs just break through in fits and bursts as Ransom holds me even tighter, pressing kisses against my scalp and rocking me gently.

"I know, baby. I know. I know." He pauses, and I can feel him looking up and over my shoulder. "Derek!" he yells and then there's another set of pounding footsteps and Muse's smoky scent is stirring up the fragrance of the violets. Ransom loosens his hug just enough that Muse can get one in there, too, pressing his warmth into me from behind.

"Holy shit, Cutie. You had us in a blind panic. We thought somebody kidnapped you."

"The buses are gone," I whisper and both boys pause, glancing toward the gates and the empty expanse of pavement behind them.

"So they are …" Muse says, trailing off as the three of us separate just enough for them to get a look at my expression. "Aw, shit," Muse says, touching the side of my face with his bat covered hand. "Did you lose your shoes again, Lil?"

I snort a little with laughter, but it's quickly drowned out in another rush of tears.

"Can you … I need to get back to the bus. I want to hold my mom," I say, trying not to sway and pass out with the sheer dizzying rush of relief that passes through me. They're still here? My boys are here? They were looking for me? "I was … I tried to find you," I whisper as Ran puts his arm around my waist and Muse picks up my heels from the pavement and takes up the spot on my other side. "I thought you'd left me …"

"No," Muse says firmly, shaking his head and leaning against me. "No way. No fucking way, Lilith. We wouldn't leave you like that, Cutie, not ever." I'm not sure how to interpret that, but at this point, I just don't have the emotional energy to try.

I'm just so … so fucking *relieved.*

I was prepared to walk barefooted, heels in hand, to a homeless shelter and try to start a new life.

But I'd much rather be with my boys.

"I just texted the others," Ran says on the end of a long, heavy sigh. The poor thing's still shaking. Just like me, I guess. We're both trembling. "The bus is parked a few blocks away in the lot of a laundromat."

Muse and Ran support me the rest of the way, but they don't speak. I feel like I can't right now, not with all of these emotions clogging up my throat.

They came for me, I think, but it still doesn't feel real, like I'm still sitting alone on the sidewalk, wishing for something impossible to happen.

"Lilith!"

It's Michael, running down the street toward us.

I reach up a hand and touch the pair of necklaces at my throat. How could I have thought he'd really leave, after he gave me these? I'm such an idiot.

He snatches me up and squeezes me so tight that my feet leave the ground, but I don't care. I don't think a person can be hugged enough by people they care for; it's impossible. Even though my story with Michael really just got started today, the connection I feel with him is intense and passionate and I feel tears streaming down my face by the time he sets me down.

"Where the fuck were you?" he asks in that angry, brisk way of his, curling his fingers around the leather shoulders of my borrowed jacket. His dark eyes are glittering with rage and relief and a ton of other emotions that I can't pick apart right now.

"I ..." I start, but then I see Pax and Cope sprinting for us and I find myself choked with tears again.

Cope reaches me first, grabbing me in one of his perfect hugs and refusing to let go until Pax gives his hair a sharp tug.

"Bloody fucking fuck, love," he says, and then he gives me a hug that's surprisingly affectionate, one that's reminiscent of the way he hugged Ransom in the kitchen the other day. See, he's not really an asshole at all. "Might have to put a leash around that neck," he adds and I narrow my eyes a little. Okay, a small part of him might just be an asshole, but the rest is ... capable of a great and terrible level of emotion.

"Where were you?" Cope asks, his voice plaintive, his turquoise eyes focused on my face, on the tears that refuse to stop tracking down my cheeks.

"I've been here the whole time," I say with a sniffle, not even really caring how and why I got back to these boys or what happened to lead up to this point. I just want to crawl into the Bat Cave with them and feel their warmth against me, inside of me, listen to the sound of their breathing and know that despite their pain, they're alive. I'm alive. And as long as we're alive, that means we all get second and third and fourth chances to get it fucking right.

"On the sidewalk, doll baby?" Ran asks, searching me carefully. "Where's your pass?"

"Kevin," I say and the boys exchange looks. "He was here for the concert, in town for that stupid lawyer thing that Vanessa's dad was going to. He saw me on my way to the store and ... he threw my pass in a locked postal box."

I reach down and take Ran's and Muse's hands again and the boys take that as a cue, walking me back toward the bus as I explain the rest of the my shitty evening in as much detail as I can. It's not much right now—I'll owe them a better story later —but for now, this is all I have the energy for.

Finding the boys hasn't cured my grief for my father, and I want my mom in my arms *now*.

"I knew that bitch was lying," Michael growls, and I reach out to grab his arm before he stalks across the cement toward his manager. I can see Octavia from here, white-faced and clutching her tablet against her chest.

"I really *am* firing her arse this time," Pax says, and nobody bothers to protest ... except for me.

"Do whatever you want tomorrow," I tell him, and I hope he can hear how serious I am right now. "I ... let's not stir up anymore drama tonight, okay?"

Pax starts to protest, but something about the expression on my face stops him and he ends up storming past and tearing open the door to the bus, completely and utterly ignoring

C. M. Stunich

Octavia's presence.

"You are just a fucking groupie, Lilith."

I stare at her as we pass by, her cruel words ringing in my head, but I know that she'll get hers eventually, tomorrow, whenever. I can't wait to see Pax fire her. But right now, I don't need anger and frustration and confusion, and somebody has to get Beauty in Lies to their next concert.

The six of us pile into the bus, and Cope shuts the door behind us, locks it.

The first thing I do is stand there and close my eyes, breathing in the familiar smells, enjoying the warmth of the heater against my frigid skin. Then I open them and drink in the sight of the leather sofa and the swivel chairs and the kitchen.

"Lilith," Muse says, drawing my attention over to him. He's looking down at the floor, biting his lip. When he looks up at me, his face is completely open and shattered into pieces. His story, I'm going to get it soon; I can tell. And it's going to hurt *bad.* That much I know for certain. "Would you like to come on our world tour with us?"

"Your ..." I start as I glance over at the others, standing around me with various expressions of relief and frustration and tenderness. "You want me to come with you?"

My shock doubles, triples, and suddenly I feel like I just need to sit down.

"Here," Ran says, digging the plastic bag with the small ceramic urn from my purse. My mom's spilled inside of it, gray-white powder coating the clear plastic, but I don't care. I take her in my arms and hold her tight, closing my eyes for a moment to try to take it all in.

Mom never got to travel much, even though she dreamed of being a jet-setter and sharing her art with the world. I could do that, couldn't I?

"As a ..."

"A friend," Muse supplies carefully, "or more if you want."

"As a groupie?" I say, glancing up and reclaiming the word that was thrown at me in hate tonight. I can make that word be whatever I want it to be. *I* can be whatever I want to be—in life, in art, in my relationships with these men. This is my choice to make.

"Whatever you want," he supplies and I smile, feeling a slight reprieve in my tears.

"That's what I want," I say and then I turn and take Mom down the hall with me into the Bat Cave, pulling out the drawer with the manila envelopes in it and nestling her carefully inside, shrugging out of Michael's jacket and using it to cushion her.

When I stand up, I loosen the ties on the sides of my dress, drop it and my slip to the floor and climb into bed.

Muse, Cope, Ran, and Pax join me without hesitation, but Michael stands awkwardly in the doorway for a moment, looking unsure but staring at me with this unbridled passion that's almost scary. We're going to be tumultuous, me and him. But then I raise my fingers to touch the necklaces and he climbs onto the bed, kicking off his boots and covering my body with his.

My fingers curl in his dark hair as he kisses me like I'm the person he's been looking for his whole life. I don't know how much of that is bullshit—Cope can kiss like that, too—but I take what I can get, letting myself go completely in his arms.

Paxton moves up beside us, brushing my hair away from my ear, kissing the side of my throat. Ransom takes up the other side while Cope and Muse each start kissing their way up my legs.

Worshipped.

That's me in that moment.

Lost, lonely girl with nobody and nothing.

Lilith, the groupie, and her rockstars.

I don't think I can be both of those things at the same time; I am more than happy to shed the first title. And no, I don't know how long this will last—I don't fucking care. Sometimes relationships look perfect from the outside but fall to pieces on the in. Well, ours looks messy and weird from the outside, but on the in … it's perfect. At least for now, it is fucking *perfect*.

For a while we're just a tangle of limbs and heat, mouths and tongue, bodies and moans and caresses. Group sex like this usually takes some maneuvering, talking, adjusting, a hell of a lot of practice. But that night, our first night as a *sixsome,* we somehow manage it intuitively.

I straddle one of the guys, sheathing him inside of me, welcoming another from behind. One of them puts a knee on either side of the bottom man's head and lets me take his cock gently between my lips. And then I use my hands on the other two, kneeling on either side of me as my body is rocked gently from behind.

It's sex—some might think kinky, strange, dirty, gritty, maybe even ugly sex—but it's more than just that with us. We're six souls bathed in darkness and pain, twisted together in this moment into one person. I might be the lynchpin holding the sex part together, but it's just a further expression of something these guys already had with each other: love. It might not be romantic love between them, but they all love each other nonetheless.

And one day, they'll all love me, too.

It isn't that night—although that's the start of it all—but it happens.

I fall in love with five rockstars; they fall in love with me.

We're all broken pieces, shattered by loss and grief and hurt, but put us together … and you get one perfect whole.

Bodies are touched and soothed, orgasms given and received, but when we end up laying together, half-asleep, catching our breaths, sharing secret smiles in the dark, I finally get it, the name of their band.

Beauty in Lies.

Sometimes, even in the worst situations, the deepest grief, the meanest look, there's a spark of light peeking through all the darkness

Like finding something beautiful … in a lie.

Beauty is everywhere—if you know how to look for it.

Roadie

Roadie

Rock-Hard Beautiful

I'm in love with five bad boy
rock stars. But is our love
strong enough to overcome our tragedy?

International Bestselling Author
C.M. STUNICH

Rock-Hard Beautiful, Book 2
COMING SOON!

Discover you next five star read

in C.M. Stunich's (aka Violet Blaze's) collection and discover more kick-ass heroines, smoking hot heroes, and stories filled with wit, humor, and heart.

KEEP UP WITH ALL THE FUN ... AND EARN SOME FREE BOOKS!

JOIN THE C.M. STUNICH NEWSLETTER – Get three free books just for signing up http://eepurl.com/DEsEf

TWEET ME ON TWITTER, BABE – Come sing the social media song with me https://twitter.com/CMStunich

SNAPCHAT WITH ME – Get exclusive behind the scenes looks at covers, blurbs, book signings and more http://www.snapchat.com/add/cmstunich

LISTEN TO MY BOOK PLAYLISTS – Share your fave music with me and I'll give you my playlists (I'm super active on here!) https://open.spotify.com/user/CMStunich

FRIEND ME ON FACEBOOK – Okay, I'm actually at the 5,000 friend limit, but if you click the "follow" button on my profile page, you'll see way more of my killer posts https://facebook.com/cmstunich

CHECK OUT THE NEW SITE – (under construction) but it looks kick-a$$ so far, right? You can order signed books here! http://www.cmstunich.com

READ VIOLET BLAZE – Read the books from my hot as hellfire pen name, Violet Blaze http://www.violetblazebooks.com

SUBSCRIBE TO MY RSS FEED – Press that little orange button in the corner and copy that RSS feed so you can get all the latest updates http://www.cmstunich.com/blog

AMAZON, BABY – If you click the follow button here, you'll get an email each time I put out a new book. Pretty sweet, huh? http://amazon.com/author/cmstunich
http://amazon.com/author/violetblaze

PINTEREST – Lots of hot half-naked men. Oh, and half-naked men. Plus, tattooed guys holding babies (who are half-naked) http://pinterest.com/cmstunich

INSTAGRAM – Cute cat pictures. And half-naked guys. Yep, that again. http://instagram.com/cmstunich

GRAB A SMOKIN' HOT READ – Check out my books, grab one or two or five. Fall in love over and over again. Satisfaction guaranteed, baby. ;)

AMAZONhttp://amazon.com/author/cmstunich
B&Nhttp://tinyurl.com/cmbarnes
iTUNEShttp://tinyurl.com/cmitunesbooks
GOOGLE PLAYhttp://tinyurl.com/cmgoogle
KOBOhttp://tinyurl.com/cmkobobooks
VIOLET BLAZEhttp://amazon.com/author/violetblaze

P.S. I heart the f*ck out of you! Thanks for reading! I love your faces.

<3 C.M. Stunich aka Violet Blaze

ABOUT THE AUTHOR

C.M. Stunich is a self-admitted bibliophile with a love for exotic teas and a whole host of characters who live full time inside the strange, swirling vortex of her thoughts. Some folks might call this crazy, but Caitlin Morgan doesn't mind – especially considering she has to write biographies in the third person. Oh, and half the host of characters in her head are searing hot bad boys with dirty mouths and skillful hands (among other things). If being crazy means hanging out with them everyday, C.M. has decided to have herself committed.

She hates tapioca pudding, loves to binge on cheesy horror movies, and is a slave to many cats. When she's not vacuuming fur off of her couch, C.M. can be found with her nose buried in a book or her eyes glued to a computer screen. She's the author of over thirty novels – romance, new adult, fantasy, and young adult included. Please, come and join her inside her crazy. There's a heck of a lot to do there.

Oh, and Caitlin loves to chat (incessantly), so feel free to e-mail her, send her a Facebook message, or put up smoke signals. She's already looking forward to it.